DECEIT

Also by Clare Francis

Fiction

Night Sky
Red Crystal
Wolf Winter
Requiem

Non-Fiction

Come Hell or High Water
Come Wind or Weather
The Commanding Sea

DECEIT

Clare Francis

HEINEMANN : LONDON

First published in Great Britain 1993
by William Heinemann Ltd
an imprint of Reed Consumer Books Ltd
Michelin House, 81 Fulham Road, London SW3 6RB
and Auckland, Melbourne, Singapore and Toronto

A CIP catalogue record for this book
is available at the British Library

ISBN 0 434 27043 1

Typeset by Keyboard Services, Luton
Printed in Great Britain
by Clays Ltd, St Ives plc

For James

ONE

The organ booms out its summons, a single ragged chord. The reverberations are quelled by the rustle of people rising, the clearing of throats, the reopening of service sheets. I am late getting to my feet and Josh, who has jumped up with transparent and unashamed haste, turns questioningly, his mouth puckered in a look of mild impatience. Josh, our nine-year-old. Not mine alone, not yet; still ours. Though Harry has been dead almost three months I can't bring myself to think of Josh as fatherless. It seems too final somehow.

The last hymn. I am relieved. I shouldn't be, I suppose, but the service has been rather long, there have been no less than three eulogies, some of which, though well meant, did not seem to have much to do with the Harry I knew. And I am tired, so tired. My legs are leaden, my brain heavy.

At the same time I am aware of the morning having rushed by with bewildering speed. I wish I could rewind it and start again. From the moment I woke the children and we sat down to our silent breakfast, my mind has steadfastly refused to involve itself in the day's proceedings. It is part of my blocking out process. Even after so long I think I am still in a state of disbelief, and the seamless succession of prayers, addresses and hymns have passed in a dream, as if I were watching through a dark screen.

I am acutely aware that I should be making the most of this ceremony, that it provides an unrepeatable chance for me and the children to come to terms with Harry's death; yet for me at

1

least the opportunity has largely been missed. The only sensation I can identify with any certainty is emptiness; that, and a dread tightness in my stomach, which, after all this time, has grown so familiar as to be almost unnoticeable.

We launch into the second verse. Katie, on my left, is standing very close. Her hand holds mine, as it has from the beginning of the service. Her touch, which is cool and firm and permits no wavering, gives me immeasurable support, and I know that she is drawing as much strength, if not more, from mine. Stand or fall, we are together.

Katie is not Harry's daughter, though for much of her young life she would have liked to be. Katie, now fifteen, is the daughter of my early marriage to a musician who faded from her life – and mine – many years ago. He was last heard of living in a beach commune in Mexico. Thus to all intents and purposes Katie has lost not one but two fathers, a double blow that she, with her anxious and fragile nature, isn't well equipped to deal with. She has taken Harry's death badly. For a time I thought she would never come to terms with it. If it hadn't been for our seven weeks in California, I think maybe she never would.

She is stronger now, but not so strong that I dare glance at her in case one or the other of us should betray an emotion that we would rather keep to ourselves. This is not, anyway, an occasion for sadness. It is, I remind myself, a time for thanksgiving. For Harry's life.

The choir bursts into soaring harmony. They are really very good, this choir, some fine voices among them. I find my place on the sheet and mouth the refrain, 'O hear us when we cry to Thee, For those in peril on the sea'. This hymn, like everything else in the service, has been chosen by Harry's sister Anne. The selection was left to her partly because I have not been around to deal with such things, partly because Anne desperately wanted the job of organising the service. She too has taken Harry's death badly.

This hymn was an obvious, not to say inevitable, choice – Harry was lost at sea – but it is such an emotive piece that

I find myself wishing it might have been left out. But I mustn't quibble; Anne has taken enormous pains over the arrangements. The flowers, enormous sprays of them, are spectacular, the service sheet beautifully printed, the turn-out strong – Anne has, I know, contacted great numbers of people by phone and letter in case they missed the newspaper announcement.

The final verse at last. A suppressed sob comes from close by. It is Anne, standing on the other side of Josh. She is fumbling with a handkerchief, she buries her nose in it. Beyond the trembling feathers of her hat, her husband Charles blinks uncertainly and, catching my eye, flashes me a glance of mild alarm. I give him a reassuring look. His mouth twitches in a grateful smile which does not quite conceal his discomfort. A product of Eton, hunting fields and Cirencester Agricultural College, Charles is more at ease with farming accounts than emotional crises.

As we sing the final lines something shifts inside me, the darkness moves aside, and I am at last able to focus on Harry, on the image of him that I want to keep, the Harry who gave me many years of contentment, who gave me Josh, who, during Katie's young years, gave her the father-figure she longed for; who was never, despite his inadequacies and inconsistencies, the failure he feared himself to be.

These thoughts, coming so abruptly, threaten to tip me over an emotional drop that I instinctively avoid. Hastily I look down at Josh's shining hair. Taking after me, he is tall for his age, already approaching my shoulder. As he raises his head, I catch his profile, with its ski-jump nose, full mouth and long lashes. Never an ardent singer he has finally dropped all pretence at mouthing the words, and is staring at something high above the altar. His expression is one of duty and resignation that has long worn thin. I feel a stab of love for him, this strange child of mine, so contained, so extraordinarily unconcerned. He has an acceptance of events that baffles and impresses me in turns.

We kneel, the priest incants the commendation and blessing, there is a hush and I say my last prayers for Harry, gripping Katie's hand more tightly as I do so. I was never much of a one for prayer before, but I have prayed regularly since Harry's death. Hypocritical, I suppose, but the need is strong. I pray for the Harry that I loved. For the Harry that I loved and cared for to the best of my ability, that I supported in his many ventures, that I wish so very much were still alive.

We stand up. I risk a glance at Katie. Her mouth is firmly set, her eyes expressionless. Only her nostrils betray a rapid breathing. She catches my stare. Our eyes exchange enquiries and receive reassurances – a glance that says we are both all right this far. I reach for Josh's hand and prepare for the moment I dread, the walk down the wide aisle through the banks of faces.

But as I gather my things, Anne reaches past Josh to touch my arm and indicate that I must wait. I realise: I have forgotten the item that has been tacked onto the end of the programme, the item so dear to Anne's heart.

From the back of the church, a lone bugle rings out. The last post. I tried to persuade Anne to change her mind about this, I tried gently and diplomatically, and now I wish I had tried a little harder. In his days in the Parachute Regiment Harry served in the Falklands War, but he said he never got involved in any real battles, and it certainly wasn't a time he remembered with any great pride or pleasure. This didn't stop him from acquiring a war hero tag, drummed up by his supporters to bolster his election campaign. It was an embellishment that became overplayed to the point of embarrassment, even for Harry. I felt that this service was not the moment to perpetuate the idea, that it would have been a good opportunity to play it down. But it seemed I was the only member of the family to think so, or at least the only one prepared to voice concern about it. Yet I am not good at fighting my corner, not in family matters which risk upset and resentment anyway, and when Anne mounted an emotionally charged defence I gave way.

The bugle call has a reputation for bringing tears to the driest eye. I realise that Katie, having managed reasonably well so far, has finally run into trouble. She has dropped her head, her

4

mouth is skewed, she is frowning fiercely. I give her hand a rough shake. 'Almost there,' I whisper hoarsely. She shows no sign of hearing, and I cajole her. 'Hold on, baby. Hold on.'

The sound of the bugle dies away, the clergy start to progress out of the church. It's over at last.

I look up to see Jack gliding to a halt in front of Katie. Jack used to be Harry's business partner. He is also a godfather to Josh. I realise that he is intending to escort us to the church door. I am reluctant, I hold back. For this particular journey I would prefer that the children and I walked alone.

But Jack isn't someone who is easily deterred and I, as much as anyone, seem incapable of deterring him. Even here in the subdued atmosphere of the church he seems to overwhelm me and with an inevitability that dismays me I let him take my elbow.

We begin to walk. I force myself to meet the numerous eyes, even to smile, and am suddenly glad that I have made the effort, for though people stare – forced by tradition to wait for my departure they have little choice – the stares are warm and kind. There are so many people. And so many I had not expected to see, people from my past, neighbours from Suffolk, parents of Katie and Josh's school friends. I am deeply touched.

In the porch an usher is opening the heavy church doors. The London air flows in, heavy and hot with traffic fumes. I pause just short of the doors and turn, gathering the children on either side, ready for the line-up and ritual handshaking. Before I can stop myself I look questioningly to Jack, as if seeking his approval for this move.

Taking this as his due, he grips my arm lightly and narrows his eyes in a look that contains the appropriate mixture of understanding and solidarity. 'All right?' His voice is rough with sympathy. 'You did so well, Ellen. *So* well.' I suppose he means that I produced no tears, no embarrassments, no behaviour that could be judged to be anything less than immaculate.

Remembering the children, he adds emphatically, 'You *all* did well. Your father would have been proud of you.' He

5

throws an avuncular smile at Katie, who, having no time for Jack, doggedly avoids his gaze. Undaunted, Jack runs a hand playfully over Josh's head.

I notice how beautifully dressed Jack is in a lightweight suit that must have come from Savile Row, how beneath the concerned expression he has a barely suppressed exuberance. But then, despite the business interests they still had in common, the recession never seemed to touch Jack as it did Harry. I recognise this inner light as the glow of success. Some new conquest, no doubt. Financial or female, it is hard to tell with Jack. Quietly, as soon as his attention is elsewhere, I disengage my arm.

'I'll give you people's names as they come to you,' Jack says, surveying the advancing line with a glint of relish.

'Thank you.'

'You know Reynolds is here? And Draycott.'

'Reynolds?'

He gives an awkward laugh, as if I have cracked a dubious joke. 'The party chairman,' he says firmly.

I was only checking. And Draycott, I remember, is a junior minister of health. Ever since I let Harry down by confusing a minister of the environment with a Labour back-bencher, thus mixing not only party – a heinous enough crime – but rank too, I have gone to great pains to make sure I have the names and jobs right. Harry, who always felt humiliation keenly, did not let me forget my gaffe for weeks afterwards.

The effort of preparing myself for this final test must show in my face because Jack says in his most soothing voice, 'I'll keep you briefed, don't worry.'

I smile my gratitude, which is real enough.

He squeezes my arm again. 'Sure you're all right?'

'Oh yes. Really.' I give a half-smile to prove it.

He leans close. 'Good girl. Knew you would be,' he says with a glance that is all largesse and pride. The role of family stalwart is one he seems to enjoy.

Anne and Charles approach. Jack, who has the remark for every occasion, says to Anne, 'A beautiful service. Congratulations.'

But Anne has her sights on me. She hisses over Katie's head in a not-so-low whisper, 'What about the children, Ellen? Shouldn't we get them to the hotel? They'll have had enough. Bound to. Haven't you, darlings? *Must* have had enough. You'll be longing for your lunch, I know you will. They've got meringues at the hotel, Josh. *And* chocolate cake.' Anne, childless herself, prides herself on her rapport with children, a conviction based on the belief that children are only happy when filled with rich food. Anne herself has perhaps never passed this stage in her own development, for at forty-three she is by any standards large and has never to anyone's knowledge tried to diet.

Aware of the danger of giving offence – always a risk with Anne – I say lightly, 'It's good of you, Anne, but I think they'd really prefer to stay. For the time being anyway.'

Anne gives me a look of irritation and bafflement, as if I am being unreasonable. In fact we have discussed this several times. I have told her from the beginning that it is my intention to keep the children with me at this stage of the proceedings. I have explained how I want them to meet their father's friends and acquaintances, to hear at first hand all the nice things they will say about him, so that they will see him through other people's eyes as well as their own.

Anne gives way, if only because of the crush of people building up behind her. Most of the family are already grouped on the far side of the porch – my father on a rare visit from Cornwall, wearing the expression of abandonment and defencelessness that he acquired long before Mother's death four years ago; my mother-in-law Diana, mother to Harry and Anne, glaring fiercely into the sunlight; and the faithful Margaret, Harry's secretary, keeper of birthdays and anniversaries, organiser of impossible schedules, who, although she is not strictly family, is treated as such by us all.

Jack, expansive and commanding, very much in his element, begins to announce people: an MP who shared a cramped office with Harry during Harry's all too brief spell in Parliament; the health minister, his presence apparently wrenched from the teeth of a busy schedule; business associates of

7

Harry's, many of them unknown to me, courteous men with firm handshakes and evasive smiles who murmur gruff words to the children.

I check on Katie. We agreed that she could change her mind about this right up until the last minute, could go back to the hotel if she wished, but she seems to be doing all right. By way of confirmation she gives a careless glance that drifts past me and over the gathering. Josh, as usual, is taking things in his stride. Fidgeting, pulling impatient faces, impervious as ever.

Suffolk people now. The women kiss and hug me and look on me with worried eyes. They want to know what they can do now that I'm back, how they can help out. They make me swear to call them. They tell the children that their friends have missed them and are looking forward to seeing them again. The men kiss me a little more sedately and echo their wives, a nodding chorus. Anything they can do, anything at all.

Then Molly, who gives me a hug that almost robs me of breath. Molly is my closest friend. Irrepressible – some might say impossible – she works for a half-way house project for young offenders which she bamboozled me into raising money for.

'Oh, Ellen!' she cries, and when she pulls back her eyes are bright and fierce. 'God, you're thin!'

I make a face.

'You're back now?'

'I'm back.'

'Staying put?'

'Oh yes.'

'When am I going to see you?'

'Well . . . soon.'

'Soon!' she exclaims, refusing to interpret this as a rebuff. 'How soon? Tomorrow?'

I gesture possible difficulties. 'I don't know yet. I'll have to see . . .'

She gives me a look that is both disappointed and questioning. 'Why didn't you call?' she whispers harshly. 'Before you left?'

I shake my head. I can't begin to explain.

'I waited. I would have done anything, *anything*.'

I touch her hand. 'I know.'

She gives me another all-enveloping hug that drives her sleeve hard into my eye and makes me blink. I hug her back, but a little more hesitantly. The children apart, I love and trust Molly more than anyone else in the world, but just at the moment my equilibrium is too fragile to survive too much tender inspection and unconditional support.

Molly moves on reluctantly, her mouth pursed in a mixture of affection and rebuke.

A tall man of perhaps fifty stands before me. His stiff bearing, the cut of his double-breasted suit, the tap of his metal-tipped heels on the flagstones declare his military status well before Jack introduces him as Harry's CO, a colonel whose name as usual I do not catch. This is the first time I have met anyone from Harry's Falkland days. I was never sure why this should be, why Harry, unlike most men of his background, of the well-connected officer class, failed to keep in touch with his regimental comrades. I assumed Harry's world had diverged too much from theirs, that business and politics left him too little time for the niceties of the past. But if I used to feel mild curiosity about this it is largely gone, and today is not anyway the time to satisfy it. I accept the colonel's formal words, his imaculately expressed regrets. His grey unblinking eyes are cool and unreadable, though not, I think, unsympathetic. I wonder how well he knew Harry.

A small bow and the colonel turns away.

More Suffolk people – the local builder, who spent the best part of a year renovating Pennygate; Jill Hooper, who cleans the house and looks after Josh when I am away; and Maurice, our gardener. I tell them how much I appreciate their coming all this way.

I find myself greeting a man with sideburns and a stern well-weathered face who, since Jack has got side-tracked, is forced to introduce himself. He has a Suffolk accent, an indistinct manner of speaking. It takes me a moment to grasp that he is attached to the coastguard service, and a further moment to

9

understand that it was he who organised the search for Harry. To compensate for my initial blankness, I lurch into excessive thanks. I thank him for coming, I thank him for instigating what was, I feel sure, an extremely thorough search, I thank him for doing all he could. This effusiveness only serves to darken his expression. He shakes his head, he will not have it. From his point of view I suppose he judges the whole thing a professional failure, a blot on his record. The yacht not found. Nor the body. I assure him I do not blame him in the slightest for what I euphemistically call 'the way things have worked out'. I am sure no one could have done more. He shrugs grudgingly. We stumble on for a few moments, then I grip his hand once again and, grateful to be released, he is gone.

The line keeps coming. I did not realise that Harry and I knew so many people. I have difficulty in remembering what I have just said and to whom. Falling back on my long months as a candidate's wife, I confine myself to a resolute smile and repeated thanks.

The stream of faces and outstretched hands begins to dwindle at last. Not an instant too soon. My legs are starting to go. The stress affects me this way, a sudden draining of energy from the limbs, a leaden sensation in the muscles. In California, where every trial of existence is confronted and analysed into submission, Katie and I went on a stress management course. Remembering our lessons, I concentrate on my breathing, I force the tension from my shoulders, I make a conscious effort to calm myself.

John Barrow, the local Conservative Association agent, has been hanging back and finally approaches. He wears his habitually lugubrious expression which gives him the air of being sorely tried. By his standards, I suppose he is. I don't think he ever really liked Harry, far less his candidature. Harry was acutely aware that, following his failure to win the seat in the 1987 election, Barrow secretly tried to oust him. Barrow had considered the seat to be winnable and blamed Harry for its loss. Even when the seat unexpectedly fell vacant almost four years later – the Liberal incumbent died of a heart attack – and Harry won the by-election by a narrow margin, Barrow was less than euphoric. Harry, who had an almost obsessive need to know what people were saying about him, discovered that Barrow was already expressing doubts about Harry's ability to hang on to the seat at the forthcoming general election. Barrow put Harry's by-election win down to the short-term publicity Harry had gained from organising a concert in aid of Rumanian orphans. The concert certainly got publicity – Harry managed to persuade two chart-topping pop groups and an Oscar-winning actress to take part – but Harry didn't figure much in the photocalls and I don't think it boosted his profile as much as Barrow thought it did.

Barrow's concerns about Harry's long-term prospects were well-founded. In the 1992 general election, which came just five months after Harry entered Parliament, his constituents, bucking the national trend, voted Harry out.

Barrow shakes my hand and says the service was very good and that he is pleased at how many people have been able to come. He means, considering it has taken place in London. Like him, I would have preferred the service to have been held closer to home, in Woodbridge or, at a stretch, Ipswich. But Anne would not hear of it. The MPs and ministers by whom she sets such store would never travel that far from Westminster; and a service in London does, I realise, have a certain cachet.

'I feel you should know – we're selecting a new candidate. We've got a shortlist,' says Barrow in a confidential voice. He watches me closely and I realise he is concerned at how I will react to this news. 'We left it a while,' he adds. 'But after so long . . . well, we hoped it wouldn't be unacceptable to go ahead.' Wouldn't be unacceptable. To me, I suppose. Did he think I was going to be offended? Did he think I wanted the candidature left empty?

'Oh no, of course not. You must go ahead. I know Ha—' Oddly, I still stumble over Harry's name when talking to people I don't know well. 'I'm sure Harry would have approved.' Then I add, more for something to say than out of any real interest, 'You've got some promising people lined up?'

11

'I think so.' From the way his eyes spark I would guess that he already has a strong candidate.

Katie pulls at my hand. She wants to go. And Josh, who has been gently and insistently prodding my leg for some minutes, has also reached the limits of his nine-year-old endurance. Margaret, who, as Harry's secretary for almost ten years, has perfected the art of appearing on cue, catches my signal and comes to scoop them up. Without meeting my eye Katie says 'See you later, Mum,' and strides off with Josh in tow. As they're swallowed up by the dusty sunlight I feel a small pang. Whatever you do for your children, however much love and support you give them, you can't entirely protect them, they still have to face great chunks of life on their own.

'The final selection won't be till the end of the month,' Barrow says. 'Perhaps you might be able to come along then, to meet the new candidate? Nice if you could give your blessing. Pass on the torch, so to speak. People would appreciate that.'

The thought of a public event, of photographers and chattering party faithful fills me with dread, but for a moment I can't think of how to refuse. 'Well—'

'There's no hurry.'

'It's hard to plan. I—'

'Say no more.' Barrow attempts a rare smile which pulls his heavy face in directions it is not accustomed to go. Whatever he felt about Harry's abilities as a candidate, he has always been more than kind to me. 'We'll talk about it again, nearer the time.' He begins to move away then pauses, as if considering the wisdom of what he is about to say. Finally he says, 'You might want to know – I'd like it to be Crawley.'

'Crawley?' I am momentarily confused. Crawley is Jack. I repeat with a laugh, 'Crawley?'

Barrow confirms – it is Jack. And suddenly I understand what has given Jack his aura of suppressed excitement. He has in his sights a prize which for him will be as great a conquest as money or women. Jack has put himself up for Harry's candidature.

On the far side of the porch Jack is standing with some men I

12

do not know. He is looking intent, his arms crossed, his well-defined features creased with concentration. Even as I watch, he goes into rapid and animated speech accompanied by strong precise gestures. The man of the moment.

Politics are, of course, an obvious step for him. If I had thought about it, which in the trauma of the last months I certainly have not, I might have seen this coming. Of striking appearance, exuding success of the most obvious kind, possessed of a persuasive and charming manner, he is ideal material for the candidature. With Barrow's support, I imagine he will almost certainly get it.

'You did know?' Barrow asks hesitantly, and from his expression I guess that someone – presumably Jack – was meant to have told me.

I make light of it. 'It's taking me time to catch up.' I show by my expression that I really don't mind not having been told, which in truth I don't. Harry's political career was only important to me while it was important to him. Now that he is dead I have no interest in the candidature, and if I feel anything at all it is relief at no longer having to live up to the standards of being a politician's wife. The days when I earnestly mugged up on local history and social issues and wore suitable clothes already seem blessedly remote.

Barrow interprets my indifference as approval for Jack's candidature. At least he looks pleased, though if he imagines my opinion counts for anything, I think he's mistaken.

Barrow, seeing that someone else is waiting to speak to me, makes way for a young man who I recognise but can't immediately place. My expression must give me away because the young man hastily announces himself as Tim Schwartz. I have him now. He is the director of the Rumanian orphans charity that Harry's concert raised all the money for. I met him once at a pre-concert reception, then again in the scrum of the concert itself. He is an earnest and rather severe young man with small unusually round eyes, like the watchful eyes of a small animal. He has the air of someone who is permanently irritated. I imagine that he is extremely able. I apologise for my lapse.

He dismisses this with a quick lift of his mouth, and fixes me with his odd gaze. 'Mrs Richmond, I'm sorry to bother you about this. But I was wondering, did you get my letter?'

'I've only just got back from America,' I explain. 'I haven't had a chance to look at anything yet, I'm afraid.'

He narrows his thin mouth and looks decidedly put out.

'I'll be getting down to the mail soon,' I offer. 'Next week . . .'

But his eyes are absorbed, as if he is already on to the next thought. 'I was wondering – I'm coming your way on Sunday. Would it be possible – could I drop by? It would only be for half an hour.'

I smile vaguely as I try to work out how I can put him off. I have been back just two days, but the weekend already seems precious to me, a breathing space. I murmur, 'Sunday's rather difficult, I'm afraid.'

'It would only be half an hour,' he repeats, forcing an unconvincing smile that vanishes as rapidly as it came. 'It is rather urgent,' he adds with a tinge of impatience. 'It's the concert accounts, you see. We can't get moving on anything, not until they're sorted out . . .' He trails off, frowning, as if it is really too complex for him to explain or for me to understand.

'If it's about the concert I'm not sure I'll be able to help,' I say. 'I didn't have much to do with the organisation or anything, I'm afraid.'

'Maybe not, but I've tried your husband's advisers, I've tried them several times and . . .' He gestures the hopelessness of this avenue. 'Look – would Monday be better?'

'My husband's advisers?'

'Your solicitor – Leonard Braithwaite? And Gillespie at your accountants.'

'Oh. And they can't help?'

'They say not.'

'Well, then—'

'You're the only person who might be able to, you see.'

This argument is altogether too neat for me, and in my tiredness I can't find a way past it. 'Oh.'

'Monday then?'

'Monday?' I echo tautly. 'I'm not sure. I've so much . . .'

14

'I would appreciate it. It's really very important.'

I have the feeling that whatever argument I put up he will outmanœuvre me. 'Well...' I say wearily and realise that I have drifted into agreement, and that I will have to commit myself to a time. We settle on noon. Immediately Tim Schwartz has gone I wish I had put him off until later in the week. Monday will be fraught enough as it is, with the post to face and all the other problems that I know are lying in wait for me.

For a moment no one notices that I am alone. I push my head back against the tightness in my shoulders, I knead a muscle in my neck, I think ahead to tonight when I will be home again, to when Anne and the rest of the family will have left and I won't have to make this effort any more. It's strange, but in California I dreaded the thought of being home again, of having to face the house alone. I thought it would bring Harry's death back, that it would make me relive it all, but as soon as we got back on Wednesday and I walked into the house, I knew it was going to be all right. The anticipation had been far worse than the event.

'Ellen!'

It is Charles, who takes me by the elbow and leads me towards the light. 'Got to look after you!' he states gravely. 'Must be absolutely worn out, poor old thing.'

Anne, who has been talking to one of the clergy, hurries forward. 'Absolutely!' she declares firmly, apropos of what I'm not quite sure, since she cannot have heard what Charles said. Signalling her farewells to the clergyman, she takes my other side and with Charles guides me through the doors. I am not so unsteady that I need this support, but I don't want to risk upsetting anyone by refusing it.

Emerging into the glare I see my father standing uncertainly at the top of the steps. With suitable explanations I unfasten myself and go across to him. Anne calls after me, 'Tell your father he's expected for lunch, won't you?'

Pa shuffles his feet at my approach and looks away. He is finding this whole episode difficult. Even when I was a child we never quite knew how to establish communications. We are so very different, he and I. Often when he looks at me I think he is amazed that we should be related at all. I am tall and fair, he of medium height and, before he went grey and thin on top, strikingly dark. He does not follow politics; I do not follow the sports results. After Mother died, it was a job to find common ground. We do our best. I phone him once a week, and we diligently go through our list of common interests: the children, our health, the state of our gardens.

His mouth forms into what is intended to be a smile but is closer to a grimace. I can see that he is longing to get away. Lunch can only be an ordeal for him. Also, though he has not actually said so, I think he has a woman friend down in Cornwall, someone he will want to be getting back to. And why not? He is still a robust man, a good catch for a lonely woman. I am pleased for him.

'No need to stay, Pa. Why don't you get an early train?'

He begins to protest, but not so strongly that I cannot win him over.

'Well – don't suppose I'll be much use,' he says finally.

'No, Pa.'

'And the food – you know.' Father is a plain-food man and does not hold with the sort of French restaurant where Anne and Charles have arranged for us to eat.

I put an arm round his neck and kiss him. He pecks my cheek awkwardly and pulls firmly back, anxious to be on his way now that it is all settled. He raises his hand in the direction of Harry's family, a wave so insignificant that there is little risk of it being noticed. He starts down the steps and turns to look back at me, but if he was going to say anything more he decides against it and with a last stab at a smile he continues down to the street. I watch him hail a cab and climb in. I wave but he does not look back.

Anne arrives breathlessly at my side. 'He's gone! Did he have to go?' She is put out, as she always is when her plans are upset. 'What will he do for lunch?'

'I think he wasn't very hungry. He had to get back. He sent his apologies.'

She gives me an odd look, as if she blames me for

16

encouraging him to slip away, before gripping my arm again. Charles takes up station on my other side, giving my hand a small squeeze, and we prepare to start off again.

Jack, easing himself away from the last remaining mourners, takes charge of Diana, who seems far more in need of support than I. Diana has withered visibly since Harry's death. Her shoulders are stooped, her skin is grey and hangs loosely about her jaw, her dress floats voluminously over skeletal bones. She looks far older than her sixty-six years. The loss of a son is of course a terrible burden for any mother to bear, even Diana, who, despite her physical frailties and her drinking, has always given the impression of immense strength.

The sun is bright and we are half way down the steps before I spot two photographers who seem to have come from nowhere. For an irrational moment and before I see the absurdity of the idea, I wonder if Anne has laid them on as one lays on photographers for a wedding.

'A bit much,' Charles mutters darkly, as close to anger as he ever gets. 'A bit unnecessary.'

I, too, wonder why they have come. Harry was not an MP for very long. He was not especially rich or powerful. There was nothing particularly newsworthy about him. Except the way he died, perhaps.

Anne has her chin up, showing a courageous face. I keep my eyes down, my face blank. I do not want anyone to read anything into my expression, or to see things that are not there.

Anne and Charles guide me towards a chauffeur driven car, one of the three that Jack has laid on for the day.

A man is waiting to intercept us. Coming so soon after the photographers my first thought is that he must a reporter. I prepare to pass quickly by, but Anne and Charles slow down, we come face to face.

I realise my mistake: the man is a mourner, well-dressed, wearing a black tie and holding a service sheet. I half recognise him from the line-up, one of the many faces I did not know.

'Richard Moreland,' he says immediately, as if he wouldn't expect me to remember. 'I knew Harry from the Falklands.'

'Richard Moreland!' exclaims Anne, as if she knows the name. 'Well!' She clasps his hand. 'How very good of you to come. How very kind! You and Harry – well, my goodness!' She laughs her gracious laugh which after the trials of the day has become a little high-pitched.

Moreland smiles politely and brings his eyes back to mine. 'I just wanted to say that I'm staying not far from you, and if there's anything at all I can do . . .'

'That's very kind.'

Anne beams into Moreland's face. 'It's so nice to meet one of Harry's army friends,' she says in her nervous rapid speech. 'He hardly talked about his army days, you know, hardly at all. He wasn't one to dwell on the past – too much going on, of course, with Parliament and so on. But what a pleasure to meet you! A friend of Harry's from the Falklands, Charles! Did you hear that? It must have been amazing. I mean – the experience.'

Moreland's eyes glint slightly, his mouth tightens a little. He murmurs a perfunctory reply and says quietly to me, 'I'm just on the other side of the river, near Waldringfield. Perhaps I could come by one day?'

'Well . . . I . . .'

'When you've a moment,' he adds quickly. 'I'll phone, of course – if I may.'

Trapped, I gesture agreement.

The rituals we go through, the things we say. How many people have said that they will be coming to see me? I can't begin to count. Thirty? Forty? I hope they don't all mean it. Or if they do, that they will be easily dissuaded. All I really want is to be alone with Josh and with Katie when she's home from school, and for the three of us to be left to get on with things in our own way. I don't want endless reminiscences, long overblown talks of a golden past.

Richard Moreland, however, gives the impression of being quietly determined and I rather suspect he will not be put off.

'It was all Harry ever wanted,' Anne declares, 'the Paras. Because of Father, of course. You were in action together?'

18

'Not exactly. I was a Royal Marine, you see,' he says in his calm voice.

'Ohhh.' Anne draws the sound out while she adjusts to this news. 'But you and Harry—?' She regains momentum. 'Harry certainly mentioned your name. I remember it clearly. Aren't you—?' She smiles coyly, inviting revelations.

The heat closes in around me, the sun is very bright. I blink hard against the light. Perhaps I look unsteady because the next moment Moreland takes my arm and asks me if I'm all right. He opens the car door and, while Anne fusses in the background, he helps me inside.

I sink into the seat. On the pavement there is a flurry of discussion while Anne decides on who is to go in which car. I close my eyes for a second. When I reopen them Moreland is crouching in the still-open door.

'All right?' he repeats in that soft voice.

'I'm very tired.' Why I should tell him that, I'm not sure.

He says gravely, 'Be careful, won't you.'

Careful? I nod vaguely.

He watches me for a moment. No, studies me, as if fixing an idea of me in his mind.

'I'll call you tomorrow then,' he says. He rises, only to reappear in the frame of the open door. 'By the way – does your boy like fishing? I thought I might go out some time. Perhaps he'd be interested?'

Interested? I'm not sure. When it comes to fishing Josh is rather fussy.

Moreland says diplomatically, 'Well, one of these days. If he feels like it.' He smiles again, a gentle smile, and closes the door. As he walks away he stops to talk to Leonard Braithwaite, my solicitor. They seem to know each other. Leonard smiles a lot. They shake hands as they part.

'That Richard Moreland,' Anne says, settling into the front seat. 'I'm *sure* Harry mentioned him. Isn't he a cousin of the Fenimores? I remember Harry saying he'd met a cousin of the Fenimores.'

'You're thinking of the Moore-Ingham chap,' Charles replies.

'Oh!' Anne makes a small exclamation of annoyance. 'Well! How confusing!'

I withdraw and, as always in my quiet moments, think of the children. I worry most about Katie, who was born with uncertainty and apprehension etched into her heart, who seemed to survive the trials of life by the narrowest of margins. As a baby she clung to me, at the mercy of the slightest trauma, and any confidence she has felt in the outside world has been achieved only by an effort of will.

My vision of our future tends to fluctuate. Sometimes it seems to stretch out before us, smooth and steady, so that we progress across it with hardly a ripple. At other times – usually in the night – it is grim and threatening and mountainous with difficulties and I feel sure we are going to founder. At these times I am stabbed by fear so violent that it shakes me awake in the darkness. But the more intense the fears, the more I try to conquer them.

We have come so far, we have survived so much. As I keep reminding myself, all we have to do now is hold on.

TWO

'Drop me by the gates!' Katie says suddenly, her voice high and brittle. I glance at her in surprise. She was all right a moment ago.

'But your stuff,' I reply faintly. 'How are you going to get it to the house?' I am thinking of the size of the school grounds, of the distance from the gates to Katie's house. 'And I told Mrs Anderson I'd go in and see her.'

Katie doesn't answer. She is staring ahead, her mouth pulled into a hard line, her gaze determinedly avoiding mine. I can't guess why she has made this abrupt decision. Perhaps, afflicted by teenage embarrassment, she does not want her friends to catch sight of me. Perhaps she is dreading her friends' sympathy and wants to face them alone.

I understand all this, but at the same time I can't help fretting over the practicalities. I sent her main trunk over yesterday but she still has two heavy bags and a CD-player to carry. Yet I'm too emotional to argue about it. I can only think that soon we will be separated, soon we will go through the lunatic ritual of parting. After so many weeks together, after all we have been through, I can hardly bear to think about it.

The gates come into sight. I do not approve of this place. Oh, it's pretty enough. The white stucco dormitory buildings are dotted among smooth lawns, colourful rose beds and woodland. According to the prospectus the school boasts an unusual number of sports facilities including an Olympic-size pool and I've forgotten how many tennis courts. And the

21

academic results, so everyone keeps telling me, are good. The staff expect Katie to win a place at a decent university in three years' time.

But I can't approve. Here parents give up their children to strangers for weeks on end and, unlike me, seem to do it gladly. You are told it does your child no harm, that things like unconditional love and physical contact and parental support will not be missed. I can't buy this. Boarding schools, it seems to me, are a peculiarly British madness, an inexplicable relic of Dickensian times that should have gone the same way as child labour and other primitive practices.

I used to say that I would never send the children away, no matter what, and I would say it with enough passion to belie my easygoing image. At first Harry argued for Josh to board. He himself had been sent away at seven and, like many who had survived the system, he believed it had done him more good than he'd realised at the time – in his case, with his problematic relationship with his mother, even I had to admit he may have been right. Also, though he never said so openly, I think he believed the old myth that an all-male school would make a better man of Josh, that I, as an unashamedly loving mother, was in danger of undermining Josh's masculinity. I used to challenge him about this in a light-hearted way – which was the only way with Harry – but he would simply laugh it off. In the end I got so upset that Harry relented and agreed to day school, at least until Josh was thirteen.

With Katie it was different. There was never any question of her going away. When Harry and I married, Katie was five and, it has to be said, at her most difficult and demanding. But Harry, who had taken on his role as surrogate father with some qualms, showed a tolerance that touched and delighted me. He appreciated Katie's overwhelming need for security and a home life.

This of course was long before Katie made up her mind.

I see the same stubbornness in her expression now.

I draw up just inside the gates. 'I could drop you here and

take your stuff up to the house,' I offer. 'Put everything inside the door . . .'

Katie sighs harshly and exclaims, 'No point!' Her anger has always been volcanic, even as a small child. It is a trait she hates passionately and has tried very hard to control.

'Okay,' I say reasonably. 'Why don't you go ahead with your stuff and I'll wait here for a while, until you're inside. Then I'll pop in and see Mrs Anderson.'

'No!' She is trembling visibly, near lift-off.

I leave it a moment before saying quietly, 'Do you want to talk about it?'

She turns away to look out of the window. My question has made her pause, as I'd hoped it would. While in California I went to an excellent therapist, a man with the unpromising name of Bob Block. After a time Katie agreed to see him too and, though she found the idea of talking to a stranger quite hard, she soon warmed to him and her sessions seemed to help her at least as much as mine helped me. Bob's favourite prompt was: 'Do you want to talk about it?'

Suddenly we're through the storm. The tension slips from Katie's body. She grimaces and rocks her head. 'Sorry, Mum.'

I grasp her arm. For a while neither of us speak. 'It's been a long day,' I say eventually. This is true in every sense. Lunch started and finished late and we got caught in the Friday afternoon jam out of London, then, just twenty minutes from home, we met an accident on the Ipswich bypass. The journey, which normally takes two and a quarter hours, took well over three. It was very hot, the three of us spoke only to complain, Josh got a headache.

But Katie, always her own harshest critic, is not prepared to forgive herself her momentary loss of control. She shakes her head in self-disgust.

I try to jolly her along. 'Josh got fairly ratty,' I point out. 'And Anne was absolutely exhausted.'

A humph of disapproval. 'Anne was drunk.'

'Oh,' I say. 'Was she?'

'She drank almost as much as Granny.' Katie is a bit of a

23

puritan; she notices these things. She doesn't like excessive drinking in the family, nor any other kind of immoderate behaviour. 'And she stuffed herself. She had *three* lots of profiteroles.'

'Good God, did she? Oh well, you know how she is. She hates waste.'

Katie looks cross with me for making her smile, and we sit in companionable silence for a time, contemplating Anne and the profiteroles. The air is much cooler here than in the city, and there is the shimmer of a breeze in the heavy-leafed oaks.

'So . . .' I say at last.

'Take me to the house. Please. Sorry.'

I give her a quick kiss, which is just about permissible under the rules. No hugs, no farewell scenes allowed. This was agreed two days ago. This doesn't prevent me from feeling a fresh stab of impending loss as we drive slowly through the grounds and draw up in front of Oakwood, Katie's house.

Katie fairly leaps out. She throws open the boot and I hear a bag thudding onto the ground. She bobs down at the window, fans out her fingers in a brief goodbye, and turns quickly away.

I watch her struggle towards the entrance, tottering under the weight of her CD-player and overstuffed bags. In the doorway she turns and throws me a brief almost garish smile, which I return as best I can. 'See you soon,' I mouth at her through the windscreen.

This smile of hers is a good sign, a declaration of her intention to get on with life and make a success of school. It was Bob Block who proposed that she and I should segment our lives, should create set times for work, for amusement, for deliberate and studied grief. I hope Katie has decided that school will be about work and laughter, that whatever anxiety and guilt remains, she will keep it for me and Pennygate. I want Katie to be happy and carefree, though this has always been difficult for her to achieve, even before life came and knocked her sideways.

Mrs Anderson, the housemistress, has a businesslike compassion that gets us quickly through the condolences, which I always find difficult, and on to Katie's welfare. We discuss how Katie is going to make up the schooling she's missed without feeling she is under pressure. We discuss the number of weekends she will come home. We agree that Katie should decide this for herself, that she should come out as often as she wishes. Mrs Anderson does not think it would be a good idea for her to come out mid-week, although, as the school is only fifteen minutes from Pennygate, it would be easy for her to do so. I have immediate visions of Katie getting into a state on a Tuesday night and having nobody to turn to. I know that I am probably worrying too much, that Katie is probably more resilient than I give her credit for. At the same time she is so easily knocked off-balance by the smaller obstacles of life that I cannot imagine she won't have some difficult moments.

In the end we compromise. We agree that Katie will be able to call me at any time from the relative privacy of Mrs Anderson's rooms.

I can do no more. To keep my mind off Katie, to suppress the heat behind my eyes, I drive back to Pennygate unusually fast. Fast by my standards, anyway. The local drivers and the narrow roads in this part of Suffolk frightened me into submission many years ago and I have long driven with care, though for some reason Anne has persuaded herself that I drive recklessly, and often recounts cautionary tales of fatal accidents for my benefit. It is part of her image of me, an image that is all artistic unreliability and lack of common sense, and bears very little relation to the person I am now. I think her idea of me stems from my art student days when I earned money singing blues with a semi-professional band that toured the universities; a brief enough era, God only knows, but one which to Anne appears sufficiently exotic to have fixed itself indelibly in her mind.

Pennygate stands at the end of a mile-long drive which passes through the Pennygate Estate. Most of the estate was sold to the neighbouring landowners in the sixties, and Harry sold the last few fields when we bought the house four years ago. Now only the drive and the fifteen acres immediately around the house remain.

I love the drive. It starts at a tiny gatehouse, long unoccupied, and carries on in a straight chestnut-lined avenue across broad fields towards the undulations and hidden dips that mark the banks of the unseen river. Turning to run parallel to the river, it follows the high ground through groves of pine and beech and mixed woodland. The track has a poor surface and has to be taken slowly – the recession hit us before we had time to repair it – but I rather like it that way. It gives me time to notice the seasons, to appreciate the loveliness of the place.

In my absence it has become full summer. The chestnuts under which I pass, the grass and the nearby woodland have turned a uniform shade of green. In the fields the crops are up – wheat, barley, rye, I'm never sure which. Far away across the river a field of vivid rape-seed blinks through the trees.

As a town person I took to country life with unexpected enthusiasm – unexpected even to me. Nothing I had read or seen, none of my occasional country weekends had prepared me for the extent of my conversion. Friends said I had become more countryfied than the locals, and I suppose I had. I liked village life, I liked knowing everyone, I enjoyed making cakes for the fête and collecting for the church fund. The very parochialism of the life gave me a sense of security and ease. The life; and of course my marriage to Harry.

When Harry and I were first married – ten years ago this February – we lived on the outskirts of the village at the edge of the heath, where I would take Katie for walks. In those early days Harry and I would sometimes go for walks too, though he preferred to drive down to the river and walk along the marsh paths in the direction of the sea.

It was on one of those early river walks that Harry first pointed Pennygate out to me. We must have been quite far downriver because you can only see Pennygate from a distance, perched as it is quite high up and screened by trees from below. He said it was the best house on the river. There are few enough houses on the river – by a miraculous combination of private ownership and protection schemes the river, despite being a couple of hours from London, is almost completely undeveloped – but he was right. Pennygate, though it will never win prizes for architectural beauty, has by far the best view.

With hindsight I can see that Harry already had a gleam in his eye when he said this, that he had already set his sights on the house, but it was not in his nature to reveal his most private ambitions, even to me, not, at any rate, until they were within an inch of attainment. The one thing that he feared more than failure itself was the idea of having to admit it to anyone. Even with me, who was never less than supportive – or tried very hard to be – he found it hard to discuss his ambitions. At the beginning I used to feel rather hurt at this lack of trust. I tried to prise his plans gently out of him, to open up some sort of dialogue, but after a while I began to appreciate just how difficult this was for him, how paper-thin was his confidence, how for him the prospect of failure was almost like dying, and I learnt to suppress my curiosity, hard though it sometimes was.

After almost a mile the beech wood, which has never seemed taller, blots out the light, and then I am taking the last bend and ahead of me lie the four cottages which mark the boundary of the estate and the beginning of our land. Harry tried to persuade the landowners to sell us one of these cottages to house the staff we were planning to hire, but money got short and we never did acquire anything so grand as a permanent housekeeper.

Jill Hooper, who with her farm-worker husband occupies the second cottage and comes to clean for me three mornings a week, is standing in her gateway. She has changed the blue suit she wore at the service for her usual T-shirt and floral skirt. She waves heartily then lets her hand fall abruptly, as if uncertain as to the appropriateness of such a cheery gesture. Suddenly she waves again, signalling me to stop. She calls, 'Shall I have Josh for tea? I've got a lovely shepherd's pie in the oven.'

I thank her, I say Josh is fine and could not anyway eat

another thing for hours. Waving, I drive on. I am lucky to have Jill. Not the most thorough cleaner in the world – even I who am far from fussy can't help noticing the dust she has missed – she is nevertheless immensely kind-hearted and will always look after Josh at short notice.

Pennygate is fifty yards on, hidden from the cottages by the high walls of the kitchen garden and the trees lining the circular sweep of the drive.

Margaret's car is parked in front of the house, alongside Anne and Charles's, and the stately blue Volvo of Leonard, our solicitor. I am relieved to see there is no sign of Jack's BMW. I park further to one side than normal. As I get out I notice that a drain-pipe beside a first-floor bathroom at the side of the house has been leaking, discolouring the Suffolk-pink rendering with streaks of brown. I suppose I will have to get it seen to, though I can't feel much enthusiasm. While I have always appreciated the wonderful location of the place, the large airy rooms on the garden side looking down to the river, I have never really loved the house itself. I am not absolutely sure why. Perhaps because, with seven bedrooms, it is too large to make me feel comfortable. Perhaps because I had no say in choosing it. Perhaps because we never found the happiness here that we had known at Heath End.

The house was built in the twenties, solidly. On this side it is at its plainest, the windows too small, the walls of the kitchen extensions too angular, the trees too close, so that, by contrast with the garden side, it seems dark and damp.

I slip in by the kitchen door and go straight up the back stairs to Josh's room. It is empty, which doesn't entirely surprise me. Josh may have looked exhausted when we got back from London, but he has extraordinary powers of recovery. Even as Katie and I left for the school he was edging towards the garden. He'll be in one of his hide-outs by now, or shooting home-made arrows at trees.

I stand for a moment in front of his desk with its pile of Disneyland memorabilia which will probably find its way onto the walls between the Batman stickers and posters of whale flukes rising high out of the sea. We went to Disneyland twice, but the second time wasn't a success. I hadn't appreciated how homesick Josh was, how impatient he was to return to his outdoor life. I had been devoting so much time to Katie that I think Josh often felt bored, even a little neglected.

Now we're back I'll be lucky to see him except at meal times. Sometimes I get uneasy when he's gone a long time, but he knows the rules, to stay in the grounds and never go down to the river unaccompanied. I have always worried about the children being near water. Also, though we own the land all the way down to the river, there's a public footpath which follows the bank and brings all kinds of strangers, especially in summer.

I go silently up the corridor to my bedroom. My half-unpacked bags still lie on the floor. In the dressing-room a light has been left on, illuminating Harry's suits where they hang in an orderly row. I notice that several of his shirts have been hung on the wrong rail and absently rearrange them. I stare at the suits. They will have to be disposed of. The thought touches me with quiet dread, but I decide it is a job best done sooner rather than later, perhaps as early as next week if I can find the time. They can go into the next sale in aid of the church fund, where they should raise a few pounds for the roof.

As I touch the cloth I catch the scent of Harry, a subdued blend of cologne and indefinable male odour which I recognise instantly. After all that's happened, it is this that finally unlocks the emotions of the day. No unreality now, just the enormity of what has happened. I lean against the shelving and cry silent tears that carve hot trails down my cheeks. I am not sure what I am feeling. I am never sure what I am feeling. Pain. Bewilderment. Rage.

Small darts of despair, too. But since despair is not something I allow into my repertoire of emotions, I quickly pad into the bathroom and scoop cold water onto my face until the heat is gone.

I glance in the mirror. I suppose I look the same, but I don't feel it. There is no avoiding my eyes, in which I see not only the person I used to be – someone increasingly, bafflingly

29

remote – but also, looming ever larger, this strange new person I have become. This person has qualities I never realised I had, qualities which I do not particularly like but which I know I must hold on to with grim determination. If I ever lose sight of this, if I feel myself faltering, I only have to remember the children.

Instantly my mind flies to Katie and something lurches inside me. I do not dare to think of how much I am missing her already.

I splash more cold water over my eyes, then hot water, as hot as I can bear. Briskly I dry my face and brush my hair. I go and stand at the bedroom window, a moment of quiet before going down to the family.

I notice the lawn has patches of yellow; Charles told me yesterday there has been a shortage of rain. The formal garden, which is to the left and protected by a high wall from the frost-laden winter easterlies, does not seem too badly affected. If anything the roses look more abundant than usual. To the right the band of shrubs, oaks and wind-bent pines which conceal the track down to the quay is as dense as ever.

Ahead, the long expanse of lawn stretches out to a hidden ditch – I can never bring myself to call it a ha-ha – and beyond, a broad field that falls slowly away to the river where it meanders round in front of the house. The field is soft with some half-grown cereal which glows a limy yellow in the afternoon sun. The river, curving elegantly into the distance, is palest blue. In its middle reaches near Waldringfield several white-hulled yachts form dots of brightness.

When I first saw this view – the day that Harry finally announced he had bought the house – I was confused and dazzled by it. The way the river winds through the marshes as far as the eye can see – which on a clear day is the whole seven miles to the open sea – the way woods slope down to the marshes, the way the garden is so carefully designed to frame the scene: it is almost too perfect. After four years I am still in awe of it. Sometimes I feel it was intended for someone else altogether, and that I am here by accident.

Anne's voice drifts up from the terrace. I realise my absence will be holding things up. Making my way downstairs, I can't pretend I don't have to brace myself a little to meet Harry's family.

The drawing-room is a room that Harry encouraged me to have interior-designed in English chintz, a style that in the end proved a little too crisp and cool to make it congenial. But Harry was pleased with it, and I never said I was anything less than happy with the result.

Diana is sitting in a chair by the window, silhouetted by the brilliance of the sunlit garden. Margaret is opposite her, perched on the large footstool. As I come in, Margaret catches my eye and raises her eyebrows slightly, a signal that things could be easier. With my mother-in-law things are rarely easy. Diana has a large drink in her hand – gin or vodka, she switches between the two – and it won't be her first of the evening, although Margaret will doubtless have tried to water them down. Diana has been a widow for almost forty years and a drinker of great resourcefulness and determination for perhaps thirty-five, although, since this is something the family discuss with emotion rather than detachment, the exact time scale is hard to establish.

At lunch Diana put away enough for two large men, but on this day of all days no one was going to try and stop her, least of all me. Even now she shows few signs of her prodigious intake; her control, while it lasts, is formidable.

She frowns, sucking in her cheeks. This is her look of displeasure, the one that would have Harry leaping out of his seat with agitation even before she spoke.

'There you are! Thought you might have gone off again!'

'Off?' I say.

'Off. *Off.* To America or wherever.'

Half-smiling, I shake my head.

She grunts, 'You were away long enough,' and there is a wobble of resentment in her voice.

'Well – seven weeks. But it was worth it.' This, I realise, might be misinterpreted and I add, 'I mean, it was good for the children. They needed to get away.'

'Needed to get away?' She exaggerates the words. 'We could

31

all do with getting away!' She lifts her glass and takes a long gulp, fuelling her pique. 'You should have been here! Then Anne wouldn't have made such a hash of the service. All that nonsense about a pop concert, for heaven's sake! Who wants to be remembered for a pop concert?'

'Well, it was quite something, raising all that money.'

She waves this aside. 'You should have been here, Ellen! You should have put a stop to it!' She fixes me with a droopy stare.

So I am not to be forgiven for going away. Anne has already let me know her views on my absence and the considerable inconvenience it has caused her. With Diana I think it is rather different. I suspect Diana is punishing me because I wasn't around to look after her. For all the hoops she put Harry through, for all the trials she has subjected the rest of us to, I have always felt a certain sympathy for her, and, grasping this, she has always made the most of it. Under her prickly veneer which she has maintained with such vigour over the years, she is rather a forlorn and unhappy person.

'But it was a fine service,' I say. 'Anne put an enormous amount of work into it.'

'She was just trying to make an impression for Charles. Trying to get him noticed!'

There must be a logic in this but I am too tired to guess what it might be. 'Oh?'

'Politics, politics! Got it all the way back in the car. They thought I was asleep, but I heard!'

I look to Margaret for help. Margaret, who is usually the most direct of people, tucks her chin down to reduce the impact of her words. 'Charles is shortlisted for the candidature.'

I absorb this slowly. I thought Charles had given up all ideas of politics after an unsuccessful attempt to get selected for the next-door constituency eight years ago.

So many aspiring politicians in and around my family. Jack. And now Charles. 'Well. How splendid.' I take a long breath and get to my feet. 'I think I'll go and make some tea.'

'Just had tea!' Diana declares, as if this might keep me.

The kitchen is cool and quiet. This, more than any other room, is where I feel at home. It is furnished with pine that I found at country sales: a dresser whose shelves I have filled with blue china; wall units faced with old wooden shutters remade to size; a large Victorian table that has to be scrubbed hard to remove each spot of grease. Beyond, there is a lobby leading to a larder and a pantry. Late last autumn when I had thoughts of picking up my career again, I cleared out the pantry and made a small studio. I bought an expensive draughtsman's easel and a complete set of new materials. I worked on a few designs for a fund-raising poster for Molly's half-way house project, but they never seemed much good and when we couldn't get anyone to sponsor the cost of the printing I put them on one side.

I put the kettle on, find a tea-bag and perch on a stool while the water boils. I contemplate this wave of political activity that has grown up in my absence and feel profoundly grateful that I will not have to be a part of it. Political life was always an effort for me. The manœuvrings and the gossip and the backbiting never excited me as they did Harry. I didn't look forward to the evenings at the Conservative Club or the socialising with the party faithful. I hope I never let these feelings show – I tried very hard not to – and if Harry guessed how I felt he never commented on it. He merely assumed he could rely on me, which he could.

Thinking about it, Anne would make a good candidate's wife. She has the ambition and drive. I am not so sure about Charles himself though. I don't think he has the aggression, what Harry used to call the nail-down mentality, and he has never struck me as a natural speaker.

The quiet on this side of the house is almost total. On the wall in front of me is the pinboard where I keep the household lists, school calendars and details of local events. It has not been touched since I went away. The household diary, the one where I scribble the family engagements, is still showing the week of 12 April, Easter Monday, the week we left for California. I take it down and leaf slowly back until I reach Friday, 26 March. There is nothing to show what happened, to

33

mark the day in any special way. Two days earlier, on the Wednesday, I see that Josh went to a birthday party. It seems a long time ago now. And on the Thursday the engineer came to fix the washing machine. On the Friday itself there is a cryptic 'Load boat'. Then a line through the weekend, and written large: 'H & J take boat to the Hamble'. I forget now what excuse Jack gave for ducking out – a business meeting, something he couldn't get out of. It is his favourite escape clause: something I just can't get out of. But then I don't think he was ever that keen on the trip anyway. A coastal passage is not really Jack's thing. Too time-consuming, too little going on. If he sails at all, it is to take an adrenalin-charged rush around the buoys followed by a gin and tonic at the clubhouse.

There is more. On the line that divides the Friday and Saturday my handwriting says: 'Josh to Jill's. Ellen: supper at Molly's.' Then, on Saturday: 'Katie out?'

Slowly I tear the page out, followed by all the preceding ones. And all the ones leading up to the present week. I'm not sure why I am doing this, but I tear them neatly into two pieces then four.

'There you are!' says Anne, sweeping through the door. She comes as far as the sink. 'I had no idea you were back!' She looks rather cross with me.

I drop the scraps of paper in the bin. 'I was talking to Diana.'

'We've all been waiting.' She can't entirely hide the exasperation in her voice. 'Leonard too.'

'I'm sorry,' I smile quickly. 'I had to see Katie's house-mistress.'

'Yes, well ... There's an awful lot to sort out here, you know. We've had to make a lot of decisions while you were away. Letters, bills, staff ... *Mother*. It's been an awful job.'

'I do appreciate it, really.'

She blinks rapidly, not entirely mollified.

'I would like to say, Anne – thank you for the service. I know how much work you put into it. It was lovely.'

'Oh.' She's not sure how to take this, not sure if I'm just trying to humour her. For some reason, I have always managed to baffle Anne, to send her confusing signals. 'Well, I

34

thought it was the least we could do,' she states with great dignity.

'And so many people.'

'Oh, you thought so? Really? Well, I was quite pleased, I must say. People are so busy nowadays. But most came – most people Harry would have wanted anyway.'

The people Harry would have wanted. Yes, I suppose they were. Harry knew many people, but his favourites were either successful types who had a buzz about them and made him feel alive, which he liked more than anything else, or, by complete contrast, very ordinary people, like the locals he used to meet occasionally at the village pub on Sunday evenings, the sort who, according to Harry, kept him in touch with reality. I think they also made him feel good because they reminded him of how much he had achieved.

For some reason, I also think of the people who were not there, the people that Harry fell out with over the years – early business associates, political allies, friends from the past. Harry could be abrasive under pressure; he did not keep his friends easily.

Anne's face creases into a grimace of anguish. 'I still can't believe he's gone, you know. There are whole times when I just...' She makes a despairing gesture. 'It's the not *knowing*. I wish – I wish they would *find* him! I really can't bear it! Having him out there – just *out* there somewhere. It's *awful!*'

I pour the hot water and keep pressing the tea bag with a spoon until the liquid is almost black.

Anne sniffs fiercely. 'We haven't let them give up, you know!'

I hesitate for an instant before pulling a stool out from under the counter and offering it to her. 'Haven't let who give up?' I ask.

She perches on the stool grudgingly as if she doesn't really mean to stay. 'The coastguard!'

I must look blank or alarmed, or both, because she explains loudly, as if I might be having trouble hearing, 'Give up the *search*. They would have given up – oh, weeks ago. But we weren't having any of that! No, Charles got hold of some

Felixstowe fishermen. Got them to chart the tides and everything, to say where the yacht was most likely to have gone down. Took the chart along to the coastguard. Otherwise they'd have been quite happy just to sit back and wait, you know. They kept saying it was bound to turn up sooner or later. I mean!'

My heart knocks once against my ribs. 'The boat?'

She blinks at the crassness of my question. 'Yes – the *boat*.' Her face folds into an expression of pain. 'Though they don't say anything about Harry, they don't say . . .' She presses the back of her fist to her lips, she takes a deep breath.

I extract the tea-bag and squeeze it harshly. My throat is dry, I long to drink, but when I take a sip the tea scorches my tongue. 'Why do they think it's likely to turn up?' I ask.

Anne shrugs impatiently. 'Oh, I don't know. Something to do with the fishing boats – I don't know. *Anyway*, the point is they're having a proper look. *That's* the important thing!'

I stir the tea repeatedly in an effort to cool it down. When I don't respond, Anne is driven to repeat testily, 'They really would have given up, you know!'

'Yes, I see. I hadn't realised.' I try not to think of the yacht, but I see it lying there on the sea floor, I imagine its white hull reflecting light dimly back to the surface.

But why are they bound to find it? So much sea, such a small boat. I don't understand.

And why do they want to keep looking for it? After all this time I had assumed they would have given up. In fact, I had convinced myself. Forgetting how hot the tea is, I take a gulp and burn my throat.

Anne has returned to an earlier theme. 'There's been *so* much to sort out,' she sighs. 'Honestly! The staff weren't getting paid – did you realise? And Mother's allowance, the bank stopped it – just like that, if you please. *We've* been paying it ever since – quite happy to, of course – but that's not the point.' Anne finds it impossible to talk calmly about money. Harry was the same. Their father, who lived in some style while he was alive, left heavy debts and Diana had a struggle to meet the school fees. There wasn't enough for

36

skiing trips and expensive treats, and even thirty years later Harry still smarted at the memory of not being able to keep up with his schoolfriends.

'I hadn't realised you'd done so much,' I say. 'Thank you.'

'Well, someone had to!' The sharpness of her tone leaves me in no doubt that I have been derelict in my duty. 'You left so soon! So quickly! As if – well, as if you'd given up hope!'

'It was almost three weeks, Anne.'

'Just over two, I think, Ellen.'

I am not going to be drawn into an argument that is unlikely to achieve anything but bad feeling. 'I would have gone mad if I'd stayed,' I explain with sudden candour. 'And the children – I wanted to get them away.'

'Well, it's one thing to go away, and quite another to go just like that! At two day's notice, leaving everything in a mess! And as for the children – well I would have thought it was very unsettling for them, being away from their friends in a strange place.'

I don't have the energy to defend myself. I shrug in mild apology. 'I did what I thought was right at the time.' I stand up. 'And now, forgive me, but if Leonard's waiting . . .'

Conflict passes over Anne's face. She doesn't like her flow being cut short, not when she is still brimming with things to say. She busies herself with a fresh handkerchief. I cross the distance between us and hold out my hands. My time away, my sessions with Bob Block, have only reinforced my belief that life is too short for resentments and petty grievances.

After a moment's hesitation – I think I have taken her by surprise – Anne brings her arms up and we embrace clumsily. Her cheek is warm and soft, her well-cushioned back rigid under its corsetry.

Charles has appeared in the doorway. Reading the emotional temperature, his face loops into a lazy smile. He, like me, prefers a life without discord. I decide, not for the first time, that he is a nice man, certainly too nice for politics.

I shake my head at him as I approach. 'I'm told you're going to throw yourself to the wolves.'

'What? Oh, that.' He attempts a solemn expression. 'It's

not settled yet. Not too late to pull out. What do you think? I wanted to talk to you about it.'

'Me? Why me?'

'Well, I thought— You don't mind then?'

'Why should I?' I grasp his arm. 'Good luck to you.'

From behind, Anne says hurriedly, 'We were going to tell you, weren't we, Charles? We thought it would be wonderful to keep the seat in the family.' Much taken by the idea, her voice quivers, her eyes moisten. 'Make it into a bit of a tradition. Carry on Harry's work.'

I look back at Charles. He meets my eye. It might be my imagination, but I think there is a trace of sheepishness in his good-natured smile.

Anne leads the way into the hall. I touch Charles's arm and we fall behind. 'Anne tells me you went to see the coastguard,' I say as soon as she is out of earshot.

He stops, his expression both forthright and uneasy, as though he is worried about upsetting me. I give him my most unemotional expression.

'We felt they could be doing more, Ellen,' he says gruffly.

'And are they?'

He folds his arms and frowns at his feet. 'Well, they've agreed to focus things a bit more. Look at the most likely area.'

'They're searching then?'

He shakes his head grimly. 'No resources, I'm afraid. And they say the area is too wide anyway.'

I feel a rush of relief.

'No,' Charles continues in his stately manner, 'they rely on the local fishermen to keep a look-out for things that snag their nets or show up on their sonar, that kind of thing. But they do say that small vessels often get found that way, by the fishermen. Surprisingly often, in fact.'

The anxiety returns, and it must show in my face because Charles says worriedly, 'Now that's why I didn't tell you before, you see. I didn't want to raise your hopes.'

Raise my hopes? I find myself looking at him in open bewilderment before glancing away. 'Where's this new area then?'

'Oh, along the route south, as before. But also a bit to one side, to allow for the tides. We're not sure the coastguard took the tides properly into account before, you see. Well, the inshore fishermen didn't think so anyway.'

'A bit to one side?'

He nods, thinking this is all the answer I need.

'Where exactly?' I ask lightly.

'Oh, west a bit,' he says. 'Inside the Gunfleet Sand. The tide sets in there, you see, in towards the mouth of the Thames. *If* Harry hadn't allowed for that, *if* the yacht had drifted . . . d'you see?'

I absorb this slowly. 'I see.'

He takes another reading of my face. Reaching awkwardly for my hand, he grasps it unhappily and says, 'Please don't hope for too much, Ellen.'

I put on my most robust look. 'No, I won't. But thanks. For taking the trouble.'

He smiles his bashful smile. 'The least I could do.' He releases my hand and pushes his shoulders back and looks suddenly much brighter.

Anne reappears and summons us impatiently to the drawing-room, where she is trying to persuade a haughty and belligerent Diana that it is time to go home. It takes the combined efforts of us all to persuade her into the car.

Before climbing into the driving seat, Charles gives me a brisk embrace. 'I don't think you should be here on your own,' he says with a frown.

I have Josh, I tell him. I'll be all right. In fact I'm not at all sure I will be all right, but I have learnt that at times like these, times when I am feeling unsettled, I am better off on my own, that indeed it is the only situation in which I feel safe.

As the car draws away Diana puts her face to the window and pulls a face at me, a face that says I have let her down. I give her a wave.

Margaret comes back into the house with me. She is certain there must be something she can do. She, like Charles, worries about leaving me alone, but I tell her to go home, that I will be fine and that I will see her on Monday when we tackle the paperwork. I have looked into the study and seen the neat piles of letters and bills waiting on Harry's desk, beautifully ordered and marked.

'You're sure?' asks Margaret, who can't bear the idea of leaving any task undone. Normally Margaret is based at Harry's office in Ipswich. She came to him nine years ago when he and Jack set up Ainswick Properties and started their first project, a shop and office development down by Ipswich station. She was newly divorced then after a long and, I think, difficult marriage. She must be in her mid-fifties now, a wiry agile woman of great energy and common sense who is a devil at golf and was for several years women's county champion.

'No, you go home.' I pause, trying to grasp a half-remembered thought, the echo of some conversation from earlier in this endless day. Finally it comes back. 'The Rumanian orphans concert, Margaret. Do we have anything on it? I don't know – records, files?'

'There's a bit,' she says. 'Mainly fund-raising and correspondence. The files are at the office. Do you want me to bring them over?'

'No. Well, I don't think so. It's just that the charity director is keen to see me for some reason. He's coming on Monday.'

'Tim Schwartz? But that's ridiculous,' Margaret declares. 'He's already been on to me. He's already been in touch with Mr Gillespie. I'll have a word with him. He shouldn't be bothering you, and certainly not when you've only just got back. That's very naughty.'

'He said he'd tried Gillespie but had no luck.'

'Well, there you are! Even less reason to bother *you*. I'll put him off, shall I?'

I almost say yes, but the memory of Schwartz's insistent manner holds me back. 'Did he say what he wanted when he spoke to you?'

'Not really.' Immediately Margaret indicates that this is not strictly true. 'What he *asked* for were details of the banking arrangements for the concert. But when I gave them to him he said it wasn't enough. He needed access to the invoices. That was when I put him in touch with Mr Gillespie.'

'Invoices?' I repeat, trying to maintain interest.

'I don't think we ever saw any,' says Margaret. 'Not that I remember. The bookkeeping was done by someone attached to the charity. *If* we had invoices they'd have been in the accounts file that I sent to Mr Gillespie some time ago.' Instantly she is concerned that she might have done the wrong thing. 'I can check with Mr Gillespie, if you like.'

Gillespie was Harry's accountant, and now, I suppose, he must be mine. I have met him only twice and what I remember of him is somewhat daunting. I shake my head.

'I'll put Mr Schwartz off then, shall I?'

I am tempted, but if I don't see Tim Schwartz then I'm not sure who will, and I don't think he'll take kindly to being palmed off. Also, if there's any problem that involves Harry, anything that needs sorting out, then I feel I should know about it. While I was away I made this decision to face up to situations, however difficult or unpleasant they might be, something I hadn't always managed to achieve in the past.

'No, I'll see him. It'll be better to see him.'

As she gets into her car, Margaret says, 'Why don't I check with Mr Gillespie anyway, just so we're clear on who's got what?'

I would have preferred to avoid even this small fuss but I can't think of a reason not to agree.

Before joining Leonard, waiting patiently in the drawing-room, I go outside and call half-heartedly for Josh.

The garden is overwhelming, the air warm and heavy with the scent of pine and grass, the lawn streaked with long golden light. An insect buzzes idly past, and floating up from the river comes the reedy call of a marsh bird.

I feel a sudden relief at being home, an unexpected gratitude at being returned to this small corner of the world, which, through some miracle, seems to continue as before, altered but unchanged. I thought it would be far harder coming back, that I'd find it agonising to see the river again, to sleep in our bed, to see and touch Harry's clothes. But I am stronger than I realise. I think I always have been.

I call again, but if Josh hears me he doesn't reply, and after a

41

time I go back inside. Crossing the hall, I step lightly past the drawing-room door and enter the passage that leads to Harry's study. The walls are decorated with assorted hunting prints and antique maps of Suffolk, and, half-way along, a large framed nautical chart. This too is a bit of an antique. The markings are faint, intricate and closely packed and, in the poor light, it is a moment or two before I manage to find the Gunfleet Sand, which appears to be a long shoal radiating outwards from the mouth of the Thames. Comparing it to Harry's planned route, I see that it lies well off to the left as you look at the chart.

If they have to focus their attention anywhere, I suppose this is as good a place as any.

But I wish they would leave Harry in peace. The thought of them finding him gives me actual physical pain. All it could possibly achieve is heartache for the children and me. No one seems to have thought of that. Probably because no one has asked me. I should speak out; there is nothing to stop me. But I would have to argue long and hard, and I'm not sure I could do it convincingly.

THREE

The drawing room is bright after the gloom of the passage. Leonard is sitting in an armchair on the far side of the flower-filled hearth. He pulls his tall frame hastily out of the chair. 'Ellen.' He pats my hand with light fluttering strokes, as if I am made of something more fragile than flesh and bone. His pepper-and-salt eyebrows, which protrude like porcupine quills, are pulled together in a frown. 'You must be *very* tired. We could easily leave this until another day, you know.' He releases my hand abruptly, as if he has already held it too long.

'I'd rather not.'

'It'd be *no* trouble to come back over the weekend. *Any* time at all.'

'I'd rather go ahead. If you don't mind.' I realise the news isn't going to be good – there have been hints and meaningful pauses from the family – and now it has got to the point where I would prefer to know the worst.

Leonard hovers a moment. 'You *are* taking care of yourself, Ellen? You've got someone in the house tonight? You shouldn't be alone, you know. Can't Molly stay with you?'

There is something about me – my appearance, my manner, I'm not sure what – that has always made people feel they must worry about me, people like Leonard and Charles and Molly anyway. And with Harry's death their concern has been given full rein.

'Leonard,' I almost laugh, 'I'm all right.'

He stares at me, not entirely convinced, then gives a resigned nod.

We sit down. Leonard pulls his briefcase onto his lap and extracts a batch of papers from a folder. 'I'll start with the *legal situation*, if that's all right. Everything else rather *stems* from that.' Leonard, who must be nearer sixty than fifty, comes from the old breed of solicitor, the kind who cares for you from cradle to grave. Harry took him on soon after we married. The choice rather surprised me. Harry's other advisers – his accountants, financial consultants, corporate lawyers – were always young and assertive. But it was probably Leonard's very staidness, the very solidity of his values that recommended him to Harry.

'Since we last spoke, things have become a *little* clearer,' Leonard begins carefully. 'But I'm afraid that, generally speaking, the situation is rather – *difficult*, Ellen.' He pulls his cadaverous face into a regretful expression. 'As you know, the will is relatively straightforward, and under *normal* circumstances probate would be granted within months. But as things stand – well, I'm afraid we can't hope to have it proved for some *considerable* time—'

'The will,' I interrupt tentatively. 'I'm sorry – you wouldn't go through it for me?'

'What, the *terms*, you mean?'

'Yes.'

'Oh . . .' He is reluctant. I think he was keen to get the bad news over with and I have put him off his stride. 'Very well,' he says hesitantly. 'Is it one or two things you're not clear about, Ellen, or . . . ?'

'Well, I think . . . just the basics, really.'

He gives me a sharp look, alive with sudden apprehension. 'But you *have* seen the will?'

'Well . . . not actually seen it, no.'

He tries again, gently. 'But you saw it some time ago?'

'Harry told me about it.'

'Oh!' Leonard's sense of propriety is offended. 'I thought— You said on the *phone*—'

I apologise. I explain that I was not at my brightest during that conversation which, if I remember correctly, took place at the unpromising hour of six a.m. just two days after the

44

children and I arrived in California. I was awake, as it happened, but groggy with sleeping pills and whatever else I was taking at the time.

'Well, if Harry told you...' Leonard says, somewhat mollified.

When Josh was born Harry told me that if anything should happen to him we would be taken care of. He took a certain pride in being able to provide for us, something which, by his reckoning, his father had singularly failed to do for him. He told me there would be a trust fund but did not go into detail. He was never a person to reveal more than he chose to. Secrecy came naturally to him, a form of self-preservation that he had learnt in his troubled childhood.

It was two years ago that Harry mentioned he was setting up a special trust fund for Katie. I was proud, grateful, touched. Generally I don't believe inherited money does young people many favours, but for someone as insecure as Kate it would be a blessing, something to give her some much needed independence. Typically, Harry did not tell me how much was involved and, just as typically, I did not ask.

It wasn't until a few weeks before Harry died, when the extent of his troubles was becoming clear even to me, that I thought about Katie's trust again, anxious in case Harry should change his mind about it. I went so far as to ask an accountant I met at a constituency gathering how trust funds operated. He assured me that a trust could not be dissolved once it was set up.

Leonard draws back his lips. 'It'll take some time to go through it.'

'Just the main points. That's all.'

Rallying, Leonard says in a brisk voice, 'Right.' He extracts a document from another of the folders on his lap.

'As I think I told you, Harry's last will is dated just after Josh's birth, with two codicils added to cover a few minor points. The essence of it is *this* ... the bulk of the estate is to be formed into a *trust*, with myself and Jack Crawley as trustees. Diana will be one of the beneficiaries of this trust during her *lifetime.'* He gives me a quick glance to see if I am with him so far. 'As you know, Harry set up various annuities for her over the years, but under the terms of the will, she will receive an *income* from the trust, to replace her present allowance. The income is determined by various calculations. Er . . . Did you want the details?'

I shake my head.

'Well, once Diana is taken care of, then the trust will be for the *exclusive* benefit of *you*, as Harry's widow, and the *children* of the marriage – that is, Joshua. Now, so far as the administration of the trust goes, the trustees will have *wide* discretionary powers—'

The implications of what he is saying dawn slowly and strike me with sudden weight. 'But Katie—' I interrupt. 'What about Katie?' At the far end of the sofa the telephone starts to ring. I stare at Leonard. 'I thought – I thought there was a trust for Katie.'

Distracted, Leonard glances towards the telephone.

I say again, 'I thought there was a trust.'

My anxiety sends him back to his notes, though he must be aware of the answer. I am conscious of my heart beating away long seconds marked by the rhythmic warbling of the phone. 'A trust. Yes, *yes*,' he says in his deliberate voice, drawing out a paper. 'Thirty thousand pounds. But it was a gift in Harry's lifetime, you see. So it doesn't appear in the will. No *need* to have it in the will.' He gives a smile that was probably intended to reassure me but comes out as a grimace.

'I see,' I say uncertainly. I should be relieved – I am – but this doesn't stop a small knot of uneasiness collecting in my stomach. The phone rings on.

'Er . . .?' Leonard glances at the phone, longing to see it answered.

Suddenly I realise it might be Katie. I get to the receiver in time to hear the line buzzing emptily.

I return to my seat. I look at Leonard and grapple with an old suspicion that has resurfaced abruptly.

I ask, 'Katie's trust – when was it set up?'

46

'What? Oh . . .' He takes another look at his piece of paper. 'Er . . . Yes, two years ago. Almost exactly. *June.*'

'And before that?'

Leonard's head comes forward, he peers at me like an ancient bird. 'I'm sorry?'

'Before Harry set up the trust, what were the arrangements for Katie?'

'Well . . .' He blinks at me, suddenly a little wary. He waves a hand. 'Well, I could check back, *of course.* But Ellen dear' – he gives me his most benign smile – 'for the moment it might be best to press on. Otherwise we won't get through it all, and I don't want to keep you too late.'

'I only wanted to know . . . I just wanted to be clear . . . There was no particular provision for Katie? Before?'

He stares at me. 'Well . . . no.' Hurriedly he leans forward and, resting his elbows on his knees, gestures reassurance with the spread of his long hands. 'But Ellen, don't take that to mean— Well, don't imagine that Harry intended Katie to be badly off. Not for a moment. In fact *quite* the opposite. This little trust was just a bonus for her, an *extra.* No, he assumed there'd be *plenty* in the main trust, that you would be so well provided for that you'd be able to support Katie *amply. Amply.*'

I nod slowly. 'I see. Thank you.'

Leonard searches my face. He says urgently, 'But listen, I would *not* get too concerned about all this if I were you, Ellen. Not at this stage. You see . . .' He proceeds awkwardly, 'When everything is finally *valued,* when all the calls on the estate are met, we might well find that everything is rather *different . . .*' He comes to a halt, pushing out his lip. 'Well, perhaps we'd better come on to that later. I will need to explain it in some *detail.*'

He is laying the ground for this bad news of his.

'I see,' I say. 'Go on.'

He peers at me anxiously. 'You're sure?'

I manage a smile. 'Sure.'

Leonard finds his place. 'The trust, as I say, is allowed considerable *flexibility.* The trustees will have discretion to provide either *capital* or *income . . .*'

47

I hardly hear him. I am still thinking of Katie's inheritance. Why nothing for her in the will? How could Harry have been so unfair? When Harry and I married he said he would do his best for Katie. He always spoke of her as his daughter, he encouraged her to call him Daddy. After Josh was born he talked about 'the children'. I had always assumed he wouldn't differentiate between them. I had always assumed – what an irony – that he loved her equally.

I digest this, I let it settle. It is not so very hard. Really, this is just one more small hurt in a long line of hurts that Harry dealt me in the last few months. As I absorb it, it begins to take on the colour of an older and more familiar emotion, one that I felt last autumn at the start of what was the most painful time for Harry and me. This emotion is a blend of misery and bafflement, and now it reopens like an old wound.

I become aware of silence, of Leonard watching me. 'I'm sorry, Leonard, I . . .'

He is half way to his feet. 'Can I get you something? Water? Coffee?'

'No. You are sweet, but I'm fine.'

'You look completely worn out.'

I shake my head, I give a crooked grin. 'Honestly.'

'Do you want me to run over that last bit again?'

'No, no. Go on. Please.'

But something must have shown in my face because, after a moment's hesitation, Leonard brings himself to say, 'Did you think Katie would be getting a share of the main trust? Is that it?'

I spread my palms wide. A sudden heat pricks my eyes. I suppress it rapidly. What does it matter what I thought?

'It's not important now,' I say brightly, hoping he hasn't noticed the unsteadiness in my voice, the shine in my eyes. Whatever happens, I don't want to draw attention to how I feel about Harry's behaviour on this.

For a moment I think Leonard is going to say more but, reading my expression, he settles slowly back into his seat, though not without the occasional troubled glance in my direction.

'Now *probate* . . .' he says in a tired voice. 'Perhaps I should explain a few of the problems we're likely to encounter in obtaining probate. The main obstacle, as you might imagine, is the lack of a *death* certificate. Normally, in circumstances where – well –'

I help him along. 'Where there's no body.'

His mouth jerks up at the corners, a sort of nervous reflex. 'Er – *yes*. Where there's no *direct* evidence of death . . . then the statutory period for presumption of death is *seven* years. Now we wouldn't expect to have to wait *that* long, of course. Not in this case. The seven year rule is really designed for people who just up and off. You know, walk out of the door and are never seen again. No, in this sort of case, where there are *special* circumstances, one can apply for leave to swear to the death *within* the statutory period. But having said that, I have to warn you – it can be a long drawn-out process. There are certain *conditions* which have to be met. Even then it's up to the court, and they may not grant leave for some time, not until they're *absolutely* satisfied.' He crinkles up his eyes, he sucks in his breath. 'It could take years.'

I hadn't imagined that any of the legalities would be simple. At the same time I had rather hoped they could be cleared up in a matter of months rather than years. 'These conditions, what sort of thing . . . ?'

'Well, they're designed for quite *different* circumstances, of course.' Seeing that I am not to be denied the detail, he assembles his fingers and counts them off slowly. 'First, nothing must be *heard* from the deceased, not by anyone who would normally expect to hear from him. Second, nothing must be *seen* of him – again by anyone who would normally expect to see him. And lastly, and I would imagine most importantly, the *circumstances* of the presumed death have to be taken into account. These would have to be sufficient to establish in the court's mind that death was very much *more* likely to have occurred than *not*.'

'But these circumstances, our circumstances – aren't they enough?'

He is not going to commit himself. 'It's really a matter for the experts, Ellen. They're coming back to me shortly. It's taken some time to assemble all the, er – appropriate information.'

'Appropriate information?' I echo mildly. 'The weather, you mean? The people who saw him. That ship.'

'The weather – yes, that must count for *something*, of course. But the sightings – well, they're not so sure. You see, it's not a matter of establishing whether or not Harry *left*. There's absolutely no doubt about that. So whether the yacht that fellow at Waldringfield saw going down the river was actually *Minerva* or some other yacht is slightly by the way. And the crew of the coaster, they couldn't actually identify the yacht they saw that night. But as I say, it's all rather *academic*, because we know that Harry and the yacht left the river. There's no doubt about that. D'you see?'

I give a tiny nod. 'What about the dory, then?'

'Well, yes, that *does* mean something, of course it does. But again . . .' He creases up his face regretfully. 'It's not quite *enough*.'

'But . . .' I give a small laugh of incredulity. 'It was found drifting. I mean, it wouldn't be drifting if something hadn't happened.'

Leonard draws a long breath. 'N-o-o,' he says in the tone of a parent humouring a child.

'I don't see . . .'

'I'm sorry?'

'Why isn't it important?'

'Because, umm . . .' He swivels a hand and claws the fingers slowly into his palm. 'Because, you see, in *theory*, the dinghy – the dory, you call it – could simply have come *loose*. Drifted away from the yacht without Harry realising it. It doesn't follow that the yacht itself got into trouble. D'you see?'

I am trying very hard to see. I look out of the window for a moment. 'What about *Minerva* being missing?' I ask, disliking the sarcasm in my voice. 'Isn't that significant either?'

'Ah! Well, that's significant, of *course*. Very. But from the soundings I've taken—' His face twitches at the unfortunate choice of words and he gestures apology before hurrying on. 'From what I can *glean*, it would be much more – well, *useful* if it were actually *found*. That would be the most powerful *evidence* of all, d'you see?'

I say abruptly, 'You mean, otherwise it could be assumed that Harry was half-way down the Atlantic, heading for South America!'

'No, no.' He attempts a dismissive laugh that doesn't quite come off. 'No—'

'Well, why else would they be so keen to find it?' The peevish edge is back in my voice. 'I mean, he was seen leaving the river. The weather was foul. He only had food for a couple of days. What else would he be doing but sailing for South America?'

Leonard looks vaguely alarmed. I don't think he has seen me in an abrasive mood before. 'I can assure you that no one's ever mentioned *anything* like that. Not for one moment, Ellen. No, it's simply a question of the weight of evidence.'

I sigh heavily. I know I shouldn't let this get to me, I know I am achieving nothing but anxiety and grief for myself, but I can't seem to prevent it.

Leonard explains patiently. 'Evidence can take *time* to—' He pulls himself up hastily, on the point, I guess, of saying to surface. 'To *turn up*,' he states carefully. 'The court really can't afford to be hasty. There have been cases . . . Well, you can imagine.'

'I don't want it to drag on . . .'

What I really mean is that I don't want Harry's life subjected to constant re-examination, though I don't say that.

Leonard makes a sympathetic face. 'No. I suppose we *could* try to apply for leave straight away . . .' He doesn't sound confident.

We are silent for a time. The garden has turned a rich gold in the evening sun. A vision leaps into my mind, one that I normally manage to keep at a tolerable distance. It catches me unawares, arriving by a side door that I have failed to defend. For a moment it overwhelms my imagination. I see Harry's body. It is lying in icy water, deep in the North Sea. I wish there were no detail, but the image is merciless. His eyes are open, his skin is grey and swollen, his body is rocked to and

51

fro by the current. It is an image so ghastly that I cannot think it for very long without feeling I will go mad.

Leonard stirs. 'Um . . . Shall I go on or . . . ?'

I get to my feet and go to the drinks tray. 'Do you want anything, Leonard?' He shakes his head. I am no drinker; the occasional glass of white wine is usually my limit. But I have a need for something to take me through the rest of the conversation. I stare indecisively at the bottles and finally pour myself a small brandy. I take a sip and wait for the unfamiliar warmth to fire my stomach before returning slowly to my seat.

'Sorry, Leonard. Do go on.'

He draws a breath to get himself going again. 'Until the death certificate is issued—' The phone interrupts. He looks at me plaintively. I go and answer it. It is Molly. She says she tried to call five minutes ago.

'Now listen,' she says in her no-nonsense voice, 'shall I come over? Have you eaten? You're not on your own, are you?'

I fend her off, though it's not easy.

'You may think you're doing fine, my love,' she says, 'but you *can't* be doing fine. And why can't I come over? Won't you at least bring Josh to lunch tomorrow?'

I promise I'll think about lunch and let her know in the morning. I would promise anything at the moment.

Leonard, who has picked up the gist of this conversation, looks approving as I sink back into my seat. 'Good to get out and about,' he says firmly. Like most people he seems to think solitude is the worst possible thing, that activity is the only effective antidote to bereavement. It would be useless to explain that I feel much stronger on my own than with other people.

Leonard resumes his troubled expression. 'Until the death certificate is issued there are going to be certain *difficulties*, I'm afraid. Particularly – well, *mainly* on the money front. For the time being you can continue to sign cheques on your *joint* account, there's no problem there. And the deposit account that feeds it still has *some* funds.'

'Anne said something about people not being paid.'

He makes a dismissive gesture. 'That was just the fools at the bank. For some reason known only to themselves they froze the deposit account. I soon pointed out their *error*.' This he says with heavy irony. 'Harry had an automatic top-up arrangement. They had *no* authority to stop it.' He pauses delicately. 'But I have to mention . . . the funds in the deposit account *are* getting low. Just over five thousand, to be precise. Er – would you be having any calls against this in the next few weeks? Calls of any *size*?'

I presume he means bills from California. I try to think. Some will have come through already – the rent of the house in La Jolla, the airline tickets, the hire car. But some will still be in the pipeline – Bob Block's fees from my last few visits, the cost of the week we took in Yosemite Park.

'It depends what you mean by size.'

He nods sagely, as if this was an answer.

I ask, 'And when the five thousand's gone?'

His eyes slide away, he contorts his mouth inward. Even before he speaks, he has told me everything I need to know.

'That bad?' I give a dry laugh.

'There *are* assets, Ellen. A portfolio of stocks and shares. A life insurance policy. Something to be claimed for the loss of the yacht. And of course Harry's holding in Ainswick Properties. But the shares – well, they're in *Harry's* name, you see, and—'

'Couldn't I borrow against them or something?'

'In theory, *maybe*. But so far as I can tell at the moment – from what Gillespie says – well . . .' He sighs. 'The assets seem to be heavily encumbered.'

Encumbered. A strange archaic word. But I understand it well enough.

Leonard continues ponderously. 'I had a long meeting with Gillespie – now what I'm going to tell you is *totally* confidential, Ellen; he said to impress on you that it *really* mustn't go beyond the three of us – but apparently Ainswick has two major *creditors*, and one of them – a Middle Eastern bank – called in its loan straight away, within a *week* of Harry's death. Very hasty, but that's the way these people are, I'm afraid.

53

And the financial climate being what it is...' He gestures gloom.

'Ainswick couldn't pay?'

He shakes his head in agreement. 'The recession... A cash shortage... I don't think there're many property companies that could satisfy a sudden demand for cash in today's climate.' He fixes me with a sorrowful gaze. 'It seems Harry put up a large proportion of his *personal* portfolio as a guarantee – almost seventy-five per cent, Gillespie estimates – and, well... The bank has gone and *cashed* the shares.'

I chew on my lip, I raise my eyebrows. Leonard takes this as some sort of technical query and adds hastily, 'Oh, nothing illegal about it. Nothing *improper*. No, the bank was fully entitled apparently.' He frowns at his hands for a moment. 'Gillespie is holding the other bank off, but he tells me that negotiations are fairly *critical*. They're holding all Harry's remaining securities as a guarantee, along with an interest in Ainswick's most valuable property. Somewhere in London, I believe.'

'Shoreditch,' I murmur. 'An office block in Shoreditch.'

'Oh, is it? Gillespie didn't say. But anyway everything depends on the sale of this building apparently. According to Gillespie the whole things is, er ... fairly *critical* ...' He peers at me unhappily from under his substantial eyebrows. He wants to make sure that I have read this message correctly, that I have understood that Ainswick may go under. 'I'm sorry, Ellen. I'm really sorry.'

I take my time. I let this settle over me gently.

I knew that Ainswick was in trouble. I had guessed long ago, months before Harry finally, angrily, admitted to it. It wasn't a great feat of deduction. The bitter disappointment that Harry felt at losing his parliamentary seat was considerable – we lived through some black weeks – but even that couldn't account for the stress that he showed later last summer. While success made him calm and controlled, pressure made him hyper-active. As the recession bit deeper he spent less and less time at home, he propelled himself into a spiral of meetings, the few times he was home he drove nowhere – or maybe somewhere

– late at night, he woke early to scribble in his study, as if by throwing time and energy at his problems he could simply wear them down.

Once I dared suggest that he might achieve more by slowing down a little. But Harry disliked even the mildest criticism, especially from me. Not because I wielded it often – quite the opposite – but because, I realise, it was in his relationship with me that he felt most vulnerable.

So there will be virtually no money, not from the estate anyway. I feel oddly unmoved. Maybe because there are many worse things that could happen, maybe because I can't believe I will be left entirely destitute. And because there's still the life insurance policy to be discussed.

'And Katie's trust?'

'Ah, *that's* unaffected. D'you see what I mean now, about things turning out rather differently? About the intentions of the will not meaning a great deal?'

I feel a small satisfaction at this unexpected turn. Nothing for me and Josh, something for Katie: there's a sort of justice in there somewhere. Thirty thousand was not a great deal by Harry's standards of course, but it's quite a bit by mine.

I dwell on this thought for a moment before asking, 'What about the house?'

'It's in *joint* names,' Leonard explains carefully, 'which means it can't be sold yet. But it *might* be possible to raise a further mortgage on it.' He puts a suitable note of caution into his voice. 'The existing mortgages and liens are quite large, of course. But it might be possible to *extend* them. So Gillespie says, anyway.'

I knew from something Harry said soon after he bought Pennygate that there was a mortgage, but I never gave it much thought until Leonard called me in California. I was sitting in my swimsuit in the air-conditioned cool of the La Jolla apartment, I remember, clutching the receiver – slippery with sun oil – to my shoulder, watching the children swimming in the communal pool under the harsh sun, when Leonard said that the debts against the house – two mortgages and a charge registered by a bank – totalled almost three hundred thousand.

'Of course,' Leonard says now, as he said then, 'the house is worth at least seventy or eighty thousand more. As long as prices stand up.'

But prices are not standing up, so the newspapers keep saying, and I can see that, by the time the house is finally sold, there may not be much left after interest payments.

'The insurance pay-out on the yacht should fetch fifty thousand or so – *eventually*. I've spoken to the insurance people. They're basically sympathetic, but because there's no actual wreck as yet . . . Well, I think it might be a *year* before terms are agreed.'

There is a pause. I wonder why Leonard does not return to the life policy. I know it is very substantial.

As if reading my mind, his face brightens a little. 'There *is* the life insurance, of course,' he says. 'It could be worth quite a bit – *eventually*. No claim can be made, of course, until the death certificate is issued. Even then it might be a while before they pay out. Insurance companies aren't exactly *forthcoming* in these circumstances.'

'How much is it worth?' I ask.

'In death benefit, you mean? Rather than cashing-in value?'

'Yes.'

'Five hundred and forty thousand.'

This is an enormous amount to me. I feel a surge of optimism. It will be more than enough for what I have in mind.

'And it would come straight to me, the money? Not into any trust?'

'Straight to you.'

I'd rather hoped as much.

'What about for now?' I ask. 'Couldn't I borrow against it?'

His brightness dims. 'It's back to the difficulty of establishing death. The whole thing's too uncertain, you see, from a potential *lender's* point of view.'

'Uncertain? But . . . they'll have to pay out, surely. Whatever happens.'

'Ah . . .' Leonard goes carefully again. '*We* may know that, Ellen. But to the insurers, you see, the facts will be looking *less* than conclusive. They will be forced to keep their minds open to *every* possibility you could ever imagine.' He gives an odd chuckle.

'Ah.' I nod sagely. 'You mean—?'

'Well – they have to consider things like suicide.' In his anxiety to make light of this he almost laughs. 'Intentional disappearance. That sort of thing. *Mad*, I know. But they're bureaucrats, that's the way they see things.'

'I see. And suicide would—?'

'I'm sorry?'

'It would affect things?'

'Oh yes. It would make the policy void.'

I knew this. Everyone knows this, whether they have life insurance or not. But I want to get everything absolutely clear, I want every question answered, every detail in place so that I can feel fully prepared.

'I was wondering . . . assets. You've nothing of your *own*?' Leonard asks diffidently. 'No savings?'

I shake my head. I started my marriage with an old car, a tiny rented flat, and about a thousand in the bank. As a graphic designer in a small advertising agency, as a mother who believed in buying the best possible childcare, I was lucky to have that much.

Leonard leans forward again, hands latched over the front of his briefcase. 'Now you're *not* to worry, Ellen,' he says, forcing a note of cheer into his voice. 'Gillespie and I will go through the options. We'll arrange the best possible financial plan for you.'

'It doesn't sound as though there's a lot to arrange.'

He looks blank.

'Not a lot of money,' I explain with a sort of laugh.

But Leonard is beyond jokes, however feeble. 'There will be something left,' he says earnestly, 'It's just a question of finding the most cost-effective way of tiding you over. Until we can apply for the death certificate. Until that building sells.'

'Of course.' I grin at him.

He clicks his briefcase closed and regards me solemnly. 'I'm not sure I should have burdened you with all this.'

I drain the last of my brandy and stand up. 'For heaven's

sake, Leonard!' I say half in exasperation, half in affection. 'What else were you going to do!'

My brittle tone seems to catch him by surprise. I think Leonard has always had this rather old-fashioned image of me as the quiet wife.

I walk with him towards the door. I pause. 'What about Jack? Is he having problems too?'

Leonard looks puzzled. 'Problems? I don't think so.'

'Isn't he affected by Ainswick?'

Leonard follows me thoughtfully into the hall. 'I don't think so. He severed all connection some time ago. I'll check. But...' He puts on his doubtful expression. 'I'm pretty sure.'

I knew that in their business life Jack and Harry had been going increasingly separate ways for some time, that Jack had other companies and other directorships. Yet for some reason I imagined that Jack had maintained an interest in Ainswick. In retrospect I see that this was naive of me. Jack, who has a rodent's instinct for doomed situations, would be far too canny to stay with a sinking ship.

Leonard chatters as we walk to his car: the service, how honoured and proud I must feel, the number of people who came, the great esteem they all felt for Harry.

We reach the car. Leonard slides his briefcase onto the back seat. He grasps me by the shoulders. 'Ellen *dear*.' He plants a paternal kiss on my forehead. 'You will take care? You will see people? If you want us to have Josh at all, we'd be delighted...' Leonard has a nice wife somewhere, a dedicated grandmother who rarely emerges except to go to church.

'He'll be going back to school after the weekend.'

'Well, if in the meantime ... My nephew goes fishing most Sundays. If Josh wanted to go I'm sure it could be arranged.'

The talk of fishing reminds me of Richard Moreland crouching in the open door of the car. I ask Leonard if he knows him.

'Oh yes!' Approval brightens Leonard's face. '*Nice* chap! Friend of the Dartingtons. Renting their cottage at Waldring-field.'

The Dartingtons are a family who live on the other side of

Woodbridge. They are substantial landowners, effortlessly and unobtrusively upper class, people who Anne and Charles count triumphantly among their friends. The father is a retired admiral and former ADC to one of the royal family, while two of the three sons are, if I remember, currently serving in the Navy. In this community it is more than enough to know that someone is a friend of people like the Dartingtons.

'But you know Moreland, surely?' Leonard blinks at me. 'I thought you must know him! He served in the Falklands with Harry.'

'No.'

'Oh . . .' A momentary adjustment and he brightens again. 'But you met this morning? Someone introduced you? Such an *immensely* nice man.'

I kiss him on the cheek. 'Goodbye, Leonard. And thank you.'

He drives a few yards before halting and thrusting his head out of the window. 'You're sure you'll be all right?'

I reassure him several times, and he is gone at last.

I go back into the house. My first thought is: no Katie, and my heart squeezes painfully. I shut the door and am struck by the absolute stillness of the place. Even when Harry wasn't here he used to leave a sort of energy behind him, a sense that things were about to happen, which they usually were. He was constantly asking me to put on goodwill events for the constituency, drinks parties for local worthies, dinner parties for the more influential. It took some time, but I like to think I became an efficient hostess.

It is almost half past nine, high time Josh appeared, if only for food. I go to the boot room to find some walking shoes. The footwear is arranged in racks. Most of it is Harry's: waders for salmon fishing – a short-lived interest this, Scotland was too far, the sport too static; brogues for pheasant shooting, a sport he returned to spasmodically in the winter; tennis shoes, almost new; squash shoes, unworn. When it came to hobbies Harry was a man of sudden enthusiasms, but as he lacked the time to improve his skills and could not bear to be less than proficient at whatever he did, his interest was apt to wane

59

almost as rapidly as it had sprung up. Sailing, though it took me a long while to realise it, was the one exception.

I circle the lawn, calling Josh's name. I let myself out through the side gate and start down the track towards the river. Many times in the last weeks I have tried to picture this moment, tried to imagine how I would feel taking the path again after all this time. Oddly, I feel little. Just a tightness in my throat, a lightness in my stomach.

The sky is fading. Under the long arch of trees the light is already deep with shadows. I call Josh again. His hide-out is somewhere ahead. I am not sure of its exact location – I have never been invited to inspect it. A crow caws above. An outboard hums on the river.

Emerging from the vault of trees, I reach the point beyond which Josh is not permitted to go unaccompanied, and call again.

I wait, I listen. Finally I walk on towards the river. The track levels off and passes briefly between pastures inhabited by black-faced sheep before falling once more to the flatness of the river bank and a copse of oak, hawthorn and birch. The copse encircles a clearing of tussock grass and patches of flinty sand. On the far side of the clearing is the quay, an ancient stone-built structure some twelve feet wide protruding thirty or forty feet into the river, matted with couch grass and guarded by a tall stand of pines. Beside the quay is an equally ancient slipway, crumbling and uneven.

I don't resist the memories. I see *Minerva* as she was that day, tied up alongside, her silvery spars bare of sails, her decks cluttered with rope and sail-bags. I see Harry lifting boxes of provisions over the rails onto the deck, I see the darkening sky, the curtains of rain. The memory is clear, but oddly bearable for all that, probably because I have been here in my mind so many times before.

I see Harry's expression under the hood of his waterproofs, the grim determination that pushed his face into a mass of lines, and I wonder if he was ever really happy, even in the early years of our marriage. He tried very hard to be; he applied himself to marriage as he applied himself to most things, with close attention. But there was a part of himself he could never risk, a sort of inner shame that held him back. He knew I loved him, I used to tell him often enough, but he could never quite accept this outpouring of affection, which to him was too unconditional. He found it hard to understand why I didn't judge him as harshly as he judged himself. In those days, of course, I had no reason to.

I know the dory isn't here any more, I know it's being stored at the boatyard at Waldringfield, but this doesn't stop me from glancing down to where it used to lie tied up to the quay. At low tide it was unusable, squatting on the slipway at a drunken angle, but at anything above half tide Harry would jump into it, fire the outboard and, paying token obedience to the speed limit, race off to the pub at Waldringfield.

Tonight the tide is low, and the river winds sluggishly through the mud flats, looking as though it has no depth to it at all. A small boat makes its way upstream under outboard. On the far bank a group of walkers strides in single file along the embankment that straddles the marshes. A mile or so downstream, by the boatyard on the opposite shore, yachts are tightly clustered around the visitors' moorings. It is high season and the start of the weekend; by tomorrow the river, regarded as one of the prettiest on this coast, will be noisy with boats and shouting people.

The last time I came down here was with the senior police officer, Dawson, to show him the quay, to point out the mooring, to tell him what little I could. It was a Thursday, I remember, five days after Harry disappeared, and cold, the river wind-blown and deserted.

I remember the day for another reason. It was the day that I realised I must get myself and the children away from Pennygate as soon as possible, that with so many pressures if we stayed any longer we would be in danger of falling apart. Self-control is an oddly treacherous thing. The instant you think you have mastered it, it deserts you, suddenly and without warning. It had almost happened once. I lived in dread of it happening again.

Climbing back up the track, I call for Josh with increasing

frustration. As I pause for breath half-way up, his voice comes from close behind. 'Mum.'

I give a great start and jerk my head round. 'Where have you been?' I cry in fear and anger.

His lips pucker, he frowns.

I look around and see that we are just within the boundary of his permitted territory. I let my breath out slowly. 'Didn't you hear me?' I say weakly.

He shakes his head.

'I thought . . .' I gesture helplessly. 'I thought you were down at the river.'

Another shake of the head, more rapid.

'Sorry,' I sigh. 'Sorry.'

Josh contorts his mouth, a small peace offering. Feeling a rush of emotion, I put an arm round his shoulders and squeeze him to me.

'Supper?'

He greets the idea without much interest. We start up the hill.

'Long day,' I remark. I know he is tired, I sense he is not particularly keen to talk, but I am anxious to re-establish communications after the disruptions of the last few days. 'Had a good time?' I ask.

He lifts his shoulders high in another of these shrugs he uses as a substitute for conversation. Noticing that his clothes are still relatively clean, I wonder what he has been doing all this time. 'The hide-out okay?'

He pushes out his lip in partial agreement.

I trawl for questions. 'So what's new?'

'Someone's been there.'

'Where?'

'In the woods.'

'Oh? What – camping?'

He nods. 'In the bushes.'

My mind leaps to unsavoury thoughts of tramps and child molesters. 'You didn't see anyone?'

He shakes his head. 'The signs were pretty ancient.'

The signs. This is part of Josh's outdoor survival language

which covers a range of expertise I don't pretend to grasp. But ancient I understand all right. 'This someone wasn't using your hide-out?'

He frowns at the stupidity of my question, from which I gather that his hide-out is so well concealed as to be undiscoverable.

The track steepens. We climb slowly through the darkening woods. Josh kicks at stones.

'Shall we get a schoolfriend over tomorrow?' I say brightly. 'Dan or someone?' Josh always resists these attempts to get him together with boys of his own age. He enjoys the days he spends with Dan, but he is just as happy on his own, if not more so. This time, however, I intend to push the idea. Josh will be going back to school on Monday and seeing Dan will ease his passage. 'I might be able to arrange for Dan's dad to take you fishing.'

He says matter-of-factly, 'Richard's taking me.'

'Richard? Richard who?'

He looks puzzled that I do not know. 'Dad's friend,' he explains.

'Ah.' Visions of the face framed by the open car door. 'You mean, Richard Moreland?'

'He was in the Marines.'

'Yes. Yes, I . . . heard. When did he ask you?'

This forces Josh to think. He has never been good with time. 'Umm . . . Teatime. About.'

'When I was taking Katie back?'

'Yup.'

'But – did he phone?'

'No. I saw him.'

'Where?'

'He came up here.'

'Did he now?' I say defensively. 'I thought I told you never to talk to strangers.'

Josh thinks about this for a moment. 'But he came and talked to me this morning. With Uncle Leonard.'

'What – at the service?'

He nods.

'Oh.' We walk on. 'I didn't realise. Oh. Well . . . we'll see.'

'He said he'd phone you.'

I hear the hope in his voice. Josh loves fishing more than almost anything else. And after spending so many weeks cooped up with Katie and me in what was inevitably a charged atmosphere, a trip in male company can only do him good.

'All right,' I say. 'But I'll need to know there are things like life-jackets and food, and where you're going, and when you're due back.' I try not to fuss over Josh but really I'm a born worrier.

We pass through the gate into the garden. A bird sings overhead, an astonishingly rich sound. I stand for a moment under the heavy trees, looking for it. When I glance round Josh has almost disappeared.

'Hey!'

He turns.

I catch up with him and give him an impulsive hug. 'Good to be home, eh?'

He does not push me away, but he does not hug me back either. He has been broadcasting this faint remoteness ever since his father died. I am never sure if it is part of his coping mechanism, or whether he is punishing me for some crime. I drop my arms. 'Well,' I say, filling my voice with cheer. 'What do you fancy? Pizza? Baked beans?'

In the dusk his expression has reverted to its usual breezy unconcern. 'Not hungry.'

He knows this ploy has no chance and as we turn for the house I am already telling him that unless he feels strongly about it he is going to get baked beans.

A dark figure emerges from the shadows of the conservatory. My heart gives a small bump, I come stiffly to a halt. For a split second I seem to see Harry.

'There you are,' calls Jack, striding across the lawn towards us. 'I was beginning to think you'd vanished. *Hello*, Josh. How's the fishing?' He grips Josh's shoulder and gives him the benefit of his broadest smile. 'How about you taking me out one day? Catch a few bass, hmm? You'll have to tell me what's what, of course. Never could get bait to stay on the hook.' He laughs and drops his voice conspiratorially. 'Just the two of us, eh? And a few beers. Well—' He slides a theatrical glance in my direction. 'Coke, then. Now, listen, old chap, would you give me a minute with your mum?' He winks and, gripping Josh's shoulder, turns him deftly towards the house.

I suppress a faint resentment. It is partly the way Jack has arrived without warning, partly his use of this blatant and practised charm which, directed at a child, seems vaguely offensive.

I say more sharply than I mean to, 'No.' Then, aware that I have sounded unreasonable, I add, 'I really can't talk now, Jack. I've got to make supper.'

I start after Josh.

'Ellen. *Ellen.*' Jack has my elbow. He slows me down. 'Hold on, hold on. It won't take a minute.' His tone suggests that I am being childish. 'Ellen.' His voice becomes soft, coaxing.

I hesitate. I half turn. I say in all honesty, 'I'm very tired, Jack. Perhaps another time. If you wouldn't mind.'

He moves in front of me, very close. This is a way of his, to come so close that you are forced to tilt your head back or look away. He reaches up and pushes a strand of hair away from my eye. 'Poor love, you *are* in a state.'

I draw back. 'I'm not in a state.' This is not strictly true – I am near my limits – but I am not about to admit this to Jack, who likes to feel that he has a disturbing effect on all women. 'It's just that I've had enough for one day.'

'*Ellen.*' He spreads his hands wide, looking misunderstood. 'I only came to find out if you needed anything. Any help. I know the situation is – well, far from easy. Leonard's kept me in touch. But I just wanted you to know that *whatever* happens, Ellen, *whatever* support you need – I'm here.' There is intimacy and compassion in his voice. Jack can do almost anything with his voice. It is rich and dark, like an actor's.

'Thank you. That's very kind. I do appreciate it.' I wonder just how much Jack knows about my financial situation.

'Ellen!' His tone is half-injured, half-amused. 'You seem cross with me. *Are* you?' He ducks his head to read my expression in the half-light.

65

If I try to answer this I will only get embroiled in ever decreasing explanations, in a sort of word game which, with Jack, will be impossible to win. I shake my head and turn for the house.

Jack walks at my side, watching me. 'You know, it isn't just because I *have* to be involved – as a trustee and all that. It's because' – his voice swoops low and soft – 'I *want* to help. Because I *care*.' He lets the thought hang in the air, gaining significance. He can't stop himself drawing closer, brushing his fingers across my hand. Physical contact with the opposite sex is a compulsion with Jack. 'I can't bear to think of you trying to get through this on your own, you know.'

'I've got Leonard.'

'Yes... Of course.' He makes Leonard sound like a decidedly mixed blessing. 'But Leonard can't do everything.' He strides ahead to put a restraining hand on the open door of the conservatory.

He leaves me too little room and as I turn sideways to pass through he catches me softly by the shoulder. 'Ellen – you're not cross with me, are you? *Are* you?' He tips me a self-mocking grin.

Drained, I sink back against the door frame. I sigh, 'Jack...'

'I'd be most upset if you were. You're very special to me, Ellen. Very special indeed.' His voice has acquired a rough edge, as if he is fighting some deep emotion. This is the trouble with Jack; he can make any statement sound plausible.

Yet I cannot take him seriously. For Jack, the moment is everything, and once it has passed he is easily distracted. I am not, anyway, his sort. Jack goes for super-confident, highly packaged women, the kind that proclaim a man's status like an expensive car.

I mumble that I am not cross with him, not in the least. Then, disentangling myself gently but unequivocally, I make for the kitchen.

The last time Jack offered to take care of me, it did not end well. Remembering it now, I feel an echo of mortification. He had caught me at my lowest ebb, one evening last November, soon after the truth of Harry's behaviour had been brought home to me in the most inescapable way. I was not so adept at hiding my feelings then. I let misery undermine my judgement. It only needed Jack to slip his arm round my shoulder for me to cry wretchedly, to discharge great bursts of despair. Such was my anguish that I almost – so nearly – revealed my most bitter, most secret emotions to him.

Jack wasn't the best person to turn to, of course. I should have known this. I should have realised that he would instinctively offer the only sort of comfort that had any meaning for him. But when his mouth, which had been resting on my hair, travelled down my cheek and brushed my lips, I was held by inertia and surprise, like a mindless sixteen-year-old. I doubted my interpretation of what was happening. It wasn't until his hand arrived on my breast and squeezed it gently that I reacted. And, having delayed, I over-reacted. I was seized by a strange anger which probably had more to do with my feelings towards Harry than Jack. I did something I never knew I was capable of, although even as my hand flew out it seemed to travel in slow motion and I watched it with fascination, as if I might yet pull it back. I pushed my hand into his face and thrust it away from me, a hard shove. His head arced back, he caught himself just before he fell off the chair. I don't know which of us was more surprised by this show of force. Jack exclaimed 'Christ!' over and over again and glared at me and muttered something, I think it was, 'So it's like that, is it?' Then, beginning to recover himself, his expression changed to one of grim amusement. 'I think you misunderstood me a little there,' he breathed. He even managed a thin laugh. Then he said ingenuously, 'Just trying to help,' and rested his fingers lightly on my hand: the misunderstood child asking forgiveness.

It was a long time ago now; it has no importance. I go quickly into the kitchen, flick on the lights and pull a can of baked beans out of the cupboard.

Jack strolls in behind me. 'Now, the first thing is to get you *settled* financially.' His voice has taken on a note of casual authority. 'The legal situation – Leonard has explained it all, has he?' He catches my nod. 'Well, it's obviously going to take time to sort out. Nothing we can do to hurry it up. So I've arranged with Gillespie for you to have something to tide you over. Call it a loan. But you're to have it for as long as you need it.' He leans against the counter and flourishes a hand. 'Just as long as you need it.'

I finish pouring the beans into a pan. 'It's very kind of you. I'm very touched. Very. And I'll certainly bear it in mind. But hopefully it won't be necessary.'

He takes this as an understandable show of reluctance, a necessary prelude to my accepting the money. He cajoles me gently to accept it straight away, finally he lets the subject drop, but with the knowing look of someone who is convinced I will see the light eventually.

He watches me saw bread into ragged slices. 'You could have done without Ainswick, too.'

I grunt non-committally.

'Leonard told you, did he?'

I give a vague shrug.

'There's still a chance, of course. If a buyer can be found for that damned Shoreditch property.'

'I thought you weren't involved in Ainswick any more.'

He picks up a piece of fallen crust and examines it for a moment before propelling it neatly into his mouth. 'I'm not,' he says with a heavy sigh, as if it were a great sadness to him.

The bread is too thick for the toaster and I have to manœuvre it down into the slot. 'I never knew – why did you leave?'

'What?' He seems a little surprised that I should ask. 'I suppose because Harry's ideas didn't mesh with mine any more,' he says at last. 'Partly that, and partly . . .' He chews pensively. 'Because Harry thought I'd done him a bad deal.'

'And had you?'

He looks suitably offended at my question then ignores it. 'The point is, he *thought* I had. I took a no-hope proposition off Ainswick's books when it needed some cash. Gave a bloody good price for it too. Probably twice what it was worth. Scrubland with no planning, and no prospects of getting it either. Then two years ago, right out of the blue, damn me if the planners don't suddenly reverse their policy and zone it for low-cost housing.' He makes an extravagant gesture of disbelief. 'Harry decided I must have had wind of it. God, if only I had – I'd have bought up more land.' He raises an eyebrow. 'Anyway if anyone should have got wind of it, it was Harry. He was the one with friends in the right places, not me.'

It seems to me that Jack, like Harry, always made it his business to know the people who might be useful to him, but I let it pass.

The toaster pops. I extricate the slices and drop them onto a plate. 'If you don't mind, Jack ... I want to give Josh his supper.'

He draws himself elegantly away from the counter. 'Of course.' In one continuous movement he comes closer and drops a hand onto my neck. 'But we'll talk again soon, eh? You *will* let me take care of that money, won't you? Mmm?'

He smiles the lazy low-lidded smile he keeps for all women who are not old or hopelessly plain. His fingers stir against my skin. I move away, touching a distancing hand against his chest. I feel him stiffen. It is the hand: he has not forgiven me for pushing him away all those months ago.

'You can be very hard on people, Ellen.'

I shrug wordlessly.

'You were very hard on Harry,' he comments coldly.

'Was I?'

'All that business ... you took it far too seriously, you know.'

The beans are sizzling. I reach for the switch and turn the gas off.

'You made it into something it wasn't,' Jack goes on. 'She was nothing, just a ...' He wheels a hand, searching for the word.

'A younger, prettier, smarter version?' I attempt an ironic laugh which comes out wrong, almost like a gasp.

'It was just an *affair*, Ellen. It would never have come to anything. He would never have left you.'

This is Jack's view of adultery – just an affair. But then he has never been married, he has never seen it from the other side. 'I

69

never thought he was going to leave me,' I say in a resentful manner which I instantly regret.

'Come on, Ellen,' Jack argues in a soft unyielding tone. 'You watched him like a hawk. You were obsessed. God – you could have cut the atmosphere with a knife. Even the best men stray, Ellen, but it's not the end of the world, you know.'

I cannot deal with this discussion. My breath is band-tight in my chest. I am desperate to be alone. 'Jack, please . . .'

He shakes his head sadly, as if I am a lost cause. When he kisses me goodbye he has a patriarchal smile, and, though I am not crying, he brushes my cheeks lightly with his thumbs as if to wipe away tears.

As he lets himself out I stare sightlessly at the overcooked beans and think about Caroline Palmer.

FOUR

The phone pulls me out of a dark sleep. I open my eyes, half frightened that it will be night and that the nightmares are still to come. But grey light fills the room and I absorb the familiar shapes, the well-remembered pattern of the partly drawn curtains with something close to relief. For better or worse, I am home.

Rolling over, I reach for the phone. It is Molly. She wants to know if she has woken me.

The bedside clock says it is just before eleven. I try to remember when I finally fell asleep. Four or so. 'No,' I say. 'I was just getting up.'

'What about lunch?' She tempts me with favourite things, smoked salmon, artichokes, strawberries. 'And there's the most adorable puppy next door that Josh can play with.'

'Molly, I'd love to, but—'

'Ellen! I want to hear about America, I want to hear about *you*.'

'I've got to wait for Josh to get back from his fishing.'

'Come on your own then! Come on!'

'He's due back at lunchtime.'

Unabashed, Molly regroups. 'Who are these people he's gone with? Can't they keep him for a while? Or I could bring lunch over, a picnic.'

'Molly – I'm not sure. Can I call you later?'

'When?' she growls.

'As soon as I'm up?'

'Ellen . . .' she sighs. 'You know – I'm not at all sure what to do with you.'

71

'Oh, I'm all right.'

'Are you? I worry about you. I have this silly idea that you're bottling things up, that you're making yourself ill. I've never seen anyone so thin, Ellen. I couldn't believe it when I saw you yesterday. You haven't developed a *thing* about food, have you? You're not feeling guilty or something stupid? Everyone feels guilty when someone dies, you know. You're not tormenting yourself, are you?'

This is Molly's way, everything up front, nothing left unsaid. It is one of the reasons I am so fond of her. 'No,' I say carefully, 'it's not like that, Molly.'

'It's not— You don't blame yourself over that stupid business? That woman?'

I never told Molly about my troubles with Harry. I didn't have to. Being a person who misses little, she soon guessed that something was wrong. At first she contained her curiosity – though with obvious effort – and gave me silent unquestioning support, but then, as my unhappiness deepened, she began to ask questions. The other-woman scenario was almost the first thing she suggested. This surprised and grieved me; I hadn't realised people saw Harry as such an obvious candidate for adultery. I didn't bother to contradict her. There wasn't much point. At the same time I wouldn't talk about it. I didn't dare. With Molly, I was afraid I would say too much.

'I don't blame anyone, Molly. Really.' Even as I say it my heart tightens, I feel the old unsteadiness in my stomach.

'You'll call me straight back then?' Her voice has a lurking reproach. She is preparing herself for the fact that I will put her off again.

I find Josh's note on the kitchen table, anchored by the salt grinder. The writing is uneven, the spelling erratic, there are capitals in odd places. I can imagine him labouring over what for him is an exceptionally long message.

'We are trying other side of Waldringfield' – this misspelt and amended – 'and Kirton Creek. Have life-jacket and food. Back at lunchtime with fish.'

The assurance of this last statement is characteristic of Josh, who, whatever his failings at school, does not lack confidence out of doors. Reading the message again, I realise that, left to his own devices, he would never have provided half this information. Moreland must have stood over him, telling him what to write.

A bowl stands in the sink, whiskers of Josh's favourite cereal floating on the milk. Next to it is a plate dotted with crumbs and smears of butter, and a glass with a tidemark of orange juice, testaments to a proper breakfast.

On my way back I find another note, one that has been posted through the front door. It comes from two of my Heath End neighbours and directs me to the kitchen door where I find a cardboard box containing two quiches, an apple pie, a large bag of tomatoes, a selection of soft fruit, cream, two bottles of wine, a fruit cake, and a parcel of five or six gingerbread men. The gingerbread men have been made with the loving care of young hands that have rolled the mixture rather too thin in places and have pressed the button eyes too hard into the face, so that the sides of the head have ballooned out. There is a card for Katie, Josh and me, sent with 'tons of love' from the mothers and many carefully wrought kisses from the children.

My gratitude is touched with apprehension. What will these people expect of me? Brave widow, grieving wife. I'm not sure I can manage either role.

As I load the perishables into the fridge, I think of Katie. Her absence is like a constant ache, lurking just below my consciousness. We have become so close over the last months that we are almost like those twins you read about, hardly needing to voice our thoughts to each other. Quite apart from loving her in a passionately maternal way, I admire her so much. She is such a fine person, so generous, so brave, so easily wounded. So bad at being alone. And that is how I think of her now, among her noisy schoolmates – alone. I long to talk to her, but she has classes at this time on a Saturday morning and I won't be able to reach her until one-thirty.

I put off my call to Molly until I have had a shower and dressed and got a stiff coffee inside me. Even then I have to brace myself to tell her that lunch of any sort is going to be too difficult. Only half-jokingly, she accuses me of trying to avoid her. I placate her by asking her to lunch on Monday.

It is twelve. If I'm lucky I might have an hour before Josh comes back. The study is on the north side of the house, facing the vegetable garden. Harry always wanted a study like this, imposing, heavyweight, with tall ornamental bookshelves, bottle-green brocade curtains, silk wall hangings to match, and a wide mahogany knee-hole desk. In all but the brightest weather, however, the room is gloomy, and today it is positively dark. I turn on the concealed lighting, and splashes of light spring across the ceiling and the rows of reference books, the copies of *Hansard*, and the Victorian hunting scenes on either side of the window.

A table and office chair have been brought in and placed to the left of the door, facing a wall of books. Typewriter and paper stand on the table, ready for Margaret to start work on Monday.

The surface of Harry's desk is covered with sorted, clipped and weighted stacks of letters and papers, and I have to slide some to one side before I can place the desk lamp at the front where it will shine down into the drawers as I open them.

I have been through the desk once before, about three days before I left for America. I removed everything I thought Leonard might need, everything of an official or vaguely legal nature – Harry's birth certificate, passport, insurance certificates. The financial papers – share transaction and bank statements and so on – I gave to Margaret.

I go through what is left. Foreign money; travel and hotel guides; bills scored with a single ink-stroke and the date of payment; medical insurance leaflets; brochures for garden machinery, conservatories and solar heating; theatre and music programmes – though Harry went to this sort of thing out of duty rather than enjoyment. For him theatre was far less dramatic than real life, while classical music simply passed him by.

In a bottom drawer there is a box of unmounted snapshots from Harry's school and army days. He used to keep them in a battered old trunk at Heath End. When we were first married I had to persuade him to show them to me. He wasn't very keen. For some reason the past irritated – or bored – him, it was hard to know which.

There is a picture from a skiing trip – a grinning Harry standing outside a Verbier chalet in a group of young people vying with each other to strike the silliest pose; then a more formal group taken on an army climbing expedition in the barren hills of what looks like Scotland – a serious Harry here, stiff and grimly determined, scowling as he often did when he had his personal barriers up; then a shot of Harry with three fellow guests at a wedding reception. The party was held in Berkshire in a flapping marquee on a wind-blown Saturday in September 1982. I know exactly how it was, because it was here that Harry and I met. We were introduced by a former flatmate of mine and later that day, when seven or eight of us went on to dinner at an Indonesian restaurant off the Brompton Road, Harry and I were squashed next to each other at the cramped table.

I felt no instantaneous attraction for Harry. Rather, a sort of awe. It was hard not to be impressed by him. He was striking in a robust sort of way, broad-shouldered and athletic, exuding an overwhelming well-being with his lightly tanned skin, his clear eyes, his barely suppressed energy. Quick, sharp, poised effortlessly on the leading edge of the conversation, he was an exhilarating if daunting dinner companion. Rather than air my ignorance and my altogether slower wit, I kept my contributions to a minimum. It didn't worry me that I wasn't making an impression; I didn't think I was Harry's type. I didn't appreciate that for Harry it was my very lack of competitiveness, my relatively placid nature which were my greatest assets. Later he told me he came to a decision about me almost straight away. He couldn't say why. I suppose it was a sort of blind recognition. I think I made him feel safe.

By then my marriage had been over for two years and I was ripe for Harry's steady, almost circumspect, courtship. Not that I was immediately convinced. It took me some time to begin to appreciate the qualities that he took care to keep well hidden – an underlying vulnerability, an absurd generosity – and to realise that the things he most needed from me, trust and emotional security, were the very things that I could supply in abundance. He needed me and, for me, being needed is very close to love.

Now, looking at Harry as I first saw him, dressed in his wedding regalia, I remember the weeks and months after our own marriage, the feeling of unreserved happiness, of pride, and I wonder when the next great turning point came – when he stopped needing me. The awful thing is, I don't know, and I realise now that I probably never will. But at some point he slipped away from me into a dark world of his own. I can't help being haunted by the thought that I missed the signs, that he sent warnings which I chose not to read, that if only I hadn't been so wrapped up in the children and the satisfactions of my existence I might have realised something was wrong. When I'm being kind to myself I tell myself that times were difficult, that he was in such a stressed state that it would have been impossible for me to identify his separate preoccupations and obsessions. This thought, when I can keep any sort of hold on it, eases my guilt a little.

I glance through the remaining pictures. School, foreign holidays, army, an earlier skiing trip. In the drawer above are bunches of letters held together with elastic bands. Most date from the late seventies when Harry was posted to Germany and Northern Ireland. Several come from his girlfriend of the time, a bouncy girl called Susie whom I met some years ago. The letters are boisterous and devoid of intimacy.

The remaining drawers yield nothing, though even now I am not absolutely sure what I am looking for. A note perhaps. A letter. Some clue as to Harry's state of mind in the week before he died. A copy of the will, some sort of explanation as to why Katie was to be left so little. Anything, really, that might throw some light on those last six months, on what made Harry do what he did. I want so much to be rid of my anger, I want so much to understand.

I also want to be able to destroy anything before anyone else should find it.

I go round the desk and check the back for hidden compartments that I know perfectly well are not there. I search the cupboards that support the tall piers of bookshelves. Completing the circle, I sink back into the chair and open the centre drawer again. There are airline vouchers, Eurocheques, old pocket diaries from two and three years back, an abandoned address book. I flick through the diaries, but the entries, some in Margaret's neat hand, some in Harry's scrawl, have the innocent rhythm of happy days. The pocket address book, overfilled and well thumbed, is not dated, but is, I think, quite recent, last used perhaps eighteen months ago. I cannot help looking for Caroline Palmer's name, though I'm pretty sure Harry didn't know her at that time. I find nothing under either P or C.

At the back of the book, on an unprinted flysheet, Harry has printed several lists of numbers in his distinctive boxy handwriting. Credit card numbers identified by their prefixes: Amex, Visa, M/card. And what look like bank account numbers, prefixed by such abbreviations as P/A and D/A – personal account, deposit account.

I put the book to one side. While Harry was alive I only looked in this drawer twice, three times at the most, and that was when he phoned and asked me to see if he'd left his cheque-book behind. Once he had forgotten his keys. They aren't here now, I notice. There are only desk keys, spare outhouse keys, and, hidden at the back, one of the two keys to the gun cabinet.

The phone rings. I feel a dart of hope that it will be Katie until I see it's barely half past twelve. Anne greets me in a taut voice. Closing the drawer, I hunch down over the desk, my elbows anchored in the gaps between the stacks of paper, while she recounts the full difficulties of having Diana to stay for the night, how she complained about her supper, how, having refused to go to bed, she fell asleep in her chair.

I make sympathetic noises. I suggest that maybe Diana was upset by the service and the talk of Charles's candidature and will feel calmer in a couple of days. Anne is not so sure. Listening as best I can, murmuring appropriately, my eyes stray to the papers by my right elbow, to one of Harry's credit card statements that Margaret has marked 'paid'. It is for March. I notice that Harry did not stint himself, even though we were under financial strain. The bill totals over five hundred pounds. There are charges for petrol and other mundane things, but also for goods from Turnbull and Asser – shirts presumably – and meals in London restaurants – a couple of fashionable places with prices to match, and two that I have never heard of with more modest prices. I wonder if it was Caroline Palmer that Harry took to these cheaper restaurants where presumably there was less chance of being recognised.

I wonder what Caroline Palmer is doing nowadays, I wonder if she is grieving for Harry. Somehow, I don't think so.

Anne's tone has changed. She has put on her petitioning voice, brusque and defensive. She says that Diana is due to return home to her cottage after the weekend, but that she is not at all sure it is safe to leave her alone for long, that someone will need keep an eye on her, but that it will be difficult for she herself or Charles to manage this every day while Charles is busy preparing for the selection proceedings.

I take up my cue. 'I'll look in,' I say, 'whenever I can.'

'Well, *if* you don't mind. We've had to deal with it all, you know. While you've been away.'

'Yes. Of course.'

There is a silence through which she conveys her considerable dissatisfaction with me.

'So . . .' she says at last. 'How did it go with Leonard?'

I tell her Leonard is sorting everything out. Then, in an attempt to restore family harmony, for which, it seems, I am to be held responsible, I recount the problems stemming from the lack of a death certificate and ask Anne's advice about the house, and whether she thinks I should try to let it. She warms a little to this appeal to her wisdom, she says she thinks I should stay put for the moment. By the time we ring off we have managed to re-establish some feeling of mutual support. It is always like this with Anne and me: shaky bridges in constant need of rebuilding.

I stare at the desk. I remember Harry's keys. I remember that somewhere on the bunch there should be a key to the one place that I haven't yet searched.

Harry kept two sets of keys; the spares should be in the house somewhere. I start for the stairs, then, reminded of another key, in need of maximum reassurance, I divert into the kitchen and feel inside the right-hand door of the old pine dresser that takes up most of the end wall. The second key to the gun cabinet is in its usual place, on a hook hidden behind the frame.

The phone again. I stop in the doorway, reluctant and indecisive. When the ringing finally stops, I cross the kitchen and switch on the answering machine.

The hall table – large and Jacobean, and something I suspect Harry paid far too much for – is very tidy. Some newly delivered country and sporting magazines stand in a pile next to a stupendous flower arrangement, a bowl of white roses, presented by a neighbour. The various hats Harry liked to scatter over the table have been removed, probably to the coat cupboard. The silver tray holds a neat stack of cards and circulars.

Harry sometimes left keys here but more often than not he kept them in his dressing-room. But when I go upstairs and look in the china bowl on top of the chest of drawers where he would drop them with a loud clink I find nothing but a few brass coins.

In the bedroom the phone rings again. I start slightly, I don't know why. The answering machine stifles the sound at the fourth ring.

In the top right-hand drawer of the chest are folded handkerchiefs, a dress tie, some unloved cufflinks relegated from the leather box in front of the mirror. Moving the handkerchiefs aside, I search the drawer. Though I have been

79

to this chest countless times in the past to put clean linen away, this act, more than any other since I returned, makes me feel uncomfortable, like an intruder. I am struck by the irrational illusion that Harry is close by, that he has been gone only five minutes, that he will step round the door at any moment and demand to know what I am doing. Old guilt, new guilt. In the general well of remorse, it's hard to separate them.

There are no keys in here.

A door bangs downstairs, light feet run into the hall. My heart gives a small thump, I pull my hand back, I close the drawer.

'Mum!' Josh cries. 'Mum!'

I draw a slow breath. 'Here,' I call. 'Upstairs.'

Without thought, I pull open the left-hand drawer and glance quickly inside. Socks arranged in rank according to colour and thickness, a legacy of Harry's army days. And at the front, for anyone to see, the keys.

'Mum!' Josh arrives panting. 'We've got the fire going! It's already good and hot. And we've got tons of mullet. They're really hard to catch usually, but we've got a whole lot.' He gasps, '*Five.*'

'Five!' I look impressed. I slip the keys into my pocket.

'The fire's not ready yet. It's got to die down a bit.'

'Is there anything you need?' I make for the stairs. 'Bread or anything?'

'Oh no!'

'Nothing at all?'

'Richard's got everything.' He races past me to drape the top half of his body over the banister rail and slide rapidly down into the hall.

'What about ketchup?'

He snakes round the newel-post and drops onto the floor. 'Umm ... I don't think so.' There is doubt in his voice. Ketchup is Josh's great weakness. I raise a questioning eyebrow at him.

'No,' he says, with abrupt decision.

I nod wisely. Ketchup wouldn't perhaps be appropriate in the wild. I lead the way into the kitchen. 'Coke, then?'

'We've got lemonade.'

'You have everything then.' I lean against the kitchen table and regard my son with an upwelling of satisfaction and sudden optimism. I would love to reach out and touch him, but in this mannish self-sufficent mood of his I do not think he will take kindly to such an open display of affection. 'So . . . ?' I say. 'What can I do for you?'

'Oh!' exclaims Josh, remembering why he has come. 'There's enough for you. I mean, if you want to have some.'

'Well, thank you.' I give a slight bow. 'But wouldn't you rather have it all to yourselves?'

'There's too much.' He shuffles his feet.

I chew thoughtfully on my lip. 'But would you *like* me to come?'

'*Course!*' He rounds his eyes in rebuke, then spoils it by averting his gaze, which sends me a more confused message. 'Richard said—' He pauses, beset by some inner debate. The words, when they finally come, are delivered with a frown. 'He said to ask you nicely so you'd be sure to come.'

'Ah . . .' I nod gravely. 'In that case . . .' I accept, won over not so much by Josh's manner, beguiling though it is in a backhanded way, but by my desire to earn back that part of his approval which I sense I have lost.

I tell Josh I'll be down in twenty minutes or so. The phone rings. My eyes dart to the clock. Five past one. I turn up the answering machine, hoping for Katie, and hear Jack's sinuous voice. I turn the volume down again. When I look back Josh is gone.

I wait another five minutes, sitting at the counter with a second cup of coffee. In my mind's eye, I see Katie leaving the dining hall and walking towards her house. I try not to impose an expression on her face because, in my present mood, I know I will paint it dark and lost.

The phone is answered by a senior girl and I have to hang on for what seems a long time while she finds Katie.

'Mum?' Katie's voice has a lift to it. She tells me she is fine, that everyone is letting her get on with things, not paying her special attention – well, not so much that she can't deal with it.

81

I listen for shades of false cheer, for signs that she is putting on a front for my benefit, that underneath it all she is is struggling, but if there's anything to be heard in her voice it's relief.

'I'm so pleased, darling,' I say. 'That's wonderful.' I cannot help adding, 'But you will phone, won't you? If you need to talk?'

'I will, Mum. Don't worry. *Please*.'

'Okay. I promise!' I laugh to help the moment along. 'So . . . what's the news?'

She takes me through a change of teachers, a girl she liked who has had to leave because her parents can no longer pay the fees.

I say I am sorry about her friend. Then, in my brightest tone, I start to talk about what we will do next Saturday afternoon when she comes out for the weekend.

'Mum—' Her voice takes an uncertain swoop. 'I'm not so sure . . .'

'About what, honey?'

A whisper: 'Coming home.'

I take my time. 'Oh. I see.'

'Mum, you know I want to see you more than anything, you know I'm longing to see you, but . . .' Her voice is so faint I can hardly hear it.

I wait. I don't want to rush her. 'But what, darling?' I ask at last.

'I just . . .' A pause. 'I've got so much work, and . . .' She sighs. She takes a moment to sort it out in her mind. 'I can't deal with it just at the moment.'

I stare unseeing at the pinboard in front of me. 'I understand.'

'I'd feel so low, Mum.'

'Yes, darling,' I say. 'In that case it'd be a bad idea.' Against all reason, tears prick the back of my eyes.

'You don't mind, Mummy?'

'No! Of course not! No!' I give another laugh to persuade her that this is true. 'But I can't bear not to see you at all, darling.'

'Course not.'

'Shall we have tea then? Go to that ridiculous place with the cream buns? Or Sunday lunch. With Molly perhaps. You know she'd love to see us. She keeps asking—' Aware that I am burbling on, I halt abruptly.

'That'd be lovely, Mum.'

I send a smile into the phone, as if this could be transmitted in some way. 'Katie,' I venture, 'you will say, won't you, if . . . even for a moment . . .'

'Yes, Mum. Promise.'

'I just need to know you're okay.'

'I'm okay.'

We are silent for a moment.

'Love you, Mum.'

'I love you too, darling.'

I tell her that I am going to leave the answering machine on for the time being, and that to be sure of reaching me she should use what used to be Harry's line, the one he kept for business and political calls. I start to remind her of the number, but she has it off by heart. As I ring off, I tell her once again that I love her.

I'm going to be late. I throw a bottle of wine, plastic glasses, napkins, fruit and – unthinkingly – ketchup into a basket, and make my way past the boot room to the side door. There is no trace of yesterday's sun; the heat already belongs to another world. The clouds are low and heavy, there is a strong wind bounding up from the river. My blood must have grown thin in America because as I set off down the track I feel chilled almost immediately. In no mood to turn back, I press on, walking faster.

As the track flattens out by the ribbon of pasture, I see streaks of smoke, torn from the tree-tops by the wind. I picture the man and boy tending the fire, and am struck by a powerful sense of *déjà vu*. It is a trick of memory, I realise, a confusion with a time soon after we moved here, when Harry brought Josh down to the quay to cook sausages on an open fire. In the summers that followed they often talked of doing it again but, what with Harry's campaigning and increasingly hectic business activities, they never quite managed it. Josh had to make do with humble barbecues, organised – and, more often than not, overcooked – by me at the house.

The two figures are crouched on the far side of the clearing, by an ancient fallen tree. Even at this distance I realise that the camp-fire is an impressive affair, encircled by stones, with a spit of impaled fish supported by crutches of forked branches, like some diagram in a Scout manual.

Moreland looks round, as if he has been expecting me at this precise moment, and, rising, comes to meet me. In old jeans and a sweater he looks leaner than before, and a little shorter, though he must be five foot ten. At five-nine, I am perhaps more aware of people's height than most women. We shake hands. He offers a cheerful smile, an open gaze. I am reminded of his frank appraisal of me as I sat in the car yesterday, and my impression – rightly or wrongly – that I had passed muster.

'You found the note this morning,' he says easily, reaching out to take my basket.

'Oh yes.' We begin to walk towards the fire. 'I was most honoured. It was the longest communication I've ever had from Josh.'

Moreland's mouth creases down, he looks across at me. Seeing that I have long since guessed how the note came about, he gives a sudden laugh that illuminates his face. 'Well . . . any prompting was purely accidental.'

'It's really most kind of you to go to all this trouble.'

'No trouble.' He seems surprised that I should think it was. 'I've enjoyed it. Josh's quite a character. And it's good to get out on the river.'

'You fish a lot?'

'Now and then—'

Josh calls loudly for us to hurry, that the meal is cooked. He shows me to the best – indeed, the only – seat, a sturdy branch protruding from the massive trunk of the fallen tree. He presents me with a whole fish accompanied by two slices of raggedly carved bread, served on a child's plastic plate of violent purple. His own plate is an equally turbulent puce.

Catching my expression, Moreland says, 'A little bright,

aren't they? But the cottage is rather limited for picnic gear. It was either these or a set of bone china with dragons and fire-eaters on it.'

Josh raises his head and laughs, a sound that takes me by surprise. 'Dragons and fire-eaters!' he exclaims and laughs again. Moreland grins back and I wonder if he has made up the dragons and fire-eaters for Josh's benefit.

'You're staying in the Dartington's place?' I ask Moreland, revealing my limited knowledge of him.

'For the moment. But they want it back in a month. Then I'll have to find somewhere else. And I'm afraid' – he directs a rueful face towards Josh – 'a new place is unlikely to come with boats.'

He has brought wine, I notice. It stands ready opened, the cork pushed back into the neck as a temporary stopper. And two wine glasses – proper glass, not plastic.

'You're here for long?' I ask.

'Most of the summer – well, I hope so. Apart from a few trips to Saudi. I'm working on a project for them.' He pours the wine and hands me a glass. 'Patrol boats. Being built in Ipswich.'

'You're a boatbuilder?'

'What?' He examines the thought for an instant and laughs softly. 'No. Oh, that I were! No, I'm ... well...' He shrugs self-deprecatingly. 'Just a glorified overseer, really.'

Josh is hovering impatiently. '*Mummy.*' He pushes at my plate, anxious for me to sample the fruits of his labours.

I accept Moreland's offer to fillet my fish. He uses a long thin-bladed knife which must be exceptionally sharp because it scythes effortlessly through the flesh, leaving hardly anything on the bone. He slips the fillets onto my plate with a deft movement. Watching him, I get the impression he is expert in all such practical things.

We eat like three seasoned campers, sitting around the open fire. I am not too proud to use a fork. Josh, rejecting such refinements, kneels in front of his meal and stabs at it with a short knife, then, when he thinks no one is looking, resorts to his fingers. Moreland, sitting cross-legged, fillets his fish and, laying it on the bread, constructs a giant sandwich. As he bites into it he drops a wink at Josh.

We talk of fishing and expeditions. We discuss survival techniques, how you find food in unlikely places, how you collect water in the desert. Or rather, Moreland and Josh pass these ideas back and forth while I pick at my fish. Moreland has a way of talking to Josh – of asking questions, of deferring to him – that has Josh discharging thoughts and ideas at a rate I rarely see nowadays. Occasionally Moreland glances at me with the ghost of a smile, a blink of the eyes, as if to reassure me that I am not excluded.

Moreland has a strong face, with blunt features and close-cropped brown hair that would probably be wavy if it were left to grow. His eyes, dark and wide-set, give an impression of self-possession, of preoccupation, but his smile gives a rather different message, of kindness and accessability. It is a confusing face, hard to read. I wonder, not for the first time, why he is here.

He and Josh start to talk about sailing. I try to communicate some interest, then give up. Harry may have developed an infatuation with the water but it never transferred itself to me, and I maintained a strictly supportive role, as cabin cleaner, buyer of provisions, and – very occasionally, if Harry promised not to take us beyond the mouth of the river – inept and uncertain crew.

I drift with the moment. The wine, light and crisp, stills my brain. The wind hardly reaches into this corner of the clearing. I am no longer cold, I feel oddly safe.

Josh, abandoning the rest of his fish, which is now inextricably mashed up with the bones, departs with a bucket to obtain washing-up water from the end of the quay.

Moreland pours me another glass. He tells me what a fine service it was yesterday. 'It must have been a strain, though.'

'It was rather hot,' I agree. 'And there were so many people.' I examine the fire for a moment. 'How did you meet Harry?' I ask.

He hesitates for the tiniest instant, but it is enough to make me feel I am about to get a modified version of the truth.

'We met in pitch darkness,' he says lightly. 'In a bog. We gave each other a terrible fright. Neither of us realised the other was there.'

'This was in the Falklands?'

He nods.

I try to imagine Harry and Moreland in this Falkland bog, in fear of the enemy, but the picture refuses to form, if only because it doesn't mesh with the little I gleaned from Harry. All Harry told me was that one of his men was badly injured by a sniper, and getting him to the medics delayed his unit so much that they missed much of the fighting.

'You knew him well?' I ask.

'No. Not then, anyway. We met again a couple of years ago, of course, over the Saudi deal.' I smile ignorance and he explains, 'The yard here,' – he points a hand in the general direction of Ipswich – 'was tendering for the patrol boat order against several places in Europe. They needed all the help they could get. Harry persuaded the government to get behind it, got things going on the diplomatic front.' He gives a slow nod of acknowledgment. 'And very effective he was too, so they say.'

This does not surprise me. Harry loved manœuvring people and situations towards a goal, enjoyed using his power as an MP. Most of all, of course, he loved being at the centre of things.

'And then,' Moreland continues in a voice that is oddly diffident, 'he did me a great favour once.'

I do not doubt this either. Harry was a firm believer in the bestowing and collecting of favours; it was the currency by which he operated. If I am at all surprised, it is that Moreland should have been the beneficiary of Harry's largesse. As an overseer of boatbuilding projects, I would not have thought Moreland particularly influential.

I do not ask what this favour might have been. In the way of favours traded between men, I imagine it is something that Moreland would rather not discuss.

'Harry never talked about the Falklands,' I say reminiscently. 'Nor about the Paras, either. I don't think—' I pause, examining the remark for disloyalty. 'I don't think he ever really enjoyed soldiering.'

Moreland opens his mouth to speak, then changes his mind. Finally he says with a shrug, 'Well, it's a fairly dubious way to earn a living, isn't it, even at the best of times.'

'Dubious?' An odd word.

'Oh, I don't mean dishonourable.' He chuckles drily. 'I mean that you join up because – in my case anyway – your father was in the Marines, and his father before him, and in your eighteen-year-old innocence you think it'd be a good idea to do a few years' service, have a few years of stretching yourself in very well-defined directions.'

'And then you go to war.'

'Yes, strange that. You get to think you'll never do any real fighting and then suddenly there you are. It's the real thing.' His eyes veer towards the fire. He says with a grunt of disdain, 'People being killed. Friends. Nobody really warns you how you're going to feel about that.' His face tautens. His eyes swing back to mine.

I glance quickly away. I stare at the ashes. I'm not sure I am in the right state of mind for this sort of discussion. When I glance back, it is to find Moreland watching me.

'I think Harry was rather like you,' I remark. 'I think he joined because of his father. I mean, if one's looking for reasons. Losing his father so young, there was a sort of inevitability. A psychiatrist would probably say so, anyway.'

Moreland nods pensively, though I have the feeling that his thoughts, whatever they may be, are directed less at Harry than at me.

Josh comes into view, staggering under the weight of a slopping bucket. Moreland, catching my flicker of amusement, follows my gaze and, jumping to his feet, hails him. 'Easier to take the plates to the bucket, Josh.' Collecting the plates, Moreland scoops the bones into the embers and, shooting a quick smile in my direction, goes to meet Josh, who, having lowered the bucket to the ground, is resting athlete-style, bent forward, hands braced on knees.

I am on a downward slide from the wine, sleepy, mildly befuddled, pleasantly detached. As Moreland demonstrates dish-washing techniques to Josh, I get off my wooden perch and stretch out on the grass, eyes closed. It would be easy to doze but if I do I know I'll have trouble sleeping tonight, and it is the nights I've come to dread.

After a time I hear feet approaching and the sound of someone dropping onto the ground not far away.

'I trust Josh is going to maintain this sudden enthusiasm for washing up,' I murmur.

'Ahhh.' Moreland draws the sound out into a small laugh. 'I've done my best to encourage him.'

'Funny how men are perfectly capable of these things when it suits them.' I soften my voice to show there is no rancour in this.

'Ha! Now there's a statement that a man answers at his peril!' But his voice is warm; he enjoys this sort of debate. 'But you're right. Of course you're right. Guilty as charged. *Most* men, anyway. Naturally I am a glowing exception. But in our general defence, I must say that we used to be encouraged – still are, really – by, dare I say it, women, who make us feel unwelcome and incompetent in the kitchen.'

'No man in my life has ever been made to feel unwelcome in the kitchen,' I say.

He laughs, but a little awkwardly, and I sense Harry's presence, a shadow that falls across the conversation.

Then, as if in reply to some question, Moreland says, 'But he'll be all right, Josh. He'll be fine, you know. He's got . . .' He hums as he searches for the word. '*Passion*. Real enthusiasm.'

I ponder this compliment. Passion is not something that I would immediately consider in relation to Josh – or many other children for that matter – but in a sense Moreland is right; it is a good and positive thing to possess. Unless it is powerful and dark, like Harry's.

Moreland continues in what I realise is a single chain of thought, 'But you . . .' He is unusually hesitant. '. . . well, I imagine things are not going to be so easy for you.' He adds quickly, 'I mean, legally. Financially.'

89

I open my eyes a fraction. The clouds bulge darkly overhead. 'Well, no. I don't think these things ever are.'

'I had a friend once . . . Her father was lost at sea. The family had a terrible job sorting it out.' I turn my head. He is sitting with his arms resting on his knees, squinting sideways at me. I sense an element of preparation in this, that he has guided the conversation towards this point. He goes on, 'The first lawyers got it wrong and wasted two years. The family ended up having to sell their house. I just wondered . . .' The slight awkwardness again, which seems uncharacteristic of him. 'You're all right for advice, are you? I know you've got Leonard. But what about experts? Has he managed to find the right people for you?'

It occurs to me that I could take this as an intrusion, that Moreland is overstepping the marks of our new acquaintance, but for some reason his interest does not bother me, perhaps because it is purely practical – about the only sort of interest I can deal with – and clearly well-meant.

'I think so.'

He nods sagely. 'And the money side? Who's . . . ?'

'Harry's accountant, Gillespie. He's meant to be good, so they say. Well – *sharp*. Which probably amounts to the same thing.'

Moreland seems content with this; he nods anyway. I pull myself up into a sitting position and yawn and stretch my arms, though my drowsiness has quite gone.

'I was wondering . . .' Moreland begins with an abrupt, frowning smile. 'I hope you don't mind my asking . . . but I'd be interested to know . . . what the weather was like that day? The day Harry set out. Here in the river. Was it misty?'

It is strange how the unease can fade, almost without my realising it, only to rush back with an unpleasant little lurch. I wonder why he wants to know. The question must show in my face because Moreland says, 'It's just that someone said it was foggy, someone else said it was was quite clear. I've sailed off this coast. I was curious. Academic interest. But look, it doesn't matter if . . .'

I shrug, 'I don't mind.' I nearly say: It helps to talk about it. I look across the clearing to where Josh labours over his dishes, to the track just the other side of him and, beyond, to the trees, which, tormented by the wind, writhe and shiver continuously. 'Early on it was quite like this, but even windier. Harry thought of cancelling the trip. He phoned the weather people. But they told him the wind was going to drop and by mid-morning it did. In fact by noon, when Harry brought *Minerva* into the quay, there was hardly any wind at all. He was relieved. He didn't feel too confident in a blow. Not singlehanded anyway. Then, as we were loading up, the rain started. A steady downpour. Then – yes, I suppose you couldn't see very far.' The memory is vivid, a vision of the boat disappearing into an indistinct wall of grey until I could see nothing but the brilliant orange of Harry's waterproofs, a small blob of colour suspended as if in space. 'When the rain eased it was misty. But I wouldn't have said it was foggy. It might have got foggy in the evening, of course – I don't know. I'd gone out by then. I was the other side of Woodbridge. It certainly wasn't foggy there.'

Moreland absorbs this slowly. 'Harry didn't go straight off?'

I am miles away. 'What?' I say, coming back with an effort. 'Oh no. He went to the mooring to wait for the tide. It wasn't right for going south, not till later. He'd worked it out – he had all the tide-tables. He was aiming to leave at five or six – something like that. But he couldn't wait at the quay, you see. *Minerva* had a deep keel. There wasn't enough water for her except at high tide. He had to take her out to the mooring as soon as we'd finished loading. He was going to spend the afternoon doing jobs on the boat then potter down to the end of the river and wait the last half hour there.'

'You don't know when he left?'

'No. By the time I got back from dinner it was too dark to go and check. But he was seen going down river by someone at Waldringfield at about five. Then a coaster saw a yacht through the mist or fog or whatever it was, later that evening.'

'Ah.' He nods slowly. 'No one else saw him?'

91

'I don't think so.'

'And he was aiming for the Hamble River?'

'Yes. But not in one go. He was going to stop on the way. He wasn't sure where. He was going to wait until he got tired, and then put in somewhere. Ramsgate. Brighton. He wasn't sure. Originally he was going with a friend – Jack Crawley – but Jack couldn't make it.'

Moreland contemplates the ground for a moment. 'He couldn't find anyone else?'

'Oh, he *could* have, but . . .'

Moreland waits silently. Eventually he murmurs, 'He wanted to go singlehanded?'

I spread my palms in bafflement. 'It was a challenge, I suppose. Something he'd never done before – a long passage, I mean, on his own. I think it frightened him rigid. But then,' I comment almost to myself, 'that was part of the attraction. At least I think so.' How do I explain? How do I explain this person, my husband, who walled off enormous areas of himself, who did not himself know what drove him?

'He hadn't sailed much before?' The softness of Moreland's voice does not conceal its attentiveness.

'Hardly at all, no. He was brought up not far from here – just north of Woodbridge – but he never sailed as a child. It was the quay that got him going – I mean, the fact that it came with the house. He didn't like to waste it. And then he was offered a good deal on *Minerva*, and that was that. He had to learn everything from scratch. He bought books, got one of the lads from the local yard to teach him the rudiments, went racing a bit. Then, when *Minerva* came back from the yard, after she'd been refitted, he used to take friends out with him, people who knew the river – it's quite dangerous out by the entrance, the sandbanks shift—'

Moreland nods to show that he knows about the hazards of the bar. 'You never went with him?'

'Me? Oh no. Well – now and then, when he promised to keep in the river. And once or twice further out, when it was very calm. But I didn't enjoy it, I'm afraid. The water terrifies me.' I laugh at myself. 'Pathetic, really.'

'Not at all.' He says this in a kindly abstract way, although, having been a Royal Marine, he must find my lack of spirit quite alien.

'He took Josh sometimes,' I say, 'but Josh got bored. *Minerva* went too fast to catch fish.'

Moreland grins briefly. I notice that his eyes are more hazel than brown, and that when he smiles they lose all their pensiveness and glint with vitality.

We fall into an easy silence. Josh is still at the bucket. He has elongated the sleeve of his sweatshirt to cover his hand and form a dish-cloth with which to rub the plates. Drying, I hope vaguely, rather than washing.

'They think he must have been run down in the night,' I say, feeling compelled to complete the story, as much for myself as for Moreland. 'A ship that never saw him, never realised what had happened.'

Moreland looks towards some distant horizon then back at me, his face creased with renewed seriousness. 'It happens,' he murmurs.

In the silence that follows I picture the scene as Moreland must be seeing it, the small yacht, the ship bearing down on it in the dark, the lone figure failing to keep a proper watch, asleep perhaps, slouched over in the cockpit; then, with no warning, the cataclysmic impact.

'One thing . . .' Moreland asks almost casually. 'Why did Harry decide to take the dory, do you know?'

I am surprised at how well informed he is. 'The dory . . . ?'

'It just seemed . . . Well, it's not really the sort of boat one would normally take on a long passage,' he explains with care. 'Impossible to stow on deck – impossible even to lift out of the water – and large and heavy to tow behind. It would have slowed him down a lot, and in any sort of sea, well . . . it could have filled up, broken loose – all sorts of things. He didn't have an inflatable? Something he could stow on deck?'

Leonard must have told him, I realise. Or – yes, of course – the lads at the boatyard in Waldringfield, the regulars in the pub. All the details of *Minerva*'s disappearance would have been thoroughly chewed over, country style.

I take my time. 'We had an inflatable, yes. A Zodiac. But he left it behind. It's in the garage, I think.'

'I see.' He still looks puzzled. He is on the point of asking something else when I point towards Josh, jogging towards us with the clanking bucket dancing lightly from one hand. Arriving, he pulls the cutlery from the bucket, gives it a last-minute polish on the much abused sleeve-end and holds it up for Moreland's inspection.

I hadn't realised how late it was. Kneeling, I sit back on my heels. 'Well . . .' I say with finality. 'It's been very nice.'

Moreland takes his cue. 'Thank you for lending me Josh for the morning.' He offers a hand and pulls me to my feet.

I look to where Josh is packing the lurid plastic plates into a rucksack. 'He seems to have enjoyed himself.'

'Well, perhaps I could take him again, while I still have the use of a boat. If that's all right?'

Instinctively I pause to weigh the idea, as I weigh every decision and response nowadays. 'Yes, of course.'

Moreland closes his rucksack and picks up my basket. With Josh in the lead, we start across the clearing.

'Harry was planning to cruise the South Coast, was he?' Moreland asks quietly, as if our conversation hadn't been interrupted.

I walk on for a moment. 'He was going to base the boat in the Hamble for the summer,' I say. 'Use it as a hopping off point for gastronomic weekends in France.' I remember Harry telling me this. He had paused in the doorway of the kitchen on his way to the study. I remember his obvious irritation at being forced into this lie. He knew that I was aware of his real reason for taking the boat to a place far from home yet convenient for London. We both knew he was going to use it for his sessions with Caroline Palmer. I chose not to say anything. I had decided long before never to say anything.

Now I faithfully recount Harry's version. I recount his lie. Like most lies I have to tell nowadays, I manage it with conviction.

Later, when Moreland has been gone for some time and Josh is playing with his Game Boy and there is no one else about, I wander into the garden, making a slow circle that takes me round the perimeter of the lawn, through the wind-buffeted rose garden, past the glass-houses and lines of vegetables, and out into the drive by the door set into the high wall. Coming to the outbuildings, I pass the double garage that houses Harry's Mercedes and my far from shiny estate car and stop at the small single garage that we use for storage. Going in by the side door, I flick on the light and look straight into the far corner. Next to the surplus furniture and sundry yacht gear and the four-horse outboard motor, I see the Zodiac inflatable, exactly where Maurice, our gardener, left it.

The Zodiac has been incompletely deflated and inexpertly folded. Maurice offered to pack it away for me, and in my weariness that day I was quick to accept. From the look of it he didn't find the job easy. The folds are too bulky for the tall green bag and the boat bulges out from the top like a sluggish sea creature emerging from a pod. The grey rubberised fabric still has a smear of what at a distance looks like a pale wash of paint but which on closer examination is in fact encrusted mud that has dried into a craze of fine cracks.

The mud dried the same way on my skin, I remember. There were patches of it all over my upper arms and shins when I woke, confused and stiff, from that first exhausted sleep. The mud had smeared the sheets as well, and was stuck to my clothes in thick grey scabs. I scrubbed myself under the shower, I pulled the sheets off the bed, I put on some clean clothes before I went in search of Maurice to ask for help in bringing the Zodiac up from the quay.

I can see how strange the choice of the dory must look to Moreland. The dory is a wide, flat-bottomed dinghy with a powerful outboard. I can understand how it must bother him that Harry didn't choose to take the inflatable. But then Moreland is well versed in these things and Harry wasn't.

I should have mentioned that, I should have made it clear that Harry often made mistakes. Like misreading charts and going aground. Like getting ropes around the propeller.

I should have mentioned it. If the opportunity arises, I will.

I close the door behind me, wishing that I wasn't beset by so many well-meaning people. Moreland probably thinks he is being helpful in some way, just as Charles and Anne and Leonard are driven by the firm conviction that they are acting in my best interests. That is the irony. And there is little I can do to stop them.

FIVE

F orgive me, but in your letter you said you were having difficulty in getting hold of the concert accounts,' I say to Tim Schwartz. 'And now – unless I'm getting this wrong – you're saying that you've got them after all.'

Schwartz sits stiffly on the edge of a cane chair, his arms resting on his knees, his narrow head framed by a weeping fig which, in my long absence, has lost most of its leaves. He sucks in his cheeks slightly, he regards me with an unyielding stare. I get the feeling that my slow grasp of the situation is a trial to him.

'What the auditors have,' he says in his tight voice, 'are the ledgers, the entries, that sort of thing. What they're missing is the necessary information to . . .' He gives a small gesture of what might be irritation. '. . . well, *interpret* the accounts.'

I pick up his letter from the table beside me. It is dated some weeks ago. I have read it several times since Margaret unearthed it from the waiting mail first thing this morning.

Glancing through it again now, I find that Tim Schwartz is no more precise on paper than he is in person. *Information relating to the concert accounts . . .*

'This information,' I ask. 'Could you perhaps be a bit more definite? It would help to know what to look for.'

'Well—' He gives a tense shrug. 'Anything, really. Correspondence, invoices, contracts, agreements . . .'

'I see.' The sun breaks through the heavy cloud and bathes the conservatory in a sudden burst of light. We blink at each other, re-establishing contact.

'The problem, Mrs Richmond,' he says abruptly, 'is that everything has come to a complete standstill. All our work, all our planning. Not a single child is benefiting or is likely to benefit until . . .' He breaks off and draws in his lips. 'You see, as things stand, the auditors can't pass the accounts for the concert – for ROC, which was the company set up especially for the concert. And while there are no accounts, the money's locked into the system. The charity can't receive the profits, not a penny. And to say we're desperate for the money . . .' He splays a hand and rolls his eyes.

I nod slowly. I explain cautiously, 'Well, after what you told me on Friday, we did have another look. Margaret – my husband's secretary – went through everything again over the weekend. She didn't find very much, I'm afraid. She doesn't think so anyway. Just some correspondence. But she's made up a list of the senders' names and the subject matter of each letter, just in case.' I take Margaret's neatly typed sheet from the seat next to me and hand it to him.

The spark that glimmers in Schwartz's eyes soon fades as he skims the page. 'I don't think . . .' He scans it again and shakes his head. 'No.' He gives a weary sigh. 'Nothing.' He hands it back.

Maybe it is the speed with which he reaches this conclusion, maybe it is his palpable gloom, but I have the feeling that he knows exactly what he is looking for and has at this very moment despaired of finding it. I also have the feeling that he thinks Harry is in some way to blame for these papers having gone missing. This realisation lodges uncomfortably in my mind. Part of me would like to retreat, to leave Schwartz and his problem to other people, as I used to leave everything that was at all difficult to Harry and his staff. But I promised myself some weeks ago that I would not run from anything, however trivial, however troublesome.

'Mr Schwartz— Tim—' I signal my uncertainty with an awkward laugh. 'You know, when . . . when you lose someone . . . When something terrible happens to you and your family . . . Well, people are very kind. Astonishingly kind. In fact I've been overwhelmed. So many letters. Such wonderful messages. And I know – I appreciate – how very difficult it is for them. I mean, lifting the phone, finding the right thing to say . . .' Tim Schwartz is listening with the wary attention of someone who fears gratuitous and embarrassing confidences. I press on, 'But sometimes in their efforts to spare you pain, friends – people – can be almost too kind. They try to keep things from you. They mean well, of course – *of course* – but it doesn't actually help. Quite the opposite. You just end up getting surprises you'd rather not have.'

I don't need to go on; he has understood me very well. 'I did give the details to your accountant,' he says virtuously.

Since my return Gillespie has been conspicuous by his silence, a lapse – very probably innocent – into which I now read some significance. This, and Schwartz's wariness, revive my determination to hear more, and I press him for the details.

He contemplates the floor crossly for a moment. He does not want to get embroiled in further explanations and difficulties. But when he brings his flat gaze back to mine I can see that, tedious though it is for him, he has decided to humour me. 'A major invoice seems to have gone astray,' he says briskly, as if, having made his decision, he is now in a hurry to get the information off his chest. 'It was – well, in theory, it *should* have been sent in by a company called Mountbay. They received a large cheque, at any rate. Though what services they provided to the concert, we have no idea. Anyway, this invoice is missing. Also, some of the other invoices from this Mountbay company, the ones that we *do* have, are inadequate for auditing purposes. They don't say anything about what Mountbay did or supplied. The auditors have looked into it, but as far as they can tell the company doesn't operate in the audio or stage equipment line – no one's ever heard of it anyway. And it didn't handle any of the artists who appeared. The auditors can't find any contract, any agreement – *nothing* to tell them what the company was about.' He stops abruptly and looks darkly away.

'So . . .' I pick my question carefully. I do not want to look any more ignorant than I need to. 'Mountbay was paid by you—'

'Not by us,' he corrects me. 'Not by the charity. By The Rumanian Orphans Concert Limited – ROC. We thought it was safer to make it a separate limited company.' Struck by the irony of this, he gives a bitter laugh.

'By ROC. But surely—' I cast around for ideas. 'The people at Mountbay, can't they help? There must be someone there who remembers what they supplied to the concert.'

Schwartz leans back in his seat. He explains distantly, 'It's an offshore company, based in Guernsey. With nominee shareholders. There are no staff.'

'Oh.' I don't quite understand how a company can have no staff. 'Aren't there owners, people who would know?'

'The whole point of having nominee shareholders, so I'm told, is that no one ever gets to find out who the owners are.' His tone contrives to suggest that I should interpret this in a sinister way.

A movement catches my eye. Maurice is trudging across the lawn, a heavy bag of fertiliser or peat or something similar in his arms. 'Is there much involved?' I ask. 'Much money?'

'You could say that!' declares Schwartz. 'Over three hundred thousand pounds.'

Always such massive quantities of money. I find it hard to relate to them. Harry's debts, the mortgage, Ainswick; nothing with less than a long series of noughts on the end.

Maurice stops in front of a flower bed and lowers the bag. He contemplates the bed for a moment then turns away and starts back across the lawn. How much does he get paid? I try to remember, and wonder how much longer I can afford to keep him.

Finally I face the question that I will have to ask Schwartz sooner or later. With a small ache of foreboding, I say, 'Why did you think the invoice might be here?'

'Because your husband was the only person who dealt with Mountbay, Mrs Richmond. Who knew anything about them.

Well, let's put it this way – we can't find anyone else who did! And' – his eyes fasten on mine – 'it was your husband who signed the cheques that went out to Mountbay, and took them for countersignature.' His tone, his stare are loaded with some meaning he wants me to read.

My God, Harry, what is this?

I search for something to say. 'This person who countersigned, what about him?'

Schwartz's eyes register a bleak amusement. 'It was our oldest trustee, Sir John Elphon.' He explains drily, 'Sir John is not a great detail man.'

There is a silence, we sit for a moment contemplating our different and common problems, then Tim Schwartz gets abruptly to his feet.

Rising more slowly, I try not to look as though I am staring down at him, though he is considerably shorter than I am. 'We'll take another look,' I say. 'Just in case.'

He gestures pessimism at this thought then pauses, hovering on the point of some disclosure. Righteousness finally overcomes reticence, and he says, 'I have to say that if things aren't resolved, if Mountbay doesn't have a proper claim to all this money they received, then there's going to have to be an investigation.'

I frown, I say sorrowfully, 'I see.'

To make sure I am left in no doubt as to the outcome, he adds, 'And the auditors seem to think that your husband will be held responsible.'

'But my husband is dead, Mr Schwartz.'

'Yes.' He gives a tiny sigh of forbearance, as though he is labouring under difficult circumstances. 'But if the auditors are unable to pass the accounts – which seems likely – then they will have to say *why*. They will have to allocate responsibility.' He adds brusquely, 'I'm sorry.'

I take him to the door. He tucks his briefcase high under his arm and surveys the drive with a frown.

'When you say Harry was responsible,' I say, 'you mean that he should have taken more care?'

'Mrs Richmond . . .' he gasps, momentarily at a loss. 'Your

husband knew exactly what he was doing! He removed that money. He knew all about Mountbay. He—' Pulling up short, Schwartz looks away and glares angrily at the trees.

Unease pulls at my stomach. 'You're saying ... terrible things, Mr Schwartz.'

He makes a token gesture of regret.

'Surely ... there must be some way to avoid anything—' I want to say *public*.

'Well, the auditors won't wait forever,' Schwartz exclaims with a bark of indignation. 'And nor, I have to say, will *we!* We've been banking on that money. It's getting to the point where the next shipment is going to have to be postponed. Medical supplies for the kids. Meant to be leaving in two weeks. It's them who're going to suffer, Mrs Richmond. The *kids*.' His glare is fired by moral outrage.

'How long before the auditors . . . ?'

Calming himself a little, he says, 'No more than a couple of weeks.'

As soon as he is gone I take refuge in the kitchen and make a strong coffee. I sit at the counter, my head in my hands. I concentrate on my breathing. I fight down an impulse towards alarm and self-pity. I take my time. If I have learnt nothing else, it is that to have any hope of gaining control of myself and events around me, I have to think problems through slowly, at my own pace.

Those heavy glances of Schwartz's, those insinuations that he meant me to read, I read them now, I reject them, I re-examine them. Schwartz thinks not only that Harry was involved with Mountbay, but that this involvement was dishonourable. He thinks that Harry transferred the money for some motives of his own. This idea scares me, yet I am not sure how much weight I should attach to it.

But what worries me even more is that, whatever led to this business, whether or not Harry was at all negligent, enormous damage will be done if it gets out. Any investigation, however small, will look very bad for Harry. At best it will imply incompetance and high-handedness, at the worst, dishonesty.

102

And the taint of dishonesty, however unjustly earned, would undo everything that I have fought so hard to achieve for the children. The loss of their father is hard enough for them to bear, but at least tragedy is straightforward and honourable, even, in some people's eyes, romantic. Dishonesty, though, is impossible to live down.

And money that belonged to a charity! Money that was bound for of all people – orphans!

God, Harry.

The coffee charges my blood. I have wild ideas – to rally Harry's friends in some way; to approach the charity auditors and explain to them – what? The ideas collapse. I feel muddled and anxious again.

I can't help wondering: did Harry realise this was coming down on him? Was this the last terrible problem that drove him over the edge?

I remember the last weekend before he died. I remember finding him at three in the morning in the drawing-room, lying on a sofa in semi-darkness. The light from the hall illuminated the glass of whisky which he held loosely on his stomach. As I came in he opened his eyes. I think he had been waiting for me. He gave a sardonic smile which seemed to contain all the resentment that I seemed to engender in him at the time and, though I see it only now, to contain, also, glimmers of despair. And maybe, if I'm really going to torture myself, I can also see in that derisive expression a cry for help.

There was no hope of my reading this or any other message, of course; by that time I was too bound up in his betrayal, which still loomed grotesquely, still produced such bewilderment and deep feelings of failure in me that, even after all those months, I couldn't see beyond it. I couldn't see beyond Harry's unwillingness to confront the issue, beyond his refusal to explain himself to me and acknowledge the damage and pain he was causing us. We were two immovable objects, trapped in mutual bafflement and guilt, our communications reduced to a series of set pieces.

We started one then.

'Just checking?' His tone was mocking, his voice thick with drink or tiredness or both.

I stood there, feeling useless. Then, as so often before, I tried diversion. 'I thought maybe we'd all go out for lunch tomorrow.'

But he wasn't going to be deflected that easily. 'Where d'you think I'd be, mmm?' he asked in a tone that was altogether more dangerous.

I could not answer this.

Turning his head to see me better, he demanded, 'Well?'

I sank wearily onto a chair.

He blew dismissively through his lips and murmured, 'Christ. Such faith, such faith.'

'I couldn't sleep, that was all.'

'Must be difficult with one eye open.' He snorted with feeble amusement.

The remark struck home, just as he intended it to. I couldn't help watching him. I did it all the time. When he disappeared at odd times I felt such a gnawing anxiety that I couldn't concentrate on anything until I had established where he was and what he was doing. When he was in the house, I had to know precisely where. It had, I suppose, become an obsession.

'Lunch,' he murmured. 'That's allowed, is it?'

'Katie and Josh would love it.' I tried to keep a light note to my voice, something that would leave the conversational door open.

A long pause, and he murmured, 'Too much work.'

'Oh? What a pity.' I wanted to sound reasonable, or at least understanding. 'Well – tea, then? At home, I mean. I could make a cake.' God, I thought, to such depths of subterfuge am I driven.

Harry gave me a strange unfocused stare, as if he was looking beyond me to some half-formed future that excluded me. Eventually he turned away and closed his eyes.

I waited but he never replied.

I was struck then by the realisation that despite all my hopes, despite all my efforts to bring us together again as a family, we were not going to make it. Simply, Harry's determination to make us fail was greater than mine to succeed, and I wasn't sure I could hold out against him any more. Until then, the possibility of us falling apart as a family had been unthinkable, a last and remote resort. But in the long silence of that dreary night I finally faced the fact that it might happen. Faced it – and could not bear it. The thought made me ill. I was wrenched by a sense of loss and outrage.

I spoke his name. I got up and knelt on the floor at his side.

His eyes stayed closed. His lips tightened.

The ghosts of countless failed conversations hung over me. I struggled for something new to say. But it was no good. All I could find was: 'I just want to understand. I just want to ... understand.' I heard the emotion wobbling ignobly in my voice. I knew I was doing everything wrong. By this time he resented me touching him, but that didn't stop me from reaching out and putting a hand on his arm. His tension was tangible, like an electric charge.

'Come to bed,' I said. My voice sounded thin and pathetic in my ears. 'Why don't you ... ?' How I had the courage to say this I'm not sure, not when my confidence in this department was at rock-bottom, not when we hadn't slept together for weeks, not when I had long agonised over the thought that it might have been some failure of mine that had first started all our troubles.

I suppose it was simply that this age-old move was the only one I had left. But even as I made my clumsy offering I was tense with dread and hopelessness.

Harry opened his eyes and stared at the ceiling. He didn't say anything, he let me wait – he made me wait. Then he turned his bleary gaze slowly on mine, and gave me a narrow look of such bitterness and disgust that I surged with humiliation. It seemed to me that he had done this with the simple aim of hurting me. My throat swelled, my pulse beat violently in my head, my stomach filled with violence. I had never known real rage before, but I felt it then, a hot tide of resentment and fury that shot me blindly forward. I thought of everything he was doing to hurt our family, of the selfishness, and the damage. I thought of Katie. I forgot he was in the grip of what was really a sickness, I forgot the terrible strains he was under. I felt so angry at what he had reduced me to, at this unbearable sense of powerlessness, that for the first time in my life I wanted to strike out. I wanted to hurt him back, as he had hurt me. I wanted, for a moment, to kill him.

The moment passed, I'm not sure how. Somehow I held on to my rage and struggled to my feet and got away. But something terrible had happened in that moment, some Rubicon had been crossed. Both of us had glimpsed the depths we were capable of descending to.

The ragged tapping of the typewriter ceases as I open the study door. Margaret twists in her chair. 'Well?'

'Well,' I say with a shrug, 'nothing, really. The file – your list – didn't interest him.'

I sit down at Harry's desk. Margaret has explained how the paperwork is sorted. Directly in front of me are the typed letters awaiting my signature; to the right the letters that I will have to answer by hand – no dent in this pile yet; also the paid bills and a number of unpaid invoices with queries; to the left, documents and forms, most of them with yellow stickers bearing memos in Margaret's neat script. There is also a list of answering-machine messages from the weekend – about fifteen – and another six or seven calls taken by Margaret this morning.

Looking at all this, I feel engulfed again.

I pull the nearest pile towards me and stare unseeing at the first letter. I am still thinking of Schwartz.

'Margaret, do we have Harry's address books? His diaries?'

'The desk diaries are at the office,' she says in her measured voice. 'But I've got an address book here. And this year's pocket diary.'

I lean back from Harry's desk and, opening the centre drawer, pull out the old pocket diaries and hand them to her. 'I wondered – could you look through them for me? See if you can find anything about a company called Mountbay. It's based in Guernsey, I think.'

'Oh, but . . .' She hesitates. 'I've already looked. Mr Gillespie asked me to.' She adds quickly, 'We didn't find anything.'

I stare out through the window at the vegetable garden, at the glass-houses which lean against the vine-covered perimeter wall and, rising high above them, the tall beech wood beyond. I notice that the glass-houses have been whitewashed against the sun.

I half turn back to Margaret. 'What about meetings?'

'I'm sorry?'

'Did Harry have any meetings with people who – I don't know – could have had anything to do with this Mountbay company?'

'I can look.' Her tone betrays her doubts. 'I'm not sure if I'll find anything. He was a bit vague sometimes.' Harry was rarely vague. I think this is her way of saying he could be secretive.

'Well,' I say ponderously, 'what about people who weren't with any particular company then. Any meeting you can't place. I just thought, maybe . . .'

'Yes. Yes, I understand.' She sounds marginally more optimistic.

I wonder how Harry entered his appointments with Caroline Palmer. Presumably he wouldn't have used her name openly. Just her initials, perhaps. Or a code name. I wonder how much Margaret knew about this. She is a perceptive woman, she has a way of identifying people's foibles, of gently mocking their vanities. It's hard to believe that she could have been totally unaware of Harry's activities.

'I'd be most grateful,' I say. 'Then at least we can say we tried.'

She would like me to explain this, she would like to know what we're trying for, but she checks herself and turns back to her work.

I read the first of the letters that Margaret has composed for me – to the Inland Revenue, informing them of my changed circumstances – and put my best signature at the bottom. I begin to fold the letter, but Margaret calls, 'I'll do that!'

There are letters to the Department of Social Security, to

banks, insurance companies, building societies. I sign the rest of these letters without reading them.

I skip over the personal letters, which I cannot face just at the moment, and alight uncertainly on a pile of official-looking forms. A transfer form from the bank. Some sort of release form from Leonard's firm. And renewal forms. Do I want to renew our family subscription to the local sailing club? Do I want to renew the service contract on the house security system? Or the one on Harry's personal computer? My instinct is to rid myself of everything that I have no use for. I have modest dreams that encompass no service contracts, no staff, just a small cottage, a functional car, and enough money to ensure the children's security.

A claim form from a marine insurance company, presumably for the yacht. The stick-on note from Margaret asks me to sign it on the last page where marked, saying that Leonard will fill in the details.

Then, a household insurance form. In the claim box various items have been typed in. Clothing, cash, camera. And: Cellphone handset.

Margaret misses nothing.

'Margaret . . .'

She twists round and sees the claim form in my hand. 'Yes?'

'The mobile phone. It's definitely gone, is it?'

'Well, I rather assumed so. Mr Richmond always took it with him on the yacht, I think, didn't he? Oh, and there was the bill,' she adds rapidly. 'It showed several calls that Friday evening.'

'Yes . . . Could I see it – the bill?'

'It's at the office. I could bring it in tomorrow.'

'Thanks. I'd just be . . .' I gesture uncertainty. '. . . interested to see.'

'Of course!' Margaret exclaims in a voice of deep understanding. 'Of course. I'll bring it in.'

Thanking her, I sign the claim and, putting it aside, go to the next form. At first I think I'm misreading it, but no, it's an application for a firearms certificate, issued by the Suffolk Constabulary, itemising two shotguns.

I am puzzled. Harry's licence was only renewed last autumn, some time in October. I remember the police coming round to inspect the guns and check the security arrangements. When they'd finished their work Harry sat them down with some coffee – his offer of whisky was politely refused – and told them how scandalously underfunded he believed the Force to be and how he had fought hard in Parliament to get things improved.

I am baffled as to why the licence should need renewing again so soon. I am also bemused to see that the form is made out in my name.

At the top Margaret has attached a note on a yellow sticker. *Police will need to make inspection. Have suggested 8th.*

'Margaret, I'm sorry to bother you again.'

The typing ceases. 'No problem.'

'This firearms thing – I don't understand. We've already got a licence.'

'Oh yes, but it's in Mr Richmond's name, and since I thought you'd probably want to get rid of the guns I took it on myself to arrange the transfer. I do hope that was all right? They should be worth quite a bit. Four thousand or so. Well, that's what I've been told. The police explained the transfer to me. They said this was the best way. A bureaucratic thing. Any dealer'll take them, so long as they have the licence and proof of identity.'

'I see.' I study the form again. The eighth is tomorrow. I can't face the police so soon. 'Can we put them off?'

'Of course. Easily. But no need for you to be bothered. I could show them all the arrangements, the locker and so on. I was intending to do it anyway. They'd probably only need you for a signature.'

I duck my head into my hands and give my face a savage rub. 'No . . . Thanks all the same. I'll do it.'

'Are you sure?'

I tell her I'm sure.

'When would you like them to come then?'

'Not tomorrow. I won't be here tomorrow. Some other time.'

'Next week?'

'No, I think—' I stare out at the sky, I have a brief desire to be in the open, walking over the heath with Katie as we used to in the old days. 'No, let's get it over with. This week.'

The phone rings. Margaret crosses swiftly behind me to answer it. Capping the mouthpiece, she announces Leonard.

I take the phone.

'A bit of *good* news,' Leonard declares. 'Some money's come in. I thought I'd let you know straight away. It should be in your account by the end of the week. Ten *thousand*. Better, as they say, than a kick in the head.' He makes a wheezing sound that is something like a chuckle.

'Come in?' I echo vaguely. 'Where from?'

'From? Oh ... a business loan. Something Harry set up some years ago. It came due this week.'

With the firearms certificate still in front of me I am finding it hard to focus on this, far less to identify what is bothering me about the news. 'And it's coming to me?'

'Yes!' he says triumphantly.

'Who from?'

'A business associate of Harry's.'

I hesitate. I don't want to seem ungrateful, but at the same time I have to ask, 'This individual, Leonard, is it – would I know him?'

A pause. I can imagine Leonard's expression of forbearance. He is thinking: why does she have to be difficult? 'Ellen . . . The thing is – I can't actually *say*. It was a confidential arrangement. One of those things ... Nothing *sinister*, I assure you.' He gives his wheeze-like chuckle again.

I bristle. 'It's from Jack, isn't it?'

'What? No. Why should it be from Jack?'

'If it's from Jack I can't take it.'

'Ellen, I assure you it's not from Jack.'

I do not believe him. The whole thing bears Jack's stamp – a cosy little arrangement between men, the assumption that I would accept this unlikely story without question, that I wouldn't notice the astonishingly convenient timing of this magic money. I can imagine the two men congratulating themselves on their harmless little subterfuge.

But they have caught me at a sensitive time.

'I can't accept it, Leonard. I'm sorry. Not unless I know who it's from.'

'*Ellen.* I assure you this is the *genuine* repayment of a *genuine* loan. I guarantee it.'

'I don't want it,' I repeat stubbornly.

I imagine Leonard blinking in puzzlement, sighing inaudibly beyond the mouthpiece.

'Leonard? Please understand . . .'

'Well, I'm trying to. But you're wrong, you know.'

I feel a flicker of doubt, but I can't very well concede now. I change the subject. 'While you're on . . .'

'Yes?'

I tell him that Tim Schwartz came to see me today.

'Oh, did he? Oh. *Oh.* I'm sorry about that. I'm sorry he's *bothered* you. You should have told me.'

Aware that Margaret has stopped typing, I drop my voice a little. 'What's it about, Leonard?'

'Gillespie would be the best person to talk to about that, Ellen.'

'But is it serious? He made it sound serious.'

'*Serious*? I can't hear you. Did you say *serious*? In what way?'

'Well . . .' I cup my hand round the phone. I hate having to say this, even to Leonard. 'He seems to think they're going to blame Harry for the accounts not being right.'

Leonard makes calming noises. 'Oh, no, no. I don't think so. No. *Gillespie* doesn't think there's a problem. He seems quite happy.'

In the hall the doorbell sounds. I swing round. Margaret is already getting up to answer it.

'But Leonard,' I say as the door closes behind her, 'it's not just the accounts themselves, it's some money that Harry was responsible for. It seems that it might be' – I choose the most neutral word I can find – 'unaccounted for.'

A short silence. 'That *can't* be right.' Leonard has put on his most paternalistic tone. 'I'm sure that's not right, Ellen.'

I knead my forehead ferociously. For some reason Leonard's simple faith causes me fresh darts of anxiety.

111

'Leonard, would you do something for me?'

'Well – if I can.'

'If it wouldn't be too much trouble, would you look into this company that Tim Schwartz seems worried about? It's called Mountbay. And he said it was based in Guernsey.'

'*Guernsey* . . .' He pulls in his breath doubtfully. 'A different legal system, Ellen. I'm not sure . . . A bit outside my scope.'

I am easily defeated by such arguments. 'Oh,' I say weakly.

'And really, Gillespie would be better placed.'

Gillespie, it seems, is best placed to know most things. It is I who feel badly placed to ask him.

Before ringing off, Leonard makes me promise to reconsider the issue of the returned loan. I promise, and even as I do so I think he is right and that I must be mad to consider turning down this money. Pride is all very well, but only when you can afford it.

The doorbell will have been Molly, arriving for the lunch I have not even begun to prepare. I linger at the desk a while longer. Finally, without enthusiasm, I reach for a pad to scribble a note to Margaret, asking her to arrange a meeting with Gillespie in London tomorrow.

I find Molly in the hall, chattering to Margaret. She greets me with an exclamation of joy and gives me one of her all-enveloping hugs.

'I'm taking you out!' she declares.

I make only token resistance. One of the delights of knowing Molly is her enthusiasm for bursts of indulgence.

She talks exuberantly as she drives, one hand on the wheel, the other weaving explanatory patterns in the air. She gives me news from the Project, stories of two protegés who have managed against the odds to land jobs, tales of several past residents – and one present – who have reoffended. She recounts their misdemeanours with the feigned scorn and cheerful resignation of someone who has learnt to live with frequent disappointment. She mocks their efforts at crime and condemns their fecklessness at being caught, as if she could do a lot better herself, which, given the many tales she has heard, she probably could. 'Stupid boy! Went for a

Mercedes at a house up a long drive with an insomniac owner! Got collared before he reached the motorway. I ask you! When there're dozens of Cortinas on the Chantery Estate just begging to be had, and half of them nicked anyway! Really – what can you do?' She throws back her head and laughs her explosive belly laugh, which frequently turns heads in public places.

Molly is quite a bit older than me, I forget by how much – sixteen years perhaps – but sometimes I think she is younger. She has never lost her enthusiasm for people or life. And this despite ten years of loving a man she cheerfully called 'the rat', who, when he finally left his wife to move in with her, got cancer and died. Two years ago, when going through what she called her mid-life apex, she took up with a twenty-three year-old bricklayer. She treated him as if he was lucky to have her which, by any reasonable standards, he was. He adored her in a startled bovine sort of way but the affair faded last autumn. 'Lovely but wearing,' Molly declared. She pleaded a need for independence, but I think he simply bored her.

Molly makes no concessions to time or fashion. Her dark hair, now salted with grey, grows in a vast uncontrolled cloud like something from a Beardsley picture. She wears seventies radical – ethnic, flowing; or else her own version of eighties casual – jeans and hugging T-shirts with scanty patterned waistcoats. In the last few years her beam has broadened, her bosom burgeoned, but she carries her weight unrepentantly. With her olive skin, oval eyes and chinking jewellery, she has the look of a stage gypsy.

For our lunch she has chosen a new Thai restaurant in Woodbridge. Austere in correct nineties style, it is a blur of white walls, grey floor-tiles and white table-cloths relieved only by a splattering of single red carnations at each table, like specks of blood. As we glance indecisively down the packed menu, Molly gets onto the heated subject of the second half-way house which she has been trying to set up for as long as I have known her. It was Molly who, meeting me for the first time at a mayoral inauguration dinner, cornered me and, during an exhilarating and bemusing ten minutes, talked me into heading the fund-raising committee. We managed to raise three-quarters of the money by last September. The trustees approved the purchase of two adjacent properties for conversion into a fifteen-bedroom centre, but now there appears to be a problem with the planning department.

'It's this great toad Meacher,' Molly announces with narrow eyes. 'The chairman of the planning committee. I know he's blocking it. His minions mumble about fire regulations and access and all that stuff, but it's just excuses. It's Meacher himself – he's on the take. *That's* the real problem!' She pauses to make sure I have hoisted this in, that I am not showing disbelief at what might seem like a rather wild claim. 'I reckon he's been nobbled by the not-in-my-backyard mafia, led by the local builder who – wouldn't you believe it? – lives round the corner from our building. A neighbourhood lad-made-good – you know the sort – gold cufflinks, a house tarted up to within an inch of its life, a Mitsubishi Shogun in the drive.' She blows out her lips with disdain. 'Anyway him and Meacher are as thick as two banknotes in a bookie's pocket. We haven't a hope, not without an *in*.' She raises a finger. 'Could have done with Harry batting for us.'

'I'm not sure he knew Meacher,' I say. 'He never mentioned the name.'

She raises an eyebrow. 'Well, Jack knows him all right.' When I don't respond, she continues, 'I mean, Jack got permission for this development out by the bypass, didn't he?' She holds up her hands as if to pre-empt me. 'Oh, I'm not saying Jack bought his way in. God forbid! What I'm saying is' – she narrows her eyes theatrically – 'clout carries a lot of weight!'

The waiter hovers for the order but Molly asks for more time.

'If Jack knows him,' I suggest tentatively, 'couldn't he put in a word?'

'You mean, I should ask him?' Molly drops her chin and shoots me a look that tells me I should know better. 'I think not,' she says forcefully. She and Jack have never got on. She has never been able to resist discomfiting him, something he

114

finds hard to forgive in a woman, and, though he makes attempts to laugh off her well-honed verbal shots, his smiles are decidedly stiff-lipped.

I can see where this is leading. I sigh inwardly. 'Molly, I would ask him myself. But I can't. Not at the moment.'

She reaches across the table and grabs my hand. 'No, no, my love, I didn't mean you to! No! Would I throw you to that lion? No – that wasn't what I meant! No . . .' She swings back in her seat and waves airily, her eyes sparking. 'No, I'm doing my own nobbling! Taming my own councillor. Bribing him with long lingering evenings over coffee and biscuits in the Project kitchen.' She drops a slow wink. 'Putty in my hands.'

Laughing, I shake my head.

'Food!' She thrusts the menu under my nose.

Indecisive, I let the waiter choose for me. I would have been happy with a single glass of wine but Molly orders a bottle. 'My treat,' she says.

I did not get round to eating any breakfast and the wine is sharp on my stomach. I sip cautiously. I catch Molly watching me.

'Friends should never give advice,' she states with something approaching solemnity, 'friends should only ever listen. So what am I going to do?' She makes a show of leaning her arms on the table in an overtly interfering manner that is designed to disarm me. 'I'm going to say that I think you look terrible, that you're ludicrously thin, and that you should go and see someone.'

'Molly,' I smile. 'And who should I go and see?'

'A therapist. Someone to help you through all this.'

'I saw a therapist in America.'

She absorbs this. 'Well, perhaps you should go and see another one here.'

'I'm all right, Molly.'

'I haven't finished yet,' she says firmly as if I have tried to stop her. '*Normally* I think that what they say about not making any major decisions for at least six months after something like this happens is absolutely right. But not for *you*, not in *this* situation. I think you should leave that house as soon as

115

possible, like instantly. I think you should move away. *That's* what I think.'

'But I don't want to move away.' I tell her about my plans, how I want a cottage in the village, a job that will fit around the children's school hours, but how it will take time because of the legal difficulties.

'But why stay in the village? Claustrophobic.'

'Well . . . the children. They have their friends here.'

'But what about you?'

'I have my friends here too.'

She clicks her tongue. 'You worry too much about the children!' She frowns at me, she would like to pursue this further, but we are interrupted by the arrival of the food.

'How was your weekend?' she asks brightly.

'Saturday was good,' I answer with equal brightness, as if we are in the business of cheering each other up. 'Josh caught some fish. We had a barbecue. Yesterday . . .' I indicate it was a little more mixed, which indeed it was. I sat down to reply to some letters first thing, only to find that I couldn't bring myself to trip out the ritual platitudes – the solemn thanks, the brave but understated acceptance of Harry's loss, the plucky little end note about how well the children were coping. The words jammed in my craw, I simply couldn't put them down, and when Josh thundered down for breakfast I broke off with relief. After the long night perhaps I overdid my welcome – I scooped him up and bear-hugged him and blew noisy kisses into his neck – but he soon wriggled free. If this little rebuff hadn't been so blithely and innocently delivered I might have thought he was punishing me again. I planned to spend the whole morning with him; we did some painting and played a bit of ping-pong. But it wasn't long before he slipped away into the garden. When I tracked him down, he announced that he was watching a bird's nest and needed to be alone. I felt a small pang. Then, hardening my heart, I got on with my day. When all is said and done, I am good at hardening my heart.

I say to Molly, 'I miss Katie so much. It's awful.'

An odd look comes over Molly's face. 'Katie'll be all right, you know. If you'll let her.'

I cannot entirely hide the dart of resentment I feel at this remark. Katie is not a subject on which I take criticism easily, even from Molly. I manage an uneasy half smile. 'I don't think I've . . . *hindered* her in any way.'

'Of course not, love, of course not,' Molly says a little too quickly. 'I'm just saying that she needs space. She needs to breathe. She's fifteen. She's almost grown up.'

'Molly—' I shrug my incomprehension. 'Since when haven't I given her space?'

'Since . . . well – last Christmas.'

I put my fork down very slowly and stare at my plate for a moment. The wine has made me emotional. 'I don't think that's true, Molly.'

'It was when things got bad with Harry. I noticed straight away. You sort of took refuge in Katie. I mean, nothing wrong with that, love. *Nothing*. It was just that I think it was a little too much for her. She sort of took on a hunted look.' She gives a pained sigh. 'God, I'm saying this all wrong . . . Bugger it, my sweet – *sorry*.' She reaches for my hand again. 'What I mean is, I love you both and I just think that . . .' She screws up her face into an expression of remorse.

'That Katie needs her space,' I echo flatly.

'Well – yes.'

I give an ambiguous shrug, as if I might be conceding the point, and after a moment we move self-consciously on to other things.

Molly chides me for not eating. 'What are you trying to do, darling! Give yourself anorexia? Get deficient in all your minerals? *Then* you'll really get depressed!'

Still trying to lighten the mood, she moves on again, entertaining me with a story of a bald and rotund Project trustee who has got caught out in a mundane sexual indiscretion.

I respond, I laugh, I am as thankful as ever to have Molly as a friend. But her remarks about Katie linger, a grain of discord that rubs at our affection. There was a similar wariness between us last autumn when my problems with Harry became too painful for me to discuss with her. She didn't say so, but I knew she was offended by my unwillingness to confide in her.

She chatters as she drives me home, but she is subdued, preoccupied. Drawing up in front of the house, she turns off the engine and says in a rush, 'Listen, you're not blaming yourself about Harry, are you, sweetie? If so, you really mustn't, you know!'

I laugh awkwardly. 'No.'

She stares at me fiercely, then looks away to the trees. 'He wasn't the easiest of men. Christ, I wouldn't have lasted five minutes with him!' Her eyes dart back. 'Sometimes I thought you were an absolute saint.'

She has never said this before. I rather wish she wasn't saying it now. 'He took good care of me, Molly.'

She makes a doubtful face. 'Yes, well – in his own fashion, I suppose.'

'He did,' I insist, feeling oddly distressed. 'And he was never unkind, Molly. I mean, he never *meant* to be unkind. He was just . . . unhappy about himself sometimes.'

Molly takes a long breath. 'Yes.'

'And he loved me,' I state solemnly. 'He always loved me.'

'So much that he hit you?' she says with sudden heat.

I look at her in astonishment. 'What? Where on earth did you get that idea?'

She makes a face that is both apologetic and knowing.

'He never hit me,' I say with quiet vehemence. 'Never!'

She says a small 'Oh.' Then: 'Sorry, darling, I didn't mean to upset you.'

'But it's not true.'

'No, of course,' she says placatingly.

'Why did you think it was?' I say, hearing my voice rise, wishing I had not drunk all that wine.

'Well . . .' She puts on a show of reluctance. 'It was hard *not* to notice.'

'Notice what?'

She won't say.

'*What?*' I insist.

118

'The bruises,' she says at last.

'You mean – on my arms? The time I fell in the boat? I told you – I fell. On the side of the cockpit.'

She nods slowly, as if bowing to the rules of some game which require the maximum denial on both sides. Then, switching mood, she says breezily, 'Well, anyway!'

But I can't leave it alone. 'Molly, he never hit me,' I repeat doggedly. 'I fell.'

'Okay, darling. Okay.' But I sense a lingering doubt.

Frustrated, close to anger, I turn away, I grope for the door.

Molly cries, 'Oh, honey! I can't bear it!' She won't let me go. 'I do love you!' she says. 'I do so want everything to be all right for you!'

She throws an arm round my neck and pulls me into an awkward hug. She says she is sorry. She says that of course she believes me, that she had just got this stupid idea, that it was silly. The more she tries to persuade me the more certain I am that she doesn't believe me, and I feel inexpressibly weary.

She walks with me to the door. She gets me talking about the week ahead, about the people I have to see.

'The police?' she says, hearing about the gun licence. She is silent for a moment. 'Look, before I forget, just to let you know . . . They came to see me after you'd gone away.' There is a note of rehearsal in her offhand tone. 'They were just checking up. You know.'

'Oh?'

'It was just routine, darling, like in the movies. They asked about the night Harry left – disappeared. They were perfectly happy. I told them that you came at six, we had supper together and you left about eleven-thirty.'

'Eleven-thirty?' I echo quietly. 'Why did you say that?'

'Because. Well, it seemed a normal sort of time to leave.'

I stare at her. 'You didn't have to say that.' I am still absorbing the fact that the police thought it necessary to check up on me.

'Well, I wasn't going to tell them things they didn't need to know, was I?' retorts Molly.

I look at the shimmering trees, I hear an indistinct sound

119

rising from the river, a whistle, a call. 'You should have told them the truth,' I say. The truth was that Katie phoned at about eight-thirty, in a bit of a state, and I went to see her. 'It wouldn't have mattered.'

'None of their business,' declares Molly.

I stand in the open door for some time after she has gone. Did the police think I was trying to hide something? Is that why they checked up on me? Worrying thoughts leap into my mind – that they know Harry was bankrupt, that Tim Schwartz has told them about the missing charity money, that – my heart sinks – they think Harry committed suicide and I am covering up in some way.

It takes me a moment to remind myself that this visit of theirs happened many weeks ago and that they have not been back since.

I have an hour left before I need to collect Josh from school. Margaret is still hard at work. She has drafted several more letters to officials and government departments, letters that I wouldn't have known how to begin. They are beautifully written, with authority and clarity. As I glance over them I remind myself that I mustn't get too accustomed to being looked after in this way. Margaret, like Maurice, is a luxury I cannot really afford.

She reports that she has fixed a meeting with Gillespie for eleven tomorrow at his office in the City. Also, that she has searched Harry's pocket diaries and found nothing. There are one or two entries she wants to check more thoroughly with Jane Furlow, who was Harry's parliamentary secretary during his time as an MP, but she is pretty sure there are no names or meetings that cannot be accounted for. She looks me straight in the eye as she says this, and I wonder if perhaps she didn't know about Caroline Palmer after all.

She guides me through a few pages from last year's diary. Her own entries are clear, Harry's less so but still decipherable. I query a few. Barber, tailor, business associate: Margaret knows them all.

Some of the evenings when he was in London have single pencil lines drawn through them, sometimes two in a week.

'And these?'

'To be kept free.'

'You mean . . . ?'

'For meetings Mr Richmond arranged personally. Informal meetings.'

So that was how he did it.

I glance up at Margaret, but she is leafing studiously through the pages again. Suddenly I feel certain she knew about Caroline Palmer. Guessed, at least. Maybe she closed her mind out of loyalty, an unwitting collaborator. Maybe she thought a man like Harry was bound to have affairs and that it was of no great importance.

'So . . . nothing about the concert?' I sigh.

She shakes her head. 'I checked, but I remembered most of the meetings anyway. Nearly all of them were with the promotion company. The rest with artists' agents, PR companies – that sort of thing.' She regards me solemnly.

'Thank you, Margaret.' What else did I expect? Part of me is relieved at failing to unearth anything disturbing, part of me feels a twinge of unease because, whatever we find or do not find here, the Mountbay situation is not going to go away.

While Margaret resumes her typing, I take another desultory look through the diaries and the office address book. The address book has nothing that could be Caroline Palmer under either P or C. But then, he probably knew her number by heart.

Remembering the obsolete address book I found on Saturday, I pull it out of the drawer and riffle through to the back and look at the lists of account numbers again. I debate whether to bother Margaret with them. Finally I take them over to her.

'Credit cards,' she agrees. She studies the second list. 'And these, yes, bank accounts. This one' – she points to the first, marked P/A – 'is Mr Richmond's personal account at Barclays in Woodbridge.' Her finger travels down. 'This is your joint account. Well, let's just make sure.' She refers to a memo card in her Filofax. 'Yes, your joint account. And this – the D/A – is the deposit account at Woodbridge. And these two, they're the

Ainswick number one and number two accounts.' She lingers over a shorter number at the end of the list, which has no prefix or abbreviation. 'I don't know this one,' she says. She stares at it intently as if her gaze might force it to yield some information, then goes on to the bottom of the page, where a number stands on its own, prefixed by the letters 'S & M'. 'Nor this one, although I think it might be a building society account. The S & M sounds like a building society, doesn't it? But I'm not sure. I have no record of it. Though . . .' She pulls in her chin with concentration. '. . . I did see a statement once – well, just the heading. It was from S and something. It could have been S & M. I just glimpsed it, a financial statement. Some time ago.' I think she is trying to tell me she wasn't actually prying.

She is about to say more when the phone rings.

It is Josh's school. Instantly disorientated, thinking that time must somehow have evaporated and that I am late in picking Josh up, I look at my watch. Three-thirty. Or has it stopped?

The headmistress's voice is crisp and matter-of-fact as she tells me that they cannot find Josh.

Something lurches heavily against my chest, a knocking dread that belongs to my worst imaginings.

He was there at lunchtime, she continues in her unemotional way, and in the playground during playtime. One of the children saw him just before double art at one forty-five, taking his overall from his peg. He was not missed until the art teacher counted heads for a project.

And Josh loves art. I stare blankly into the garden.

She informs me that the staff are still searching and have not lost hope of finding him in the grounds. The gardener, who has been working near the gates all day, has not seen him pass through. She has called the police because it is school policy to do so, but her tone suggests that she thinks this step will prove excessive.

I say I am on my way. Ringing off, I gather a measure of control, I suppress my imaginings because I know this is the only way I will get through the next few minutes. I hear myself giving Margaret the bare facts in a calm voice. She follows me to the door. She offers to drive me, but I ask her if she'd be so kind as to stay by the phone. She hands me my car keys and opens the door.

A strange car is standing in the drive. A man in a grey suit is getting out. My first thought is that the police have got here very quickly, that they are going to tell me something awful about Josh. The scene freezes, I feel an instant disconnection. Then I see that the car is small and dirty and the man is on his own. He turns and, above the city clothes, I recognise Moreland.

A fleeting relief, a momentary impatience at myself, and I hurry towards my car. Moreland calls to me, a soft hail of surprise. Signalling impossibilities, I wave him towards Margaret. Driving off I glimpse him still watching me before he turns towards Margaret.

St Edmund's is fifteen minutes away, on the edge of Woodbridge. During the journey I try to put myself into Josh's head. I try to imagine what would make him walk out. He seemed to be looking forward to getting back to school. Or was he? There are never any certainties with Josh. Immediately I start blaming myself. Missing the signs. Again.

Turning into the gates I do not see any gardener, and for the first time I notice how insecure the grounds are: low fences at the perimeter with rows of narrow gardens beyond, and lines of semi-detached houses with miserly windows and frilly net curtains that bob up in the centre, like watching eyes. Inside the grounds, shrubberies, outbuildings, playing fields: not so many places for a small boy to hide.

The headmistress sees me coming and meets me at the front door. Mrs Rothsay, a young self-contained forty. She shakes her head to indicate a lack of news then ushers me into her room where I stand uneasily, like a child awaiting interview. The police are searching, Mrs Rothsay says. So are three of the staff. Everything possible is being done. In the meantime, may she ask me about Josh?

My instinct is to be gone, to be out searching, but when she invites me to sit I sink meekly onto a small wooden chair that inhabits the wide open spaces beyond her desk.

How was Josh's behaviour over the last few days? she asks. Did he appear disturbed?

'He seemed all right,' I answer humbly.

'No signs of stress?'

'No.' But I am beginning to doubt my own judgement. 'Well, I don't think so. Not that I could see.'

'Was he worried about school?'

I shake my head numbly, remembering that I never actually asked him.

Mrs Rothsay regards me with sympathy. 'Would he make his way straight home, do you think?'

This question defeats me. Under the power of Mrs Rothsay's gaze, I rise and go to the window. Cars are creeping sedately into the drive, rocking over the sleeping policemen, as parents arrive to collect their children. I have a sudden yearning for the days when I had nothing more to absorb me than the school run.

Where would Josh go? 'I don't know,' I say. In voicing this, I see beyond the house to the woods. I see Josh in the clearing by the quay, stoking the open fire, glancing to Moreland with an expression of earnest contentment on his face.

I turn back. 'May I use the phone?'

I phone home. Margaret tells me that there is no news, that Moreland has gone out in search of Josh. She is not sure where he has gone exactly; down to the river, she thinks. Anyway, he has left his car.

I offer Mrs Rothsay a stumbled explanation and leave. In the drive the buzz of conversation fades, the mothers, standing in clusters, stare at me with droop-eyed pity. Two friends, Ruth and Mary, descend on me with fussy concern and fierce avowals of help. Mary announces that she has already despatched her husband to join the search. Other parents, they tell me, are organising themselves into search parties. Ruth takes my arm and guides me to my car. It takes all my meagre powers of persuasion to convince her that I am safe to drive back on my own.

Slamming the car door, gunning the ignition, I run the gauntlet of concerned faces and speed for home. A heavy lorry and a school bus slow my progress along the main road, but once onto the estate I racket down the length of the drive, the potholes sending booming ricochets against the suspension. More cars have appeared in front of the house – a white police car with an orange stripe, and, unbelievably, Anne's estate car – how did she know? But the car I am looking for, Moreland's, is still there, parked untidily in the middle of the sweep. The sight of the muddy Golf, once black, a long way from new, fills me with a wild unreasoned confidence. I carry on past the house and, unlatching the cattle gate, swing it open and drive down the track to the river.

A solitary crow stalks the quay and rises languorously at my approach. The river, grey and swollen with fast-running tide, ripples furtively. The air is still. There is no one in sight except two fishermen on the opposite bank sitting immobile behind their rods.

I stand in the open and bellow a loud hello. The trees throw back a bleak silence. I start along the footpath that runs the length of the river-bank in the direction of Woodbridge. My shoes, smooth-soled and narrow-heeled, slip on the muddy surface. I am driven by the certainty that Moreland guessed right, that Josh would head for the river and that this is the way he would have come – this way or over the fields, through the wheat. No – not over the top. No. It has always been the river for Josh.

I try to calculate how far Moreland would have got by now, at what point he would converge with Josh. It never occurs to me that he might have given up. I see him searching in a systematic and knowledgeable way, I see him using an almost mystical skill that he has gained from his service days.

I slip and almost fall. I move onto tussock grass in search of more grip but my soles slide just as uselessly. I stop for a moment, getting my breath back. There is nothing ahead. Nothing but the narrow path meandering along the top of the embankment, the long bend of the river with its wide plateaux of marsh and bog intersected by tiny dried-out waterways. And, at the edge of the marsh, clearly visible at this state of the tide, the patch of mud where I found the Zodiac.

125

Starting off again, I can't help looking for signs of that day, of my blundering progress through the glutinous mud, as if something of my struggle to reach the boat might still be visible after all these weeks. But though each step took me up to my knees and the sucking mud tipped me over at least twice and the marks I left must have looked like those of a floundering animal, there's nothing left now. The mud flat is as smooth as burnished rock.

I catch the muffled sound of a car coming down the track behind me. When the engine note floats clear of the woods, I take a backward glance. It looks like – it can only be – the black Golf. I stop, bewildered.

A figure climbs out – Moreland – and, with a sharp wave, runs towards me. He runs easily, lightly, his shirt ballooning out behind him.

Suddenly I know that Josh is safe, I know by the way Moreland is running, I know even before his voice carries across to me, 'Found!' Before he repeats it in case I have not heard.

I start towards him, slither again, shoot my arms out to keep my balance.

'He's fine, *fine*,' Moreland calls as he covers the last few yards.

We come to a halt in front of each other. 'No harm done,' Moreland pants.

I nod wordlessly.

Perhaps in my relief I look angry because he adds, 'There was no reason. He can't say why. I honestly don't think he realised.' He grips my shoulder and gives me a smile that seems to contain understanding of everything that I am feeling.

'Where did you—?' I ask.

'Up by the old ferry. He'd crossed the road at the roundabout and was coming along the river.'

'But when—?'

'We'd just got home when you rushed past.'

I bow my head, I give a long sigh. 'Well, thank you,' I say simply. 'Thank you.'

We stand for a while, his grip firm on my arm.

I give a feeble laugh and look up at him. 'These things . . . they give you a shock.'

He nods slowly. 'Yes.'

'I didn't realise he was . . . I thought . . .' But I can't express it.

'I'm sure he'll be fine. He *is* fine. But maybe . . .' He shrugs to show it's just an idea. 'Coming back after so long, the service . . . perhaps it brought everything home to him. And then it must have been a bit of a shock, having to go back to school.'

'And he didn't say anything?'

'No.' I sense a slight hesitation in his answer, but if he was going to say more he thinks better of it and we start back along the path. My soles slither on the mud and he takes me by the hand, he holds me firmly so I can't fall, and I think what a luxury it is to have someone to lean on, even for so brief a time.

SIX

It's quite a time since I came to Shoreditch. Seven – no, eight months ago. It was October, a Wednesday. I remember it in some detail, though I would rather I didn't. Dense rain had brought an early darkness, the trains out of Liverpool Street had been halted after a bomb scare, and I needed somewhere to wait. The cab driver overshot the building and squealed to a halt three doors down. He offered to reverse back but it looked dangerous in the rain and traffic, and I told him not to bother. My umbrella, one of those tiny collapsable jobs, saved my head and shoulders, but not my legs or shoes which were quickly soaked by the bouncing spray. Reaching the door, I couldn't raise the security guard and had to let myself in through the side door with the keys. I had my own keys then.

Now, as the cab draws up, I step out into harsh sunlight with Harry's keys ready in my hand. Three years after refurbishment, the five-storey building still reflects a confident sheen, the tinted windows mirror-sharp, the cladding gleaming palely. But the pavement in front of the grand post-modern doorway is uneven and marked with those strange black streaks and blobs that afflict the less salubrious London streets, while the hotchpotch of neighbouring buildings, long abandoned by the boom which so nearly reached them, have sunk into apathy and shabby disrepair.

An agent's sign has been fixed over the doorway offering fifty thousand square feet of air-conditioned office space at ten pounds per square foot. A previous offer of twelve pounds has been ostentatiously cancelled out with a red cross. A poster affixed to the inside of the glass doors and illustrated with the profile of a fierce Alsation announces the name of a security company.

When Harry bought the building it was renamed Richmond House and the letters etched into the stone lintel over the door. There was a naming ceremony. It was at this party that I got my first inkling of the gamble Harry was taking with this project when someone – a prospective tenant, I suppose – not realising who I was, remarked baldly that the building was a street too far. Too far from the City proper.

The side door has locks at ground and eye level. Going through Harry's keys I pick the right one first time. Inside, the air is heavy with stagnant London heat, overlaid by a faint chemical tang. There are no signs of security guards. I avoid the lift and take the stairs to the fourth floor. The flat, described in the sales brochure as a director's *pied-à-terre* or dining/overnight suite, was interior-decorated and furnished as a sales lure. But when the building was still unlet after several months, after Harry, having lost his seat, could no longer justify a separate flat near the Commons, he began to use it himself.

The door to the flat is made of panelled mahogany which has been varnished to an excessive and rather garish shine. Standing in front of it, facing my blurred and distorted reflection, I remember when I last stood here, bedraggled and cold, looking forward to getting inside and taking off my wet shoes and grabbing the early news before trying for another train. I was rather pleased at having got myself this far, at not letting the terrorists or whoever it was at Liverpool Street get the better of me.

Entering the carpeted hall now, I close the door softly behind me and listen to the silence.

By chance I also closed the door softly that other time, although I wasn't expecting to hear anything. Bending down to flip off my shoes, the sound took me by surprise. I stood very still, faintly puzzled, faintly alarmed. Awareness came slowly and unevenly, in disconnected darts. First the sound itself – a rustle, the brush of fabric, very muffled. Then the direction – from beyond the bedroom door which was slightly ajar and showing a sliver of dull light. My first reaction was to retreat hastily in embarrassment. I thought I must have blundered into a situation where the flat was being used by someone else – I still had a fragment of naivety then.

But I didn't retreat. I didn't even move. I listened, my senses reaching out across the hallway. There was rustling again, then a creak, and another creak. Irregular creaks but gaining a sort of rhythm. I knew that rhythm; everyone knows that rhythm.

A sharp ache pulled at my chest. I tried not to think of Harry, but once the idea lodged in my mind it wouldn't go away. I felt a foreboding, matched only by my need to see into the room, a compulsion which drove me slowly but doggedly across the hall.

The door was open only a little way and I had to push it further to see the bed. Strange how at moments like that you think of something, anything, which does not involve the reality of what is in front of you. I thought that I had never seen people making love from this angle before, feet on. In fact I had never watched anyone making love from any angle whatsoever, though if you go to films nowadays it's easy to imagine that you have.

The bedcovers were off. The woman – she didn't have a name then – had her legs arched high over Harry's back. Her feet traced circles in the air as she rolled and swayed to Harry's rhythm. Harry's buttocks looked broad and white and oddly shapeless as they flexed and pumped. I tried to persuade myself that for all its familiarity this straining body might after all belong to someone else – such shimmers of hope – but even as I thought it Harry raised his head a little as if to look into the woman's face and I saw the distinctive shape of his head, the hair that curled down behind his ears, his quarter profile.

I didn't move for what must have been several seconds. Violent sensations rushed at me, vivid, immensely confusing. My throat seized with shame, I was crippled by the sort of

130

withering humiliation that I had not felt since childhood. Strangely, or perhaps not so strangely, the one thing I did not feel was jealousy.

It was the ragged grunts of pleasure-pain from Harry and the series of harsher cries from the woman that brought me to life again. That, and a certain brutality in their actions which made me want to shrink away. As I backed silently into the hall and pulled the door softly to, a long raw sound followed me; I couldn't make out whose. Then a deep laugh: hers.

I stood just inside the hall, my limbs locked with tension and shame. I thought wretched tormenting thoughts, some self-punishing, most riddled with half-focused anger. I wondered how many other dark obsessions Harry had been harbouring, what else he thought about in those secret compulsive moments of his.

Or was this simply an escape valve for him? Was this his way of keeping some sort of control over his life?

I clung to this idea. I kept some sort of a hold on it as I crept over to my shoes and pulled them hastily on and, suddenly desperate to be gone, let myself quietly out.

The place is silent now, the only sound the subdued murmurs of the city from beyond the heavy glazing. I notice that a fine layer of dust sits over the reproduction Regency table and that the carpet is flecked with lint.

I push open the door of the bedroom. Whatever emotions I felt that day have long since faded. If I feel anything at all it's indifference. The hanging rails are empty, the drawers also. There is a used tissue in the bedside table, a few pennies, a grocery receipt. A half-empty box of tissues lies under the bed.

A perfunctory look around the bathroom, which contains a packet of disposable razors and a tube of shampoo that has lost its cap, and then into the main room which is furnished in candy stripes, co-ordinated florals and contrasting blinds, like a display window in a fabric shop. Only two drawers here, both empty. I look behind the colour-matched prints that hang at precise intervals around the walls, but there is no safe. Nor, as far as I can tell, is there one of those cunning devices set into the floor or power points. In the kitchen the fridge contains a carton of coagulated milk and a can of beer. Jars of instant coffee and Coffeemate, both almost empty, sit in the cupboard.

The place is like a hotel suite, bland and anonymous. I don't know why I thought I would find anything here. I had the idea that Harry used the place regularly, but perhaps he went to Caroline Palmer's. I used to phone sometimes, but if Harry was here he didn't answer.

Those phone calls – what an effort it took me to make them. I would sit at Pennygate in the long evenings, trying to hold on to the idea that things weren't irretrievable, that all it needed was for Harry and me to talk. But sometimes the silence and the loneliness would get to me. Then, hating myself, wishing I could stop myself, I would reach for the phone.

There's nothing here. At least, no evidence of Caroline Palmer's presence, which is the important thing. No papers either, though I'm not too sure what I was hoping to find. An invoice, I suppose. A file of accounts.

But I feel better for having come. And safer.

I take a last look in some unlikely places – the top of the kitchen cabinets, the back of the cleaning cupboard. Mindful of my grandmother who kept her jewellery in the back of the oven during the blitz, I peer into the microwave and fan oven.

Leaving, I close the door stealthily, as if by habit, with no more than a click.

Gillespie's office is a twenty-minute walk away in the City proper. If the recession has bitten deeply into the financial world you wouldn't know it from the polished buildings, the glossy fascias of the banks, and the purposeful manner of the sleek young people who criss-cross the streets.

I arrive fifteen minutes early. I am left to wait until eleven precisely, when a secretary with glowing blonde hair and a confident stride ushers me into a conference room with no windows, a ceiling of harsh lights and wallpaper that plays tricks on your eyes. The long table is set with a dozen or so blotters, overlaid with writing pads and shop-new pencils. After some thought I choose a place half way along the table, facing the door. As I sit down Gillespie enters.

'Mrs Richmond.'

He offers a thin hand. Reaching for it, I spill my handbag to the floor. Wishing I hadn't chosen this moment to look quite so inept, I duck to retrieve the contents.

As I re-emerge the secretary appears with coffee, though I have not asked for any.

Gillespie has taken a seat opposite me and placed a slim file on the table in front of him. 'I'm sorry I wasn't able to come to the service,' he says. 'An unavoidable crisis.' He regards me with a flat gaze. He is a slim, sleek man in his thirties with a narrow head and sharp features, slicked-back mousy hair and very white skin. His eyes are expressionless and unusually pale, almost without colour. 'I trust you received my letter? Of condolence?'

I don't remember seeing it, but I nod anyway.

'Now, how can I help you?' he asks. He sits erect, his hands laced loosely together on the table. 'I'm afraid your financial restructuring proposal isn't quite complete yet. We're waiting for a few final negotiations. I hope to have something to show you next week.'

I'm not sure what to make of this easy confidence. 'There's not going to be a problem then?'

'Oh, I think we'll be able to arrange something.'

'Leonard gave me the impression there wasn't much left.'

His eyebrows lift a fraction. 'There were large debts, certainly, but in the long term there should be sufficient assets for you to settle reasonably comfortably. The life insurance and so on.'

I dare to ask, 'And in the short term?'

'It's a question of finding satisfactory collateral and negotiating the best terms.'

'You mean, I'll have to borrow?'

The heavy lids droop in confirmation. 'Though I understand from Jack Crawley that he's willing to help out?' Reading the hesitation in my face, he continues, 'It would ease things considerably. Finding sufficient guarantees for the bank is proving something of a problem.' When I don't respond, he explains, 'The estate doesn't have many assets to borrow against, you see.'

'I see,' I echo slowly, thinking of Jack.

Gillespie's eyes flicker down towards his watch. 'So. How can I help you?'

'Oh ... I just had a few questions...' I made a list of them on the train, to be sure I didn't forget anything, which can happen to me quite easily when I'm on uncertain ground.

While I extricate the list from the confusion of my bag, I ask about Ainswick, about how it's going.

'Well, as I think you'll appreciate by now, things are tough.' He has a flat hard-edged voice. 'There's no interest in the Shoreditch building. None. Well, we had one offer, but it was a complete flyer.'

My incomprehension must show in my face because he explains, 'Someone trying to pick up a desperation bargain. A derisory offer.'

I take this in, but slowly. 'So people realise Ainswick's in difficulties?' I ask tentatively.

'Everyone's in trouble. Everyone's getting stupid offers. Making bad deals or holding off until the market improves. The problem with Ainswick is that it can't hold off.'

I nod, as if I had understood this all along. 'I'm just trying to get things clear,' I explain. 'This offer, what would happen if Ainswick accepted it?'

He looks down at his hands. 'It would be a waste of time. The cash raised wouldn't cover the company's liabilities, and without further realisable assets it would have to go into liquidation. More coffee?'

I have barely touched the first cup. 'Thank you, no.' I take a sip to make up for lost time. 'But – forgive me – isn't there a risk that Ainswick will be in trouble anyway? I mean, if the building stays unsold?' I speak slowly to reduce the chances of sounding foolish. 'Wouldn't some sort of sale be better than none?'

A flicker of what might be amusement crosses Gillespie's face. 'It doesn't quite work that way. The directors have a duty to sell at a fair market price. This isn't by any stretch of the imagination a fair market price.'

I ask more cautiously, 'And these people won't increase their price?'

'It was a take-it-or-leave-it offer. No, the best thing is to hold off as long as we can and *hope* for a genuine buyer.'

'The chances aren't good then?'

For a moment I think he has not heard, then I realise that the low-lidded, down-turned expression he has taken on, the spreading of the palm just above the table, are his answer. I interpret this to mean there is no chance, or so little as makes no difference.

I give a false laugh. It is an old habit of mine, to try to ease difficult moments along in this way. It comes from having a mother who used silence as a weapon of attrition. 'Pretty hopeless then?' I say, making a face.

He squeezes his lips together by way of reply. His lips are thin and dry. He seems to be losing interest.

I might have left it there, but something about Gillespie's laconic manner rekindles my determination not to be put off.

I study my list. 'Who are the directors of Ainswick now?' I ask.

He blinks slowly. 'Myself. And, more recently, Raymond Kerr. He has experience in marketing difficult properties.'

I ask studiously, 'And the estate agents – they're doing everything they can, are they?' Like everyone else I have heard stories about the offhandedness and general incompetence of estate agents, though most of these tales probably stemmed from before the recession.

Gillespie tilts his head a little and frowns, as if this is tantamount to questioning his judgement. 'Most certainly. They're a top firm. Extremely capable.'

The next question is probably naive but I ask it anyway. 'And the price – it's realistic?'

'Absolutely.' His tone is torpid, his eyes severe. 'But you must understand that twenty per cent of office space nation-wide – on the fringes of the City more like thirty per cent – is unlet. We're still deep in recession. It's a buyer's market.'

'I see.' I read out the next question word for word. 'How long can Ainswick survive if Shoreditch doesn't sell?'

He takes a long breath. 'I think we might be able to *squeeze* four months. Which is a great deal longer than we deserve.' I don't ask why we're undeserving of this extra time; I don't want to hear about all the things that Harry should or shouldn't have done.

There are more questions I should probably ask, but Gillespie flusters me and I can't seem to pin them down.

I move on. I explain about the account numbers I found in Harry's old address book, how Margaret can't place two of them. I pass him the sheet that Margaret typed out for me.

Gillespie gives the numbers a perfunctory glance before tucking the paper into the file in front of him. 'I'll check,' he says.

This is all too abrupt for me. I lean forward, I make a smiling gesture towards the file. 'But what about those initials – S & M. Aren't they something? We thought a building society perhaps.'

He turns an ear, as if he hasn't quite caught what I'm saying. 'A building society? No . . . I don't believe so.'

'A bank, then?'

'I'll see if I can find out.'

I stare at him, not sure whether I am being palmed off. 'But what about the other number?'

'I'm sorry?' He opens his hand and cranes his head in a practised display of incomprehension.

'I thought perhaps . . . you might recognise it?'

Languidly, he slips Margaret's paper from his file and takes another look. 'A number,' he says in the exaggerated tones of someone who is being forced to explain the obvious, 'could be almost anything. It could be a balance, a payment, a reference. One has no way of knowing . . .' He lifts his shoulders elegantly.

'But it could be an account number?'

'It could be. Of course.'

'You don't have a record of Harry's accounts?'

'An accountant only knows what his client chooses to tell him, Mrs Richmond,' he says piously. 'But may I suggest,' he gives a patronising little smile, 'that you don't live in any great hope of finding undiscovered accounts filled with money.'

I regard him for a moment, the narrow face, the pale eyes. 'I'm not expecting anything like that, Mr Gillespie.'

'Fine,' he says, still with a hint of condescension. 'Fine.'

Letting this pass, I stare at the next heading on my list. 'The Rumanian concert,' I begin with a small sigh. 'Tim Schwartz came to see me. He asked about this company, Mountbay. It supplied something – he isn't sure what – to the concert. He said the invoices had gone astray—'

'Schwartz has been on to me about that,' Gillespie cuts in smoothly. 'I've already told him I can't help.'

'Margaret thought you might have some accounts.'

'I wasn't in charge of the accounts.'

'But there were some figures she sent you?'

'They weren't accounts.'

I wonder if he is being unhelpful, or whether he just appears that way. 'The papers you *do* have, they don't shed any light on the thing?'

'No.'

I look away. The wallpaper, the latest thing in geometric black lines on grey zigzags, strobes violently. Blinking, I come back to Gillespie's level gaze. 'Tim Schwartz seems to think . . .' I hesitate. Though Gillespie is meant to be on my side, though I'm meant to be able to confide in him, I cannot get rid of the feeling that his interests don't entirely coincide with mine. But who else am I going to ask? I plunge forward. 'He thinks that Harry can be held legally responsible in some way.'

'Nonsense.'

'Well . . . he seems to think that the auditors will pick Harry out, that it'll look bad, as if he'd done it intentionally—'

'Done what? Schwartz doesn't know what he's talking about,' Gillespie says with emphasis. 'His own people did the bookkeeping, for heaven's sake.'

'Oh.' I can't judge the significance of this. 'You mean . . . ?'

'If there was a problem, they should have spotted it.'

'So . . . Harry can't be held responsible?' I'd love to believe this is true.

He flips a hand dismissively, sparking with sudden annoyance. 'Listen, these charity people have made good money out of the concert, something over a million. They shouldn't be whingeing.'

I venture, 'But Schwartz says the auditors won't sign the books – or whatever it is they have to do. And the charity can't get hold of any of the money.'

'Not your problem.' He bites the words off crisply, with satisfaction, someone who enjoys combative situations.

I venture, 'Wouldn't it – don't you think – it might be an idea to get a second opinion?'

'What? Legal advice, you mean?' He takes a breath, he leans forward, he slides his elbows onto the table, he fixes me with his gaze. 'Listen, Mrs Richmond, the charity is *not* going to make a fuss, believe me. Not at the end of the day. It's not in their interests to do so. They'll distance themselves from the concert, maybe. They'll disown whoever they want to disown. But not publicly. You see, they can't get away from the fact that they themselves were meant to be keeping the books. If something's gone wrong with the accounts it's the trustees as a whole who must be held responsible. They can't try to pin it on the first convenient scapegoat.' He gives a derisory grunt. 'They want that million too badly. A million, I might add, that they would never have got otherwise. Believe me, they'll get the auditors to sign some sort of modified accounts, they'll get it through their committee somehow. They'll take the million and be very glad of it, which indeed they should be. It really *isn't* in their interests to make a fuss.'

I feel as though something is creeping over my skin. Gillespie's cynicism perhaps.

'But as far as you're concerned, the important thing is to do nothing,' he says. 'Be polite, whatever. But ignore them. Do nothing. They'll go away eventually. Just say that you're very sorry but you can't help.'

I gaze at him for several seconds. I want to say: *You mean, do as you're doing?* But I don't say that; I don't say anything. Slowly I gather my things.

Gillespie gets to his feet. 'You see the point?' he asks.

I take a moment to answer. I say, 'Yes.'

He almost looks pleased with me. I don't think he expected me to be so quick on the uptake.

He takes me to the lift. We talk about the weather.

I think I am gone from his mind even before the doors close.

I catch the 12.48 with half a minute to spare. Closing my eyes for what I mean to be a short doze, I sleep heavily most of the way home. I wake when the train judders to a halt somewhere outside Ipswich, my head twisted uncomfortably against the window, my mouth hanging inelegantly open for what, judging by the dryness of my tongue, must have been some time. I feel exhausted and refreshed at the same time. I probably had three hours' sleep last night. It was ten before Anne and Charles finally left, and for a long time afterwards I lay on the bed next to Josh's, listening to his soft breathing, occasionally raising my head to catch the outline of his head, going over things endlessly in my mind.

My thoughts hardly need direction, such well-worn grooves do they follow. Episodes rerun themselves in minute detail. And when I feel more than usually baffled by the past I switch to the present. I assess how I am doing. I try to see how my actions might appear to others, how I can incur even less attention than I hope I do already. I measure situations, I gauge dangers.

Round and round. I am very good at going round and round.

Now, to add to everything else, I have Josh to worry about.

I pick up the car from the station and, though it's far too early, drive straight to St Edmund's and wait in a quiet corner of the car-park in the vague hope of going unnoticed by the other parents. This, I should have realised, is too much to wish for. Ruth, who is also early, finds me immediately, followed by two or three other mothers, who treat me with a sympathy that is warm but also scrutinising. They say their own children have given them dreadful moments. They say they are immensely relieved that Josh came to no harm. I tell them I am too. I make light of it. I say Josh was finding school a bit of a shock after lying on a beach for so long. By the time Josh finally emerges ten minutes late, I am desperate to be gone.

He kisses my cheek in a half-hearted way. He seems tired. At any rate he is not in a mood to talk. Once I have unwound a bit, I start to chatter about what we might do at the weekend, about sport, about the films that are showing in Ipswich. I don't talk about yesterday. I don't feel it would be helpful to ask him why he ran away. The experience will have been quite traumatic enough, finding the police waiting at home, realising the alarm he had caused, having Anne besiege him with a battery of dire warnings and tearful pleadings never to frighten her like that again. Besides, I have never believed in harping on about the children's mistakes. Life is tough enough already.

I don't appreciate the depth of Josh's mood until we're into the drive and half-way down the long straight that leads into the shadows of the beech wood, just moments from home. Then I catch something in his profile that makes me look again and ask if there's something the matter.

He doesn't answer.

'What is it, honey? Tell me.'

His lower lip pushes out, a battle rages across his features, then he says in a thin voice, 'I'd like to go to another school. Please.' It comes out fully formed, as if he has been rehearsing it in his mind.

'Darling...' I look at him so hard and so long that I nearly drive into the rough. Swinging back, hitting a hole that makes the car lurch, I say with sudden heat, 'Are the other children saying things? Are they bullying you? Is that it?'

He shakes his head bleakly.

'Darling, you don't have to put up with it, you know. You really don't! These kids, they just don't know what they're saying...'

He shakes his head more vehemently and, clamping his mouth tight shut, bunching up his eyes, he turns away to stare out of the window. This makes me think I'm on the right track.

We are there at last. I come up to the house too fast and brake in a cascade of gravel. Turning off the engine, I make

140

myself wait for a second or two before saying softly: 'Honey, you know how kids are. Stupid. They're probably just jealous of all the attention you're getting. In fact, I would say that was definitely what it was about. Wouldn't you? I mean, you having had all this time off. And then yesterday. And well – everything.'

Josh looks down at his lap, he picks at the hem of his shorts. He shakes his head with world weariness, as if he knew I was bound to misunderstand.

I wait while he winds himself up to speak.

'I want to go somewhere else. Away.'

'Away? What do you mean away?'

But I know what he means, and knowing it, I am already shrinking inside.

He can't seem to come out and say it, so I say it for him. 'You mean, board? Go to boarding school?'

He nods, avoiding my eye.

I give a short laugh. 'But darling, that's not going to solve anything. I'll go and see Mrs Rothsay. I'll—'

'*Mum.*' He glares at me, his face taut with exasperation and anxiety. 'There's nothing wrong with school!' he almost shouts. 'I want to go somewhere else, that's all.' He drops his head again.

I gaze at him, fighting down the hurt. It is a while before I say, 'But why, darling? You have to tell me why.'

He pulls at the long thread that has prised loose from his shorts. He hunts for the words, almost speaks, hesitates again, and finally says in a voice that has almost faded away, 'It'd be more fun, that's all.'

More fun. This takes me aback. Fun. It's not a word that has come into my vocabulary too often recently. It's not something I have considered in relation to Josh's future – or Katie's, for that matter. I've thought a great deal about the importance of being together, of supporting each other while we find our feet. But fun? I suppose he has a point. Neither Katie nor I have exactly been a barrel of laughs in the last two months.

'Well . . . okay. I mean . . . we'll talk about it, darling.'

He tips me a look that contains more than a little scepticism and I feel bound to add: 'I promise I'll – we'll – think about it, okay? It's a big thing to decide just like that.' I make a terrible stab at humour. 'Not trying to get away from your old mum, are you?'

This is unfair, the sort of question that comes uncomfortably close to the kind of emotional blackmail that I dreaded in my own mother. The moment it's out of my mouth I wish it unsaid. But before I can retreat, Josh gives a fierce shake of his head and, gathering his satchel, jumps out of the car and heads for the kitchen door.

I climb out wearily, wondering where I have gone wrong.

The gibbering of TV cartoons comes from the sitting-room. As I start to make Josh his favourite Marmite and cucumber sandwiches Margaret comes in, hunting for tea.

I tell her the meeting with Gillespie went reasonably well. I don't offer any detail.

She tells me that she might have had some success with tracking down the S & M in Harry's old address book. 'There's a company called Simmonds Mitchell,' she says. 'They used to have an "and" between their names, but now they're just plain Simmonds Mitchell. It may not be the *only* S & M around, of course – or rather SM – but it's the only one I can find in London that's even half likely, and I've searched the whole of the S section in the business directory.'

I pour some juice for Josh. 'Who are they?'

'Commodity brokers.'

'Oh,' I say as if I know what this means. But I'm talking to Margaret and I don't have to pretend. 'I've heard of commodity brokers,' I tell her, 'I've always been impressed by people who are commodity brokers, but I don't think I've ever had the slightest idea what they do.'

'I think they're like stockbrokers,' she laughs, 'except that they buy and sell commodities instead of shares. Wheat, sugar, corn, tea – that sort of thing.'

Balancing the sandwiches and juice in one hand, I take them through to Josh. He is sitting on the floor just feet from the TV. Knowing I don't like him to sit so close, he slithers backwards, eyes still firmly on the screen, and taking his tea, mumbles his thanks. I linger for a moment, looking down at the spindly child-legs that extend from the bright shorts, more knee joints and angular bones than muscle, at his ski-jump nose, at his rounded cheeks filled hamster-like with food; I look, and confusions bunch uncomfortably in my chest. So familiar, this child of mine; and so mystifying. Why boarding school? Why this wish to escape? Have the two of us lost some vital thread? Does he feel I have failed him in some way?

I can't begin to grasp the beginnings of an answer.

'I think what happens is that people trade against the future prices of commodities,' Margaret says as I come back into the kitchen. 'Like they think sugar will go up so they buy some and sell it at a profit a few months later. Simmonds Mitchell act as brokers and take a commission.'

'So people would have accounts there?'

'I checked.' She holds up a hand hastily. 'Oh, I didn't say who I was. I wasn't specific. I just asked them if their account numbers ran to six or seven digits. They said six.'

'And that—'

'Tallies.'

We wander down the passage to the study.

'Would it work like a bank account?' I say this almost to myself, since I don't really expect Margaret to have an answer.

'Well, I know Mr Richmond used to leave the proceeds from share sales with his stockbrokers while he decided what to buy next. Perhaps it was the same with these people.'

Coming into the study, I remember Gillespie's narrow white face and the way he glanced dismissively over the sheet of account numbers. 'And is it a big company?'

'I don't know, it was hard to gauge, but the entry in the directory is in large print, and its address is right in the middle of the City.'

Probably large then; probably important. Gillespie must have heard of it. I wonder why he couldn't take a guess at the initials.

'I've got the Cellphone bill for you.' Margaret lifts it momentarily off the desk. 'And there are quite a few

143

messages.' Since I haven't called anyone back since the weekend, the new messages have only served to lengthen the list. My father. Neighbours wondering if Josh would like to come over. Distant relations on Harry's side. Molly. Leonard. Jack, who has called twice since Saturday, the last time only a couple of hours ago to say that he will come and see me tomorrow 'if it would be convenient'.

'I said it was unlikely,' Margaret declares. 'I could ring him if you like, and put him off.' Although Margaret enjoys a brisk relationship with Jack, liberally peppered with banter, she has no illusions about him and her patience with his perennial charm has worn thin.

'What did he want?'

'Didn't say.'

'When's he thinking of coming?'

'Ten. But I made a lot of unlikely noises because I fixed the police for eleven' – she points to the message on the pad – 'and I thought it wouldn't leave you enough time to get anything done.'

'The gun inspection?'

'I could still put them off.'

I say, 'No.' Then, feeling I have to explain: 'I'd rather get them out of the way.'

'Of course. And Mr Crawley?'

'I'd like to get him out of the way too.'

Margaret sniggers, 'Wouldn't we all?'

A movement in the garden catches my eye. It is Maurice, carrying a laden trug out of the glass-house.

Watching him tramping towards the rose garden, I murmur, 'That policeman who came round when Harry died . . .'

'Dawson.'

'Dawson. Has he been in touch? Did he come back?'

'No, not since . . .' She thinks for a moment. 'Oooh, since just after you'd gone to America.'

'After?'

'Just a few days. A week maybe.'

'Here?'

'Oh no. He came to the office.'

Maurice passes out of sight. I turn back to Margaret. 'What did he want?'

'Oh, nothing really. He just asked a few standard questions. Well, I imagine they were standard.'

I wait for her to tell me.

Her eyes flick away, she says in a determinedly offhand manner, 'He just wanted to know what had happened in the weeks before Mr Richmond died. If Mr Richmond had any particular worries – that sort of thing. I said that like everyone else in the recession he had a few problems, but nothing that he couldn't deal with.'

'No . . . that's absolutely right. Thank you, Margaret.'

She looks quietly relieved at having passed this test.

'Oh, and Richard Moreland was hoping to see you.' She slides a message slip across the desk. 'He wondered if you were free for a short time tomorrow evening. Something he was coming to ask you yesterday when Josh went missing.'

Moreland. I am grateful for what he did yesterday, very grateful. But his attention worries me in some unidentifiable way.

'He didn't say what it was?'

'No. He just left his number.'

I take the slip of paper and place it on top of the message pad.

Margaret gathers her things. At the door she gives me a small self-conscious hug. She has never done this before. I don't know why she should choose this moment to feel sorry for me. I smile as best I can, to show her I'm all right.

I get Josh to bed early and read him a long story, which I animate with actorish voices and exaggerated actions. He is not fooled, of course. He can see that I am pulling out all the stops, that with these risible antics I am trying to re-establish my standing as a worthy and entertaining companion. When he thinks I'm not looking he steals the occasional glance at me, now and again his mouth twitches in the direction of a smile, but for the most part he stares idly into space, pulling his face into ever more varied contortions.

As we hug good-night I sense in the perfunctory clutch of

his arms a tinge of reproach because I have not yet met my promise to bring up the subject of boarding school.

I go downstairs in a forlorn mood, feeling that in some unavoidable way I have lost the battle of the boarding school even before it has begun. If his mind is made up and I force him to stay home, he will only resent me for it.

I take a plate of bread and cheese to the study and sit dejectedly at the desk. I pull the Cellphone bill towards me. It covers the month of March and runs to three full pages. About a hundred calls in all, each itemised. I go immediately to the end of the list, to 26 March, the day that Harry died. He made several calls – six, I count – all of them after midday, all, therefore, from the boat. His last call was timed at 23.50, to the house. Earlier there was a call to Katie, or rather to the Oakwood House staff number, which is the only one parents can call in on. Going back through the other calls, I look for numbers I don't know, I look for numbers I know well. There is nothing I don't expect to find.

I fold the bill and place it in the centre drawer of the desk.

Moreland's number faces me from the message pad. As I dial I wonder briefly what he does in the evenings. Whether he goes to the pub, or out to dinner with people like the Dartingtons, or swaps sailing stories around the yacht club bar. I place him everywhere, and nowhere.

He answers straight away. 'How are you?'

'I'm all right.'

'And Josh?'

'I don't really know.' Which is the truth, though I hadn't meant to say it. 'He's got it into his head that he wants to go to boarding school.'

'Ah. Not a good idea?'

'I'm trying to keep an open mind. I'm trying to—' My throat seizes, I dry up.

Filling the silence, Moreland says, 'Perhaps he'll forget about it in a few days.'

'Perhaps.' But I say it without conviction.

It occurs to me that Moreland would be a good person to talk to Josh. His opinion, being male, neutral and greatly respected, is likely to carry more weight than mine. At the same time I'm wary of involving him more deeply in our affairs. It is partly my lingering confusion about his motives, partly an instinct to keep him at a manageable distance.

I compromise. 'You were sent away at eight, weren't you? You should explain the minus side to him,' I say, tying him down to a limited role. 'Tell him how homesick he'll get, how the other boys'll bully him if he cries, how they'll force him into becoming a regular-issue public schoolboy – all male bonding and locked-in English emotions and suppressed anger—' I halt, aware of the harshness in my voice.

Moreland gives a soft laugh. 'I could warn him, of course. But these places are much better than they used to be, Ellen.'

Old emotions barrel down on me. 'They still produce people who're unhappy with their feelings,' I say with sudden heat, 'who bottle things up, who, after their parents have dumped them there, never really trust or relate to anyone ever again. Who learn to live on two levels, to hide things, to deny their real emotions—' I break off.

'We're not all as bad as that, I hope!'

'Maybe not. But it can never be right. Not at eight! They're just babies at eight.'

'Ah, now that's another argument altogether.'

'It certainly is!'

I'm glad when he lets it go and says after a short silence, 'I'll do what I can, Ellen.'

I exhale slowly. 'Margaret said you wanted to see me about something?'

'Would you mind? It won't take long. Shall I come over tomorrow evening?'

'No,' I say immediately, calculating that I can make a duty call to Diana on the way. 'No. I'll come to you.'

We fix on eight.

I answer three more letters of condolence. If I had qualms about what to say, they seem to have faded, and I pitch my reply in the sort of brave understatement and widowly fortitude that is expected of me. By the end of the third letter I have polished one or two phrases until they have something of a ring to them. The more poignant the words, the less they seem to relate to me or Harry, though writing 'We will miss him very much' still fills my throat with sadness.

I put my pen down and watch the darkness creep out from beneath the thick canopy of beech trees. I am beginning to miss my talks with Bob Block; I miss his robust guidance, his benign good sense, his refusal to register the slightest shock. I try to imagine what he would tell me now. To take one day at a time? To start to put the past behind me and get on with my life? But how, Bob? How can I take one day at a time when each day brings new and disturbing shifts? How can I get on with my life when the past blocks every turn?

It is eleven a.m. California time. Bob will be with a client and, even if he calls me back, he's unlikely to have more than a minute or so to spare. A letter would, anyway, be better. The writing will be cathartic; I might not even need to send it.

I've never learnt to use Harry's personal computer, and Margaret's electronic typewriter, which has come from the office, has complicated things like memories and deletion systems that I don't understand. In the end I fetch my comfortable old portable from its home on a high shelf in the utility room.

I set it up, dusty and battered, on the shiny surface of Harry's desk, and search for paper. The desk drawers contain nothing but a few sheets of Ainswick stationery, and some notepaper headed 'Harry Richmond' in grey 24-point Times Europa Bold. I designed the letterhead, my only direct contribution to Harry's business. The rest of the stationery is kept in one of the cupboards that support the long line of bookshelves. Inside, on the top shelf, are boxes of printed paper in various styles, with a sample of its contents fixed to the lid. Below are the headed cards and compliments slips. And on the bottom shelf the plain A4, three boxes of it, from which I draw five or six sheets.

I wind a sheet into the machine. I sit and look at the last streaks of colour in the sky, I think about turning on more lights, I consider what I will say to Bob Block. Then, following some instinct to leave no corner of Harry's world unexplored, I go back to the plain A4 and riffle through each box in turn. The sheets fan past my fingers, blank and innocent.

I move to the boxes of printed stationery and go through each one: the two-thirds A4 headed 'Pennygate', the full size A4 of the same, the cards, the compliments slips, the 'Harry Richmond' paper in two different sizes. The box whose lid announces 'Ainswick Properties Ltd' (in scarlet 30-point Medici Script) contains a collection of different paper sizes, envelopes and compliments slips culminating, at the bottom, in full A4. I lift the block of A4 and let it ripple past my thumb, *Ainswick* ... *Ainswick* ... in a flickering lantern show of red print.

The streak of black disturbs the flow of scarlet like a flaw in a jewel. Even as I go back and draw out the sheet, I know what I will see. Ever since Tim Schwartz's visit I have been glimpsing this in some recess of my imagination.

I sink back on my heels and read in black 36-point Century Old Style: *Mountbay (Guernsey) Ltd*.

SEVEN

'Simmonds Mitchell.' A female voice, professionally up-lifting.

To my annoyance I stumble, I explain myself awkwardly.

'Do you want billing or broking?'

I hesitate. I say I'm not sure. 'I want the person who deals with individual accounts. In general. Someone who . . .'

'One moment.'

Clicks on the line, then a brisk male voice against the drone of what I take to be the broking floor. 'Alan Bicknall.'

'I wanted to ask about an account.'

'Who do you normally deal with?'

'I don't know.'

'You don't have an account with us?'

'Well, I have a number.'

'Which is?'

I give him the number from Harry's address book with the sinking feeling that I am about to be found out. But he doesn't round on me. After a pause, he merely informs me that the broker isn't at his desk at present. Can he take a message?

I leave my name and number, wondering whether the absent broker will work out who I am, whether he will return the call.

I sink back in my seat with a fleeting sense of achievement. At least I have made the call, and for me that is something.

Outside, the garden is suffused with a thin troubled light beneath a mackerel sky. A wind has sprung up, bending the poplars into a silvery blur. Earlier, just after dawn, I went for a walk in the woods. The mist was tangled around the branches like wreaths of smoke. The air was filled with bird-song and hushed animal sounds. The loveliness made me sad. I concentrated on my breathing – slowly from the diaphragm: one of Bob Block's six so-called 'Paths to Progress' – and tried to come to terms with some uncomfortable truths. This was more difficult than the breathing. There was the realisation that Molly believes that Harry beat me, and that whatever I say she is not going to change her mind. Then there is Josh, who, it would appear, no longer wants to live with me. And finally it seems that my husband was involved in some shady dealing, possibly to the extent of knowingly removing money from a charity. Knowingly. But fraudulently too? In law I rather suspect there is no difference. Harry was many things – and a few things that some people found hard to take – but I can't believe he would have done something quite so cold-hearted. And something which carried such a very high risk of being found out.

When he started in politics he was scrupulous about avoiding situations that might compromise him in any way. He always repaid his personal debts. Once he insisted on driving back five miles to sort out a matter of some mistaken change.

He would have been highly sensitive to any risks, he would have been extremely wary.

But we had money then; perhaps that was the difference. Perhaps he simply got desperate.

Finally – and looming ever larger as I circled the woodland – I knew I had to brace myself for the visit from the police, something which filled me with quiet dread.

My walk lasted for the best part of an hour. Returning at six-thirty, I finished the letter to Bob Block. I told him everything – from the beginning I always told him everything. I reported on Katie and Josh. I went through the Mountbay business, Katie's legacy, the debts, the legal delays. I also told him how at the strangest moments I missed Harry

151

dreadfully. The completed letter ran to four double-sided pages.

Then I wrote two drafts of a letter that I wasn't at all sure about sending, and which I put on one side while I got Josh his breakfast and drove him to school.

I take the drafts out again now. Though still undecided about the wisdom of it, I thread a sheet of the house note-paper into the portable and begin a fair copy. I had thought of addressing it to 'The Director, Mountbay (Guernsey) Ltd', but now I leave the company name on its own. The address, taken from the letterhead, is a Guernsey post office box number.

Dear Sirs, I write to make enquiries following the death of my husband, Harry Richmond. I wish to know if my late husband was associated with your company, and if so in what capacity. I would also be very grateful for information concerning any dealings your company may have had with the concert in aid of The Rumanian Orphans Appeal that my husband helped organise eighteen months ago. After some thought, I add: *I would be extremely grateful for any information of any nature that you are able to give me.*

I sign it (Mrs) E. Richmond. As I start on the envelope, I hear Margaret's footsteps in the passage and slide the Mountbay notepaper into a drawer.

'Good morning,' Margaret calls brightly, passing the desk and putting her bag on a chair. She does a double take on the portable. 'Wow! What a machine!'

I pull the unfinished envelope out of the roller. 'It was my mother's.' I scoop up the typed letter and drafts and, keeping their faces towards me, clip them together with the envelope.

Margaret glances at the bundle. 'Did you want something posted?'

I look blank for a moment. 'Oh no . . . I need to have another look at it. I . . . It's not right yet.' Without thinking I open the drawer containing the Mountbay paper and slip the bundle on top. The Mountbay paper is lying face up and in the instant before it is covered I am aware of Margaret's eyes flicking down towards the letterhead.

I close the drawer rather more forcefully than I mean to, and make a surprised face at the noise. I wonder at my instinct for concealment; I wonder at my belief in the need for it. This, after all, is Margaret, who is not going to broadcast anything detrimental about Harry.

Margaret clasps her hands together and says gaily, 'Well, how about breakfast? Toast? Juice?'

'Just coffee, please.'

She tilts her head with gentle disapproval. She thinks I am letting myself go. She may be right. If I am gaining weight it's very little. And though I have always been a neat person, I can't have spent more than five minutes on my appearance this morning. I pulled my hair back into a band, I threw on jeans and a loose T-shirt. I am wearing old trainers, and without makeup my eyes tend to fade away and my skin to look washed out.

But whatever comment Margaret is about to make, the phone cuts her short. She scoops it up before I have begun to reach for it. She asks who is calling and, raising her eyebrows at me in a mixture of surprise and enquiry, announces Mr Noakes of Simmonds Mitchell.

'Mrs Richmond? Brian Noakes here. What can I do for you?' It is a chirpy voice with a cockney accent.

I begin, 'It's about an account . . .'

'And your client number?'

I read it out, aware that Margaret is getting to her feet and leaving the room.

'Just getting it up on my screen,' says Brian Noakes. 'There . . . How can I help?'

'I was wondering . . . is it possible to tell me the balance in the account?'

His voice changes. 'We haven't dealt before, have we, Mrs Richmond? I would normally speak to—?'

'My husband.'

'He isn't available?'

'My husband died in March.'

A tactful pause, and he says, 'Yes, of course. I was sorry to hear about it, Mrs Richmond. My condolences.'

'I was wondering what the balance was. We're trying to trace everything, you see.'

'Ummm.' He is consulting something, or considering. 'I can tell you that all right, Mrs Richmond. It's nil.'

'Ah.' I hadn't expected much else.

'Sorry not to be able to help more.' He sounds polite but pressed.

'Can I ask – has there been much money in the account in the past?'

'Ummm.' I imagine him scrolling back through the file. 'No recent dealing, Mrs Richmond. In fact nothing for almost a year.'

'I see. And then?'

'A buy of fifteen thousand pounds. A buy of ten. Before that . . . a sale of five thousand. Then . . . nothing back another six months.'

I expect him to ring off, but he says, 'Your husband – I read about it. I'm truly sorry.'

'Thanks.'

'Anything more I can do, please don't hesitate to call again.'

He sounds nice. 'Thank you.'

Ringing off, I draw a line through Simmonds Mitchell on my list. Disconsolately, I pull out the address book and flick through to the last page. All the numbers are accounted for now bar the one without prefix or identification at the end of the list of bank account numbers. This is a six-digit number. All the bank account numbers were eight-digit. The only other six-digit number belonged to the Simmonds Mitchell account.

I should have thought of that. I should have mentioned it.

I put the idea to one side, then change my mind and redial Simmonds Mitchell.

'I'm so sorry to bother you again,' I say when I get through to Brian Noakes. I explain about the unclaimed number. 'I'm sure it's nothing to do with you, but I thought I'd just check.'

'Hang on a mo.' A pause. 'Yes, that's one of ours.'

He's startled me. 'I'm sorry?'

'I dealt with your husband on that account.'

Now I'm simply confused. 'I don't understand.'

'It was another account of ours – a company account.'

But I need it spelt out for me. 'And the person you dealt with was my husband?'

'That's right.'

'Can you . . .' I am groping. '. . . tell me which company?'

'I can't really say anything about that, Mrs Richmond. You see, while I can tell you about a personal account that's in the family, so to speak, company accounts are confidential.'

'Not even the name?'

He groans with suitable regret. 'No. Sorry.'

'*Nothing?*' Taking his silence as something less than a refusal, I plead gently, 'I do realise your position, but if there was anything at all . . . You see, everything was left in rather a mess. It's going to take months to sort out. It would help so much, Mr Noakes.'

He gives a deep sigh. 'Well, I don't suppose I'd be giving too much away by telling you that the balance in this account is also nil.'

'Was any money put through recently?'

'Now I really can't tell you that, Mrs Richmond, much as I would like to.'

'Just an idea?'

'Brokers have had the chop for less, Mrs Richmond.'

'I wouldn't pass it on to anyone, I promise.'

'They could have my guts for garters.' But he is softening. His voice takes a conspiratorial swoop. 'What can I say?' In the pause that follows I see him tapping at his keboard. 'There was regular trading over – let me see – most of the last year.'

'When you say regular . . . ?'

'Regular. Every week or so.'

'How much?'

'Mrs Richmond,' he sucks in his breath as if I were causing him pain. '*Please.*'

'Were they large amounts?'

'You could say so.'

'And what happened to the money?'

'Happened?' There is something in his tone, a briskness, that warns me of what is coming next. 'Had to call for the margins. Yes...'

'Meaning?'

'Losses...' I can see him scrolling back through the screen again. 'Yes,' he says firmly. 'No good news at all, I'm afraid.'

'Forgive me, I want to be clear – all the money was lost?'

'That's about the size of it, Mrs Richmond.'

It's a moment before I remember to thank him.

'It was a pleasure, Mrs Richmond.'

For some minutes I sit staring into the garden.

How much was it, I wonder? And where did it come from? Ainswick money or charity money? If it is all gone I suppose it doesn't make much difference.

Rousing myself at last, I see that Jack is due at any moment. Jack is not someone I can face without a strong coffee, not when I am going to have to swallow my pride and ask him for money, and I pad down the corridor in search of Margaret and the percolator.

I hear the voices before I reach the kitchen; they stop as I open the door. Margaret looks at me with an over-bright expression that is slightly contrite, Jack with an instantaneous smile.

'Ellen!' Jack advances, arms outstretched, face creased up with pleasure, and grasps me in a fluid embrace. This is his you're-so-special embrace, which I am not so foolish as to imagine is reserved exclusively for me. He smells newly scrubbed; a blend of mouthwash and eau-de-Cologne. He pulls back, holding me by the shoulders, and shakes his head. 'I really don't know,' he tuts with fond exasperation. 'I really don't know.'

Letting this pass, I make for the coffee, which Margaret is pouring into oversized cups. A spray of hastily arranged red roses sits in a vase beside the percolator. It is typical of Jack to have brought the one flower that my garden produces in abundance, typical of him to have brought roses, and red ones at that, which must by any standards be inappropriate. I begin to wonder what he wants from me.

He drapes himself over the counter and eyes me with a proprietorial air. He is wearing an immaculate grey suit with an unusually sober shirt in plain white, and a business tie. His shiny dark hair, which he has long worn rakishly over the forehead, is now shorter and combed back. The politically correct Jack, attuned to his new image.

'We were saying how thin you were,' he announces boldly. This is a way of his, to disarm you with his frankness.

Margaret, picking up her cup, winces slightly and throws me a look of denial and apology.

Jack rearranges his long limbs onto a stool. 'I was thinking that I should take you to that new restaurant at Aldeburgh.' Pleased with this idea, he surveys the room, awaiting our approval.

The phone rings and Margaret hurries away to answer it.

Instinctively seeking distance from Jack, I cross the kitchen and sit at the breakfast table. Jack twists on his stool to face me. 'So . . . How's it going?' He drops his voice intimately. 'I mean, *really*?'

'I'm managing.'

The distance does not suit him. He slides from his seat and brings his cup to the table. 'Mmm,' he grunts, drawing out a chair. 'I'm not sure about that.' He sprawls in the chair, holding the cup against his chest, fixing me with a languid gaze. 'You don't have to do this on your own, you know, Ellen. Friends are there to be used. They enjoy helping.'

'People are being very kind,' I say evasively. I describe just how kind, telling him of all the things that Leonard is doing for me, of all the neighbours' offers of help.

He drains his cup, pushes it onto the table and glances towards his watch. Realising how this might be interpreted, he seeks to camouflage the gesture by continuing the movement into a smooth adjustment of his cuff. Catching my look, seeing he has been caught out, he gives a grin of complicity, a blast of

157

sparkling charm, as if to say: Would I be in a hurry to leave you?

I suppress a small smile.

Jack leans across the table, his eyes lizard-like, and lays his hand over mine. Immediately I want to pull away. It's not the touching that disturbs me – I love being touched – it's the way Jack turns the most basic contact into an understanding.

'Am I so terrible?' he chuckles, not expecting an answer from this ancient gambit which he has been using for as long as I can remember. 'All I ever needed,' he declares, 'was a good woman.'

'You've been going through good women all your life, Jack.'

He is delighted at my response. 'But what did they do to me? They threw me out!' This, too, is an old refrain, a blatant untruth delivered with a well-practised blend of regret and satisfaction.

'How's the candidacy going?' I remove my hand to pick up my coffee.

'Ah.' Instantly serious, he twists in his seat and, hooking an arm over the back of the chair, says in an altogether crisper tone, 'Well the favourite appears to be this Mrs Emma Reeves. With four children, for heaven's sake!' He shakes his head, in amazement or disapproval or both. 'Anyway, she's got this incredibly *correct* track record. You know – years sacrificed to hopeless seats, years canvassing tirelessly through the most deprived inner cities, years making brilliant speeches at the party conference. And now – lo! She is seeking her reward. A winnable seat on a cushy patch. Needless to say, she's also *tipped for great things . . .*' He slides me an sardonic glance. 'They always are, aren't they? She's getting a lot of push from Central Office – unofficial of *course*. But' – he raises a long index finger – 'all this correctness isn't going to count for as much as she may think. Barrow says the committee don't really want a star, they want someone who's going to do a good job for the constituency. Well, I mean—!' He flips a hand over, as if the point is self-evident. 'She's not *local*, is she? Doesn't know one end of the patch from the other. When it comes down to it, there's nothing like knowing the ground. That *has* to be my strongest selling point.' He cuts the air with the edge of his hand – a politician's gesture – then looks up with a flash of humour. 'That, and my grasp of economic affairs, and European Community regulations, and farming subsidies, and opting-out procedures. It's like being back at school – three hours' homework every night.'

'I'm sure you'll pass,' I say. 'I don't suppose you're the right person to ask, but how do you rate Charles's chances?'

'What? Oh . . .' He screws up his face into an expression of open doubt. 'I'm surprised he's got this far, frankly.' He shrugs, rapidly losing interest. 'But far be it for me . . .' He taps his long fingers rhythmically on the table, as if we are in a business meeting and must get back to the agenda. 'What I really need, you know, is a wife.' He laughs, though without visible humour. 'Candidates need wives.'

'I didn't think these things mattered nowadays.'

'Huh, you'd be amazed! The more the family unit becomes an endangered species, the more candidates must conform. The committee like to see the standard set-up. I'm non-standard. That bothers them.'

'Wouldn't it be rather a rush job, finding someone in time?'

'What?' He looks at me blankly for a moment before smiling. 'Ha, ha. Yes, *quite* . . . Which reminds me . . .' He slides his elbows onto the table and, balancing his chin on the thumbs of his clasped hands, fixes me with his most provocative smile, devilish, low-lidded, eyes laden with messages, some self-deprecating, most blatantly appealing. 'I was wondering if you'd come and hold my hand next week. Stand in, so to speak. It's an informal get-together with some of the committee. A sort of preliminary vetting. Next Monday.'

So this is it, I think. This is why you have come. 'Jack, I'm flattered to be asked. But really, I can't, it would be . . .' I trail off, remembering what I am going to ask him in a few short minutes, realising that he is unlikely to take kindly to it if I refuse him this favour. 'Let's go into the garden,' I say, to give myself time. 'Before it rains.'

He isn't overwhelmed by the idea, but follows me through the house into the conservatory where we find we are already too late and the rain is patting heavily onto the glass in slow drops.

We stand at the french windows. 'Can I let you know about Monday?' I say. 'Apart from anything else, I'd have to explain it to Charles and Anne. They'd think I was taking sides. It'd be more than my life was worth.'

He pushes out his handsome mouth. 'I can't see it would make much difference to Charles, quite honestly.'

This is untrue, he must know it's untrue, but I don't say so. Instead I gather my resources and say, 'Jack, you kindly mentioned the possibility of a loan the other day.'

He hardly blinks. 'Of course. I told you ... I'd be only too glad...' He spreads his hands like a street vendor. 'Just tell me what you need.'

'It'd just be until various bits of money come through – the sale of the house, the life insurance, things like that. Though it could be longer. I can't promise – Leonard's a bit vague about the timing.'

'A bridging loan. Of course. How much?'

'That's the thing – I'm not sure yet.'

'But you must have some idea? What does Gillespie say? He must have told you how much is involved?'

'Roughly.'

'Well – shall I talk to him then?'

'No. No ... I know how much.'

He looks at me expectantly.

I take a wild stab at a number, I leap headlong. 'A hundred and fifty thousand.' It emerges half as a request, half as a plea for mercy.

He pulls back. He gives a forced laugh as if responding to some poor joke, all the time searching my face. Seeing that I am serious, his smile falters, his eyes glint with conflicting emotions. 'Gillespie said it would be twenty at the most!'

So they have already discussed numbers, these two. How stupid of me not to realise.

Reading my confusion, Jack tips me an odd look. 'Unless this is about something else altogether?' He raises his eyebrows, he peers at me. 'Well, is it?'

Quick Jack. Jack who doesn't miss a trick. Jack who can't be fooled on matters of money. I realise that I've misjudged this conversation.

'Something that came up recently,' I admit, looking away.

The rain is beating more steadily, a growing tattoo which blurs the glass and gives our voices a strange resonance.

Jack ducks his head into my sightline. 'It's not this charity business, is it, Ellen?' My silence feeds his suspicions. 'They're not talking you into thinking you owe them something, are they? They're not leaning on you for money, for God's sake?'

It hadn't occurred to me that Jack would know about this. I stare at him, wondering why I hadn't realised he would know. Gillespie – or maybe it's Leonard – seems to tell him everything else. I feel exposed and rather foolish.

'No,' I say rapidly, 'it's not that.'

'If they made mistakes, it's *their* business, Ellen,' says Jack, ignoring my remark. 'Nothing to do with you. *Not* your problem. You mustn't even *think* of talking to these people.'

I hear Gillespie's voice in this; I have no further doubts as to who told Jack. 'It's nothing to do with the charity,' I protest more strongly. 'The money's for me.'

He examines my face, he looks doubtful. I feel as though I have the word *liar* tattooed on my forehead.

'What do you want it for then?'

Impressed at my own talent for improvisation, I declare, 'I want to buy a house. I can't bear to stay at Pennygate a second longer than I have to. I'm miserable here. I feel I can't begin to have a life again until I get out.'

'A *house*? Why didn't you say so?' Jack's expression softens a little to compensate for the irritation in his voice.

'I felt you wouldn't understand. It seemed like such an extravagance.'

'I understand,' says Jack, making a visible effort to do so. 'Have you got somewhere in mind?'

'No, but I've got a good idea of what I want.'

'Why can't you rent? It would be more sensible to rent.'

I am so deep into this lie that I am forced deeper still. 'I want a permanent home. For the children's sake. I don't want them to feel unsettled.'

Jack frowns at this, then, labouring his puzzlement, wheels a hand slowly in the air by his head, as if to assist the workings of his brain. 'Well...' He stares at me in an unfocused way before turning to look tight-lipped into the garden, 'It's rather more than I...' Catching my eye once more, he says defensively, 'The recession ... Things are a bit tight, even for me. And if Gillespie comes to me for this twenty thousand to cover your general expenses...'

Aware that I must shift this moment to my advantage, I suppress what is left of my pride and, using tactics that Jack himself would recognise, I touch his arm, I hold his gaze for much longer than I need to, I put into my expression messages that say: I will be in your debt, I will be suitably appreciative.

The light of calculation and reassessment crosses his face. He says stiffly, 'I can't promise.'

But in saying this, I know he can. Jack isn't short of cash, whatever he may say, but like Harry, like many people who have experienced life without money, it pains him to be parted from it.

As I show him to the door I make my own offering. 'That party. Perhaps if we all arrived together, me and Anne and Charles and you? But I left with you?'

He considers, he sees instantly that he will have the best of this arrangement. We exchange a glance of understanding that, for me at least, owes more to commerce than feeling. He nods slowly. Then in a gesture that shows he is leaving nothing of the old Jack behind, he reaches out to brush my cheek.

The police are late. I use the time to remake my list for the day, pushing some of the calls onto tomorrow so that the afternoon will be clear. I try to picture Dawson as I saw him on his second and last visit, the day before I left for America. I remember the inspector as a dapper man in his mid-forties, on the short side, with a broken nose, slow-moving eyes and the beginnings of a beer belly. He stayed for half an hour or so, sitting in a wing chair, solidly at ease, gazing down the garden towards the river. Like most policemen, he seemed in no particular hurry. We talked about the hazards of sailing the coast, although, like me, he knew almost nothing about tides, currents or small boats. Finally he came to what I took to be the point of his visit, and asked me whether *Minerva* was fully equipped with lifesaving gear. I told him I thought so but suggested he check with the boatyard, who would know exactly what was on board. We hardly talked about Harry.

The coffee has overheated my taut nerves. My mouth is dry, I feel sweat under my shirt, my pulse beats high in my head. I tidy the desk. I crumple the redundant list and drop it into the bin. The scored out 'Simmonds Mitchell' stares back at me from the rumpled paper.

The tension and the heat give me a sort of energy, a false courage. With Margaret busy on the other line, talking to a builder about the broken gutter, I lift the phone and call the City number, and get through to Brian Noakes.

'It's me again.'

'Well, hello, Mrs Richmond.' The jaunty voice betrays only the slightest wariness.

'I've just one question. I want to know ... is it a Guernsey-based company?'

Out of the stillness behind me, muffled by the heavy study door, comes the soft chime of the front doorbell.

Brian Noakes emits a sound that is half complaint, half chuckle. 'Guernsey?'

Margaret finishes her call with a bang of the phone and hurries out to answer the door.

'What can I say?' His voice takes on a theatrical ring. 'Let's put it this way, Mrs Richmond, I'm remaining silent...' He pauses for dramatic effect. 'And you can take that to mean what you like.'

But I want to hear. 'You mean ... ?'

'That I'm not saying no.'

I catch the murmur of voices in the hall. I picture Margaret on her way down the passage to summon me. 'Would it be called Mountbay?' I ask quickly.

A silence.

'You're not saying no.'

He is delighted with my progress. 'I'm not saying no, Mrs Richmond!'

'Thank you, Mr Noakes.'

'Don't mention it, Mrs Richmond.'

There are two policemen waiting in the hall, both uniformed, one of an age where he must have long since given up ideas of promotion. Sergeant Willis and Constable Deakin. I make a point of memorising their names.

They have a practised stolidity, though once the formalities are over – the murmured offer of condolence, the apology for bothering me, the recounting of the firearms regulations that demand this inspection – the sergeant slips in a little joke about the bumpiness of the drive, as if to test the conversational temperature. I give a smile which encourages them to settle into a steady well-rehearsed banter – the places they have had to find in their time, the drives they have had to negotiate.

I lead them to the boot room which Harry, in thrall to some grand houses he had visited, tried to persuade us to call the gun room.

Leaving them in front of the gun locker I go to the kitchen to fetch the second key from its hidden place in the dresser. Handing it over to the sergeant with the key from the study, I offer coffee, tea, biscuits. One coffee, one tea; both with sugar.

I go back to the kitchen and put the kettle on. In my mind's eye I see the sergeant turning the keys and swinging open the door of the gun locker. I spoon instant coffee into a mug. I drop a tea-bag into a taller mug emblazoned with Harry's name, then follow it with a second bag; I have the idea that policemen, like repair men, prefer their tea dark and viscous.

The men take longer than I thought. The kettle has boiled

and I am pouring water over the tea-bags when a soft rap comes at the door. I hold the kettle steady and lower it carefully onto the counter before turning.

The sergeant stands on the threshold. He asks if I can spare a moment. 'Of course.' I follow his deliberate steps into the boot room where Constable Deakin stands beside the gun locker. No banter now, no eye contact. We take up station in front of the open locker.

'The licence, as it stands, Mrs Richmond, is for two shotguns,' declares the sergeant. He holds up the certificate and reads from it, 'As stated here' – he taps the certificate – 'they should both be here in this cabinet. Is that your understanding, Mrs Richmond?'

I look at the open cabinet, at the shape of the long-barrelled gun in its green carrying bag and the empty slot next to it where the second gun should be and the empty carrying bag lying crumpled in the bottom of the cabinet. 'I'm sorry, I really don't know. My husband dealt with the guns. I never knew what the arrangements were...' I do not add that I disliked the things so much that I purposely ignored them, that I always thought Harry's cursory training dangerously inadequate for his careless handling of them.

'One gun appears to be missing. Could you tell me where it might be, Mrs Richmond?'

I shake my head in bafflement.

'You haven't seen it about?'

'No.'

'You didn't know that it wasn't in here?'

'I never look.' I add inconsequentially, 'I've been away.'

The sergeant purses up his mouth, a look of gravity. 'It couldn't have got left anywhere, could it by any chance?' he asks ponderously. 'Like in a car boot, for example?'

'I don't think so. I could ask someone to check.'

He doesn't respond, and we stand in silent contemplation of the cabinet with its empty bracket.

'There's been no break-in? While you were away perhaps?'

'No. Well, I don't think so. Someone would have told me.'

He inhales audibly. 'The keys, Mrs Richmond, where were they kept exactly?'

I take him to the kitchen, to the old dresser. Following my directions, he bends down and twists his hand up inside the cupboard to the hook.

'And the other one was kept in the study, in a drawer of the desk.'

'And who would know where the keys were?'

I have to think for a moment. I tell him Margaret, Maurice, Jill, although I'm not sure about Jill.

'And would there be a spare set of keys?'

'Not that I know of.'

He shakes his head. He straightens up. 'And when was the cabinet last opened, Mrs Richmond, do you know?'

'I suppose . . . when my husband last went shooting.'

'Would you remember when that was?'

'In the winter some time.' I take a stab at it. 'February?'

I hear Margaret in the passage. I call to her and explain. I ask her to go and look in Harry's Mercedes, and to see if she can find Maurice and ask him to search the garages, the store rooms and outhouses. The sergeant declines my offer to sit down and stands in the hall by the window, making notes on his pad. The constable wanders in and out of the boot room, looking at doors and windows as if for clues.

I remake the mugs of coffee and tea and take them into the men in the hall.

Margaret reports back, then Maurice. There is no gun. We stand in an uncertain tableau, while the sergeant holds a murmured conversation with Constable Deakin.

Finally the sergeant approaches me and says in a tone that is deliberately low, 'This will have to be reported, Mrs Richmond.'

Sighing, I nod slowly. 'I understand.'

When the policemen have gone, Margaret exclaims in a rare moment of irritation, 'Really! This is all we need!'

Dawson comes at five when I am alone in the house.

He is a little taller than I remember, his belly less prominent,

166

his broken nose more obviously bent. With his calm manner, his double-breasted suit, his highly polished shoes, he might be an insurance salesman, come to renew the house policy. Except that salesmen travel alone, and Dawson has two young officers with him, both plain-clothed. Tall and stiff and watchful, they seem to crowd the hall.

The back-up team sit at either end of the long sofa, while Dawson chooses the same chair as before, by the window, and stares out through the drizzle to the barely visible river. 'What a view!' he says, shaking his head and softly beating his open palm against the chair arm. 'You could look at it all day, couldn't you?' He tuts with disbelief. 'Well, well.'

He turns with the sigh of someone who must attend to business and would prefer not to. 'You realise, Mrs Richmond,' he says, 'that there will have to be an investigation into this missing shotgun? Regulations are very tight nowadays. We have to consider theft, illegal usage, all manner of things. You appreciate?'

'Yes.'

He nods benevolently and with curious intimacy, as if this mutually tedious burden has forced us into some kind of alliance. 'Sergeant Willis told me you had no idea about where the weapon might be.'

'No. I'm sorry.'

'And there was no sign of burglary or theft, I gather?'

'No.'

'But the house has been empty at night while you were away?'

'The alarm would have gone off. My neighbours in the cottages would have heard.'

'And there was no break-in before you went away?'

'No.'

'No,' he echoes vaguely, looking abstracted. He stares away through the window again, narrowing his eyes against some imaginary glare. He says almost to himself, 'Do you think your husband might have taken it with him, Mrs Richmond?' He turns with an exaggerated expression of enquiry. 'On the yacht?'

There is a moment of stillness, a moment when I feel the heat pricking my cheeks. 'I don't know. He did take it once.'

'Oh.' Dawson absorbs this, suddenly far less abstracted. 'On the yacht? And when was that?'

'Last autumn. He thought he might have a go at some duck.'

'From the yacht?'

'Yes.'

Dawson's face creases into puzzlement. 'While he was sailing along?'

'Oh no, I don't think so. No, from the mooring. In the afternoon, after he'd been sailing, when he was packing up. It was quiet then. The duck would fly up from the marshes.'

'Ah! I *see*. Of *course*.' He taps his fingertips against his forehead. 'Of course. Shooting's not one of my sports, I'm afraid. I'm a golfer . . .' His mind has already moved on. 'He took the gun just the once, did he, on the yacht?'

'I'm not sure, I'm afraid. He may have taken it several times. But . . .' I shrug.

He smiles attentively, he makes a small gesture of encouragement. 'But—?'

'Well, he probably wouldn't have told me.' I add with a false laugh, 'He knew I wasn't too keen on him shooting, you see.'

'Ahhh.' Dawson gives a slow nod of understanding. 'On the day your husband set off for his trip south, Mrs Richmond – March 26 – you helped him load the boat, if I remember?'

'I helped unload the car,' I correct him. 'My husband loaded the boat. He knew where he wanted everything. I didn't know how to stow things.'

'You didn't notice a shotgun?'

'No, I . . .' I glance away. It is strange how the truth is just as hard to deliver as lies. I look back at him. 'I don't remember seeing it.'

'It's not the sort of thing you'd miss, is it?' Dawson muses, tapping his blunt fingers idly against the chair arm. He chews the inside of his lip and looks beyond me in an unfocused way, like a visitor suddenly inexpressibly bored. Coming to, he leans forward in his chair until his stomach presses hard against his shirt buttons, and says, 'We'll just inspect the gun locker, if we may, Mrs Richmond. And if you would be so kind as to give us the details of the people who had access to the keys. Then . . .' A pause as if he can't quite recollect what he should say next. 'Then I trust we won't have to trouble you any further for the time being.'

We stand up together. Dawson takes a last look out into the rain and shakes his head. 'Amazing, that view. Really amazing.'

I collect the keys to the gun locker and, turning on lights against the gloom, lead the men down the passage to the boot room. Dawson pauses in the entrance and asks with formal courtesy if I wouldn't mind going along with the sergeant and giving him those names and addresses. It occurs to me that this is an effective way of removing me. The sergeant and I return to the drawing-room, where he takes down with slow concentration the names and addresses of Margaret, Maurice and Jill. The task finished, we wait in the silence of two people with nothing to say to each other.

Dawson reappears and takes his leave with a slow dutiful smile, like a guest who has just enjoyed a leisurely tea. 'Thank you for your time, Mrs Richmond. I'm most grateful. Oh, and if you happen to think of anything – my number.' He produces a card from an inner pocket.

I remain at the hall window after their car has gone, staring at the ghostlike trees hovering in the mist, wondering how soon the news will get out. Loyal though Jill and Maurice are, I know with a small stab of resignation that it will be too much to expect them not to talk. And that the news, being touched with drama, is bound to get embroidered in the retelling. I can imagine the story making the rounds of the ornate bar in the Wellington Arms, of the school car-park and weekend drinks parties. People will choose the most colourful interpretation. They will say that Harry must have taken the gun with him on the boat, that he probably used it on himself, that he arranged for the boat to sink in order to conceal his suicide. Needing to appear in the

169

know, they will talk of Harry having money worries, depression, and God-only-knows-what troubles.

This is the epitaph I dread for Harry.

I dread it for the children's sake, because whatever anyone says suicide is still a stigma, something they would have to live with for the rest of their lives. I dread it because these rumours have a way of travelling unbelievable distances and, if the life insurance company gets to hear about them, it may refuse the payout, and then the children's future would be destroyed in a single swoop.

After everything I have worked for.

I stand in the dark hall, fighting down a surge of frustration so violent that I contain it with difficulty.

When I'm calmer, I go to the phone and call Jill.

Josh is just about to have his meal, she reports. Ham and chips and peas and strawberries from the garden. And yes, he seems fine. Happy as Larry.

I ask if some men are arriving to see her.

Lord no, she says, taking time to look out of the window and check. Who would be stopping by to see her? She hasn't had a male visitor under sixty for weeks, not allowing for Alan her husband, who doesn't count. Her laugh fades as I tell her the police will be coming about a routine and rather trivial matter to do with the shotgun licence, how ages ago Harry left one of his guns somewhere, probably at a shooting lodge in Scotland, but that we can't track it down, and that until it turns up the police are duty bound to consider it stolen and will have to make standard 'inquiries'. I load the word with ridicule and weariness, as if I have already had enough of this tedious business.

Jill accepts this story without a murmur. 'All this form filling,' she sighs. 'It never stops, does it?'

Putting the phone down, I allow myself to believe that the absence of the gun might pass unnoticed after all.

I allow myself to hope, but not so much that I won't float the Scottish shooting lodge idea in Margaret and Maurice's direction when I see them tomorrow. And certainly not so much that I won't tell Katie about the missing gun straight away,

170

before there's the slightest risk of her hearing about it from someone else.

Katie is breathless when she comes to the phone; Mrs Anderson caught her on her way to play tennis. I start by telling her about Josh's escapade. She greets this with a dismissive 'Silly boy!' in a camp Hollywood voice that makes me laugh.

'Do you want me to have a word with him?' she adds in yet another of her actory voices, mock stern and schoolmarmish.

'You sound great, darling.'

'Yeah, well,' she drawls. 'They've let me drop history. I mean, they *finally* realised. Like I've been telling them for ever! So . . . Shall I see my stupid brother on Sunday and knock some brains into him?'

'Would you? If you could . . .? We could go for a walk after lunch. I think – well, I know he won't talk to me.' I didn't intend to tell her the rest, but I do: 'He says he wants to go away and board.'

'Oh, *Mum*.'

'Well, maybe he's right,' I say offhandedly. 'Maybe he should go.'

'Oh, Mum,' she echoes more softly. 'But what about *you*?'

'Oh, I'd survive.' I shrug it off with an airy grunt. 'But listen—' I put a lightness into my voice as I tell her that the police came about the gun licence renewal and discovered one of the guns was missing, and that they are going to have to investigate it because they always do when it's guns, and, the neighbourhood being what it is, she may hear about it from someone else.

'Oh,' she says, her voice small and tight. 'Oh. The police, were they all right?'

'Oh yes. You know, it was just a routine thing.'

A pause.

'You're okay, Mummy?'

She calls me Mummy when she is worried about me.

'Me?' I laugh. 'I'm fine, darling.'

So fine that when she rings off, I clutch my head in my hands for a long moment.

171

The phone forces me back to life. It is Diana. She complains that she is plagued by knocking sounds in her hot-water system and that her stupid plumber is more than useless – a pretext, as are so many of her calls, to talk away her loneliness.

I tell what she wants to hear. 'I was coming over anyway.'

EIGHT

This is just the sort of place I'd like to live in one day. Moreland's rented cottage is typically Suffolk, snug and thick-walled with a low-ceilinged black-beamed living room, a tiny dining-room, windows that look onto the ancient cottage garden (much in need of attention), a large open fire for the winter, and probably three bedrooms upstairs, the whole thing set among a scattering of cottages on the edge of a village which contains enough life and industry that it doesn't die a death every Monday after the weekenders have gone.

The only thing I wouldn't choose is the river. From where I sit outside the french windows, under a clematis-covered trellis, a stretch of water is visible over the tangle of the adjacent garden, between the creeper-covered corner of the next cottage and the tall side of The Maybush Inn at the river's edge. At this angle the water appears flat and lazy. Dinghies with butterfly-coloured sails dash back and forth, yachts raise their tall white mainsails and slip away towards the sea. Harmless, pretty. But if I listen too hard, I seem to catch the dim beat of wind-flogged canvas. I scent the tang of the salt. I remember, and in remembering I taste my fear again.

Moreland appears with a tray of food and more wine. 'It's rather basic, I'm afraid.' Not so basic: there is ripe Brie and brown bread and fruit.

'It looks fine.'

He puts the tray on the table and plops himself on the other chair. 'I've just been looking at the tides,' he says, raising the bottle in enquiry and refilling my glass, 'and Saturday would be best. It's high water just before eight. I could pick Josh up from the quay and we could kedge in a pool and try for mullet.' He pushes my glass towards me. 'If that's all right.' He gives a characteristic smile, warm but overlaid by seriousness.

The wine is dark and smooth. I take a long sip. From close by comes a burst of vibrant bird-song; a blackbird in the moss-covered branches of an apple tree. 'You will tell me what Josh says, won't you?' I say. 'Even if it isn't what I want to hear?'

I sense Moreland's curiosity, but all he says is, 'I'm sure it won't be anything like that.'

I'd like to agree, but I'm still smarting from one of Diana's more powerful verbal darts. After discussing plumbers and Charles's candidature and running through Diana's usual span of grievances – there is little that doesn't irritate her at some level – we touched on Josh, and I gave her a quick account of his unofficial afternoon off school. From her closed expression I realised she already knew, that Anne must have told her. Lurching forward in her seat, the vodka spilling over the edge of her glass, she fixed me with a narrow pointed look and announced, 'That boy's got out of hand. He needs to get away.' I didn't say anything; for a while I couldn't. Then, shrugging it off, I talked rapidly about other things. But Diana hadn't finished. As I made for the door, she wheezed after me and clutched my arm. Children need to be with other children, she insisted in her most dogmatic tones, not stuck in the wilds with their mother. Believe me, she said.

I drove away in voiceless indignation, wondering why Diana couldn't give me the width of understanding that I have always tried to give her, feeling, rather as Harry must have felt for much of his life, unfairly treated. Arriving at Moreland's, some of my resentment must have been locked into my face because he took a careful glance at me, put a glass of wine into my hand, sat me down in the garden and talked about inconsequential things. Perhaps it was the wine, perhaps it was the calm flow of Moreland's voice, but my anger soon gave way to something much more manageable, a blend of resignation and apathy.

Now, watching Moreland carve the bread, I say reminiscently, 'Strange, but Josh used to tell me everything. I took it for granted. I thought it would always be like that.'

Moreland pauses, his knife in mid-cut, and considers. 'Well, disturbing thoughts are always more difficult to express, aren't they? He's probably feeling lots of things he doesn't understand.'

'Yes,' I sigh, 'I see that. Of course. But he was all right in America, you see.' Abandoning this thought, I take another sip of the rich silky wine, aware that I'm drinking more than I'm used to and it's going straight to my head, but not caring too much.

Moreland puts bread and cheese onto a plate and, leaning across, places it in front of me. He taps the plate and gives me the flicker of a smile. I am being ordered to eat. Obediently, I cut some cheese and press it onto the bread.

'I think he blames me for something,' I go on. 'That's the feeling I get anyway. Something I've done. I try to think what, but I just don't know. All I can imagine is that he's been feeling left out. Katie was in such a state after Harry died that I did rather neglect him, I suppose. I don't mean *neglect*, I mean . . .' I stare unseeing into the garden while I grasp the thought. 'Well, I suppose I just assumed that he was was all right.'

Moreland has made a sandwich of his cheese and is chewing thoughtfully. 'But children always test their mothers, don't they? It's part of growing away from them. Coming to terms with the fact that their mothers are going to have to be dispensable after all. Everyone gives their mother a hard time. I certainly did. When I wanted my own way. Which, at nine, was nearly all the time.'

I try to imagine Moreland giving his mother grief. 'I don't believe you.'

With a fleeting grin, he ducks the challenge and says, 'Didn't you go through stages? Doesn't everyone?'

'Yes. I was perfectly horrible.' Forced back into these memories, my smile fades. 'But then—' I hesitate, not because I'm reluctant to tell Moreland – I sense a sympathy in him – but because even after all this time my feelings are still extra-ordinarily confused. 'My mother could be very—' What word to use? 'Difficult,' I suggest finally. 'Not just with me, with my father too. She knew how to ... twist things round. To build them up, to drag them out, to make us feel that, whatever had gone wrong, it was our fault. Sometimes it was hard to remember what our original crime was meant to be. When it got too much my father used to slip out of the house, usually to the golf club, and not come back till late. And I – well—' My throat swells, old anxieties and resentments block my words, and what I used to do at these times hangs in the air, unshaped, unspoken. 'She wasn't a happy person,' I say at last, frowning into my lap.

'You had no brothers or sisters?'

'No. A pity, really. It might have...' I shrug the thought away. 'Anyway, I escaped as soon as I could. Went to art college and got involved with the first interesting man I came across. Well, *unusual* might be a more accurate description. And that was that.'

'He was an art student too?'

'No, music. In his first year at the Royal Academy. But he used to play jazz piano in the student band I was with.'

'You were with...?' He gapes incredulously. 'Good God! What did you play?'

'Nothing. I sang.'

'Sang ... jazz?' He shakes his head and laughs in open amazement.

'I loved it. Singing was...' Normally I wouldn't attempt to explain, but the wine has given me a new voice. 'It was the only time I didn't feel socially hopeless. I was rather shy then. To put it mildly. I did my best to fade into things – walls, floors, anything really. Singing did great things for my confidence.'

'I bet it did, I *bet*.' Moreland gives a series of faint nods, as if this at least confirms his picture of me. 'Well...' He keeps looking at me with mild astonishment, even admiration. 'And then? What happened then?'

'Then? Oh, Katie came along and I had to give up college. So did Johnnie – Katie's father. Well, he didn't *have* to give up. He chose to. He joined a group as their keyboard player. They were into seventies-style protest numbers. Anti-apartheid, anti-injustice, that sort of thing. The band was on the road most of the time. Katie and I went along too. But it was a hard sort of life. No money, no security.' I twist the stem of my glass until the wine dances. 'And too many drugs.'

I leave this hanging in the air to tell its own story of Johnnie's slide into addiction.

We sit in thoughtful silence. The sinking sun dips below the last shreds of the rain cloud and paints the garden with shades of amber. The river, slinking away to the east, reflects only grey.

I turn brightly to Moreland. 'And you? What happened to you?'

A suddenly light in the eyes, a slow smile. 'You mean after I stopped being hard on my mother? Ah . . . not a lot, I'm afraid. I didn't have the guts to rebel.' He makes a face of mock regret. 'I thought of getting angry about things but put all my energy into playing sport instead. Then I thought about doing things like going to university but in the end I took the easy way out and went into the Marines. I didn't mean to stay long, just four years or so. It was twelve in the end. But then I did rather take to it.'

'All that self-sufficiency?'

'Well, y-e-s,' he says as if it's rather difficult to explain, 'that's a *part* of it, certainly.' He takes a large bite of his sandwich.

I watch him, I wait. Finally I prompt, 'And the other part?'

He chews slowly, he studies me as if deciding on the type of answer I should have. 'Well, they're really quite different from any other outfit, the Royal Marines. They give you a chance to show what you can do, to operate as an individual, show your initiative within a strong framework – to a degree you don't find anywhere else, not even in the Paras.' Satisfied with this statement, he continues in a lighter tone, 'In my unit we were often working in small teams, just four of us, out on our own. You have to be able to live off your wits in those situations, be totally resourceful, take your own decisions. That was the main attraction. For me anyway. The mixture of routine and not knowing what the hell's coming next. Call it *Boy's Own* adventure if you like.' He gives me a smiling glance that isn't entirely free of defensiveness. 'But while the Cold War was on, the work was important enough. It had a real purpose.' He reaches for his wine. The glass hovering at his lips, he adds, 'And there's also a tremendous sense of family in the Royal Marines.' He knocks back his wine. 'And that includes wives and children. A sense of mutual support.'

I look at him, I am very still. Moreland with a wife. The idea hits me with odd force, I see the inevitability of it, and wonder why I haven't realised it before. A man like this would hardly have reached forty or thereabouts without marrying. The thought disturbs me in some way I cannot immediately identify. A feeling of having been caught out, perhaps. A small resentment at not having guessed.

This does not stop me from being curious to know if I'm right. But by the time I frame the question, Moreland has started to talk about his father, and the moment has passed.

Clasping my wine, I ease my shoes off and curl my feet up into the chair against the evening chill, and watch Moreland's face as he tells me how his father stayed in the Marines for twenty years and started a small wine business in Berkshire on his retirement. He worked hard, held wine tastings and organised promotional weeks. The business was reasonably succesful, he thought of expanding.

Moreland looks at me often as he talks, glances that are islands of reassurance in the sea of his story. I sense that he does not tell this story often, that for some reason I have been awarded the privilege of hearing it.

I notice his hands, which are long and expressive. He gestures often, small turnings of the wrist, a spread of the fingers. He smiles ruefully at some turn in his story, and suddenly there is something in his manner, a mixture of solemnity and kindliness, that is intensely attractive.

His gaze becomes preoccupied, he looks past me, he sighs. He tells me how his father's business took a sudden downturn, how his mother died soon after. He pauses. He pulls his mouth down into a grimace. 'Then, just to cap it all, my father was a name at Lloyds. He was deep into a syndicate that was caught by two of the big disasters, the Alaskan oil spill *and* the 1984 Florida hurricane. He was hit very hard. In the end they called for virtually everything he had.'

'How awful. I'm so sorry.'

He lifts his shoulders. His hands fan out briefly. 'Well, that was the risk he took, I'm afraid.' He adds with a grunt, 'But it almost broke him. Emotionally as well as financially. Knocked the stuffing right out of him. He's never got over it. Never will, I don't think. Having to face retirement without a nest-egg, just when he thought he was all set up. Had to move into a flat and sell the house at a bad price. I did what I could of course, but . . .' After a moment of stillness he casts me a new look, one that is oddly uncertain. Sitting up, he puts his glass carefully to one side and slides his arms onto the table. 'But look – this is part of what I wanted to talk to you about. You see . . . it was Harry who helped us out.'

'Harry?' I make an incredulous sound.

'He let me have a loan. Enough to keep the wine business solvent until it could be sold. That money saved the day, really. Made all the difference between what you might call total disaster and manageable disaster. With the business sold, my father was at least left with something. Not a lot, but enough to keep him going. So you see . . . I owe Harry a great debt.'

I frown, I look away, I feel a mixture of pride and resentment. Harry. Still springing surprises on me at this distance, still living up to all his old contradictions. At least this surprise, if I understand it correctly, is something to be proud of.

Dusk is creeping under the trees. A sharp wind springs intermittently around the garden. I pull my sweater closer round my shoulders. 'I'm glad he could help.'

'I'd like you to know,' Moreland says, 'that he offered it quite spontaneously, and without security, and that he never put a time limit on it.'

'Well . . . *good!*' I nod and keep nodding long after I have finished speaking.

'In the absence of any proper arrangement—' With this curiously formal phrase Moreland runs into difficulty, looking down at his hands, pausing, as close to being unsettled as I have seen him. He takes a breath and goes at it in a rush. 'What I did was to repay the money in instalments, every month, whatever I had available. By the time Harry died, roughly half was paid off. Which left a bit over ten thousand. Now, rather than, umm' – he searches for the words with a spiral of his hand – 'worry you directly, I contacted Leonard and asked him to handle the repayment. To say it was a business arrangement.'

'Good Lord!' I stare at him, I lean forward. I shiver and laugh simultaneously. 'It was you! I thought . . .'

'I'm sorry. I didn't mean it to appear in any way – devious.'

'I thought—' But I'm not about to start explaining about Jack.

'That someone was trying to give you a handout?'

'Yes.'

'Sorry. I was simply hoping to avoid any – well, awkwardness. As it was it didn't quite work out that way.' He gives an ironic shrug. 'I was coming to tell you about it when Josh disappeared.'

'Good Lord,' I echo, still absorbing this news, seeing how someone like Moreland would wish to keep the transaction – and his father's troubles – private.

Moreland sits up. 'You're cold,' he declares. Without discussion, he scoops the food onto the tray and leads the way indoors.

I sit for another moment before following with the wine, feeling pleasantly drugged and astonishingly lucid, wondering why I don't drink more seriously more often.

Moreland is switching on lamps.

'But why pay so much back at once?' I say boldly. 'You don't need to, you know. It isn't necessary.'

He bends down to put a match to the fire and shoots me a backward look that is almost fierce. 'I had the money.'

'And you thought I needed it.'

He stands up. 'I thought you needed it more than I did,' he retorts crisply. '*And* I had the money.'

I have been rebuked. His ability to pay is not really any of my business.

'I—'

But he is already remarking, 'You haven't eaten anything.'

I inspect my bread and cheese. 'No,' I have to agree. Taking the plate, I sit on the floor next to the fire. 'Thank you for the money,' I say earnestly. 'It's very welcome. I certainly won't turn it down.'

Moreland sits in the chair opposite. 'Good!' Any lingering awkwardness evaporates in the breadth and immediacy of his smile.

We talk of other things. Or rather, I prompt him to talk while I listen. It is a relief not to have to think about myself for a change, to forget Dawson and the gun business and all the other lurking worries, to settle back and listen to Moreland's fluid voice as he tells me about his job, how he goes to Saudi Arabia for several days every month, how the itinerant life has its advantages – desert hunting trips with the Saudis, invitations to Longchamps and Ascot – and its disadvantages – the alcohol prohibition – 'not, admittedly, life-threatening, but life-dampening' – laundry always in the wrong place, goats' brains and worse for breakfast – a conspiratorial smile here, as if to admit he is teasing. He touches very briefly on the problem of keeping in contact with friends. He doesn't mention a family.

When the fire becomes too hot, I retreat to a chair, my cheeks burning, though this is probably from the wine, which I continue to consume fearlessly. As the evening drifts pleasantly on, I feel slothful and oddly content and a little euphoric. Moreland, now the subject of the loan is out of the way, speaks with an easy familiarity that assumes common ground, a bank of shared experiences, as if we were old friends for whom everything is half-read; a suggestion that is both restful and beguiling.

I have visions of freedom. I allow myself to look ahead to a time when I will be able to dine out like this with whom I choose,

181

whenever I choose, without thoughts of the past. To a time when my life will be my own again; when, in some yet more distant unformed future, who knows, I might even find someone to share it with.

I'm not so hazy with wine and fantasies of freedom that I don't recognise the danger of looking across at Moreland as I think this. But ideas are harmless and free and almost as intoxicating as wine, and I'm in no state to suppress them anyway. As Moreland chuckles at the memory of a party that he came to in this cottage years ago, the glow of the firelight illuminates one side of his face and accentuates the curve of his mouth and the strong line of his nose, and I let myself wonder how life would be with someone like him.

Before this thought races away with me, I pull myself to an abrupt halt, I bring myself rapidly to earth. A relationship – even the idea of a relationship – is an indulgence I can't afford. Even if by some wild chance Moreland were attracted to me, even if by some wilder chance he were free, it would be madness, and quite unsafe.

My imagination subsides in a rush, though not without a small dart of regret.

Perhaps Moreland catches something in my expression, perhaps it is the suddenness with which I put my glass down, but he stops and says, 'All right?'

'I'd like some coffee. Black, if you have it.'

'*Black* . . . well, I don't know . . .' he teases me gently.

When I fail to respond, he gets up wordlessly and goes to the kitchen.

By the time he comes back with the coffee, I have fought myself some way clear of my wine haze, I have got my mind back on track. Using the courage that only alcohol can bring, I ask something I have wanted to bring up with Moreland ever since I met him. 'Tell me,' I ask, 'what really happened with Harry?'

Moreland is alert. 'I'm sorry . . . ?'

'In the Falklands. Harry seemed to have no friends from those days. There was no one at the memorial service apart from the CO. And you – apart from you.'

He frowns, he contorts his mouth. 'I couldn't say, Ellen. I hardly knew Harry then. We were in different outfits.'

'But there was *something*.' I sense from his manner that I have struck on the truth.

'Ellen,' he says, looking mildly beleaguered. 'These things . . . Who knows? And after all this time – well, does it matter?'

I consider this. I say reasonably, 'I think it does matter, yes. I suppose it's that I'm bound to hear sooner or later. And that I'd rather hear it from you, now.'

He looks unconvinced.

I laugh oddly, hoarsely. 'Oh, don't think there's anything you could say that's going to surprise me! Nothing about Harry could ever surprise me. I don't have any great and unreal illusions about him, you know. No great *idea* of him that's going to take a dreadful knock.' I play this back to myself while I take a long gulp of coffee, and decide it came out a little more harshly than I intended. I add evenly, 'I just want to understand, that's all. I want to understand everything about Harry. It's my way of dealing with -- his death.' And this, I almost tell him, is the absolute truth.

'Maybe there wasn't a reason,' Moreland suggests, fiddling his long fingers. 'Maybe Harry just didn't make any friends.'

I give him a look of disappointment. I shake my head slowly.

Moreland searches my face, he reads my determination. His expression, which has been reluctant, almost obdurate, shifts to one of resignation. He exhales audibly, he shifts in his seat. 'All right,' he begins slowly, 'there *was* something. Just a rumour. The problem with these things, of course, is that you never get to hear the full story. People say things, but you never really know. They might have reasons – old scores to settle, guilt, a need to shift blame, whatever.' He looks away into the fire, his forehead a sudden mass of lines. 'But so far as it's possible to . . . *believe* these things' – he looks back at me – 'it seems Harry's platoon wasn't a very happy one. There could have been all sorts of reasons for that, of course. He could have got landed with more than his fair share of troublemakers. That can happen to anyone – it's happened to me. He could have' – he chooses his words with care – 'lost his grip. One lapse, a time when he didn't make a decision quite quickly enough – something like that. And then if he didn't regain control straight away, the men would have been right on to it. They would resent it. They wouldn't let him forget.' He gives me a quick glance, as if to acknowledge that he hasn't got to the point yet. 'It could be that leadership didn't come naturally to him, that he had to work at it, that he couldn't . . . Anyway, whatever it was . . .' He brings his eyes back to mine, he says in a voice that is suddenly flat, 'The rumour was that Harry's unit didn't advance as fast as it might have, and the men were very unhappy about it.'

The room is very quiet. Only the faint hum of damp wood in the grate.

'I thought one of Harry's men had been injured,' I say, 'that they were delayed by the need to get him to a doctor.'

'Yes. That *was* a problem, so I believe.'

His tone seems to confirm what I already suspect, that an injured man is not a sufficient excuse for lack of action.

'And this rumour,' I ask painfully, 'everyone knew about it, did they?'

'No. Well – in 3 Para, *yes*, I would imagine so. But not outside the regiment. I never heard it outside.'

The famous regimental loyalty, by which they all set such store. 'But *you* heard,' I point out softly.

Moreland's gaze becomes more fixed. 'I had a friend in 3 Para. He told me.'

Not so loyal after all then.

'This . . . failure to advance . . . when was it meant to have happened?'

'During the main push to Port Stanley.'

'About the time you came across Harry's platoon?'

His expression stiffens slightly as if I have touched on a line of questioning he would rather avoid. 'About then,' he agrees hesitantly.

'So you saw how it was?'

'I'm sorry?'

'With the soldiers. The atmosphere. What it was like.'

'Not really. We came across Harry's platoon in the dark. It

184

was hectic. All anyone wanted to do was flake out for a while. We stayed together just a short time. We swapped intelligence, that sort of thing. Then we went on. That was it.'

I want to say: Long enough to get an idea of how things were, though. Instead I ask: 'And you didn't notice anything?'

'We'd been on the move for three days without much sleep,' he says. 'Quite honestly, we weren't in a state to notice anything.'

I sense that this is all I am going to get.

'Thank you,' I say.

Moreland looks thoughtful, as if he still isn't sure he has done the right thing. 'More coffee?'

'I must go.' This comes out a little more brusquely than I intended.

He catches up with me in the hall. 'Wait. I've got something for Josh.'

He opens a door I hadn't noticed before to reveal a room even smaller than the dining-room, which contains a table and chair and a clutter of papers. He doesn't switch on the light but in the brief moment before he re-emerges I see, spread over the table, large plans of some sort and, on the windowsill behind, a folding leather-framed triptych of photographs. The light is faint but I can just make out in two of the frames indistinct groups of people, and in the right-hand frame a woman on her own, a formal head and shoulders with bare neck and long hair.

'Here,' says Moreland, closing the door behind him. He hands me a book. *Fish of the British Isles*.

He reaches ahead to switch on an outside light and follows me towards the car. The evening is cool. A breeze rattles through the shrubs.

'You don't sing any more?' he asks as we tramp across the gravel.

'What? Oh no!'

'Isn't that a pity?'

We stop by the car.

'You wouldn't think so if you heard me.'

He laughs. 'But you must have been good.'

'That's it – past tense. Out of practice. Anyway, to get the right sound, you have to live the life. Wild. Unhealthy.'

He throws back his head and laughs again, and I am rather surprised and pleased that I have the capacity to amuse him.

'Are you all right to drive?' he asks.

'Fine,' I lie.

He kisses me on the cheek. 'Good night, Ellen.'

The wine makes me sleepy on the way home and it takes all my concentration to arrive safely.

On the kitchen table at Pennygate I find a note from Josh. He must have run over from Jill's soon after I left. The note is propped up against a framed black and white photograph of *Minerva* which normally lives on a shelf in the drawing-room.

The note says: *Mum, Give to Richard. Important.*

The photograph shows the yacht bowling along under full sail with a thin strip of coastline in the background.

I stare at it thoughtfully for a while before standing it on the dresser and starting slowly up the stairs.

NINE

Saturday, my second cup of coffee, and I sign the last of the sympathy letters with a small sense of achievement. Something finished, something behind me. *We will miss him very much*. It'll be a relief not to have to write that again. My throat swells each time, my eyes prick with heat.

I have also scribbled cards to all the people, mainly women friends, who left messages earlier in the week, thanking them for their concern, telling them it would be lovely to see them, but not quite yet, not until I have sorted myself out a little more. Perhaps in a few weeks. I send my love.

I wonder what these people are thinking, if any of them has heard about the lost shotgun, if they are talking about it among themselves. I haven't spoken to many people in the last few days – friends have stopped phoning and I don't call back – but the two or three who managed to get past the answering machine didn't mention anything. But then they wouldn't. Or would they? I hover between resignation and a perverse hope. This morning, hope's riding higher, partly because I'm buoyed up by thoughts of seeing Katie for lunch tomorrow, partly because I slept quite well for once; no nightmares until shortly before I woke when, for the first time in weeks, I dreamt about the dory. It was drifting through a fog, somewhere out at sea. It crunched onto a pebble beach, it was too heavy for me to lift. Then the scene shifted subtly and it wasn't me at all but a faceless man who was lifting the boat free of the shingle and pushing it out to sea. Not Harry, though; in the dream Harry was already dead.

I woke troubled but not actually desperate. This is progress.

Carried along by the idea that I am getting somewhere, I take a sheet of paper and start to make a list of things that might raise money. The most obvious is Harry's Mercedes, an expensive model, almost new, which is sitting in the garage. I put this down with a question mark, however: I have the feeling it's owned by Ainswick and not mine to sell. From the transport stable, there is also the dory itself, with sixty horsepower outboard, the jet ski, and the inflatable Zodiac with the small outboard. From the house, the personal computer, the printer; the Jacobean chest in the hall which Harry paid too much for, the mahogany six-leaf dining table with eighteen matching chairs, the massive Victorian bookcase on the top landing: furniture that is too large for any cottage. And while I think of it, the portrait of the prim-faced man in a cavalier hat by an unknown eighteenth-century artist that hangs in the drawing-room, and which I don't think anyone is particularly fond of.

How much will these luxuries fetch in the middle of a recession? Not, I suppose, a great deal.

Void of further ideas, I look out of the window and watch Maurice working on the vegetable beds, pulling up carrots and beating the earth off them. He follows a ragged rhythm, stooping, forking, straightening with a fearful jerk, knocking the vegetables against his boot and tossing them into a basket; a study, you would think, in how to acquire back trouble. I can never look at Maurice without thinking of the inflatable, and the morning when we brought it up muddy from the quay.

Through the open windows I catch the faint scrunch of wheels on the gravel beyond the garden wall. My imagination adds the click of the letter flap, the drop of envelopes onto the mat. I hurry along the passage to the hall and there, belatedly, is the post. Five letters and two circulars. I flick through the postmarks, but there is nothing from Guernsey. I pour myself another coffee before taking this disappointing harvest back to the study.

I slide my credit card statement to one side unopened;

I need time to prepare for that. I pass over a brown envelope from Katie's school – by the look of it, a bill for some extra or another. I stop at an expensive handwritten envelope and extract a letter of condolence from someone I barely remember, an old family friend of Diana's. Optimistic of me to think I had received the last of these letters.

I pick up a flimsy undersized envelope, the sort that is sold cheaply in newsagents and sweet shops. The address is scrappily written in an arbitrary mixture of lettering. My name appears as *Mrs RicHMond*. The envelope contains a slip of folded paper and a newspaper cutting. I recognise the cutting: it's the report of Harry's memorial service from the *Telegraph*. The lower margin has been annotated in the same hand. *So rotten Scum get to be heroEs now!!!*

I stare at this for some moments before slowly unfolding the slim sheet of paper. It says: *What about Joe Congreve! A REAL Hero Betrayed by Scum. Joe's widow got NOTHING. NO fancy service. Britain stinks for Real heroes. But the Right man dEad now.*

I flatten the page out, I read it again, I lay it down, I place the cutting next to it, lining the two up symmetrically on the leather. I feel a leadenness, a sense of suspension. I take the words in, but I resent them too, the way they have intruded on me.

I refold the paper and the cutting and slide them back in the envelope. After a time I take them out once more and read the spidery script again. So Harry is scum. And scum betrayed this Joe Congreve. Thus, Harry betrayed Joe Congreve. I suppose this is what I'm meant to understand anyway.

Everyone has enemies, I tell myself. If you have a profile as high as Harry's you are bound to attract envy. This is probably just a disgruntled soldier, venting some long-harboured resentment.

Yet on a harsher level, I remember Moreland's words and cannot help being sucked into a grimmer vision of Harry's army days. Unpopularity is one thing, betrayal, as this writer well knows, another.

189

Did Harry face this sort of talk at the time? Did it, I wonder, stalk him for years afterwards?

If I am completely honest – and this is painful – part of me wants it to be true, because then it makes everything more understandable, it gives me a peg on which to hang the destructiveness of those last months. And – come on, Ellen, *come on* – if you're going to be *really* honest it assuages your guilt, it lets you some way off the hook.

With this thought, I abandon the desk and the letter and go through the drawing-room into the garden.

I call to Maurice as I approach. His movements jerk to an uneven halt. He greets me with the faint embarrassment with which he greets everyone, probably including his wife. At fifty, Maurice seems to find plants more rewarding than people. With the garden looking as glorious as it does today, I'm tempted to think he's right.

'Some could've done with leavin' a bit,' he says, indicating the carrots. 'Might need a magnifier to find 'em in the pot.' Maurice doesn't entirely approve of my preference for baby vegetables.

I tell him they look just fine. We talk about the potatoes and mangetouts, when they might be ready, what is to be planted for the autumn. The autumn: I don't know why I discuss it so earnestly. I may not be here.

At some stage I will have to talk to Maurice about his future. This would be as good a moment as any but I put it off. I tell myself that I can't take any decisions until Gillespie comes back with whatever financial package he scrapes together, but in truth I simply can't face it, not at the moment.

We wander through the larger of the two glass-houses and talk about the plum crop. The air is hot and close with the overblown scent of ripening fruit.

'Oh, by the way, did the police come and see you?' I ask.

He grunts affirmatively. 'Dinner time.'

'And it went all right?'

'Was like you said. Asked about the keys. And the cabinet. Told 'em I never went near the thing. Never touched the guns. Never knew what was in there.'

190

I spread my palm lightly over a white petunia and press the softness of the petals against my skin. 'I'm sure he must have left it in Scotland, that thing, you know. Margaret and I just can't think where.'

'Sittin' in the boot of someone's car, I shouldn't wonder.'

'Probably.' I smile at him before walking on.

I pause to admire a line of geranium cuttings, set in a row of identical pots. I turn to Maurice with a look of sudden curiosity. 'They didn't come and see you before, did they, the police? While I was away?'

'While—? No.' He thinks about it again. 'No.'

'I just wondered.'

My question has troubled him.

'They had to make inquiries,' I reassure him. 'They always have to, apparently. I just wondered if they'd bothered you, that was all.'

'No.'

'Well . . . good!' I smile again.

We pass through the far door and out into the fresh air.

'Such a magical day,' I gasp, forcing myself to come alive.

Maurice looks around with the air of someone who rarely considers days or anything else in these terms. 'Could do with more rain.'

'Maurice!' I laugh. 'Anyway, we've just had some!'

'Not enough.'

I'm still shaking my head when I see Charles's lanky figure strolling across from the house. He raises an arm in a loose-limbed wave. We meet on the lawn.

'You look better!' he exclaims when we have kissed cheeks. 'Gosh, you look better!'

'Do I? Well, yes, I'm all right, I suppose. In fact – yes!'

He blinks at me good-naturedly. 'And Josh?'

'Off on a fishing expedition. So the answer's – fine.'

I tuck my arm into his and we stroll towards the terrace.

'How's it going?' I ask. 'The dreaded candidature and everything?'

'Ah . . . quite *well*.'

191

His confidence rather surprises me. 'You've got some support then?'

'Can't be sure, naturally. Can't expect rock-solid promises. But I've met quite a lot of the committee now. And I've had a few indications.' He smiles the smile of a schoolboy who's been tipped the wink about a place in the rugby team.

'Oh.'

'You don't sound too pleased,' he says in a tone of mock offence.

'I just—' I stop and face him. 'I never thought this was your sort of thing.' I laugh. 'I thought you were *happy*.'

It's his turn to look surprised. 'I was. I am. But I don't think that's a bar to getting into Parliament.'

'But all that backbiting? All that jockeying for position?'

Ignoring this, he says solemnly, 'I may be wrong, but I like to think I'd do rather a good job. As good as the next man, at any rate. Sorry – *person!* Lord, must get that right, mustn't I!' He chuckles mischievously before rearranging his face into a suitably serious expression. 'I'd certainly work jolly hard at it, I can tell you. Harder than most.'

'I'm sure you would. I know you would. But those ghastly hours,' I remind him. 'All those late sittings. Weekend surgeries. It never stops.' Saying this, it occurs to me that for Charles, living faithfully within a childless marriage, coping with Anne's permanent state of agitated discontent, the long hours may well be a blessing.

'Oh, I wouldn't mind any of that,' he says firmly, and alongside his characteristic twinkle there's a glint of determination that I haven't noticed before.

We walk on. 'Actually, I was wondering if you'd be interested in coming along to a small do,' he says breezily. 'I realise it'll probably be an awful bore for you. Not something you'd normally leap at.' He gives a bark of a laugh. 'But – well, I'd be absolutely thrilled if you could come.'

I dust off a wrought iron chair and sit down quickly. 'You mean, the committee get-together on Monday?'

'Yes! You know about it? You're going? Has Barrow already invited you?'

'Not Barrow – Jack.'

His face goes blank. He shapes his mouth into an 'Oh.'

'I said I'd go. But only if we all went together,' I explain carefully. 'So as not to step on anyone's toes.'

'Together?' He reaches for a chair and lowers himself onto it with care.

'You and me and Jack. And Anne, of course.'

'I see.' Tugging at the knees of his trousers, he sits slowly back in his seat and peers uncertainly at me. 'I see . . .' Then a crooked, rather diffident smile spreads across his face and he shakes his head in admiration. 'You are a clever old thing.'

I make a doubtful face.

'But you're absolutely right!' he declares, brimming with sudden cheer, as if the idea were so brilliant he'd have been proud to think of it himself. 'Best to be non-partisan. Absolutely right.'

It is typical of Charles to take a set-back so graciously. He really isn't suited to politics at all.

'Anne won't mind?' I ask, harbouring the certainty that she will.

'I'll explain it to her.'

I must look less than convinced about this because he reaches across and touches my wrist briefly. 'Dear Ellen. Don't worry.'

He looks away, he acquires a preoccupied expression, he launches himself into his next subject.

'Went to the coastguard again.' He folds his arms, he crosses his legs. 'I did tell you, didn't I?' He unfolds his arms again and links his hands across the front of his ancient jacket. 'Now the upshot is . . . Look, I don't want to give you any false hopes.' He frowns by way of emphasis. 'I wouldn't like you to think that the chances of finding the boat have dramatically *improved* or anything. But well, some new thoughts have come up which do seem worth investigating.'

Beyond the lawn the corn shimmers, the river is freckled with metallic light. 'The Gunfleet Sand thing, you mean? Harry having gone off track a bit?'

'Oh no. That is, we haven't ruled that out. We're still

193

keeping an eye in that direction. Most *definitely*. But no – this is something rather new. Something which could swing the search in a completely different direction. It was Moreland who got onto it, tracked down people who'd seen the boat, worked it all out. I must say, he's absolutely first rate, that chap. Really knows his stuff—'

'*Moreland*?' I say, pushing lightness into my voice.

Charles looks abashed. 'Oh, didn't you—? Didn't I—? I . . . er, meant to say . . . But listen,' he says in the tone of someone who's about to explain everything, 'he's been a tremendous help. Done a tremendous amount of work. Really first class.'

'But why?' I protest.

'You didn't know—? Ah, but Moreland's an expert. He was in the Special Forces, one of their top chaps.' His voice beats with a sentimental pride. 'Knows all about small boats and tides and that sort of thing. These chaps get popped out of submerged submarines off the coast of Norway in midwinter, you know. Have to get ashore and survive. Jolly tough stuff. Not a lot they don't know about these things.'

I look away, suppressing a sense of resentment that contains more than a touch of fear. 'Moreland went with you on Wednesday?' I ask with perfect calm. 'To see the coastguard?'

'Oh yes. That was the whole point, you see. To go over his ideas with them. I must say, the coastguard were pretty impressed. Couldn't argue with it.'

Indignation rubs at me. I have been excluded, I have been, if not lied to, then told less than the truth, like a sheltered child for whom the adults believe they know best. I stand up, I stride to the edge of the terrace, I try to regain some sense of proportion. 'And what is this new idea of Moreland's?' I ask.

'Ah . . .' Charles's voice takes on an eager note. 'Basically, Moreland's discovered that those sightings weren't much good. Those people – the chap on the shore, the crew of the coaster – probably saw quite a different yacht. In fact, almost certainly did. And Moreland worked it out that, allowing for everything – the tides, the weather and so on – the yacht would most likely have ended up somewhere quite *different* from where we thought. Somewhere off to the north. No, what am I saying? The north-east. Yes, north-*east*. Which changes things considerably, of course. It means we could have been concentrating on the wrong area.'

The sun is very high now. Beyond the thin spread of the distant marshes, the sea has crept out of the haze, a soft grey line that makes a border for the long drop of the sky.

'Of course it's just speculation,' Charles says to fill the silence. 'But I must say, it seems to make sense. Worth looking into, anyway.' I hear the slap of his hands on his knees, the scrape of his chair. A bony hand grips my shoulder. 'But don't hold too many hopes, old girl, will you?'

I shake my head slowly. I manage a feeble smile. 'Bless you, no.'

I sit on the quay watching the dinghy snake slowly round the bend and set a steady course upriver. From head-on the craft looks flimsy, like a shell. The effect is accentuated by the smooth arch of water pushed up by the bow which further reduces the hull until the two passengers appear to be sitting in nothing more substantial than a glass bowl.

The smaller figure waves tentatively, then, as I get to my feet and wave back, with more certainty.

The boat, a battered off-white fibreglass dinghy, seems to speed up as it approaches. The gentle throb of the outboard grows to a steady putter then dies back abruptly as Moreland turns the boat towards the shore. The tide is low, the quay high and dry, and he guides the boat in to the crumbling stone ramp of the slipway, whose lower portion has long been buried under a thick layer of silt.

The boat scrunches to a halt and Josh, who has been poised in the bow, leaps out into mud that is ankle deep. I dimly notice that he's wearing his best trainers.

Moreland secures the outboard and calls a cheerful greeting. My muted reply causes him to look up. Catching my expression, he gives me a questioning glance.

Josh is busy hoisting his gear out of the boat in a manner that is affectedly grown-up, all studious nonchalance and self-awareness. I know I shouldn't bring the subject up in front of

195

Josh, I know I should wait, but I can't stop myself saying crisply to Moreland, 'Charles tells me you've been helping out.'

Moreland's eyes register something like regret. He drops his gaze for a moment. 'I didn't think it was worth bothering you.' He makes a movement of his hands, a shrug or something more dismissive.

'Bother? I wouldn't have called it *bother*,' I say, giving a strange half-laugh to offset the tartness of my voice.

'No,' he agrees quickly. 'No.'

We are distracted by Josh, who has squelched clear of the mud and is waiting silently for instructions.

'Ben's mother'll be here in half an hour,' I remind him.

He flops theatrically, he blows out his lips, he gives me a heavy look that says he doesn't want to go out to lunch.

'She's going to take you swimming later.'

He puckers his mouth into an expression of disgust then, glancing at Moreland, rearranges his face into something more reasonable.

I tell him to go up to the house and have a shower, that I'll follow shortly.

He shuffles his mud-caked feet, he casts me a last protesting glance before accepting defeat. He beams a sunny farewell to Moreland, a positive blast of enchantment. He doesn't look at me as he turns to trudge up the path.

Moreland climbs out and, planting his bare feet squarely in the mud, hauls the boat further up the slip. 'I really didn't think it was worth bothering you until something came of it,' he says as soon as Josh is out of earshot.

'But on Wednesday – you could have told me. Why didn't you tell me then? And all this tracking people down, finding the crew of that coaster – I mean, that's not just *anything*! That's . . .' I clamp my arms together, I shake my head.

He climbs up onto the quay and comes towards me. 'No one had talked to these people properly, Ellen. Certainly not the police. No one had been through any of the basics like showing them a picture of the boat. Or asking them which direction the yacht was travelling in.'

I am stubbornly silent.

'Perhaps I should have mentioned it. I'm sorry. But—'

'You didn't want to raise my hopes?' I chant childishly.

He glances away, as if to reduce our mutual embarrassment at this show of peevishness. 'I wanted to wait and see if anything came of it,' he repeats.

'But something *did* come of it!'

'What?' He's filled with quiet alarm. 'Where did you get that idea? Nothing's been found yet. That's the whole point.'

'I meant . . .' But I can't explain. I can't tell him that the news caught me off-balance, that in one lurch it rekindled all my sharpest anxieties. Yet if I'm going to be impatient with anyone, it should, I realise dully, be myself, for having thought that the uncertainty was fading.

Moreland says, 'I never intended to hide anything from you, Ellen.' His gaze is steady and open, the look of an honourable man brought up to behave honourably. How must it be, I wonder momentarily, never to have done anything you were ashamed of?

'Maybe not.' My indignation begins to seem pointless and self-defeating. I say in the tone of a peace offering. 'No . . . But in future I'd appreciate being kept in the picture.'

'In that case, come back to the cottage now. I'll take you through it all.'

'Now . . . ?' I glance downriver, already knowing that I'll go.

'It'd be hard to explain without the charts. I've got all the charts.'

'I've got to see Josh off to lunch.'

'I'll wait.'

We float out into the stream. I sit on the wooden seat spanning the centre of the boat and trail my feet over the side to wash the mud away. Moreland, sitting in the back, pivots the outboard down into the water and fires the motor with a single pull of the cord. I swing my feet inboard and sit with my back to Moreland, looking ahead.

I had forgotten how much movement there is in the water, how it swirls and ripples, how the wavelets, so insignificant

197

from the shore, slap insistently against the hull. We pass close to *Minerva*'s mooring, an orange plastic buoy with an integral handhold. The current drags at it, pulling it drunkenly over, trailing a small wake behind. The current is strong here, but not so strong as farther downstream. At the river mouth it can draw small craft onto the sand-bars, so they say, and in an easterly wind, when the sea gets rough, a boat can get pounded to death. People hereabouts enjoy telling these stories and Harry used to enjoy listening to them: they added to his craving for excitement. But they made me uncomfortable. My mind would paint the picture too clearly: the deep roar of the surf, the tug of the current, the boat grounding with a heart-stopping crash.

Moreland keeps to the side of the river, out of the stream. Raising his voice above the noise of the engine, he says, 'I talked to Josh.'

I had forgotten about the boarding school discussion. I twist round. 'What did he say?'

'I think he's hankering after the active life. Sport. Other kids. That sort of thing.'

I glance away. Sport. Other kids. The sort of answer a boy would give if he didn't want to admit to what was really bothering him.

'Nothing else?'

It's a moment before he says cautiously, 'I get the feeling he's a bit torn, Ellen. The one thing that really worries him is the thought of leaving home.'

This worries him? I'm not sure I believe it. It seems to me that the one thing which is driving Josh is his determination to leave home – or perhaps, if I can bear to face the thought, it isn't so much home that he wants to leave as me.

With a stab of self-pity, I ask, 'Basically he was keen, though, was he?'

'Well . . . interested, certainly.'

I turn slowly back to face the on-coming river. I let my self-pity roll forward unchecked. I tell myself that I must do what is best for Josh, that I must let him go, that in the long run he will love me the more for it, but these thoughts, necessary and realistic as they are, don't minimise the hurt, or lessen my dread of the loneliness to come.

The boat rocks slightly, and Moreland's hand drops onto my arm and pats it. The sympathy is like a shock.

'I'm all right,' I sing without looking around.

He withdraws his hand.

'I'm all right,' I repeat. I turn my head until he can see from my expression that this is true.

Attempting to lighten the mood, Moreland declares in a tone of mock disapproval, 'They get terribly spoilt, these kids, you know. Hot showers and heated dormitories, for heaven's sake. And videos at the weekends, and out as often as they like.' Still in character, he sighs, 'No hardship at all.'

'You're trying to convert me,' I accuse mildly.

'No,' he says, dropping back into his normal voice. 'I wouldn't do that.'

Approaching the village, the river becomes quite crowded. Boats are clustered around the moorings and pontoons. People sit on yachts with their arms looped over the guardrails, clasping drinks and talking raucously. Sunbathers lie spread-eagled on the decks or propped awkwardly against open hatches. Children in bright life-jackets row inflatables and sail tub-shaped dinghies with stubby masts to the bellowed instructions of exasperated fathers. Everything is colour and activity. The winter, with its emptiness and echoing secretiveness, seems a world away.

Moreland keeps us out of the main channel, between the outer line of moorings and the loop of marshes and shallows formed by the hook of the river. The first I see of the sailing dinghy is the flash of its rainbow sail as it surges out from behind a moored yacht and heads across our path, on collision course. I look anxiously towards Moreland to see that he's already spotted the boat and is swinging the arm of the outboard across to steer us clear. Looking again I see the face of the dinghy's occupant bob down under the all-concealing sail, the face of a boy no older than Josh. His eyes lock onto us in sudden fear, for a moment he seems immobilised by the sight of us. He vanishes behind the sail again, the bow of his boat starts to turn, as if to pass behind us. But the turn stalls, the dinghy heads straight for us again. Moreland makes an exclamation, the note of the outboard rises to a roar, our boat twists away to the left, we will just pass clear. But the sailing dinghy is in trouble. Already well heeled over, it tips still further, its mast and bulging sail tracing a seemingly inexorable downward arc towards the water. Moreland shouts above the roar and clamour, 'Let the mainsheet go! Let the sheet go!'

The boy, visible now above the sail of the slowly capsizing boat, arches his back, trying to brace himself against the violent tipping of the dinghy. Then, just as it seems that nothing can save him from a dunking, he lets something go – it must be a rope – and the sail shoots out, the mast jerks upright, and with a thunderous flapping and rattling, the dinghy falls unconcernedly back onto an even keel.

'All right?' Moreland calls, but the boy is too dazed to answer. His dinghy, now safely behind us, drifts slowly on, the sails snatching and beating at their spars.

Seeing where he is headed, I cry, 'Mind out! It's shallow there!'

The boy glances back uncertainly, then ahead to where the water, deceptive as ever, looks mild and deep.

'It's very shallow!' I call again.

At last the boy pulls the tiller over and executes a slow disorganised turn, grabbing at a trailing rope and pulling it in as he does so.

While Moreland manœuvres us across the stream towards the landing place I keep an eye on the boy as he navigates his way gingerly through the moorings. When he glances in my direction I wave, but he doesn't wave back.

I become aware of Moreland watching me. 'Well done,' he says.

'But I didn't do anything.'

'You kept him off the mud.'

I look ahead. A sunburst of inflatables and tenders blossoms out from each of the two ladders let into the side of the quay. Like an ice-breaker we have to force a passage through a complaining raft of bumping obstacles to reach the wall. When the dinghy's nose finally touches, I reach for the ladder and, taking the rope – the painter, Harry taught me to call it – I climb the rusting rungs to the top. While Moreland ships the outboard I make the rope fast to a ring.

Clambering up behind me, Moreland follows the painter to the ring and eyes the knot I have used, an unmistakable inspection procedure that I appear to pass.

We start along the road. 'You've done that before,' he says.

'Self-defence.' I add, 'I wanted to be useful at something,' which isn't much of an explanation either.

It was after one of my unhappier experiences on *Minerva* that I got a boatman to teach me the two knots that form my entire repertoire. Harry had lured me out with promises of fine weather and a short trip – 'just to the river mouth'; in the event a journey that took us well out to sea – and a plea to help him entertain his guests, three businessmen who drank a great deal of beer and told schoolboy jokes. Harry, who had a propensity for living out whatever role was demanded of him, became the complete skipper to my uncertain crew, all skill and expertise to my ineptitude. He rattled off orders and, when I foundered, slid his guests a pitying glance and took over the task with a small sigh of forbearance.

I did not love Harry at these times.

Then one of my knots jammed into an unsalvageable tangle and Harry flew at me in full hearing of the guests, his eyes bulging with an irritation that he tried to conceal behind a laugh. Our relationship – it still had life in it then – survived the incident because I knew that he was under strain, and that being on the boat often affected him this way. There was something about *Minerva* that brought out the perfectionist in Harry. When things didn't go smoothly, when the smallest item was left out of place, it was almost more than he could bear.

Moreland and I pass the boatyard sheds and come abreast of the boat storage area. At this time of year the area would normally be empty of the long rows of yachts which in winter look like so many beached whales, but this year the long recession has left a sorry tide of vessels for sale or in moth-balls, their hulls draped in faded canopies that droop low over grime-streaked paintwork. Amid the keelboats riding high on their splayed skirts of timber props, a small craft crouches squat on the ground, a white work-boat under a blue canvas cover that has retained a pristine brightness. I see the boat, but recognition takes a moment longer.

The dory.

I lose momentum, I come to a slow halt, I take in the fact that the hull is white and polished, that all signs of the boat's last voyage have been expunged, that it looks nothing like it did when I last saw it.

'The yard have fixed it up,' Moreland comments, following my gaze.

We move on. 'Fixed it up?'

'There was a bit of damage.'

I take a moment. 'What sort of damage?'

'To one side. A long scrape. And a bash or two.'

'Oh.' My mind races all over the place, I falter again, I look back. I try to work out when and how this might have happened. 'From a collision?' I ask. 'From ...' From the ship that sunk *Minerva*, I mean to say.

'Possibly,' says Moreland, but his voice is full of doubt. 'Whatever bashed it certainly left some paint behind. But it's just as likely to have come from the trawler that salvaged it, I'm afraid, attempting to come alongside in a sea. I tried to go and see the trawler, to check her paint, but she'd gone round to the West Coast of Scotland. I spoke to her owners though, and they told me her hull is black. Which is the colour they found on the dory.'

Such thoroughness. To pursue things until they can be explained. To follow each fact through to the end and leave nothing unresolved. It is almost ... *relentless* springs to mind, but that would be the wrong word for Moreland. With him I think it's more a matter of pride, a professional imperative. Also, perhaps, a misguided sense of duty.

'Well done.' Saying this, my heart beats dully at the thought of what discoveries are still to come.

*

'The dory couldn't be lifted,' says Moreland in the absorbed tone of someone going over well-trodden ground. 'It couldn't be stowed on deck. It had to be towed . . . Now the chap here at Waldringfield' – he taps the large-scale map spread over the desk in front of us – 'the one who says he saw a yacht going downriver at about five that Friday evening, now *he* doesn't remember seeing a dory or any sort of dinghy being towed behind. If it *was Minerva* it seems incredible that he didn't notice it. The dory is fourteen foot long to *Minerva*'s thirty-five – large by any standards.' His voice almost fades away. 'And hard to tow . . .' Suppressing this thought with a lift of his eyebrows and a contortion of his mouth, he slides the map onto the floor, and, almost tipping out of his chair, reaches for another from a large stack at the side of the desk.

I take this moment to glance up at the folding picture frame on the windowsill, to take another look at the woman in the photograph. The contrast of the black and white print is very strong, bleaching out everything except the perfect oval of the face, the large confident eyes, the sweep of the dark hair, the indolent mouth with its half-smile. A vivid passionate face; someone with an appetite for life.

While Moreland unfolds the new map I pass quickly over the other two pictures, one a snap of a family in a garden – a laughing couple with two wriggling children – the other a posed studio shot taken many decades ago, in the forties or early fifties, showing a good-looking man and a pretty woman in a rakish hat.

Moreland looks up and I bring my attention down to the map, which is in fact a nautical chart, rather like the one in the passage at Pennygate, but covering a larger area and printed with bright colours – the land a rather violent yellow, the sea partly white and partly blue, with insets of green, and covered with a scattering of numbers. Most of these blue and green areas abut the yellow shore, but many more float out in wide tentacles across the sea: the shoals. These tongues of colour have titles like Kentish Knock, North Falls, Gunfleet Sand, Sunk Sank.

'Such names,' I murmur.

But words are insubstantial beings to Moreland and he murmurs vaguely, 'Colourful.'

He points to the top of the chart, to a river, our river. 'Got your bearings?' he asks.

I nod. From the river the land slopes down and away to the left until, drawn into the gaping mouth of the Thames Estuary, it disappears off the edge of the chart. Directly below is the wide expanse of the estuary itself, a mass of shoals which ripple out from the river's throat like blue flames from a cold dragon. And along the bottom, forming a firm lower jaw, the north Kent coast.

Regaining his impetus, Moreland draws a line with his finger from the mouth of our river downwards across the estuary. 'Now the direct course, wind and tide permitting, takes a boat this way. A small leg round the Cork Sand, then straight down, leaving the Gunfleet Sand and the Little Sunk to starboard. Then as you come into the Black Deep' – he taps a passage that leads between the shoals – 'you have to decide exactly where you're going to cross the Long Sand.' His finger hovers over a long wedge of blue that is overlaid with slivers of green. 'The green bits are the really shallow bits. To be avoided. There are two crossing points you can use in calmish weather, both of which avoid a major detour. The one here is pretty direct.' He draws a path across the blue of the shoal. 'And safe enough, though it looks a bit frightening on the chart, doesn't it? In fact, assuming it was about 21.30, there'd have been a good nine feet at the shallowest point, and the tide still making. You'd have to be very unlucky to hit a bump. *Minerva* drew six feet. She'd have been okay. Plenty of yachts use this route. People with local knowledge. *But . . .*' Engrossed now, locked into his intellectual puzzle, he splays his fingers over the area. 'It was dark and the visibility wasn't that good. You'd have to be pretty sure of your navigation, you'd have to have worked out your tides carefully, you'd have to be absolutely confident of your position.' He doesn't say what happens if you get these calculations wrong but the green patches, which rise out of the blue shoal like bubbles, lurk clearly on either side.

'The other crossing point *here*' – his finger floats a short way along the Black Deep and draws south across the blue shoal again – 'is much deeper, but it also requires a good fix – a confident position – because you don't want to go too near this shallow here.' He prods at a green lozenge close by. 'Now with Decca neither of these routes would be a problem, even at night in poor visibility. The accuracy of the system is such that even if you hadn't bothered to track the tidal flow too accurately, you could soon see how far you were getting pushed off course and compensate accordingly. However . . .' He pushes his lips out, he frowns in thought, he fixes me briefly with his wise eyes. 'It would be a bit nerve-wracking singlehanded, and that's putting it mildly. Having to bob down to the chart to fix your position – reading the Decca, plotting it; it's quick but not *that* quick. Having to listen out for ships, having to peer through the murk for buoys and lights, having to lay off your course. Well . . .' He makes a gesture that suggests it wouldn't be something he'd undertake lightly. 'Now if you wanted to be absolutely safe, or the nav aids had broken down and you were left with nothing but guess-work and God, or the fog was really rolling in and you'd lost your nerve for shoal-hopping, *then* . . . . Well, you could go outside everything.' His hand follows a loop to the east, across a white sea devoid of blue. 'It's a bit of a detour, of course. But if you were being cautious . . .'

The idea of Harry being cautious hangs improbably in the air. Preoccupied with this or some other thought, Moreland looks across at me in an unfocused way. Then his gaze sharpens, his eyes soften, he smiles briefly before turning back.

'Now this is where the coaster made its sighting.' He lays his finger on a point in the Black Deep. 'At 23.20 hours on the Friday night. As you see, it was just to the west of the second crossing point – not too promising on the face of it. According to the captain – and he seemed fairly reliable – the yacht was heading *east*, which again wouldn't seem too promising. But if the yacht hadn't allowed enough for the south-going tide, which was pretty strong by that time, and was trying to claw her way across-tide to get back into the right position for a dash across the shoal, then it's still perfectly possible, do you see?'

I get the general idea. I give a slow nod.

'But what makes me think it wasn't *Minerva* is something else the captain said.' He sits back in his seat. His long fingers fiddle with a pencil, rotating it slowly back and forth. 'The reason the coaster noticed the yacht was that it nearly collided with her. The captain wopped on his searchlight and shone it straight at her – normal practice. Now in the blur and the confusion the captain didn't notice much – he was probably too busy swearing and cursing – but one thing he was pretty sure about was the absence of any dinghy. Nothing being towed behind. Again, it would have been extraordinary if he'd missed that dory.' He adds quickly, 'Though that doesn't necessarily mean a great deal. It's possible the dory had already broken adrift by that time. It could have broken adrift soon after *Minerva* left the river . . .' He gives me a moment to absorb this, watching me carefully, like a professor taking a student through a long and difficult exercise.

'Now what the captain *did* notice,' he begins again, 'was that both the yacht's sails had numbers on them, and that the sails looked patchy. That's what he called them – patchy. I can only think the sails were racing sails, made of Kevlar, or partly of Kevlar, which is a darkish brown fabric used in ugly great squares on racing sails and looks – well, patchy. Now . . .' His hands are still. 'The lads at the yard here tell me *Minerva* did *not* have numbers on both sails – only the mainsail. And that all the sails were made of standard Terylene, brilliant white. No Kevlar. And no patches.' He rotates his hand; his pencil describes a slow arc. 'Of course, the captain might have been mistaken . . .'

'But you don't think so?'

He shrugs, but I can see he doesn't think so.

A moment of silence passes between us. Warm air wafts in from the window.

Moreland asks with sudden concern, 'Would you like anything? A cold drink? Tea?' He moves as if to get up.

'Thanks, but no.'

'Sure?'

I nod quickly. I look back at the chart. I manage: 'So you think it wasn't *Minerva* they saw?'

He turns his head to catch my words. I realise I have been whispering. 'I'm sorry?' he says.

I repeat it a little louder.

'I think it's unlikely. Also . . . if *Minerva* had been lost in the estuary somewhere, if she'd bumped onto a shoal or been run down by a ship along this route then she'd probably have been found by now. It's mainly shallow water, you see. It's very busy water. Chances are' – he chooses his words – 'something would have trawled into the wreck by this time, or caught a blip on its depth sounder.' He is ticking off the arguments, one by one. 'The only place a wreck might be missed is the Black Deep, I suppose, or the King's Channel, where the water's much deeper. But that's just where the coastguard have been asking people to look, for that very reason.'

I stare unseeing at the chart, trying to picture the Black Deep. I see swirling water and racing tides and ships suddenly bearing down out of the fog.

'And what about here?' I ask, indicating the wide expanse of sea to the east, the route of caution.

'Yes,' he concedes immediately, 'that'd be different. A wreck would be far less likely to be found there.' But from the way he says this, I gather he doesn't think Harry went that way.

'Charles said' – I make an effort to bring my voice up to volume – 'that you'd found something new?' I look up at him.

He pulls in his mouth, he sits forward, he gestures uncertainty, as if to dampen any hopes I might be harbouring. 'Well, I wouldn't say *found* exactly. It was more of an idea, really . . . a theory.'

I wait expectantly.

'It seemed to me . . .' Breaking off, he roots around under the chart and pulls out a sheaf of papers and looks at them thoughtfully. 'I took a good look at the weather. I got all the weather reports. Local, national. I asked people who were around the river that Friday. Then I put myself in Harry's place.' He opens one hand, he pauses, finally he says, 'And I decided that unless I was hell-bent on having a miserable time I would never have left that night.'

His words seem to fade out, like a radio that has gone off tune, and it's a moment before I pick them up again.

'. . . There was a gale blowing right through Thursday night into Friday morning.' He leafs through his papers until he finds the one he's after. 'Then all that heavy rain. *Then* drizzle. *Then* mist and fog.' With each point he taps the back of his fingers against the paper. 'And on the Friday night there would still have been a large sea running.' He shakes his head. 'One way and another, I'd have been tempted to stay firmly on the mooring and turn in early with a stiff whisky.' He shuffles the paper to the back and refers to the next sheet. 'Now conditions were *much* better the next morning. Only a thin coastal mist which burnt off as the sun came up. A light northerly breeze, force two to three. Almost perfect. Although if you were being fussy, a bit more wind might have been nice. But . . .' He throws up a hand that says this would have been too much to ask. Reaching down to retrieve the first map from the floor, he spreads it out again. He points to the river mouth. 'Now on Saturday morning, at about six, a yacht was seen going through the narrows here. She was white-hulled. She had a single mast. She was about the right size. *And*' – he says with slow emphasis – 'she was towing a white dinghy. Flattish, like a dory.'

He glances my way, he looks back at the map; he is giving me time. 'It was a rambler who saw it,' he murmurs conversationally. 'He'd parked his car on the north side there. Starting off on a walk. Doesn't know much about boats, but knows what he saw. And it's narrow there, boats pass close to the shore. He'd have seen clearly, even with a mist about.'

Shaping his hands into a cathedral, he rasps the tips of his forefingers over his chin. He waits, but I have nothing to say, no questions to ask, and presently, after a glance in my direction, he picks up the thread again. 'The only thing about the timing of this is the tide. At six it—'

'So early?' My interruption comes from nowhere. I hardly

know why I've made it. For a moment I am confused by my own train of thought. 'To get there, he'd have had to start...' I shrug. 'At five? Wouldn't it have been dark? I thought it was dark...'

He makes a show of consulting his notes, although I sense that he already has the answer. 'Sunrise was a quarter to six. So...' He narrows his eyes in calculation. 'It would have been twilight from five or thereabouts. Time to leave the mooring and get down to the river mouth. The journey would've taken an hour, more or less, so...'

Nothing unexplained; nothing left out.

Gathering himself again, Moreland goes back to the chart. 'At 06.00, when this yacht was leaving the river, the tide was still running north-east. At up to two knots. If it was *Minerva*, then she would have made slow headway against it, even with the engine running. Now if something disabled her fairly soon – let's say almost immediately – then this tide would have swept her backwards' – he sweeps a hand up the chart – 'and she'd have ended up *north-east* of the river mouth, not to the south at all.' He pauses, he sucks in his lips. 'You see what I mean?'

Something bothers me, but I can't quite put my finger on it. 'When you say disabled...?'

'By whatever it was. Fire. Explosion. Collision.'

The thought comes at last. 'You mean ... the boat might not have sunk straight away?'

'It's *possible* she went straight down ... A collision with a large vessel, something cataclysmic. But if it was something less severe, a fire, a collision with some floating junk – and there's enough of that about – then she could have drifted for quite a distance.'

'But if there was time ... why didn't Harry call for help?'

Moreland accepts the point with a solemn nod. 'Well, the electrics might have blown, the radio might have been damaged... If anything can go wrong at sea, it generally does.'

Through the silence a child's laughter floats in from the lane outside. A car labours up the hill nearby.

'Of course it's just a theory,' Moreland repeats.

I am worlds away, beyond the open window. 'Why didn't he get into the dory then? Why didn't he escape?'

When Moreland doesn't reply, I turn questioningly, but his expression is an answer in itself. Who can know? he is saying. How can any of us know?

'The place where the trawler found the dory on Sunday,' he says, returning slowly to the sea chart, 'seems to fit in with the timing. Matches the flow of the tides, assuming the dory went adrift early that Saturday morning.'

I see the dory floating, empty and aimless.

'The only thing that doesn't *quite* fit—' He pulls away from the chart with a frown, the logician denied the last piece of his puzzle. 'And I was hoping I could check this with you – was the colour of Harry's waterproofs. The rambler said the person in the yacht was wearing a white or mainly white jacket.'

I see the jacket clearly. It's white with a navy band around the bottom and a green collar, made by a popular manufacturer two or three seasons ago.

I take my time. 'He was wearing orange,' I reply. This image is also strong, of Harry motoring away from the quay in the downpour that Friday lunchtime, his bright orange jacket fading slowly into the gloom.

'The rambler could've got it wrong...'

'Harry had several other waterproofs,' I say. 'At least three sets. He was always losing them, buying new ones.'

Moreland's interest has sharpened again. 'He kept some on the boat?'

'Yes.'

'White maybe?'

'Maybe. I'm not sure.'

But it's enough for Moreland. His eyes reflect the satisfaction of a loose end that promises to be tied up.

I lean over the desk. I try to translate Moreland's theory onto the chart. I take in the expanse of water to the right of the river mouth. Apart from one or two slivers of blue, it is plain unending white. Deep water. Miles and miles of it.

'Will they try to search it?' I ask.

He gives a slow shake of his head. 'Too large an area. No real reference to start from. No, if anything turns up, it'll be chance as much as anything else. A fishing boat, something like that.'

I digest this silently, I sit back. 'Then . . .'

His eyes are on me all the time, kind but also suitably detached for the business in hand, an officer's look. 'Not something to count on, I'm afraid. In fact – best not to hope.'

'Actually I—' A small warning bell sounds and I pause, trying to assess how this will sound, how it will be interpreted. 'I *wasn't* hoping,' I say at last, needing to voice at least some of my reservations. 'I've never been hoping. Everyone's assumed . . .' I stare at the chart, I pick at the edge of it. 'You see,' I admit finally, 'I'd be much happier if the boat wasn't found.'

Moreland looks away then back, his face taking on an expression of sudden understanding. 'It'll be painful, I do realise.'

'It's not that so much . . . I just think it'd be better if Harry's body was left where it is. Undisturbed. I think it would be quite – wrong – to go looking for it now. I think he should be left in peace. I'd hate it if . . . Well, I'd just hate it.'

Moreland gropes for a sympathetic approach. 'I appreciate what you're saying. But from a practical point of view, Ellen, if the boat was located, it would make an enormous difference to you. Legally, I mean.'

'But if they find the boat they'll find . . .' I can't say it.

'Ellen . . .' He leans forward, his hand hovers close to mine. 'It's unlikely Harry's body will be there.'

I stare into his face. 'What do you mean?'

'Well,' he says gravely, 'if it wasn't swept away at the time, it probably would have been soon after.'

'Why?' I hear myself asking this as if I were some distance away.

'Because it usually happens that way, Ellen.'

'Why?'

'The currents. The movement of the water.' He is trying to spare me the grim details which my imagination furnishes all too easily – the body bloating, rising, the fish, the processes of the sea.

211

'I see!' I say tightly. 'I see!' I stand up abruptly.

Moreland rises, looking unhappy. 'I really don't think you need to worry.'

I go to the door. Aware that I'm sounding unreasonable, I half turn and say in a brittle voice, 'Well, I hope you're right!'

Before he can say anything, I gesture back towards the photographs. 'Your family?'

Moreland follows my gaze. 'What? Oh, yes. And friends. And godchildren.'

'Beautiful,' I say, meaning the woman.

He throws me an odd look, laden with messages I cannot read. He glances back. 'My wife,' he says in a flat voice. 'She's in New York at the moment. Her work.'

New York and work fit the face somehow.

Letting the tension go, managing a smile, I ask if he can drive me straight home. 'I've got an awful lot to do.'

'Of course.' Scooping up his car keys, he leads the way out. Meeting the weekend traffic, we talk about the pressures of tourism and the chances of keeping the river unspoilt most of the way home.

Alone in the kitchen, I sit at the table with a full mug of tea, trying to apply some logic to my thoughts. Only when I have drained the last of the tea do I get up and go across the hall to the boot room. The sailing jackets and trousers hang in colourful bundles from the hooks nearest the window. An old jacket of Harry's in a stiff yellow plastic-coated fabric sticks an arm out into the room like an absent traffic policeman. On the next peg the children's matching waterproofs, in brilliant red, hang neatly above their boots.

On the last peg the white sleeve of my sailing jacket peeks out from under a lightweight anorak which has been draped untidily over the top. Dangling beneath are my sailing trousers in a dark blue which exactly matches the band of blue around the bottom of the jacket.

I extricate the jacket and carry it back to the kitchen and lay it out on the table. I stare at it, the distinctive whiteness, the bright green collar, the blue band around the bottom, and I fold it shop-style, sides in, arms across the back, into half and then half again, until it makes a neat rectangle. I slide it into a plastic rubbish bag and fold the plastic tightly round and seal it with tape. I push the bundle into the kitchen bin, in among the general refuse, then, gathering the top of the liner together, close it with a tier and pull it out of the bin and, carrying it outside, place it in one of the metal bins by the garages, ready for the refuse collector on Wednesday.

TEN

A gale is blustering off the sea. Not an ideal time for a walk on the heath. The wind is so strong that the children and I have to lean into it, plodding heads down, like characters from an illustration in a Dickens story. But I'm glad we came. Sunday walks over the heath were a regular event when we lived at Heath End and I feel it's important to re-establish these rituals, that by reverting to the habits of those happy days we might recapture some of their mood.

We are walking off an indifferent lunch served at an inn outside Woodbridge: overcooked roast beef, pale Yorkshire pudding and dense apple pie. The children ate with uncritical hunger, I with little enthusiasm. Keen to set the right tone for this, the first of what I want to be a string of successful family Sundays, I was too busy guiding the conversation through a series of light-hearted topics. But if I had hopes of a response from Josh, he soon put me right. Since our return he has become skilled at the art of polite inattention, a master of the unfocused gaze, the close examination of his food. Meeting this newly developed indifference, I was struck once again by the feeling that, somehow or other, I have engendered his disapproval.

Troubled by this and other thoughts, I lost momentum. By instinct or chance, Katie chose this moment to come to life. Emerging from a dreamy mood, fired by a sudden vivacity, she launched into a stream of joky gossip and extravagant tales and scathing skits on the school staff, told with her special blend of theatrical effects and flourishes. When she breaks free

214

from her doubts and sparkles like this, when she uses her extraordinary talent for mimicry, I am overcome by the most enormous pride and admiration. She has such brilliance, such gifts, that I can't help imagining a splendid future for her. Not as an actress – she's far too uncertain for that – but as a writer or journalist, maybe an artist, some occupation which would make full use of her breathtaking flair for observation.

The gossip exhausted, Katie began to tease Josh, reverting to an old banter they both know well, reducing him to grinning affection. Feeding on this, she began to laugh herself, a sound that gladdened my heart, until, in her rapidly escalating euphoria, her laughter took on a fierce, brittle edge. Then I called for the bill and we left.

Now, as Josh spreads his arms wide against the buffeting wind, an aircraft attempting take-off, Katie swoops down on him and, gripping him by the waist, steers him into a series of loops and turns. The two of them gather speed, wheeling in ever wilder arcs, heads down, legs windmilling behind, until they come to a sudden halt and look solemnly out over the heath, catching their breath. Then, draping an arm around Josh's shoulders, Katie leads him on at a slower pace. They walk head to head. I keep back, out of earshot.

They walked like this in Provence last summer, I remember, Katie's arm draped lazily over Josh's shoulders as we strolled through a vineyard one morning, before the heat came up. Harry stayed behind with me, trying to look as though this aimless wandering came naturally to him.

The holiday was unplanned, a sudden whim of Harry's. At two days' notice we flew to Marseilles, hired a car and took a large villa with swimming pool near Gordes. I said nothing about the expense, which must have been considerable, because I sensed that, for almost the first time since he'd lost his seat, Harry was reaching out to us for support, and, in some way I couldn't quite pin down, was reassessing his feelings towards us. Making an obvious effort to rise above his worries, he gave us long bursts of attention, he groaned smilingly at the children's jokes, he watched us with a sort of hungry absorption, as if something had happened to make him see us through new eyes.

Setting a fresh tone, he cut down on his drinking, he swam three times a day, he agreed with only token complaint to come with us on long ambles around the Provençal markets. Best of all, he gave time to Katie. He listened with concentration to her teenage ramblings, he bought her clothes, he encouraged her to try new styles. Once he spent a whole afternoon fine-plaiting strands of her hair.

He experimented with his own appearance too. He bought tight jeans that strained over a stomach that hadn't quite recovered from all those parliamentary lunches, shirts that he wore buttoned half-way up the front to reveal plenty of chest, tie-dyed T-shirts, even – I never thought I'd see the day – a large wallet-cum-handbag of the sort that French and Italian men frequently carry but most heterosexual British men wouldn't be seen dead with for fear of misunderstandings. His hair had grown a little and he let it flop forward over his face, making him look softer and almost boyish.

I watched his efforts with a mixture of delight and, ignoble though it seemed at the time, a creep of doubt. I couldn't help wondering if it wasn't just a phase, if he wasn't simply playing some new role. But as the days went by these questions seemed increasingly irrelevant. It gave me such pleasure to see his absorption in the children, his patience with Katie, who, full of teenage excess, was difficult and charming and exhibitionist by turns. I loved watching the two of them together, talking in the shade of the almond tree or fooling around in the pool or reading side by side on the loungers.

This was the way things should be, I told myself; this was the way I longed for them to stay. If an itch of apprehension remained, I suppressed it.

I can imagine what Molly would say if I told her this story. She would say: Didn't you *see*? The answer is, I suppose I did, but the glimmering was so dark and unimaginable, my wish for our happiness so strong, that it was invisible.

Looking back, it would be easy to say that he was setting

things up during that holiday, that there was a sly calculation in everything he did. The model father and husband, chalking up points for good behaviour, putting himself above suspicion. But I can't accept he was that devious. It suggests a sure and overwhelming purpose, and I'm not convinced he had that, not then.

If there was one thing I should have spotted, I suppose it was Harry's lack of spontaneity or joy. Though he laughed and played with the children, though he joined in our games and outings, there was a watchfulness about him, a concentration that was rather too fierce, a darkness that was like a warning. I put it down to business worries.

We had the usual trials that beset all holidays, lost car keys, fits of temper, overtiredness; from me, criticism on the mounting pile of Katie's expensive new clothes which we could have found at half the price in England. We got through these dramas, we made allowances and gave ground, we felt we were happy.

It was Katie who sabotaged the holiday half-way through the second week. For no apparent reason, and with bewildering abruptness, she withdrew into a sulk of mammoth proportions. Everything was foul, everything displeased her, none of us could do anything right. I tried reasoning with her, I tried cajoling her, I even tried being angry, but she put up such a wall of simmering resentment that my words seem to bounce back at me, loaded with tension.

It was Harry who defused the situation. He showed a degree of tolerance that made my exasperation look unreasonable. Ignoring the worst of Katie's behaviour, he smiled when she least deserved it, he looked understanding at all times, and when her guard was down he slipped an arm round her and gave her a squeeze, as if to sympathise with the tribulations of being almost fifteen. I told him he was being marvellous. Accepting this, he smiled at me inattentively, with only the tiniest glint of shame.

Now, with the children out of sight ahead, I push on across the heath. The wind takes on new resonance. Above the droning and bluster I seem to hear the drag of the sea on the clattering shingle bank that lies somewhere beyond the farthest line of trees. I see the waves pulling at the shore, I hear the thunderous rattle and bounce of the stones, I feel the water sucking at my legs. An echo of panic pulls at my chest, a tug that is like a memory. Then, listening again, the sound seems to fade, and I'm no longer sure it was ever there.

From low-lying bracken and shivering grass, the path winds between tall terraces of gorse which deflect the relentless charge of the wind. Rounding a bend, I find Katie waiting for me. She grins jauntily and, flipping a strand of hair from her eyes, loops an arm into mine.

'Beastly child,' she remarks carelessly in the general direction of Josh, scurrying ahead. 'Beastly, beastly. Quite the most revolting boy.'

'What's he done?'

'He won't let me have his Walkman.'

'Should he?'

'Definitely. Mine's bust. Only want it till next weekend. Little beast.' She chants a tuneless song, she bounces along at my side, face thrown up against the wind, hair fluttering out behind her. She is still riding high, humming with a nervous high-pitched energy.

'Oh, and he won't talk about school or why he walked out,' she says. 'Silly boy. I told him not to be so stupid. I told him doing things like that is okay so long as you do them for a *reason* and you don't get *caught*. I *mean*.' She rolls her eyes heavenward, she shapes her mouth into an exaggerated look of sisterly scorn.

'Did he say why he wanted to go away?'

'No-o-o,' she drawls dismissively. 'But I'd let him go, Mum. *Honestly*. It'll do him good. He's getting too beastly.' She adds in a bored tone, 'If he goes, I can always come home.' She hums the tune again.

This statement lies between us, burning slowly like a fuse. I say cautiously, 'Well, perhaps when we're settled in a new place. I thought of looking near the school anyway. Somewhere on the other side there, in one of those villages. But you wouldn't want to be home all the time, darling,' I say, forcing

218

balance and reason into my voice. 'Weekends would be plenty. You'd miss your friends.'

She shrugs extravagantly, lifting my arm with hers. 'Oh, I don't know. I wouldn't mind. '

This surprises me. Immediately I begin to worry. 'School not so good?' I ask.

'Oh, it's all *right* . . . But sometimes the guys are so totally *juvenile.*' For guys I read girls. 'They're stuck on the same old things. Rock music, getting married, money – *really.* Obsessed with stupidities. And they pretend to be having these great love affairs!' She makes a face of incredulity. 'They get totally hysterical about these blokes. Calls, letters, you wouldn't believe it – hysterical. I mean, as if it was *important.* Even Jo Mills – of *all* people – she's got this wild crush over some bloke. Slobbers down the phone.' There's a note of injury in her voice which she covers with a defiant, 'I mean – fine, just *fine,* if that's what they want. But I really can't' – searching for the word, she throws a wild arm into the air – '*relate.* I mean, I just feel I'm sort of *beyond* all that.'

Beyond boys. I hope not. But I can see how she needs to persuade herself of the truth of this, how important it is for her to feel she has a high degree of control over her life. And I think for the moment she has her priorities absolutely right. There'll be plenty of time for boys when she's older.

'Otherwise . . . ?' I ask.

'Oh, okay.'

'Sleeping all right? No dreams?'

She scoffs, 'Too tired.'

Josh, who has run out of steam, is loitering ahead, stripping bark from a switch of wood.

Ducking her head, Katie says something which is whipped away by the wind.

I lean closer. 'What?'

'One bad night,' she admits crossly, as if I have forced it out of her.

Katie has long had vivid dreams. Since she was twelve – or even sooner, I suppose – she has been prone to waking in the night in a state of panic. Her nightmares revolve around a

219

profound sense of powerlessness – this was how Bob Block summarised it anyway – and the urge-to-flee, inability-to-escape terror that children learn to confront and overcome through the more violent fairy stories has for Katie remained all too real.

We have almost reached Josh. 'Write the dreams down,' I urge her. 'Send them to Bob. He'll be wanting to hear from you anyway.'

She gives a shrug that tells me that she is unlikely to bother. The next moment she unloops her arm from mine and grabs for Josh's stick. They tussle, Josh strikes out with his foot, they exchange a barrage of sharp words. We start back in silence. Then, rediscovering her bright amusing persona, Katie wins Josh back with a show of abject affection and teasing flattery. By the time we sight the car, he is laughing again.

It's barely four but Katie wants to get straight back to school. This, I know, is because she wants to avoid the alternative, which is to come home. We drive in silence, a silence that is contented and united. I feel that, all things considered, it has been a successful day.

Driving into the school grounds, I try to remember how many family Sundays we managed to achieve while Harry was alive. In the early years, quite a number, probably one in every three. Later, in the political years, it became very few. There was always something going on, lunch parties which drifted on into the late afternoon, more guests for tea and evening drinks, often people the children and I barely knew. Sometimes I didn't manage to give the children any time until they were going to bed.

Katie is reaching for the door handle before the car has even stopped. She prepares to bolt, then, twisting back abruptly, leans over and gives me a breathless hug. 'Mummy . . .'

I squeeze her roughly, I feel a surge of love.

'You're all right, Mummy?' she breathes.

'Me?' I make a face of mock surprise, I grin hard. 'I'm fine.' I am not going to give her the details about the search for *Minerva*, I am not going to tell her anything unless I absolutely have to.

220

Flinging a last 'Beastly child' at Josh, Katie jumps out and, sweeping her hair off her face with a flip of one hand, swings nonchalantly into the house.

Reversing into a turning place, I come back past the house to find the housemistress Mrs Anderson outside the front door, waiting to catch me.

'I was wondering—' She looks apologetically at Josh in the back seat. 'If you could spare a few minutes.'

Mrs Anderson's sitting-room is dominated by a three-piece suite in one of William Morris's more powerful prints, a swirling whirl of brown and amber that is repeated on the footstool and curtains. I sit in an armchair next to a table piled with exercise books whose covers are almost obliterated by inky doodles.

'I'm sorry to drag you in, but I thought it'd be best.' Mrs Anderson perches on the edge of the sofa, ramrod straight, a wiry fresh-faced woman of fifty or so, with the look of someone whose duty is painful but necessary. 'Are you sure Josh wouldn't like to sit in the kitchen?'

I tell her he'll be fine.

'I'll try not to keep you. It's just that there was an incident on Friday and I wondered if Katie had told you about it.'

My breath seizes. I just manage to shake my head.

'Oh.' She raises her eyebrows. 'Well, I thought you should know about it. It was nothing *too* serious. At least not in Mr Pelham's opinion. In fact, he hasn't told anyone but me. He didn't think it was worth bothering the head.' She gives me a little glance, to make sure I have appreciated the delicacy with which the situation has been handled. 'But the thing is, Katie assaulted Mr Pelham. Well, *technically* it was an assault. During a chemistry lesson. It wasn't a blow, really, so much as a – well, Mr Pelham called it a swipe. The back of her hand. It caught him on the cheek. No damage, no marks or anything. But hard enough. There didn't seem to be any reason. At least Mr Pelham couldn't think of any. Katie just seemed to get into a terrible blinding rage suddenly.'

We both ponder this for a moment, I with a small creep of dread.

'No reason at all?'

'Oh, I did ask her,' says Mrs Anderson. 'I spent a long time with her, but she couldn't seem to explain it. She didn't seem to know why she'd done it. She *said* she hardly remembered it.' Clearly Mrs Anderson does not go along with this idea. 'Anyway, we decided to put it down to stress, to all the work she's got to make up, to coming back in the middle of term. But I thought I'd better tell you.'

'Thank you. I'm – grateful.'

'Obviously I'll keep an eye on her. Encourage her to talk. But I have to say that it's rather uphill work at present.'

I look through her and beyond, absorbed by a vision of the chemistry lab. 'Mr Pelham – he, er . . .'

'Yes?'

'Is he at all . . . off-putting?'

'Frightening, you mean? No!' she declares emphatically. 'Very easy-going. All the girls like him. That's what makes it so extraordinary. He's one of the most popular members of staff.'

I would leave it at that, but I sense that some statement is expected of me. 'I can only say that I find it very unlike Katie.' I gesture my bafflement. 'Not her at all.'

I suppose this is what all parents say when their children misbehave. Mrs Anderson's face takes on the look of someone who's been here many times before.

'Well – thank you,' I say again.

'Just as well it was Mr Pelham,' she says as she leads the way to the door.

'Oh?'

'Men don't take these things quite so personally, do they?'

When I look uncomprehending she explains with an impish smile, 'They still forgive temperament in a woman, don't they?'

The recession is unrelenting, so people keep saying, but this street seems to be escaping the worst of it. The cars are only two or three years old, the red-brick semi-detached houses have fresh paint at their doors and windows, and well-tended gardens. In the midst of this tidy uniformity the two properties stand out uneasily, not only because of their size – double-fronted four-storeyed Victorian gothic villas, with carved barge-boards and ornate glass-covered porches, they tower over their neighbours – but because of their evident dilapidation. The threadbare front gardens are littered with bricks and fast-food cartons, the ground-floor windows are boarded over, and the local vandals have ensured that not a pane of the upper windows, not even those of the highest attic, remains unbroken.

The door of the right-hand house stands open. I step into twilight and the scent of damp and decay. Pursuing intermittent rattling sounds, I find Molly in a dim back room, pushing at some shutters which are bulging away from the window.

'God,' she cries, 'I think this place is going to fall apart before we ever get near it. Hold the torch, will you, love?'

She unlatches the metal bar securing the shutters over the window and with the soft tearing sound of rotten wood one of the shutters peels away from its hinges and drops to the floor.

'Damp, damp, damp!' declares Molly, gesturing upwards. 'Probably coming all the way from the roof. Got to the stage where I daren't look.' She dusts herself off and gives me a hug which sends the torch beam arcing round the room. 'How are you? How *are* you?' Without waiting for an answer, she relieves me of the torch and leads me towards the hall.

'Looking better,' she says, inspecting me in the light from the open door.

I raise an eyebrow at her.

Molly shows me over the rest of the ground-floor rooms then we sit on the stairs and spread the conversion plans over our knees. 'Not much wrong,' Molly says airily. 'Nothing that megabucks won't cure. In the last two years these houses have been busy doing what they do best – rotting away.'

'But when it's done, Molly . . .'

'Oh, it'll be great, sure. Only thing, I'll probably be dead by then. Frustration or rage, one'll get to me first. Either way, I tell you I'll be taking Meacher with me. I'm told by a reliable source' – she lays a forefinger against her nose – 'for which

223

read local reporter, that Meacher takes expensive holidays and has a new BMW. A humble councillor with a new BMW?' She narrows her eyes and scoffs heavily, 'I bet he saved a long time for it.'

I smile at her and shake my head.

'You don't believe me!' Molly declares. 'You think I'm imagining all this, but I tell you, I've got a nose for these things. That planning commitee's got a smell about it, and it's not a pleasant one.'

Championing her young offenders against a largely uncaring world, battling the grosser absurdities of officialdom, Molly is apt to see obstruction at every turn.

'What about your tame councillor?' I ask. 'How are you getting on with him?'

'Barry. You mean, *Barry*.' She sings the name, her voice swooping low with amusement. 'Listen, I've drunk so much coffee in the last few days I've got a caffeine-rated heartbeat.' She flutters a hand against her chest. 'He drops in about six every evening. Won't leave.' She gives a cat-like smile. 'I think he's lonely.'

'And . . . ?'

'He's doing what he can. Asking Meacher awkward questions about why the permission can't go through. Trying to get the whole thing onto the agenda for the next council meeting.' She makes a wry face. 'It won't be enough, of course.'

'Why not?'

'Because the local action group's too well geared up. *Someone, somewhere* is feeding them all the right ammunition.' She throws me a significant look. 'Their latest move is to object on the grounds of noise pollution. What really worries them, of course, is that the boys are going to be junkies who'll freak out on their doorsteps.' She slants her eyes. 'Or worse, sneak in and pinch their videos.'

'Perhaps you should have an open day at the Project. Invite the local people.'

She starts to fold the plans. 'What, so they can meet the boys and stare at their long hair and torn jeans and pierced noses and tattoos and have all their prejudices confirmed?'

The sun emerges, throwing a brilliant beam through the doorway and onto the dusty floorboards. Outside, a woman propels a pushchair past the gateway and pauses to stare in at us.

'Have a good look, won't you?' Molly calls but not loudly enough for the woman to hear.

The woman moves on.

'What about Jack?' I say. 'I know you're not keen, but this is just the sort of thing he should be doing to raise his profile. And he respects you, Molly. Really.'

'But he doesn't *like* me. And he knows I don't like him.' She stands up with a rattle of arm bangles. 'I provoke him.'

I get up. I say firmly, 'Molly, he's trying to win the candidature. All you have to do is find an angle in it for him. Just give him the facts, rationally and calmly.'

'I can't argue any way but emotionally, Ellen, my darling. That's the way I am. Anyway,' she says archly, 'he and Meacher are like this' – she presses two fingers together – 'so what's the point?'

This is one of her throwaway lines, the sort of provocative statement that pitches her arguments into the realms of confrontation.

'I should be like you,' she says not too seriously. 'Sensible, reasonable, sweet—'

'*Sweet!*'

'—loved and trusted by men. Someone they feel safe with, someone who brings out the protective in them.'

I roll my eyes.

A softening comes over Molly's face. 'You've never seen it, have you? How men react to you.'

'Because they don't.'

She shakes her head. 'They admire you, they want to take care of you, they want to impress you.'

'Molly . . .' I crease up my face in protest, thinking that, even if there were some truth in this, it didn't work with Harry.

'Harry too,' says Molly, reading my mind effortlessly. 'You brought out the best in him, you know.'

'And then I didn't.' I make a move towards the door.

Molly, realising she has stumbled into sensitive territory, touches my arm, a gesture of regret, then gathers up her voluminous shoulder bag from the stairs.

Shifting to a lighter tone, she remarks, 'I suppose he's going to get selected?'

'Who?'

'Jack.'

'I have no idea. I'm trying to keep out of it.'

'But you're going to this party tonight?'

'I'm afraid so.'

Half-joking but half-serious too, she wags a finger at me. 'Well, don't let Jack use you. Don't let him get the better of you!'

She goes to the door and stares into the sunlit road. Turning back, she leans against the door jamb. 'My councillor told me something yesterday,' she says boldly. 'On our fifth coffee, this was, when he was totally out of control.' She flashes her eyes briefly and suggestively. 'It was about that development by the bypass, the one that Meacher got re-zoned for housing, the one that's going to make Jack his second fortune. Well, Barry told me that before Jack got hold of the land it used to belong to a property company.' She pauses, she eyes me meaningfully. 'By the name of Ainswick.'

Ainswick. I realise this must have significance but I can't fit it into the scheme of things, I can't assign it a value.

Molly holds up two parallel fingers, Scout-style. 'Guaranteed reliable information.'

As I try to work out what Molly's getting at, she rushes in ahead of me and brandishes a conclusion. 'Ainswick applied for re-zoning several times and never got it, right? Then Jack buys the land and – bingo!' She casts me a meaningful look, she murmurs sardonically, 'In the circumstances I don't somehow think Jack'll be in the mood to back our unpopular little half-way house project against Meacher, do you? Not when he owes him so much.'

I see Jack leaning against the kitchen counter that night after the memorial service, I see him watching me as I stir

226

Josh's baked beans, I hear him telling me how he fell out with Harry over a piece of land which he'd bought from Ainswick and which had, against all expectations, come good.

'It doesn't necessarily mean . . .' I shrug, reluctant to go into detail. 'Jack's always been lucky.'

Molly's eyebrows shoot up at this. She is longing to chop this remark off at the knees but, with a visible effort, she restrains herself. She says instead, 'There was something else. According to Barry – who doesn't get these things wrong – Ainswick still owns a patch of land on that side of the city, right next to Jack's development.'

I show suitable surprise.

'You didn't know?'

'I never knew anything about Ainswick.'

'Well, it might be worth something!' She delves deep into her bag.

'I don't know . . . The market's meant to be dead.'

'But if the land gets re-zoned! Then it'll be worth a ton. Someone's probably after it already.' She drags some keys out of her bag and gives me a sly glance. 'Maybe even Jack?' The glitter of possibilities burns bright in her eyes. She has no way of knowing, and I am forbidden to tell her, that time is running out for Ainswick.

'Well . . . I'll ask.'

'Do!' she exclaims. 'You never know!'

We step out onto the porch. The worst of yesterday's gale passed in the night, but there is still quite a wind. Small clouds speed busily across the sky and in the neglected garden a plastic bag stirs uneasily against a soft-drink can.

Molly locks the door and, flipping a heavy hasp over an equally sturdy staple, snaps the giant padlock home. 'Ironic, isn't it?' she says, surveying the securely fastened door. 'All this to keep young offenders out, when the whole aim of the project is to get them in.' She drops the keys back into her bag. She peers at me, she hums, she passes a hand laughingly in front of my eyes. 'Ellen?'

I come to.

'I lost you there, gal. No one home.'

Molly wants me to go to a café for lunch, but I tell her I have too much to do.

'Money okay?' she asks for no apparent reason, and I wonder how much she guesses of my troubles.

I kiss her cheek. 'They're sorting it out.'

Driving back to Pennygate, a shadow stirs in the back of my mind. Sitting at Harry's desk, staring out at the restless trees, I realise that this worry has been circling the edges of my thoughts for some time, that it took one of Molly's remarks to give it definition. When she talked about the patch of land next to Jack's I wondered, as I had wondered so indistinctly before, if everything possible was being done for Ainswick. There was a determined defeatism in Gillespie that seemed out of proportion to Ainswick's situation. I didn't understand then, and I don't understand now, why everything is so unmarketable. I can't help thinking that Gillespie has little incentive to spend much time or effort on Ainswick's affairs.

I also wonder if there are other assets that I haven't heard about. I'm not about to subscribe to conspiracy theories – I will leave those to Molly. I don't think that anyone is failing to tell me these things on purpose. Rather, I imagine they're sparing me these details out of the belief that I won't be interested.

Margaret, having done all she can at Pennygate, is back in the Ipswich office more or less full time. I call her there and ask for the name and number of the City estate agent who is handling the Shoreditch building.

She doesn't ask why I should want the information, though I feel bound to meander through an explanation about someone having asked me to pass it on to them.

I make myself a coffee, I sit in front of the telephone, I plan what I will say, finally I dial. My palms are already damp, my heart fluttering; I don't know why these excursions into the unknown cause me such difficulty.

A female answers in a rapid sing-song. I tell her it's about a commercial property in the Shoreditch area. She clicks me through to a cool-voiced woman who announces herself as Miranda Stephenson.

'Oh yes, we have quite a bit around that area,' says Ms Stephenson, sounding keen for business. 'May I ask who's enquiring?'

It's only a small deception to give my unmarried name and the name of the graphic design company I used to work for.

'And what sort of square footage are you looking for?'

'There was a particular building, in fact. We saw your board up. The Richmond Building?'

'Oh . . . Richmond House?'

'That's it.'

'Let me see . . . I'm pretty sure . . .' I picture her bringing it up on her screen. 'Yes . . . It's *meant* to be under offer at present.'

'Offer?' I breathe through a mouth that is suddenly dry. 'Oh.' I feel a lunge of relief, a reversal of emotion that leaves me breathless. 'This has just happened then?' I ask, trying to suppress the delight in my voice.

'Well . . .'

'The last few days?'

'No.' Her voice takes on a disgruntled note. 'Actually the property's been off the market for some time but the vendor didn't want the sign taken down.'

My emotions swing back. A moment of stillness before I ask, 'How long has it been under offer?'

'I'm sorry?'

I am speaking too softly. Raising my voice, I repeat the question.

'Well . . . it's been some weeks now.' A hesitation as if she is making up her mind about something. 'If you were interested, you could *try* a counter-offer. There's nothing to stop you. I can't guarantee anything, of course.'

I feel the clarity that weariness and a sense of injury can bring. 'The existing offer, can you tell me—?'

'We know nothing about it,' she interrupts briskly.

It is an instant before I grasp the implication. 'It didn't come through your office, then?'

'No. We were just informed that there'd been a private offer.'

'Some weeks ago?'

229

'That's right.'

I whisper, 'Thank you, er . . . Ms Stephenson.'

'Would you like details of any other properties?'

'Perhaps . . . next week,' I say, blushing inwardly. 'Can I come back to you?'

Jack fastens his seatbelt and, with a gesture of wonderment, tilts his head at me and says, 'You look absolutely gorgeous.' His voice is low and gravelly, the tone he reserves for comments like this.

I don't know why he says this; I've given him no reason to. Instead of blow-drying my hair I have let it dry naturally into odd waves and kinks. The cream dress I have chosen is plain and unadventurous, I wear no jewellery, not even studs in my ears. I have given my eyelashes only the barest dusting of mascara and have done nothing to lift the colour of my skin, which with the fading of my tan has turned a little sallow. I don't need a psychiatrist to tell me that I am trying to vanish into the background.

I'm already nervous about the time. We're due to meet Charles and Anne outside the local party chairman's house at six-thirty sharp. If we're late the look on Anne's face doesn't bear thinking about.

Making no comment, smiling benignly, Jack starts up and we move off at a leisurely pace. Manœuvring the car around the pot-holes with an idle swing of one hand, he takes a series of sidelong looks at me. 'It's all in the bones,' he announces with a lazy smile. 'A matter of structure.' His free hand describes the shape of a face, then curves neatly across to drop over my hands which I have carelessly left unattended in my lap. 'Women have either got it or they haven't.' He gives my fingers a squeeze. 'You've got it.'

'Tell me about the party,' I say, making a gesture that requires me to move my hands away. 'Who'll be there?'

'Who won't? The committee. All the shortlisted candidates. Even the terrifying Mrs Reeves.' With this thought he brings his hand back to the wheel. 'Hot from some good cause, no doubt. I'm just hoping she'll overdo the credentials. Alarm them with her good works among racially disadvantaged sex offenders or whatever it is she does when she's not being a political powerhouse.' His eyes flash with agitation or annoyance. 'I'm getting quite nervous actually.' He puts on his little-boy-lost look. 'Saturday's only five days away. I'm dreading the grilling. A solid hour in front of the committee, fielding every trick question they can throw at me, and the slightest hesitation a death warrant. And I'm still weak on agricultural policy and Europe. And I think – well, I *know* – someone's going to be gunning for me.'

'Why?'

'Oh, being successful isn't enough to make you politically correct nowadays, even among the Tories; you have to be a community benefactor as well. *Especially* when you're a developer. You're meant to be immorally rich, even in the depths of a recession. To make amends for these filthy great profits that are meant to fall into your lap, you're expected to have donated a good proportion of every development for the last ten years to first-time buyers or old people or some worthy community project. People still have an eighties image of developers – you know, easy money, fat cats in flash cars – that sort of thing.' I think of Jack's immaculate clothes, his air of self-indulgence, the quiet luxuriousness of the car in which we are travelling, and make no comment. 'They don't realise it's bloody hard graft, like any other business,' he says wistfully. 'Nor do they appreciate that the recession's hit us longer and harder than anyone else, and margins have been too tight for all this generosity.'

I almost miss the opportunity, it has come so easily. 'What about the bypass development?'

He frowns distractedly. 'What? Oh, that's *one* project which should pass muster. I've donated the city three prime acres for an out-of-town sports complex. I'm not sure about the timing though . . . Announced two weeks ago. They might think I fixed it to coincide with the candidature proceedings. Well, I *did*, of course . . .' He slides me a conspiratorial glance. 'What I don't need is this fellow standing up and suggesting that this charitable work of mine is rather sudden, that I'm doing it just

231

to earn good marks.' We hit a pot-hole and he curses softly. Slowing down, he remarks, 'Harry was much better organised about these things. Regularly made donations – though never *half* as much as people thought – and with a brilliant amount of drum-beating. But then he always had a feel for the old PR, didn't he? We used to argue like hell about Ainswick's philanthropic gestures. I said we weren't running a bloody charity. Harry said it was money well spent.'

We turn out of the drive onto the Woodbridge road and, free of the pot-holes, the Mercedes lunges forward. It's six-ten. Plenty of time; I relax a little.

'The bypass development, it's going well then?' I ask.

He glances at me blankly. 'What?'

'If you can afford to give land away.'

I sense a sharpening of his attention, but then money is a subject that Jack always discusses with concentration. 'So long as the recession lifts in the next two years, it should do all right. Why?'

'Oh, it was only . . .' Without finishing this, I say in a bit of a rush, 'I believe Ainswick still owns some land nearby.' Catching his eye, I raise my eyebrows and turn this into a question.

A beat of silence then Jack says with the air of someone who is not entirely clear, 'Nearby?'

'Close to your bypass development.'

He asks in a voice that is almost liquid, 'Did Gillespie tell you that?'

'I can't remember,' I say, not entirely truthfully.

We come up fast behind another car and Jack peers out to overtake. Thinking better of it, he brakes and tucks in behind.

'Well, I hope he also told you that it's on the wrong side of the bypass and with disputed access.'

'No, I . . . he didn't say that.'

'Well, he should have. That should have been the first thing he told you. He shouldn't have let you think it was in the same sort of class.' He keeps glancing at me as he says this. 'He *didn't*, did he?'

'We hadn't got that far.'

'Ellen, my dear lovely thing' – his hand reaches across to find me again – 'there aren't going to be any miracles, I'm afraid. No immediate restoration of Ainswick's fortunes.' He gives my leg several light pats. 'It's never going to be as simple as that.'

'I hadn't thought it would be,' I say defensively, moving my legs so that his hand slips away.

'Now you're cross with me,' he says in his misunderstood voice.

'Not at all.' Which isn't strictly true. I am upset both by his condescension and my emotional reaction to it. Putting on a businesslike voice, I ask, 'One thing I'm not clear about – perhaps you'd know. The Shoreditch building – is it meant to be on the market?'

'Ummm . . .' He blows elegantly through his teeth. 'I'm not the person to ask about that, Ellen. I wouldn't know.' He reverts to a tone of patient explanation, as if I need things spelled out for me. 'You'd have to ask Gillespie. But . . .' He makes a show of considering the matter, the line of his perfect profile contorted with concentration. 'I would think it *must* be. *Everything* must be for sale.' He asks lightly, 'Why?'

'The agents don't seem to know what's going on.'

'Oh? You've tried them, have you?'

'Yes.'

His eyes dart across. He gives a mirthless chuckle. 'What – chivvying them along?'

'Just – asking.'

'Well done,' he says, repeating it with enthusiasm, as if he is only now beginning to appreciate my resourcefulness. 'Good girl. *Good girl*. They can get bloody lazy, those agents.'

His attention returns to his driving as we pause in the centre of the road to cross the opposite carriageway and pass down a narrow side road which leads to the local party chairman's house. It is only six-sixteen.

'What do you think of Gillespie?' I ask.

'Mmm?' he says with an air of preoccupation. 'Oh, he's all right.' He spins the car through a tight bend before asking, 'Why?'

'Just wondered.'

'You've seen him since you've been back? He's sorting your finances out?'

'Yes. But . . .'

'Mmm?'

'I do find him – difficult.'

'He *is* rather a cold fish, I suppose. But *solid*. Knows his stuff. Just his manner. Doesn't frighten you, does he?' He gives a fond laugh.

'I wouldn't have said—'

'Ah, here we are!'

It is six-twenty as we turn into the driveway of the chairman's home, a sprawling house in the English hacienda style with a Spanish-tiled roof and balconies with elaborate inward-curving S-shaped wrought-iron railings and heavily rouched curtains at the windows. The lane outside and the drive itself are already lined with parked cars. Undaunted, Jack drives straight up to the house and parks on the garage apron, blocking in two cars. There is no sign of Anne or Charles.

Jack twists the driving mirror round and, squinting into it, runs his hands over his hair.

I don't know why I choose this moment, but I ask, 'Jack?'

He raises an eyebrow at the mirror and sets his jaw more firmly and narrows his eyes, refining some look.

'Mmm?'

'You would tell me, wouldn't you, if there was anything . . .' What am I trying to say? '. . . anything I should know?'

Jack is barely following me. 'What do you mean?'

I don't know how to put it. 'Anything you hadn't told me?'

'What?' Homing in at last, he turns to me in puzzlement. 'Anything I hadn't told you?' he repeats mechanically. 'You mean, to do with Harry?'

'Yes.'

He gives me a strange look, as if he isn't sure how to take this, and declares in mild protest, 'There's nothing, Ellen. Well, nothing I know about. Why? Has something happened?'

'No. It was just . . .'

234

He glances at his watch. 'Well, whatever it is, I really don't think this is the best moment to discuss it.' Flinging the door open he climbs out and comes round to help me out.

'I suppose I meant – was there anything else worrying him?'

He slams the car door shut. 'Anything *else*?' he says, looking vague again. 'I think he had quite enough to be going on with, Ellen. Don't you?'

Touching his hair once again, he takes my elbow and walks me briskly towards the front door. I look for Anne and Charles among the people straggling up the drive. Sensing that Jack is about to sweep me inside, I hold back, I remind him that we have promised to wait for the others.

'But I saw their car,' exclaims Jack, waving in the direction of the gates. 'Out in the road. They're already here.'

'We arranged to meet at the door,' I say. Anne and Charles had suggested meeting at their place, but Jack had pleaded lack of time.

'But they're already here,' Jack insists, unable to conceal a tinge of irritation. He turns aside to greet a couple of approaching guests with robust words and a broad politician's smile. Turning back, his smile pales and he says in the tone of someone who is being unreasonably tried, 'Well, I could go in and check, I suppose.'

'Please.'

Feeling conspicuous, I position myself some distance from the door beside a bed of vermilion begonias which I pretend to inspect with the attention of a keen gardener. It is no kind of cover and I'm soon spotted by some ebullient arrivals who tramp over and tell me how sorry they are about Harry and how much he will be missed. Faced by the prospect of a roomful of equally well-meaning people, I feel a shaft of panic.

Jack's laughter echoes from the porch and he reappears, grinning over his shoulder at someone inside the house. Striding quickly over, he announces, 'They're here! I asked Barrow.'

'You're sure?'

'Look, here's Alan!' Putting a firm arm around my shoulders he leads me forward to meet the rotund figure of our host, the local party chairman, who is hurrying out of the house towards us. I don't need to ask how he knew I was here.

'Ellen, my dear,' says the chairman, clutching my hand with visible emotion. '*So* delighted you're here. *So* pleased. But you must come straight in! Can't have you out here. Come in! Come in!'

'Have Charles and Anne arrived?' I ask.

'Er . . . not sure. But Sally will know. Come in, come in.'

I allow myself to be guided as far as the hall where I touch cheeks with Sally, the chairman's wife, a woman with a liking for bright colours and costume jewellery and a deep tan to set them against.

'Ellen!' she cries in a piercing voice. 'But how absolutely wonderful that you could come! And . . .' Raising her pencilled eyebrows, she looks from Jack to me and back again, a conjectural smile hovering at the corners of her mouth.

The double doors to the main reception room are wide open. Several people turn at the sound of Sally's voice; I see their eyes fasten on me and Jack, I see them pass comment. I realise, with a knot of apprehension, that I can't see either Anne or Charles. From the thick of the room Barrow, the party agent, smiles at me and raises his glass. Catching my signal, he excuses himself and comes over.

He tells me Anne and Charles have not arrived yet.

The anger flows over me like a hot sea. Wordlessly, I turn away, pass quickly behind Jack and make my way to the door.

Too late. Charles and Anne are already stationed by the flower bed, looking expectantly down the drive. As I emerge from the house, Anne glances in my direction and does a double take. Her face darkens, her mouth works rapidly. 'I see!' she hisses as I approach. 'I *see!*' She sucks in a bitter breath, she fights an inner battle. Finally she exclaims, 'So much for a united front!'

Barrow drives me back to Pennygate. Thankfully he doesn't try to talk until we arrive.

'If there's anything I can do, Mrs Richmond?' he says quietly.

'I won't be coming to any more events, I'm afraid.'

'No,' he says, having grasped something of what has been going on. 'I quite understand.'

The house envelops me in silence. Before going to Jill's to collect Josh, I pour myself a glass of wine and go and sit in the conservatory, looking out at the softness of the garden and the metallic sheen of the river, listening to the faint twittering of the birds, drawing my breath slowly from the diaphragm and counting it in and out.

Molly was right; Jack isn't one to miss a trick.

Passing through the kitchen, the red-eyed answering machine blinks lazily at me. I decide to leave it but change my mind and press the playback. A call from Leonard, his voice gruff and remote: a few matters that need discussion. A call from the mother of Josh's schoolfriend Ben.

Then Moreland.

I move closer, I listen to his voice, I picture his face.

Suddenly his words loop out and fill the air. Everything seems to slow down, I have a sense of disassociation and absolute clarity.

It has happened.

They think they have found *Minerva*.

ELEVEN

The fourth day. I wake as the first grey fingers of light touch the room. I wake instantly, with an obscure sense of alarm. I stare at the open window, looking for some movement in the wisteria, listening for a telltale rustle under the eaves.

Nothing. The leaves, black against the lightening sky, hang inert. I get up and go to the window. A mist hangs low and thin over the garden. The silence is very deep, broken only by bird calls that rise sweetly through the stillness.

The wind has gone. After four blustery days when the shipping forecast was peppered with gale warnings and I fancied I could see the whitecaps advancing across the distant horizon, it has finally died. This is the day, then, when the authorities will probably make their first attempt to examine the wreck.

I bathe and dress with care, I take particular trouble with my hair and makeup, then I go down to the study to wait until I can decently call Moreland. In the mornings I try not to call him before quarter past seven. Once – I think it was two days ago – I phoned earlier and, though he insisted he was awake and sounded as pleased as ever to talk to me, I could hear the sleep in his voice.

To pass the time, I spread the chart Moreland has given me across the desk. I know its patterns and colourings by heart, the shapes of the banks, the names of the buoys. Moreland has marked the position of the probable wreck with a pencilled star – we're careful to call it the 'probable' wreck, as if this will protect me from disappointment, though disappointment is not the word I would have chosen.

The pencilled star lies some ten miles off the mouth of our river, in a direction that Moreland calls east-northeast, beyond the northern tip of a sandbank called the Shipwash. I was convinced the water must be deep there – it's coloured white on the chart – but Moreland told me that none of the North Sea is very deep. Indeed, close by the pencilled star, in tiny print, is the figure 22, which is the depth of the water in metres: twenty-two metres, about seventy-five feet. This depth creates no difficulty for the salvage boat, so Moreland explained to me; they simply drop a closed-circuit camera with a light source over the side of their vessel, on the end of a cable. All that is required is a reasonably calm sea.

Like now, like today.

The probable wreck was discovered in just the way they said it would be: snagged on the nets of a trawler.

Moreland gives me these details when I ask for them, which is usually in the early evenings when he and I are sitting in the conservatory having a glass of wine. For some reason I can't bear to hear these snippets of information from anyone else, not even Charles or Leonard. There is something about Moreland that lets me believe against all the odds that he will not bring me bad news.

The trawler was a small one, he told me. It was dragged to a halt when its nets caught on the obstruction. Their echo-sounder had given them no warning; the printed trace showed only the smallest of blips on the sea bed. It took the crew three hours to free the nets. When they finally retrieved them they found gashes and cuts in the mesh, as if the strands had been grinding against jagged metal. No obstruction having been reported anywhere near that position, the skipper followed standard procedure and notified the coastguard.

In the evenings, when Moreland and I are sitting quietly in the conservatory, he frequently tells me that this object on the sea bed could well be a container lost off a container ship, that these containers are always getting swept overboard in bad weather, that they can float for days or weeks before sinking, often ending up many miles from where they were lost. I know he tells me this because he wants to prepare me for whatever is going to happen, and because he is, I sense, increasingly concerned about me, but I don't think either of us is really convinced by the idea.

I'm feeling cold. Folding the chart away, I go up to my bedroom in search of a sweater. Passing the dressing-room door, I open it abruptly, I'm not sure why. I stare at Harry's clothes with something close to resentment. Maybe my mourning has run its course, maybe my compassion has simply run dry, but my memories are hardening. I want his clothes gone, I want his presence removed. Too much is happening; I want my life back again.

I will ask Molly to take the clothes away when she comes over later.

Downstairs again, I make a forbidden cup of coffee – the caffeine has started to give me terrible palpitations – and return to the study. It's only quarter to seven.

I stare at a stack of letters and documents that I should have dealt with days ago, and leaf through them half-heartedly. Succumbing to restlessness, I range through the house, wandering from room to room, standing for a while, looking at objects or pictures or nothing much at all, before moving on again.

I know I'm wearing myself down, I know my nerves are bar-taut and that any weight I might have gained has dropped straight off me again. I realise I should be taking something to slow me down, Librium or one of the other downers they fed me after Harry's death. But what I need more than anything, the only medicine worth having, is an end to this waiting.

Back in the study, threatened by bleak thoughts, I drift into fantasy. This is my new indulgence, my sanity preserver.

I think about the cottage that the children and I will find, the life we will lead there, the simple pleasures we will have. I imagine picking up my career again on a freelance basis, and, to get me out of the house, perhaps doing some volunteer work at Molly's Project. An existence that will be remarkable for little but its normality.

I picture all this, but I don't try to match it too closely to reality. Not just at the moment; the gaps frighten me too much.

These fantasies feed pleasantly off each other in an addictive sort of way. I find myself going off in unexpected directions, some of them bizarre, some exciting, some forbidden.

The forbidden ones relate to Moreland. At first I thought of him in the way one thinks of people who are unavailable: I placed both of us in another context, another life. I imagined what might have happened if we'd met years ago.

But in the last day or so my thoughts have shifted and focused, and I no longer think of the two of us in some hazy hypothetical past, but in the present. These fantasies are, I'm well aware, far from harmless. But whatever the dangers, I don't make much effort to prevent them. I can only live from day to day.

I picture him now, in bed. I see him emerging slowly from sleep. And I think how smooth and firm his skin must be. How I would love to feel his body beside me in the night when I cannot sleep.

I start violently as the phone rings. Before Moreland can say anything, I'm laughing into the phone.

'All right?' he asks.

'Not much sleep,' I admit.

'You didn't take anything?'

'No.'

I said I would take some tablets, I promised in fact, but he doesn't rebuke me. 'Ellen—'

'The wind's gone.'

'Yes. The boat's left. It's on its way out there now.'

My heart is hot against my chest. 'They told you?'

'Just now.'

'It'll be today then?'

'Yes.' Typically he qualifies this, taking me through all the likely snags again. 'Assuming the position they got was accurate, assuming they can locate it. And assuming there's no technical hitch, which is always a possibility with that equipment.'

241

'Well!' I make a nervous sound. 'Let's hope then!'

Already hungry for his company, I ask him if he can come a bit earlier today, at five or so.

'I'll try. And Ellen—? Try not to think about it too much.'

I do my best. Waking Josh, I chatter incessantly through breakfast and on the drive to school. He looks baffled by my sudden wave of words, and vaguely wary. He doesn't know about the salvage boat. I have forbidden anyone to tell him. Katie doesn't know either, though strictly speaking this breaks the promise we made to each other in America.

On the way back from the school I meet the postman at the top of the drive and wait while he extracts my mail from the back of his van. I sit in the car and sort quickly through it.

Nothing from Guernsey. It is more than a week since I wrote.

There is, however, a solid packet from London EC1. I open it back at the house, fortified by another cup of coffee. It's from Gillespie and contains a two-page letter, closely typed, and a bound document entitled *Financial Plan*. The plan is twenty pages long. I flick quickly through it, I study a page at random. Under year columns there are ranks of figures, and at the sides, headings covering such things as tax liabilities, mortgages and interest. One category catches my eye. Household expenditure (estimated). It is broken down into things like food, clothing, insurance, domestic staff, equipment. The total is enormous. What is Gillespie thinking of? Does he think I'm wedded to this lifestyle? Does he imagine I can't go back?

Discouraged, I put this to one side, I go through the rest of the mail. There is a handwritten letter from Tim Schwartz. I read it with a sense of inevitability and foreboding.

'. . . I'm afraid it's becoming impossible for me to hold things off any longer,' Schwartz says. 'The trustees are asking for an explanation for the delay in finalising the accounts, and I feel duty bound to give them the facts as I know them.'

Duty bound. Yes, I can see that.

With heavy heart, I start to draft a letter. I say I'm sorry I haven't been in touch but I haven't found anything that might

242

shed light on the matter. Would it be helpful if I came and met the trustees and discussed the problem with them? In the meantime I'll continue to try to find out how the money went astray. Rereading this last sentence, I cross it out and stare at the page, no longer sure of what I'm trying to achieve.

My mind travels out to sea. I picture the salvage vessel. I imagine it as a tug-like craft, squat and functional. I see it wallowing slightly in the swell, I picture a cabin full of electronics, things that blink and flicker and buzz quietly, and in the centre a group of men huddled round a TV monitor which is relaying the picture from the sea bed.

What do they see? *God, what do they see?*

I pick up the pencil again and, crumpling the draft letter into the bin, take a fresh sheet of paper and try again.

The sentences freeze and shift, losing meaning. I reach into the back of the drawer and pull out the Mountbay notepaper, as if the sight of it might yet spring ideas into my head. A company incorporated in Guernsey. A company which is wrapped in secrecy and tax advantages, which is administered by anonymous people, leaving nothing open to public gaze.

But perhaps I'm reading too much into this secrecy. Perhaps secrecy was not the purpose of this company but merely a by-product. Perhaps the little worm of unease that eats at me whenever I think of Harry and Mountbay is misplaced. Even as I think this, the unease curls in my stomach.

I wonder if Harry put something on paper and I just haven't found it. Presumably he would have needed at least one contact number in Guernsey, and some scribbled notes, maybe a bank reference or two.

Damn you, Harry. I could have done without all this.

Damn you . . . I can say that now without any guilt at all.

I look up the dialling code for Guernsey: 0481. I search for the prefix in Harry's diary and old address book. I look through the desk. I don't really expect to find anything, but on this problematic morning the task is suitably mindless and absorbing.

Nothing in the desk, but, driven by a need to leave no corner unsearched, haunted by the thought of finding something in a couple of months' time when it'll be too late, I cannot leave it alone.

Starting on the lowest bookshelves, I remove each volume in turn, glancing at the endpapers and riffling through the text, working my way slowly round the room. The exercise is strangely cathartic; already I feel better for knowing that this one room, at least, will be free of surprises.

The house line rings several times and gets picked up by the answering machine. Jill's voice calls down the passage, announcing her arrival, and presently the low whine of the vacuum cleaner sounds from a far corner of the house.

I reach the second level of shelves and a leather-bound set of Macaulay's essays. Harry acquired these and other old books from a dealer who specialised in ready-assembled libraries of suitably venerable appearance. Harry got round to reading a number of classic political works, but not much else; he said he was too busy keeping abreast of present-day politics.

Above, and probably two hours ahead of me, are modern political biographies – three on Margaret Thatcher, a cluster of previous prime ministers, the odd chancellor – and works by political analysts. Higher still are travel books and mellow volumes of indeterminate title that have a long-untouched look. On the top shelf are neat stacks of *National Geographic*s and other journals which Harry collected years ago.

After an hour I take a break, still only a quarter of the way along the third shelf. Looking for something to read with my coffee, I take out a large-format book on India which, with several other coffee-table books, is lying end-on in a stack further along the third shelf.

Sliding it back some minutes later, I notice a slim large-format book which has been squeezed into the end of the row by standing it on its front edge.

It is an art book. Of sorts. It contains photographs of firm female bodies with high breasts, dramatically and artfully lit, set against rough stone walls or oddly proportioned rooms, the sweeps of flesh taken from unusual perspectives, curving out of deep shadows or illuminated by unexpected shafts of light. The poses are provocative but also, for all their aspirations to

244

high art, rather banal, fingertips hovering on the point of fleshly contact or idly brushing downy thighs.

Harmless, if you like that sort of thing. If it weren't for the girls. They look so young, little more than children, though it is hard to be sure because, disturbingly, their faces are obscured in each shot, either turned away or hidden in darkness or cloaked by falling hair. As if the readers' lusts required a total absence of personality, bodies chopped off at the neck.

Leafing through it, I decide that, for all the artistic gloss, it's really rather tacky stuff. I'm not sure which troubles me more, the headless bodies or my vision of Harry sitting here in the study, looking at them. I don't need to guess what face he put to these lush young bodies. Certainly not mine.

The business line rings.

'I was wondering if you'd received my letter all right, Ellen. And the financial plan?'

Recognising Gillespie's voice, I am transported back to a state of uneasiness. I am thrown, too, by his use of my first name.

I murmur thanks. I explain I haven't had time to look at the plan yet.

'Plenty of time. No hurry.' There is a odd note to his voice which I can't immediately identify. 'I just wanted to say that if it would help at all, I'd be very happy to come up to Suffolk and take you through it.' I realise now: he is attempting to sound friendly. The affability sits uncomfortably on him, like an under-rehearsed performance.

I wonder vaguely what has brought this on. I thank him again. I tell him I'll let him know.

'Of course. Take your time,' he says, as if reasonableness and understanding were his benchmarks.

I prepare to ring off but Gillespie is in a communicative mood. He tells me about the various deals he has done on the mortgage, how he is quite pleased with the terms, how he has tried to cover all contingencies, how he has managed to cover me for at least the next six months.

While he's talking, I prop myself against the desk, I look

across the room to where the art book lies open on top of the base cupboards.

'By the way,' Gillespie is saying, 'I'm appointing new agents for the Shoreditch building. I wasn't satisfied that the old ones were performing as well as they might.'

Cautiously I pull out the chair and sit at the desk.

'. . . They've been cutting back on staff, and there's always a price to pay for that. I'm not promising the new people'll find a buyer, of course, but they're highly professional and they should give the thing some new impetus. The market's bottomed out now, so you never know, there might be a bit of interest.'

The suspicion that has been floating through my mind forms and hardens. I see Jack in all this. Jack has been telling tales behind my back.

'Hello? Are you there?'

'I . . . There's never been any sort of offer on the building?' I ask.

'Just the one. But, as I told you, it was derisory.'

'No others?'

'No.' He is wary. 'Why?'

'Someone told me the place was under offer, that it'd been taken off the market.'

'Who told you that?' His voice has taken on all its old smoothness and authority.

If he's been talking to Jack, he'll know the answer to this already. 'I spoke to the agents,' I say.

'Oh, did you?' For a moment I think he's going to comment on this, but he lets it pass. 'Well, I don't know who you spoke to there, but the property's never been off the market.' He adds crossly, 'Why would it be taken off the market?'

I can't offer a reason, and lacing his voice with affability once more he says, 'You'll let me know then, will you, if you want me to go through the plan with you?'

As he rings off I know what he's thinking: he's thinking that he's got off lightly, that I'm a piece of cake.

Returning to the book search, sneezing from the dust – Jill never seems to reach these shelves – I work my way

246

mechanically along to the end of the row, to the books immediately preceding the gap where the art book had been. It's a moment before I focus on the edge of brown revealed against the exposed back wall of the bookcase. A large manila envelope that has been tucked in behind some *Good Food Guides*. Jammed into the cleft of the shelf, it resists my tug for an instant before coming away.

Unmarked, quite bulky. I slide my hand inside and pull out photographs. About fifteen of them, though I don't need to look at very many to get the flavour of them.

I feel a small descent into misery, a shrinking. Oh, Harry.

Although these pictures do not stand artistic comparison to the book of erotica, some people might still class them as artistic, I suppose, since there has been some attempt at lighting and what might be considered, by those who study these things, as moderation. The camera has kept its distance, there are no closeups, and in the legal sense, I would imagine the poses fall some way short of obscenity.

But they are explicit enough. The girls have young faces on even younger bodies, small breasts and slim boy-like hips, while the men are older and burly and rough-looking, lorry drivers off the street. But what makes the scenes disturbing is that in all but one of the shots the girls are restrained in some way, with wide straps encrusted with metalwork, or heavy chains, or by men's forearms, thick and dark and muscular. Each picture is like a prelude to rape; or an invitation.

They say even the most balanced of men like an occasional look at these things. I've seen articles where experts say it doesn't do any harm, that it doesn't affect them as lovers or husbands or fathers. I'm not sure about that. I think this stuff is insidious, I think it undermines men's views of women. I think that in the end it diminishes and demeans, and encourages appetites that are best left unexplored.

Did Harry try these things with Caroline Palmer? The thought doesn't bother me in the way it would have done a few months ago. The emotion's gone. My endless compulsion to rationalise has begun to fade. I've learnt to accept that some things are simply unexplainable.

I used to make endless treks over the same lonely ground, wondering if Harry had found me inadequate in bed, deciding that I must have disappointed him in some fundamental way, though I could never think how. But having blamed myself a thousand times I've come round to a more fatalistic view. I've decided that Bob Block was probably right – that nothing I did or didn't do would have made much difference to Harry's underlying state of mind. I've come to realise that Harry's capacity for unhappiness was always there, locked deep in his childhood.

Lovemaking became a strained and unhappy experience for us, almost an act of hostility. One night, as we lay tense and silent after a particularly unsatisfactory attempt, I dared to suggest it might be an idea for us to go and see someone.

What do you mean *see someone?* His voice was ready to pounce.

I don't know, I said, already trying to retreat. A counsellor perhaps. Someone we can talk things through with.

He laughed derisively. A *shrink*, you mean?

Someone who's trained in these things.

And what would we talk about exactly? He was goading me, daring me to dig myself in even deeper.

About our problems, I said weakly.

And what might they be?

I don't know, I said. That's the trouble. I didn't mention Caroline Palmer. I suppose I still wanted to pretend that she didn't exist.

You don't know? he asked scathingly, sitting up and glaring down at me. Well that's great, he declared, because nor do I!

I was silent. He knew perfectly well what he'd done. But while he refused to face it, while there was no hope of him acknowledging it, I couldn't see any point in saying anything.

For God's sake, he said viciously, what I need is support. And all I get is this shit!

His anger poured off him like a heat, he trembled with barely suppressed rage. For an instant he seemed to hover on the brink of something violent, but then he twisted away and stalked into the bathroom.

A few days later we had a repeat performance. I started it, as always unintentionally. I said something about needing to make the effort to be with the children, and immediately we were back into the lack of understanding I was meant to be showing him, my unreasonable behaviour. This time it was a stand-up argument late at night after too many drinks. And this time the rage rode over him and didn't stop. He grabbed me by the arms, just above the elbows, and gave me a hard shake. I don't think he realised how tightly he was holding me, but the bruises came through the next day.

He was chastened; we both were.

That didn't stop it happening again. This time he gave me a punch of frustration and resentment. It wasn't a hard blow, more of a tap really, but in many ways more hurtful than anything that had gone before.

I knew this wasn't the real Harry, that this rage was quite alien, but that didn't stop me from feeling frightened, as much for the damage it was doing to our relationship as for anything that might happen. I knew it couldn't go on, that there was a risk that we would do irretrievable things to each other. I decided to make a new commitment to our marriage, to give it everything I had, though it would mean forgetting the past and pretending nothing had ever happened.

Looking back – how clear it is, looking back – it was the biggest misjudgement I ever made.

I slide the photographs back inside the manila envelope, place the envelope inside a larger padded envelope and, stapling it shut, take it out to the rubbish bin.

I continue hunting through the shelves until early afternoon when I force myself to go and have something to eat. I take an aspirin for a lurking headache. I go through the motions of walking in the garden and leafing through the mail. I pick Josh up from school. But really I am only counting the hours.

Moreland and I go to the conservatory and sit in our usual seats, adjacent wicker chairs set at an angle to each other, facing the french windows. Moreland opens the wine. After four days this has become something of a ritual.

By common consent we don't refer to the salvage boat. We have already established that there is no news as yet, that we'll be told as soon as there is.

We sip at our wine, we talk unhurriedly. I sense myself slowing down, slipping into a small pool of contentment. He has this effect on me, Moreland. An illusion of safety.

Josh appears, clutching an assortment of books to his chest, and asks what he should write about for his English essay. He listens attentively to Moreland's opinion, less attentively to mine, and, spinning out the visit for as long as he can, finally pads off.

When he's gone, we talk of inconsequential things. Moreland tells me about a master joiner at the boatyard who got into a brawl. 'Apparently he was a bit upset about his ex-wife getting remarried, and gatecrashed the wedding party.'

I warm to the hot-blooded joiner. 'Perhaps he should have told his ex-wife how upset he was,' I suggest. 'Perhaps she would have changed her mind.'

Moreland looks doubtful. 'Do you think so? I'm not sure people change their minds about things like that. I mean, once they've decided a marriage is over.'

'But who decides when a marriage is over?' I argue mildly. 'If you believe the statistics most people seem to regret getting divorced.'

'Statistics...' he says in the tone of someone who treats them with caution. 'But it only takes one person to decide a marriage is over, doesn't it? Then that's that, whether the other person likes it or not.' He says this tightly, with something like disapproval.

'The other person can fight, though.'

'Fight?'

'Try to win the other person back, I mean.'

'Well ... I suppose. But breaking the new husband's nose could be a bit excessive.'

'I don't know,' I say, only half joking. 'It shows persistence, and persistence can be very attractive.'

'Or very unrealistic.' He adds, with a peculiar little grimace, 'Better to face the facts, it seems to me.'

A pause. We have come as far as we can on the subject without venturing into more personal territory. Now and again Moreland has mentioned his wife. Very occasionally I have asked about her. Her name is Tricia. She is an expert on medieval tapestries and works for an international dealer. They have no children. She travels a lot. She likes the theatre.

I talk about Harry in similar cocktail-party terms. Places we visited. Parliamentary occasions. Holidays. Saying these things, it occurs to me that in the absence of any other information Moreland must think that Harry and I were happy together.

Moreland starts to tell me about his forthcoming trip to Saudi Arabia, how he has tried unsuccessfully to put it off, how he must leave in two days, but will keep in touch by phone. 'I'll be back on Friday, but I may not be able to come over till Monday,' he announces in an odd voice, 'Tricia's up for the weekend, you see.' He gives me a look as if to say: that's the way it is, I'm afraid.

'Oh.' I put on an over-bright smile. 'How lovely.'

For some moments he seems to hover on the point of saying more, but, changing his mind abruptly, pours more wine instead.

We sit back. Breaking the silence, Moreland asks about my day.

I tell him I have been looking for some information.

'What sort of information?'

'I don't really know, that's half the trouble.'

'Is it important?'

'It could be.'

He waits quietly.

And then I tell him, because it's got to the point where I need to tell someone and Moreland is the only person I can tell. 'It seems some money has been mislaid, money Harry was responsible for.' As I say this, I feel the first dart of shame. 'Money from a charity concert which Harry helped organise. The charity people think' – I glance away down the lawn – 'that Harry knew what happened to it. They think that he diverted the money.' Keeping my eyes on the broken thread of the horizon, I explain about the invoices from Mountbay and, later, the absence of them, the cheques drawn on the charity account that were signed by Harry and countersigned by an elderly trustee, and the lack of paperwork or explanation for the services that Mountbay was meant to have provided. It takes longer to describe the links between Mountbay and Harry and the empty account at Simmonds Mitchell, mainly because I feel bound to paint the fairest possible picture and, wherever possible, to give Harry the benefit of the doubt. 'If Harry did use the money to invest it on the commodities market, then there must have been a good reason,' I finish lamely.

Moreland, who has been listening intently, stares past me, his eyes grave, and moves his head slightly, a gesture of disbelief or disapproval, or both. Finally he asks, 'And what was it you were hoping to find in your search?'

'Anything. An address, a name at Mountbay. Someone who could tell me what happened.'

'But nothing?'

'Not so far.'

'Have you taken legal advice?'

'No. But Gillespie's looked at it. He told me there was no proof, and since there was no proof I should leave it alone. He said the charity would never dare to sue. I'm not sure he's right about that, but even if he is, that's not the point, is it?'

'When did this happen, Ellen? When did the money go missing?'

'Over the last year,' I admit softly. 'The last Mountbay payment was made in January.'

His chair creaks as he leans forward and rests his elbows on his knees. He frowns into the garden. Twice he glances across at me, as if to search for confirmation of a new and disturbing thought, and I realise that he is groping towards a fresh interpretation of events.

'You knew nothing about this Mountbay business before?' he asks at last.

'No. All I knew was that Harry was beside himself with worry. I thought it was just the business. The recession . . .'

252

'But you think it might have been this?'

'The strain must have been terrible... The thought of having lost all that money, the shame...'

'You think—' But something holds him back, and I finish it for him.

'I've often thought it might have been suicide, yes.' I look away, I make a gesture somewhere between sorrow and resignation. 'I had a feeling, I don't know why. That's why I took the children away, in case the body turned up and he'd shot himself or something awful and it all came out. That's why I didn't want anyone to go looking for the boat.'

Realisation spreads over his face. 'Oh...'

'I didn't want the children to have it hanging over them for the rest of their lives. I didn't want them to be saddled with all that.'

'But Ellen...' He's pulling his thoughts back together. 'After all this time, they won't find anything. I mean, no body.'

'Maybe,' I say, my voice heavy with doubt. 'But I'm afraid' – the thought emerges in a whisper – 'that they might find the gun.'

Moreland stares at me.

'I can't be sure ... I told the police I wasn't sure ... But I think it went missing that day. At least – I found the locker open the next morning. I know I should have told them that, I *know*. But I couldn't bring myself to. I didn't think it would help the situation. I mean, he sometimes took the gun on the boat anyway. It could have meant nothing. I didn't want to put ideas in their heads. I didn't think it would do any harm...'

'God,' Moreland sighs, sinking back in his seat. 'And I thought it would help, to find the boat! I thought it would get you through your legal troubles. I thought...' He gestures helplessly, the first time I have seen Moreland at a loss.

'I don't blame you.'

'You should have told me.' He turns to me in vague horror. 'Why didn't you say?'

'I really didn't think there was much chance of anything being found.' I give an empty laugh. 'I didn't realise quite how good you were at tracking these things down.'

'Maybe I'm not. Maybe it isn't *Minerva*.'

But neither of us dares to believe this just at the moment.

'You should have said,' he repeats in mild rebuke.

A slamming door echoes through the house, a voice calls from the hall.

It's Anne. For once Moreland's manners fail him, and he turns his mouth down in annoyance. We exchange a look of open disappointment.

I call a hello and take a gulp of wine before getting up to greet them.

Although it is all wrong, although this shouldn't be coming from Anne and Charles, I can see what they are going to tell me. Anne's liquid eyes, her quivering mouth say it all. By the time Charles delivers his sombre statement, I am ready for it.

They have found *Minerva*.

His face creased with feeling, Charles wraps me in a tweedy embrace. Drawing back, holding me at arm's length, he says in his funny brisk way, 'A relief, old thing, eh? Goes part of the way, doesn't it? *Part* of the way.'

Antagonisms forgotten, Anne presses her cheek against mine. 'At least we know now,' she says in a voice that is rocky with emotion. 'We know where he was laid to rest.' She blinks heavily, and focuses on a distant, more heavenly prospect.

For a dreadful moment I think they have found Harry. I turn rapidly to Charles, who shakes his head. 'Just the boat so far, Ellen. Nothing but the boat.'

I look away in case the relief shows too strongly on my face.

Charles and Moreland start to talk. It takes me a while to realise that they are discussing a person called Critchley who is waiting in the hall.

Moreland touches my arm. 'Do you want to come and talk to the coastguard?'

'I'm sure she doesn't want to be bothered,' Charles interjects kindly. 'Do you, Ellen?'

But I do, I do. I want to know everything. 'Yes, please,' I say to Moreland.

Pausing only to suggest that Charles and Anne wait behind, Moreland leads me through into the hall.

It is the fierce-faced coastguard from the memorial service. He stands in uniform, clutching his cap in both hands. He seems discomforted at the sight of me. I think he would prefer to speak to Moreland alone. He greets me with indistinct words of regret. As soon as we're settled in the study, he avoids my eye and addresses his report exclusively to Moreland.

The water was murky, even when the tide was at its slackest, he relates in his soft burr, but they could see it was a yacht. And then, as the salvage vessel swung, they managed to manœuvre the camera over the stern of the yacht and saw enough of the gold-leafed lettering on the transom to identify the name.

'She's lying on 'er port side,' he continues. 'Dug herself down a bit, o' course. The mast looks like it's broken some way up. Bent right over, at any rate. A lot o' rigging about.'

'Any other damage?'

'Not so as could be seen. But then she was on 'er side, like I said.'

'Nothing else?'

He shakes his head. 'No, but . . .' A pause. He flicks a glance in my direction but fails to meet my eye. He says tightly to Moreland, 'Likely they'll be sending a diver down.'

A moment of stillness. Moreland says, 'A diver? Why?'

I notice the hatching of deep lines that fan out from the coastguard's hard eyes, the broken veins that cover his cheeks. 'Have to cut things away,' he states, 'so no more nets get caught. Mast and rigging and maybe a stanchion or two.'

'But they'll leave the hull?' Moreland asks.

'That'll dig itself right down,' the coastguard replies ponderously. 'That size o' vessel, won't take long. It's all sand.'

They talk on. Moreland goes back over several questions, asking for detail, querying things. He asks again about signs of damage, but the coastguard can offer no more information.

Hardly listening any more, I begin to consider how I will break the news to the children.

Only when the two men stand up do I realise they have finished. We walk back to the hall.

Moreland whispers to me, 'I'll just see him out.'

I find Josh in the sitting-room, planted in front of the television. Anne's round form is perched uncomfortably on the floor next to him, her plump arm gripping his shoulders, her head tilted protectively to within an inch of his, her corseted bosom pressed against his chest. Josh flashes me a fierce look, as if he blames me for this intolerable act of affection.

'Just catching up with the news from school,' Anne says briskly, sending me eye signals to show she has said nothing about the boat, signals that I can see Josh picking up rapidly. Leaning on a chair arm, panting hard, Anne pulls herself slowly to her feet. 'Well,' she exclaims with heavy tact, 'I'll go and see how Charles is getting on.'

Josh fastens his attention back on his programme, something about wildlife in Siberia. Now that he has been so thoroughly alerted to the atmosphere, I realise I will have to tell him what is going on, although this is not the moment I would have chosen.

I crouch beside him. I say simply, 'Something's happened. I'd like to have told you later, after everyone's gone, but . . .'

He says nothing. I reach for the remote control and press the mute button. In the silence I say, 'I expect you'd like to know straight away.'

Staring furiously at the flickering screen, he gives a violent shrug.

Kneeling, I put an arm round his shoulders. I begin gently, 'They've found the boat – *Minerva*. Not far away. Well – out to sea a bit. The coastguard found it today. They just came and told us.' I add, as if further explanation were needed, 'It's there on the bottom. On the sand.'

Beneath my arm, Josh's body feels stiff. He doesn't say anything.

Then I say with an enormous effort: 'They don't know yet if they'll find Daddy as well.'

Eventually I pull away a little and take a look at him. He is glaring at the carpet, his face taut with suppressed emotions.

Casting about for a point of contact, I say, 'Moreland –

Richard – might be able to tell you more. I . . . didn't get all the details. He's got them all. Shall I ask him to come and tell you about it—'

Josh makes a noise half-way between a snort and a gulp, an exclamation of frustration or anger, and, twisting away from me, rolls onto his feet and stalks head down from the room.

I call after him, 'Josh—' But I don't pursue him. I wouldn't know what to say. Sinking down onto the floor again, I am filled with a dull sense of inadequacy.

Moreland finds me there a few minutes later. Taking my hand, he helps me to my feet and onto the sofa. We sit beside each other on the edge of the seat, hunched forward, our knees touching.

'The diver, Ellen. It's not about the rigging or cutting things away . . .' His hand hovers over mine, then grasps it firmly. 'It's the police. They want to have a look inside.'

I feel a pull in my stomach, a terrible lurch. 'But I thought . . . He said . . .'

'For some reason he didn't want to mention it in front of you.'

'The police?' I echo in a dying voice.

He nods.

'But why?'

'They want to check. They more or less have to, apparently.'

A pool of coldness forms in my stomach. 'Have to?'

He sighs unhappily. 'According to Critchley, they have no choice. They're duty bound to try and find out what happened. And since the boat's fairly accessible . . .' He hesitates, locked in some internal debate. 'Also . . . because all the hatches were closed.'

I feel a sharper descent, like the beginnings of death. 'Oh?' It takes me a while to ask: 'Is that – something?'

'It's – not what one would expect.'

For an instant I free fall towards despair. Then somehow I breathe, I breathe steadily, forcing myself to respond to the slow inner count that comes back to me from the past. I take a painful step towards acceptance. I force myself to realise that nothing I can do now will prevent what is to happen.

Agonising though it is, I have to accept that I have done my best, and I have failed.

They are going to find Harry's body.

I give Moreland the faintest nod, to show that I have understood.

'I'm sorry,' he says.

He sandwiches my hand between both of his and raises my hand against his cheek. This gesture unlocks something in me, a rush of self-pity, a hunger for reassurance. I drop my head against his shoulder, I feel his arm come around me and pull me against him, I reach an arm round his neck. In the few moments before we hear Anne's steps coming along the passage, I cling to him wordlessly.

A brief moment of comfort before I too begin to sink.

TWELVE

Actual bodily harm? Oh, that's just a black eye or three!' declares Molly in answer to Katie's question. 'A tap on the chin. No more than your standard dust-up, really.' Reducing her eyes to slits, she floats a fist across the table in Josh's direction. 'Your *grievous* bodily harm, that's a bit more serious. Blood and gore. Ambulances and hospitals. Short of intent to murder, but not much.'

Katie digests this. 'And after that?'

'What? Next worst?' Molly responds brightly. 'Well ... wounding, I suppose. Knives. I've got one lad at the moment, slashed someone in a gang fight, took off the other guy's *lip*.' She acquires an astounded expression. 'I mean, how do you take off a *lip*?'

The children ponder this with suitable gravity. Conversations with Molly are seldom less than educational. I spoon the last scrapings of sauce over Josh's spaghetti and take the dish to the sink.

'And after wounding?' Katie asks, pursuing some solemn logic of her own.

'Thanks, darling,' says Molly, blowing me an airy kiss as I put the carrot and celery salad on the table, salad which she herself has brought, along with the bottle of powerful Bordeaux we have just opened and some runny Brie and the rich chocolate pudding waiting on the counter.

'After wounding...' Molly muses. 'It's robbery, armed robbery, things like that ... But my lads haven't usually got to that stage. They don't usually learn about shotguns until they're banged up on remand. Notice I said *until*.' She sighs and shoots Josh a companionable look, as if he were of an age and understanding to share her pessimism. 'Mind you, given a gun tomorrow, most of them would probably manage to shoot themselves in the leg. They generally manage to cock things up. Part of their charm.'

Josh chews his spaghetti distractedly.

Katie sips her wine-and-water and replaces the glass on the table with concentration, shifting it about until she has fixed it in some predetermined position. 'What happens to them?'

'What, when they do armed robbery? Well, depending on how many other convictions a kid's chalked up – and we're likely to be talking long lists here – then it could be I.T. – intermediate treatment. But more likely, it'd be straight to a young offenders' institution. And' – the declaration is fatalistic – 'a guaranteed life of crime.'

'After robbery?' Katie asks without looking up.

'What – *even* worse, you mean?' Rolling her eyes, Molly refills my glass in a great surge that pushes the wine to the very rim. 'Then you're into rape, attempted murder, murder . . . Spying. Treason. Have you been to the Tower, Josh? Seen what they did to traitors in the old days. *Gory.*'

Josh nods vigorously, half afraid that she will go into detail.

'But we don't get the serious offenders,' Molly resumes. 'Normally it's just theft and more theft. That's all they think about, my boys – money, money and more money. The way they see it, there's absolutely nothing wrong with acquiring it from other people. In fact they're usually surprised when we want to lock them up for it.' She takes a gulp of Bordeaux. 'Even, in some cases, honoured.'

Not for the first time since we sat down, my eyes are drawn to the trees outside, my infallible wind indicators. The copper beeches stand tall and still in the evening light, the oak too; only the fingers of the ash tremble occasionally. Calmish, then, out at sea. Did the diver get down today? Nobody has called to tell me, and I have not called to find out. Once, in my impressionable youth, I used to imagine I possessed a degree of intuition, the result of a couple of prophetic statements I made that happened to come true, undoubtedly by chance. But now, though I stretch my mind out into the distance, though I wait for some dormant instinct to flicker into life, no whisper comes back to me.

'Why don't you get them?' Katie is asking Molly.

'The serious offenders? Well – in this part of the world, though you may find it hard to believe, there aren't that many. Not *yet*. And then' – she shrugs – 'by the time they get out they don't usually count as young offenders any more.'

Katie seems satisfied, and loses interest.

'Not hungry?' I ask Josh, who's stirring wreaths of spaghetti round his plate.

He shakes his head and puckers his mouth. A hush descends. The business line rings distantly in the study – I have unplugged all the other extensions. Today is candidate selection day, and it will almost certainly be Anne or Charles or Diana, wanting to give me the news. I will be more than happy to hear about Charles' interview, how he feels it went, but not while Katie is here, not when I am anxious to make her trip home an experience she will want to repeat.

Molly, glancing round, says with a cheerfulness that is almost pitched too high. 'Well, enough of *that!* I want to know *all* about the worst excesses of the school staff. Caught any of them smoking behind the lavs, Josh? Swearing in the corridor? Mmm? Spitting in the flowerbeds?'

Josh giggles.

'And you, Katie? What're your lot up to? Does the head sneak off to raves wearing shiny black leathers, mmm?'

Katie looks up and frowns.

'They're always up to something,' Molly declares with her rich laugh.

'She's a crabby bitch,' Katie says with unexpected vehemence.

There's a sharp silence. Molly, who's used to this sort of language, doesn't blink an eyelid.

'Katie,' I say quietly. 'That's enough.'

She turns and glares at me. 'Well, she *is!*' Then, dropping her eyes, flushing angrily, she scrapes her chair back and parades out of the room.

I leave it a while before going in search of her. I find her in her room, sitting at her desk with her back to me, hunched over a magazine. 'Could you drive me straight back?' she announces without looking round.

'If you like.' I sit on the bed. I pick up one of her teddy bears and fluff up its ears. Finally I ask, 'What was all that about?'

Without looking round, she raises her shoulders almost to her ears and says nothing. I give the bear a hug and wait, in case she should change her mind.

Yesterday, when I drove to the school to tell her about the discovery of *Minerva*, she took it with extraordinary calm, as if she had prepared herself for it. I was impressed by her control, by her touching concern for me and how I was coping, but now I wonder how deep this self-possession really went. I know that visions of the boat form the stuff of her nightmares. I know that her imagination, like mine, is far too graphic for these things.

She stands up abruptly and slides me a quick look from behind a curtain of hair. 'Sorry,' she declares, exhaling sharply. 'Sorry.' She scoops her hair back. 'It's just – the bloody staff get up my nose sometimes. They're so sodding pathetic.'

I hate this language she has taken to using; it's not like her at all. But I don't say anything. I recognise that this offhand manner is part of her defence mechanism, that, among her schoolmates, it probably gives her street credibility and therefore distance. I just wish she wouldn't use it on me.

On the journey back to school, Katie puts a hand on my arm and makes a wry face. A peace offering. But not, it seems, a prelude to explanation. As soon as we draw up at the door, she plants a quick kiss and is gone.

When I get back, Molly and Josh are playing a furious card game, slapping cards loudly on the table, shouting challenges, grabbing at each other's stacks. I leave them to it.

The searching of the bookshelves has become like an old

obsession; I'm no longer sure why I'm doing it but I can't rid myself of the compulsion. As I work my way along successively higher shelves, the volumes become increasingly unlikely. Victorian books on fishing and hunting, old editions of *Who's Who*, text books from Harry's university days. I search without real hope of success, continuing only because I've so nearly reached the end.

Breaking off briefly to put Josh to bed, I climb the library ladder to the topmost shelf and tackle a collection of classic French novels in the original which I never knew we had, and which will certainly never have been read, since Harry didn't speak more than ten words of French.

'Treasure hunt?' Molly asks from below with a laugh that doesn't entirely hide her curiosity.

'Sort of.'

I flip open the final volume, and, with blatant disregard for the well-being of the spine, hold the book upside down by the covers and shake it vigorously.

'Give me a clue,' she says as I climb down the ladder.

'I'm looking for something – I don't know really – a paper, a letter . . .'

'What – from Harry?' She says nervously.

'Yes.'

'Not a *note* or something? God, you don't think . . . ?' She gives me a horrified look.

'I don't think anything.'

Molly laughs with relief. 'I was going to say . . . Whatever happened, my love, I don't think Harry killed himself. He was far too tough. A born survivor.'

I don't get to sleep until late, three or so. And then it is only to wake in the first light of dawn, roused by a thought that has arrived from nowhere, mysterious yet fully formed. It won't leave me alone until I have crept out of bed and padded downstairs. I collect the first key from the desk in the study, and go into the kitchen. Reaching into the dresser, I lift the hidden key off its hook and, passing quickly across the cold hall in my thin-soled slippers, I go into the boot room and turn the separate keys in their locks and swing open the door of the gun locker.

The lone shotgun stands in its carrying bag, the second bag crumpled and empty at its side. Crouching, I search through the clutter of cartridge boxes and belts and bags lying in the bottom of the locker, then, working my way up the inside, look along the single upper shelf. There are several dusty manila envelopes, an empty cartridge carton, four loose cartridges standing on their metal rims, a box of fishing flies with a transparent lid, and one glove. The first envelope contains an instruction booklet on shotgun maintenance. The next envelope, which has been ripped almost in two, its corners curled and dusty, holds a much-folded guarantee. The last envelope, a heavy-duty full-size A4, unlabelled and unsealed, lies beneath the empty cartridge box, and looks newer. It contains four or five sheets of paper. Drawing them out, the first thing that meets my eye is the letterhead, *Mountbay (Guernsey) Ltd*.

I stare at it for a long moment before sliding the papers back inside. The house is very quiet. Closing the locker again, I take the envelope to the kitchen and lay the papers out on the table. Diverting to put on the kettle, I sit down in front of them and space them out.

Five sheets in all. The sheet with the Mountbay heading is the first of a two-page document entitled 'Heads of Agreement'. A letter from a bank in St Peter Port, Guernsey. An unheaded page of jottings – mainly figures – in Harry's handwriting. A bill from a hotel in Palma, Mallorca.

The hotel bill, made out to a Mr J. Meacher, I relegate to one side and examine the page of jottings. But though there are dates and figures and, on the right-hand side, what appears to be a running balance, it's all very cryptic. Each entry is identified by initials and what might be dates – only days and months, no years – and the figures themselves are denoted by single or double digits with decimal points. These numbers may well represent larger amounts – hundreds or thousands or more – but there's no way to know.

Pulling my wrap closer around me against the early chill, I

turn to the letter from the Guernsey bank. Marked strictly private, addressed to Harry here at the house, it is dated just over four years ago and is signed by the manager. Under the subject reference *Mountbay (Guernsey) Ltd*, the manager writes to confirm that he is in receipt of the bank draft for fifty thousand pounds and has with effect from the above date opened a thirty-day deposit account in the name of Mountbay (Guernsey) Ltd. He quotes the account number and emphasises the need to quote the authorisation code for telegraphic transfers. Overdraft facilities will only be possible by prior arrangement.

I read this oddly tantalising letter once more before turning to the last offering, the two-page 'Heads of Agreement' on the Mountbay headed paper. The document has been word-processed, the right-hand margin neatly justified. The agreement, so the text begins, is made between Mountbay (Guernsey) Ltd and J.H. Hoch of Lichtenstein (Nominees). After three paragraphs of dense legalese, the terms of agreement are itemised, one to three on this page, four to six on the next. The text is stiff with holdings and options and rights, and the second sheet doesn't look much better, though I hardly have time to read it before my eye is caught by the signatures at the bottom.

For the Liechtenstein company there is a foreign name, precisely and legibly reproduced. For Mountbay, Harry's squiggle and flourish. And beneath it a second signature, the long loose scrawl that is unmistakably Jack's.

'Well, what a treat,' Jack declares expansively, leading me towards a deep chair in the conference area of his light-filled office. I have been here once before, about two years ago when I came to touch Jack for funds for Molly's project. The room looks different, though I couldn't say how. New decor perhaps. Or maybe it's the magnificent desk, an immaculate art-deco style piece in pale cross-grain veneers, with, at one corner, a large leather-framed photograph of the prime minister, facing outwards across the room. The Sunday quiet seems unnatural. When I was here before, there were voices and telephones and the sound of heavy traffic outside.

Jack, in weekend garb of dark blue slacks and smoky-green open-necked shirt, both immaculately pressed, stands by the chair. 'To what do I owe this pleasure?' Before I can reply, he states as if in answer to some question of mine, 'Not long now. Tomorrow. Well, the *official* announcement anyway.' He slides me a jittery grin: the candidate in an agony of suspense. 'Someone's going to slip me the wink before then, of course. Should be about seven tonight.' He waits until I'm properly settled before crossing to the opposite chair. 'I really don't think anyone could fault my interview. Didn't put a foot wrong. Even the sods who were gunning for me couldn't catch me out. Managed the two trick questions just like that.' He snaps his fingers. 'I knew it went well, of course. You sense these things.' He sits back, he beams confidently at me, though his gaze is oddly unfocused, as though fixed on some more attractive prospect. 'But who can tell?' he says with uncharacteristic equanimity. 'If I don't get selected, well—' He gives a careless shrug to suggest that losing would be no more than a minor inconvenience.

You'll be mortified, I think to myself. You'll bay about injustice. You'll probably move to another town.

Rubbing his hands together, he peers at me with fresh concentration. 'So!' He turns his palms outwards in a gesture that says: here I am, gleaming with success, no time to spare, but still at your service.

I reach into my bag for the envelope of documents.

'By the way,' Jack says, 'I did try to call you when I heard about the boat. Couldn't get through. Then what with one thing and another . . .' He screws up his handsome face in a plea for understanding.

'It's all right.'

'I'm so sorry. Poor you. What a shame.'

I blink at this.

'Well, you must be fed up with the whole thing,' he says. 'It must be a bloody nuisance, having everything dragged out like this.'

266

Odd that Jack should be the one person to appreciate this, though nuisance isn't perhaps the word I would have chosen. 'It'll hurry the formalities up, so Leonard says.'

But he isn't really listening. He's looking expectantly at the pages I have pulled out of the envelope.

I pass the heads of agreement across. Sitting forward, Jack brings the document into his lap with a deft twist and I watch his eyes fix on the Mountbay letterhead. His expression is unreadable. Quickly he skims the first page and flips over to the next. When he finally looks up, it is to raise his brows ironically. He waits for me to speak.

'What's it about?' I ask.

Casting the paper onto the low table between us, he sits slowly back and, making a cradle of his hands, watches me over the tips of his fingers. 'Mountbay was Harry's baby. I haven't had anything to do with it for years.'

'But . . . at one time?'

'I was involved, yes. But in a purely nominal capacity.'

Not sure where to take this, aware of how very still Jack is and how sharp his eyes are, I progress yet more slowly. 'When was this?'

'Oh, it must be five years ago. And then for no longer than a year – if that.'

I absorb this through the sluggishness that comes from lack of sleep. 'But what did it do exactly – Mountbay?'

'Do? It didn't do anything. It was set up as a convenience, a vehicle for moving money around.'

Again I wait for him to help me along, again I wait in vain. Finally I ask: 'What money?'

'Money,' he repeats unhelpfully.

I am struggling now. 'You mean – business money?'

He blinks lazily, though his eyes have lost none of their keenness. 'I imagine so, yes.'

The minimal response again. As if he wants to absolve himself from responsibility for this conversation.

'Jack—' Out comes my nervous laugh, sounding strident. 'I'm very tired, there's a lot going on, it would be nice if you could be a little more forthcoming.'

He gives a show of incomprehension. 'I'm answering your questions, aren't I? What else do you want to know?'

I shake my head. 'Everything.'

'Well – ask away.'

'You're not making things easy.'

'I'm telling you what I know,' he says reasonably. 'Ask away.'

Seeing that he is not to be shifted, I move wearily on. 'So – Mountbay was part of the business?'

He purses his lips. 'Oh no. It was quite separate.'

'I don't understand.'

Jack taps his forefingers against each other in what could be irritation or reflection. 'Harry needed to keep it separate because he took to using it for purposes that were – how shall I put it – that took him slightly near the mark.'

This time I wait him out.

His eyelids droop in forbearance as he explains, 'There were certain advantages to chanelling payments through Mountbay. Financial advantages. But, well – it was a grey area. Open to interpretation, you might say. The purposes of the payments would have had to be argued with the Revenue. It was easier, in the end, not to let them know.'

I am careful to show nothing, and certainly not surprise. Outside in the street, an ambulance siren whoops past. The afternoon sun glows hotly against the slatted blinds.

'Where did the money go? What was it used for?' I ask.

Jack's hands fly open briefly. 'I don't think that matters.' His tone is final. Proceed no further, he is saying, I have judged it best that you don't know. But I can't help wondering if he is sparing me this knowledge for my benefit or his own.

'I'm sorry,' I say, determined not to be put off for once, 'but are you saying you don't know? Or that you can't say?'

He lifts his shoulders. 'It's irrelevant, that's all.'

It seems I'm not to have all my questions answered after all.

Sweat is damp against my blouse. I find my thread again. 'I've discovered Harry had an account with a commodities broker called Simmonds Mitchell. Was that—'

'After my time. Harry started all that after he and I parted company.'

All that. He makes it sound ominous. 'You knew about it?'

Jack gives me a look which suggests that I have managed to strike out in another unsuitable direction. 'I knew *of* it,' he replies testily. 'Indirectly, anyway.' He tucks in his fine jaw, he tightens his lips, he says disapprovingly, 'Harry had been dabbling in commodities for some time. *Investing.*' He instils the word with scorn. 'The chances of making money in the commodities market are about on a par with winning at roulette, and probably a great deal worse. Harry made the classic error of thinking that he could cover his liabilities by doubling his risk. He thought a quick flutter on the market would fill a few yawning chasms in his cash flow. Well ... I imagine that's how it was,' he adds ingenuously. 'Harry wasn't exactly forthcoming about these things.'

I think: but you knew all the same. Just as you knew all about the charity money the other day. I glimpse Gillespie's shifting figure in the background again.

'Did Harry say anything to you?' I ask. 'About his losses?'

'He didn't have to. If he'd have won he'd have been laughing, wouldn't he?'

'He didn't say ...' I can hardly bring myself to ask, '... where the money might have come from?'

Jack gives me a look that says this is not wise to ask.

This is it then, as close to an explanation as I'm ever likely to get. But, having got this far, I'm not sure what I have really gained. A little more certainty perhaps. The knowledge that there's absolutely no hope of the missing money turning up.

'Thanks.'

Jack flutters his fingers graciously. Then, fixing me with a thin smile, he adds, 'I'm sure you'll appreciate, it wouldn't be a good idea to mention this to anyone. It doesn't bother me – I cut the ties long ago – but for the sake of Harry's reputation.'

I give an unhappy nod.

'And, Ellen – no more enquiries about Mountbay. It would only draw attention. You appreciate?'

I let his words reverberate a moment longer before asking with a laugh, 'What do you mean, more enquiries?' I'm thinking of my letter to the Guernsey bank; I'm thinking that he knows about it.

He shoots me a look in which realisation and annoyance are keenly merged and for an instant I have the wild impression that I have caught him out. 'Enquiries,' he repeats solidly, taking his time. 'As in questions to Gillespie.'

'Ah.'

He starts to get up.

'Jack—'

'Mmm?' He perches restlessly on the edge of his seat.

'There was something else. I wondered...' I draw out the photocopy of the hotel bill I made this morning. '...if this meant anything to you?'

Jack takes the copy from my hand and examines it. He pushes out his lip, his expression shifts to one of puzzlement, though not before I fancy I see a flash of something like displeasure dart over his features. Languidly he lifts his low-lidded eyes to mine and gestures ignorance.

'The guest's name...' I direct him back to the bill.

'What...?' He frowns at the paper. 'Meacher?' He glances back at me, as if he's trying to get the drift of my reasoning.

'The chairman of the planning committee. Isn't that his name?'

Jack makes a show of taking another look. 'Could be.' He regards me with sudden amusement. 'What a mind you have, Ellen!' He waves a hand loosely in the air. 'Okay. Well, if it *was* Meacher, what can I say? These things have been known to happen. It would be unrealistic to say they didn't. But it's all pretty harmless. A cheap holiday, the odd weekend, things like that. These people get paid next to nothing. They expect this sort of perk. Part of the job.' He regards me coolly. 'Harry wouldn't be the first developer to have promoted his interests in this way, Ellen.'

Molly's dark suspicions about Jack and his relationship with the planning authorities flicker through my mind and I wonder fleetingly if Meacher has taken any holidays at Jack's expense.

I start to gather up the Mountbay papers.

'I'd be careful of those,' Jack murmurs, drooping a lazy finger in their direction.

Doomed to be slow on the uptake, I look up questioningly.

'Best to get them shredded. I can do it for you, if you like.'

I hold them closer to me. 'But I thought I might write to the bank . . .' I put on an obdurate face.

'As you wish. But it's very unwise.'

I hesitate.

'I'm just telling you what's best for you.' When I don't reply he stands up and says irritably, 'Well, don't say I didn't warn you.'

I get slowly to my feet. We walk towards the door.

Pausing at the threshold, Jack reverts to his father-figure tone. 'Gillespie looking after you? Talked you out of this house-buying idea yet?'

I busy myself with the fastening of my bag, I look non-committal.

Jack stands close in front of me and shakes his head. 'There is no house, is there, Ellen? *Is* there?'

'I want to move,' I declare. 'I'm longing to move.'

He regards my protest with open scepticism. 'I talked to Gillespie. We worked out that a loan of thirty thousand should see you through for the time being. I'll be glad to top it up if necessary. But no more than that, Ellen. Sorry.'

I feel a childish resentment. 'I see,' I say stiffly. 'May I ask why?'

'We think you'll only give it to this stupid charity.'

'That's my business, I would have thought.'

'Well – *hardly*. Anyway, it's not just a matter of the money. You don't seem to understand that any talk of money or restitution—'

'I wasn't going to—'

'*Any* talk of money or restitution,' he continues firmly, '*any* discussion at all, would be as good as announcing that Harry was guilty of something. You do realise that?'

I must look unconvinced, because he steps closer and takes me lightly by the forearms and says in a tone of patience wearing thin, 'Do I have to spell it out for you? Nothing can be proved about this missing money, Ellen, because so long as there aren't any papers lying around there's no way they can trace Mountbay back to Harry. That was the whole point of Mountbay, you see, the reason it was set up the way it was – so there'd be no possibility of any comeback.' He pauses to let this sink in. 'The only way they might pin anything on him is with *those*.' He points towards my bag and the papers. 'What Harry was thinking of, I don't know, leaving that sort of stuff around.' He swivels his eyes heavenward, then, fixing his considerable gaze on me again, insists, 'Without proof all they can accuse Harry of is incompetence – something these charity people seem to be pretty good at themselves. And incompetence is a very different thing from fraud, Ellen. Putting it mildly. Now you see why you mustn't admit to anything at all. Why it would be dangerous to keep those papers . . .'

Against my will I see the wisdom of this. With bad grace I reach into my bag and pull them out. Jack plucks them from my hand and, leading the way into the outer office, switches on a large shredding machine. He leafs quickly through the sheets. 'The hotel bill – is there an original?'

I hesitate for only an instant. 'No.' This of course is untrue; the original is at home. But it isn't a Mountbay document, it can't be dangerous, and a stubborn perversity makes me reluctant to give up quite everything to Jack.

He feeds the papers into the jaws. 'You're worrying too much anyway,' he says dismissively. 'If anything does come out, there'd be a bit of whispering – well, a bit of a fuss, maybe – but in the end the whole thing would die a death.'

A bit of talk, some fuss. He makes it sound harmless, but it seems to me that a whisper, far from dying a death, is the one thing that lives for ever.

The rest of Sunday passes slowly, with unreality. I feel both connected and detached, like an actor stepping in and out of a half-learnt role. My family come and go, as if responding to a set of stage directions that I haven't had the chance to see.

By the evening I am good for little but supper in front of the television. Molly insists on staying another night, and I don't try to argue her out of it. We watch a comedy. I find myself laughing, though the programme isn't that funny.

I drive Josh off to bed at nine. We don't say much. I think he's as exhausted as I am. Downstairs, a phone rings and I hear Molly answer it. A moment later she calls for me to pick it up.

As I make my way to the bedroom extension something inside me beats a warning.

Mrs Anderson's tone is buttoned down tight, but not so tight that I can't pick up the note of indignation beneath. 'I'm going to have to ask you to collect Katie and take her home, Mrs Richmond.'

'What's happened?'

'What's happened,' she says coldly, 'is that Katie's behaviour is totally unacceptable. Under *any* circumstances, *whatever* difficulties she may be having.'

Oh, Katie.

I say, 'But what—'

'I'd prefer not to go into detail.' Her voice rises abruptly then steadies again. 'I think all future discussion should be carried out by the head.'

I start to apologise, something of a reflex action with me, then, remembering that Katie is someone I don't need to apologise for, I halt and inform her that I should be there in twenty minutes.

First there are certain rituals: the bath, the bar of old-fashioned soap, the fresh towel, the crisp white night-dress, the hair-brushing, the childhood cup of cocoa. Then we lie in my bed, side by side, my arm round her shoulder, her sweet-smelling hair against my cheek. Like old times. I have left a night light on, but Katie still shifts slightly against me as if to check that I am really here.

Finally I murmur, 'Well . . . ?'

A flutter of tension that eases again. 'St-u-pid,' she sighs at last, in a sing-song. 'Bit of a disaster. *Sorry.*'

'What happened?'

273

She moves her shoulders in what may be a shrug. 'I said something, that's all...' The bravado slips, she exhales unhappily. 'I called Mrs Anderson a stupid cow. Well, she kept on at me, kept using this awful voice, like *sickly*, trying to get me to talk about what she calls my *problems*. Putting her arm round me – I *mean*!' She shudders. 'Sick! I *told* her – I don' wanna talk about it. I told her!'

Waiting for the rest, I look out at the soft windless night and the scattering of stars.

Finally she says in a defeated voice, 'And then – well, I sort of bashed her. I didn't *mean* to, I just...'

I give it a moment before I ask, 'When you say bash...?'

'I dunno ... a sort of punch, I suppose. I didn't *hurt* her or anything. I just,' she breathes deep draughts of self-disgust, 'lost my cool.'

I say gently, 'Like with the science teacher?'

I sense her surprise. 'Sort of.'

'And what happened with him?' I ask in a neutral tone.

'He's just a creep!' she exclaims as if I should know this. 'Pure *grease*. That smarmy smile, hand on your shoulder, coming close to look at your work all the time – I mean, his face *this* close.' She closes her thumb and forefinger to within a millimetre of each other. 'Thinks he's so *wonderful!* And oh-so innocent, oh-so incredibly amazed when I told him to lay off. A total creep! And all the staff think he's so *totally perfect!*' She twitches with indignation. 'But he's *yukky*. Complete *yuk!*'

I have two pictures, one of a schoolmasterish hand patting Katie's shoulder, an innocent gesture of encouragement or congratulation that this man has probably been using for years; the other, of him looking at Katie in open admiration, as many men have been doing since she was twelve or so, and failing to take his eye away in time, leaving his hand a moment too long, overstepping the mark a fraction.

It doesn't really matter which of these pictures is closest to the truth; it's the way Katie sees it. It's the way she interprets even Mrs Anderson's fumbling attempts at kindness as an unacceptable invasion of her space. If Katie has made any progress in the last weeks, it's not in the direction of trust.

274

Mrs Anderson probably thinks Katie is a neurotic, ruined by a doting mother. She cannot appreciate, and certainly I can never tell her, what Katie has been through.

I lie awake for a long time after Katie has gone to sleep. Finally I creep downstairs to make myself a hot drink. I find Molly in the sitting-room, watching a late movie, puffing on a forbidden cigarette, a habit she was meant to have given up six months ago.

'Is she all right?' she asks anxiously.

I nod.

'What happened?'

'Nothing. She's just upset.'

'What about?'

'Everything, I suppose.'

'She hasn't said?'

'No.'

Molly, who can spot an evasion a mile off, shoots me an admonitory frown.

I admit wearily, 'She had a row with her housemistress. Then something unfortunate happened. Apparently Katie lashed out at her.'

'Oh.' Molly manages to give the sound a wealth of meaning.

Ignoring this, I go through into the kitchen.

'Look, sweetie,' says Molly, coming in behind me and settling on the opposite stool, 'don't get me wrong, *please* don't get me wrong, but you don't need this, you really don't. Not at the moment. I really think you should consider getting some help. Counselling or something.'

'I'll be all right.'

'I meant for *Katie*.'

I knew she meant for Katie. 'She'll be all right, too.'

Molly fights an internal battle that rages across her face. Finally she says, 'I just don't think you should have to deal with this on your own. Not with everything else that's going on. No one should.'

'Funny,' I say, 'the head seems to agree with you. She thinks Katie needs a psychiatrist.'

Missing the irony in my voice, Molly says quickly, 'Well, I'm not so sure about psychiatrists. They just bugger people up, if you ask me. But counselling. I've seen plenty of kids that a bit of counselling did wonders for. *Wonders*. You know – someone from *outside*. Someone who isn't involved.'

'Katie'll be all right,' I say again.

Molly stays silent with difficulty. Finally she feels bound to say, 'Sweetheart, don't rule it out. Sometimes family aren't the *best* people to deal with these things.'

I make a performance of the tea, pulling out pot, cup, saucer.

Molly sighs. 'I hate to see you getting so upset. She always makes you upset.'

'I don't think that's quite fair.'

'I'm sorry, but she does. She knows exactly how to wind you up.'

'Don't, Molly.'

'But it's true, sweetheart. Got to say it. She *does*. Somehow she always manages to get to centre stage. If there isn't a drama, then she manages to make one happen around her.' Molly looks pained. 'I'm only saying this because I love you and I worry about you and I don't think *anybody* should have to cope with this alone. I'm not saying Katie isn't feeling all this intensely, I'm sure she is, I know she loved Harry, but really...' She is going to say more in the same vein, but thinking better of it, she murmurs, 'Well, it isn't fair on you.'

So Molly also believes that Katie is a case for treatment, that I have been too indulgent.

Something heaves up inside me, an explosion of internal fury. I have the urge to shout her down, to crush these ideas of hers, to make her realise how deeply unjust they are. I want to cry, Yes, she's difficult! Yes, she's demanding! But what do you expect? How could she be any other way when she's so dreadfully and irretrievably damaged? When she was so completely deceived?

But I cannot say it, I must never say it. To do so would be to admit that Katie is the real victim in all this, and I will never add to her pain or risk her precarious balance in this way.

To rid myself of my anger, I direct it back at Harry.

There were times long before that day in March when I felt I could have killed him for what he had done to Katie.

If he were here now, I could kill him still.

Later, in the twilight, a sound. The scrunch of car wheels on gravel, growing closer. I avoid Molly's questioning glance. I take a mouthful of coffee and wait. When the doorbell rings, I get up calmly, as if I've been expecting someone. Crossing the hall I have the sensation of looking backwards at this moment from a point far in the future.

Two cars are visible through the side window. I swing the door open to a solemn triumvirate. Charles, Leonard and, in a linen suit that looks as though it's had a long day, Inspector Dawson. Or perhaps it's Chief Inspector Dawson, I've never been quite sure.

'Ellen – I would have phoned but . . .' Charles waves a hand, looking oddly stricken.

Leonard, gaunt-faced, severe, stands slightly apart, looking at a point just to one side of my head.

'May we come in, Mrs Richmond?' says Dawson in his easy, salesman's voice.

'Please.'

I put on some lights in the drawing-room. Dawson positions himself by his usual chair facing the bay and the garden. We sit down, I in the armchair opposite Dawson, Charles and Leonard deeper in the room in seats that circle the fireplace, as if we are two groups of people having separate conversations. Dawson fastens his deliberate gaze on me, he puts his stubby fingers together and says without preamble, 'Mrs Richmond, I have to inform you that earlier today we retrieved a body from the sea and that it has been formally identified as that of your husband.'

I take a long moment, I unfasten my gaze from Dawson's, I look down at my hands.

'Where?' I manage at last.

'From the boat. Inside the boat.'

'Inside,' I echo, hearing my voice die away. I feel a surge of sadness. Or relief. It's hard to tell.

277

In the well of silence that follows I half turn to Charles, who meets my eye in unhappy confirmation.

Dawson's unmoving gaze waits on mine. 'With regret,' he continues in a drab voice, 'I must also inform you that a shotgun was found beside the body' – a pause, a moment of deathly stillness – 'and that from a preliminary examination it would appear that Mr Richmond suffered wounds commensurate with having turned the shotgun on himself.'

I stare, I can only stare.

'I'm sorry.'

I close my eyes, I have a sense of disconnection.

I dimly hear someone moving across the room, then Leonard is at my side, pressing a glass into my hands. I bring the water to my lips and drink.

Leonard's dry bony hand finds its way into mine. I hear the rasp of his breath beside my ear, and he murmurs, 'Not to blame yourself, Ellen. Not to blame yourself.'

Old resentments rise, freshly charged, into my chest. I blink back sharp tears. Through this sea of feeling I'm aware of Dawson watching me with a blend of detachment and discomfort, someone who hasn't found the breaking of bad news any pleasanter with the passage of time.

He waits for my attention.

'There are certain formalities,' he begins when I look up at him again. 'Routine investigations which will take some time, I'm afraid. We are hoping, circumstances permitting, to raise the yacht. Hopefully in the next few days. Obviously we'll try to minimise the distress to yourself and your family. Keep things as low-key as possible. And I hope you'll bear with us during what I realise will be a difficult time.'

Uncertain of what he means by this, I nod vaguely. Leonard, still hovering, draws up a chair and sits close beside me.

Dawson leans forward a little, as if to exclude Leonard from our conversation. 'I realise this has come as a great shock to you, Mrs Richmond. I've no wish to keep you from your family at this time. But it would be most helpful if you could tell me what reasons you think your husband might have had for taking his own life.'

278

'There were money troubles . . .' I start tentatively, looking to Leonard, inviting him to take up the story.

But before Leonard can speak, Dawson raises an excluding hand and says, 'Go on, Mrs Richmond.'

I rest my fingers briefly on my eyelids. 'There were debts,' I say unsteadily. 'Business debts. Personal debts. I didn't realise quite how bad they were, not until recently. He never told me these things . . .' I think of the children, I force myself to go on. 'Then there was his political career. When he lost his seat in the last election it was completely unexpected. He—'

'Yes?'

It's a moment before I can say, 'It was an enormous shock. He took it very badly . . .'

'Did he seem particularly depressed in the period just before he disappeared?' Dawson presses on. 'In the last few days or so?'

'I don't know. I've thought about it a lot. But with my husband it was hard to tell. He wasn't a great talker, not about this sort of thing anyway.'

'But you've been thinking about it, you say? So it had entered your mind – that he might have taken his own life?'

'No. No. It was just those last few days I kept thinking about, that's all.'

'Any particular reason?'

My throat seizes, blocking my words. Finally, I manage, 'All the things I didn't say. All the things I wish I'd said.'

'Nothing happened around then?' he asks. 'No events that upset him in any way? Nothing that might have had a bearing?'

I go back through my memory, which has become fragmented and oddly jumbled, so that I'm no longer absolutely sure of what is real and imaginary. 'The only thing . . .'

'Yes?'

'There were some business calls that seemed to upset him. I felt – it was no more than a feeling – that there was some crisis.'

'News of some sort?'

'I can't be sure, but I think so.'

'And this news, whatever it was, he took it badly?'

I almost say, *he took everything badly*. 'He was very worried, yes.'

'But he never talked about taking his life?'

'No.' I shake my head slowly. 'No.'

Dawson takes a long breath and says almost as an afterthought, 'Would you say he was capable of taking his own life?'

I wrestle with this. When my answer emerges, it is as much an admission of my own failure as Harry's. I whisper, 'Yes.'

Thus do I condemn you, Harry.

Dawson's mouth lifts at the corners, his puffy cheeks swell. He has the answer he wanted.

THIRTEEN

We were sitting on the shady balcony of the apartment in La Jolla, staving off jet lag, when Katie began to tell me about the bad times. Josh was playing computers with some kids next door, the drone of the traffic on the boulevard two blocks away had sunk to a lazy hum, and a welcome breeze was drifting in from the ocean. We were talking in a desultory way about clothes when, grasping the opportunity such as it was, I asked her in unemotional tones about her shopping expeditions with Harry. How were they? Were they – it was always hard to find the right words – difficult?

Screwing up her eyes against the bleached light, looking out over the palm-lined street towards a vivid Astroturfed lawn opposite, Katie said just as casually, They were okay. Then, with a grudging sigh, Well, not too bad.

How do you mean? You mean – caution, caution – there were some things that weren't so good?

It was just, like, this *feeling*, she said in her flat child-voice. I dunno. She shrugged hard. I tried not to think about it. Like if I didn't think about it, it would go away. I thought that maybe if I was dead nice, if I did the trips and wore the clothes, then he'd be pleased with me and everything would be okay.

Pausing, she attacked some well-picked skin on her forefinger.

It wasn't that anything happened, she added, knowing how paranoid I was on this point, how I felt driven to ask about this even at the cost of making her retreat.

281

He didn't touch you? I couldn't help asking, my heart cold against my ribs.

He held my hand, things like that, she said briskly. That's all.

I knew she was telling the truth; it was just that I couldn't hear it too often. I had developed this retrospective distrust of Harry's every action, and, excruciating though it was, I had to rake through each event.

Another day, as we walked along the broad glaring sand, past the whooping volley-ball players and the strutting girls, Katie talked about the French holiday. As so often in the conversations that followed, her mood was at first remote and unpromising. It was as though she needed to withdraw into herself, to create some distance from me before she could talk about these things.

She'd been dead worried about the holiday, she said. She'd been worried in case she spoilt things . . .

Spoilt things. It was all I could do to let this pass.

Everything was okay for a while, she said. He seemed to . . . She groped for the words. Well, it was like he didn't *crowd* me. Like he was making an effort to be . . . okay.

With what in mind? I wondered bitterly.

Then, she went on dully, then . . . Responding to the memory, she lengthened her stride, she glared down at the sand. It was like it was before, she said. Just . . . suddenly. She didn't know why it changed so quickly. She couldn't think what she'd done. She didn't think she'd done anything.

And what did he do? I asked in my most detached voice.

For a time I thought she wouldn't answer. Sort of hugs, she said finally. Just hugs . . .

I had, I thought, become a master of impassivity, of the carefully arranged expression, but Katie, taking a glance at my face, reached for my hand and gave it a solemn pat. This role reversal that she practised then, her dutiful concern, produced terrible upwellings of emotions in me, and I had to turn away and talk of something else.

After the beach, Katie was silent for several days. Her

sessions with Bob Block were, I think, absorbing her completely. Then, when we were unpacking groceries one afternoon, stealing curls of toffee crisp ice cream from a giant tub and sucking them off the spoon, the subject of Christmas came up. It was Christmases in general, but, glancing into her face, I knew we were both thinking about the last one.

This was the time when I should have realised, the moment when the situation was first written out for me, if only I hadn't been so determined not to see. It was three days before Christmas. I came in late after ferrying Diana back from a party and, finding the study deserted, the TV off and the rest of the floor in darkness, I went upstairs in search of bed, Harry, and the children, in no particular order. Our bedroom was empty; I registered vaguely that Harry must be downstairs after all. Out of long habit I went along the corridor to check on Josh, who, as always in sleep, was completely dead to the world, lying flat on his back, making soft purring noises in the back of his throat, looking beautiful and new and miraculous, as only a child can look.

Coming to Katie's room, seeing her light was still on, I knocked briefly and reached for the knob. I remember my sense of anticipation; the holidays had just begun, I was thrilled to have her home again. I remember, too, the instant of surprise as the door was flung open and Harry stood before me, his skin flushed, his mouth slightly open, his shirt skewed at the neck, and beyond, Katie's white face stared out from the bed. As we stood in a silent tableau, the signals came at me thick and fast. A tension hummed through the space between us, and the air contained something I couldn't pin down, something ugly and disturbing. I saw in Harry's face irritation and resentment, and a strange shadow, like guilt. And in Katie, in the long moment before she turned away and buried her head in the pillows, an expression of injury.

Looking back, I realise the atmosphere positively reeked of Harry's craving. But though my instincts insisted something was wrong, though I couldn't rid myself of this unease for several days, I finally shut it out. I have always tended to push

283

uncomfortable thoughts to the back of my mind, to hope in some vague unchannelled way for the best. And when Harry told me that Katie had been difficult, that she had trounced off in a temper, that he had gone to her bedroom to make peace only to be goaded into a row, I believed him.

I believed him, I overrode my instincts, and that was my great failure, the whip with which I now beat my back.

The thought of Harry having sexual feelings for Katie, let alone putting them into practice, was to me so unthinkable that it didn't begin to enter into the realm of possibility. Such things simply didn't happen to people like us. I still thought of us as ordinary people then – though, by almost any standards, Harry was far from ordinary. Deep down – I see this now, perhaps I always knew – he was irretrievably damaged in some way.

Anyway, my limited capacity for suspicion was already filled by his infidelity with Caroline Palmer. If Harry was engineering scenes with Katie, if he was using her against me in some way – and this was how I came to interpret what had happened – then I decided it must be part of some emotional game plan, some way of driving a wedge between us. I didn't imagine for one moment that Caroline Palmer was the heroin-substitute, the methadone, to his real addiction.

But then I saw everything in terms of our relationship, and how it had failed. It was soon after the French holiday, which for a time seemed to offer such hopes, that a deep ache of anxiety lodged itself in my stomach and wouldn't go away. At first I blamed business problems, political failure; all the worries we were sharing. It was some time before it dawned on me that our relationship itself was slipping away. I began to feel Harry exercising his considerable determination against the very idea of us, as though he had weighed things up and decided our marriage simply wasn't worth the effort any more.

Agonising over this, I failed to see that there was another side to this coin of unhappiness, that Harry's fascination with Katie had grown into something altogether darker and more obsessive.

With the brilliance of hindsight, I see how it began; how, as Katie began to grow up, Harry used to watch her with a speculative expression that was midway between admiration and puzzlement, as if he couldn't quite believe how sweet and lovely she was. Since I felt the same sort of wonderment when I looked at her, since I thought it both natural and not a little miraculous that Harry should feel the same affection for Katie as he did his own son, I was thrilled at the attention he gave her. I was pleased when he used to break off from whatever he was doing to talk to her. I was touched when he stroked her hair at bedtime, or ran a knuckle softly down her cheek. It was more than I had dared hope for. I couldn't believe my good fortune.

Katie, using more instinctive touchstones, knew better, though she could never rationalise her feelings. Even when she talked it through with Bob Block she couldn't put it into words; she just knew she had to get away.

The boarding school. Why didn't I guess? Not the real nature of the problem – I could never have guessed that, not then – but why didn't I see that she didn't really want to go? That she felt driven to leave home because she felt so uncomfortable there?

As we packed the ice cream away at La Jolla and talked of Christmas, the memory of the bedroom scene hung between us. Katie wouldn't give me details then. All she would say was: it wasn't bad-bad. Later, when we had established a means of communicating the more emotional information through the neutrality of Bob Block, I learned that, if not bad, the Christmas incident had certainly been worse than anything that had happened before.

There was a certain amount of touching, Bob relayed.

Touching, I echoed, dying quietly inside. You mean assault.

After Christmas, Katie kept telling me, things were better. The rest of the school holidays and the first half of the spring term there were no shopping expeditions, no unexpected visits to school.

This, of course, was because I was watching him. Tracking

his movements. Looking for evidence of Caroline Palmer. Ironic. The hunter on the false trail.

Wretched Katie, wretched me. Both deceived.

I've thought a lot about the nature of blame and forgiveness. I don't blame Harry for being the way he was. I loved him as much for his faults as his more obvious strengths.

But this isn't to say I can ever forgive him; I can't. Understanding is quite separate from forgiveness. You can only forgive acts that people commit unthinkingly, in a rush of weakness, in the heat of the moment; things that you yourself might have done under the same circumstances.

But Harry didn't do what he did unthinkingly. He planned it. It was this realisation, more than anything, that suspended all feeling, that gave me the strength to do what I did. It was this realisation that eats away at me still.

I find the office of The Rumanian Orphans Relief Fund tucked away above a print shop in a run-down terrace of late-night grocery stores and kebab houses and launderettes between Queensway and the Russian Orthodox church. The lino on the stairs has seen better days and there's a smell of stale spices and disinfectant. The door at the top sports the charity's logo and, tacked on beneath, a stencilled sign inviting entry. Inside, two work-weary women sit tapping at computers amid stacks of mail. The walls are papered with press cuttings and photographs of volunteers grouped around relief lorries at what I presume to be Rumanian orphanages.

Tim Schwartz's office, which leads off the outer office, is a more spacious but no less overstretched room. The surfaces of the metal and melamine desk and conference table and the tops of the battered grey filing cabinets are stacked with documents and box files.

Schwartz looks mildly disconcerted at seeing me, as if I have come unannounced and he is having to tear himself away from something important.

He is wearing a voluminous shirt tucked unevenly into his jeans. His narrow face is made more severe by a pair of metal-framed Einstein spectacles. He clears a seat for me then wheels his own chair round the desk and leans back in it, his arms crossed in the attitude of someone who is not likely to be impressed by what he is about to hear.

I unfold my prepared piece, written in the late hours of last night. Mindful of Jack's warning, I am anxious that there should be no misunderstandings.

'While in no way accepting . . .' My voice cracks. I clear my throat and start again. 'While in no way accepting that my husband had any responsibility for any funds . . .' I pause over the awkward phraseology. '. . . that might have been due to your charity, and on the understanding that what I am about to offer should in no way be seen as connected to any other matter, such as these funds, I would nevertheless like to offer, as a gesture of good faith, a contribution to your charity. In view of my present finances, this contribution will be smaller than I would like, in the region of twenty thousand pounds for this year.' I glance up and find Schwartz's eyes glinting with what looks like a hostile light. 'In future years,' I continue uncertainly, 'I would expect to make further donations. These donations will continue for as long as I am able to make them, and for as much as I can afford.'

Schwartz's mouth twitches downward. 'That's it?'

'I'm sorry?'

'These future donations,' he says tautly, 'you can't specify . . . ?'

'No, I . . . Not at the moment. Though I should have a better idea in a couple of months.'

He screws up his mouth. 'Mrs Richmond, frankly your offer amazes me. *Amazes* me . . .' He lifts an unbelieving hand. 'I mean, this money never belonged to your husband. It wasn't some kind of *loan* to be repaid at his – or your – convenience. It belonged to *this charity* . . .'

I see slippery slopes before me, just as Jack prophesied. 'It's the best offer—'

He cuts in aggressively, 'I mean, we *are* in agreement as to who the money belonged to, aren't we?'

'I don't think . . . I don't really feel I can . . .' I hear my voice ebbing away. '. . . discuss it.'

'We're going to pretend your offer is unconnected, is that it?'

Reluctant to be cornered, I waver, only to realise that hesitation is an answer in itself.

'We're going to say you're making these donations out of the blue, are we?' he continues derisively. 'And the charity's meant to show extreme gratitude, I suppose?' He gives a faint snort. 'The fact is, Mrs Richmond, that we need this money *now*. We have major capital projects that have got to be carried out before we can even begin to think about the children's emotional and educational needs. We've got to get the orphanages functioning. I don't think you realise – these children are still having to live in the most basic conditions. The staff spend all their time wrestling with prehistoric laundry and kitchen equipment. The plumbing doesn't work, the heating fails—'

'I've no doubt you need the money,' I interrupt unhappily. 'And if it was in my power to wave a magic wand and send enormous quantities your way, believe me, I would, I *would*.'

Partially mollified, he falls into a grudging silence.

'And if I personally had anything else to give,' I say, 'then I would give it. But my husband's estate isn't going to be worth very much. I have the house, but there's a big mortgage, and by the time it's sold . . . There should have been some shares, I thought there were some shares, but it seems they're not mine after all.'

'I'm sure you're doing your best, Mrs Richmond. I don't doubt your goodwill. That's not the point.'

We eye each other uneasily as we both ponder the point, which, I don't need reminding, is that the charity is without its money.

I refold the paper. 'My offer . . .' I venture at last. 'It's not a lot . . . I realise . . . But hopefully it would go some way . . . ?'

'Forgive me,' Schwartz retorts, 'but it's really pointless to discuss this. A large sum of money has gone missing. And the simple fact is that it belongs to us.' His hands fly out in indignation. 'We want it back.'

'I don't think . . . that'll be possible.'

He slowly refolds his arms. 'Oh? Why?'

'Because it isn't there.'

'You know this?'

'Well . . . I'm pretty sure,' I murmur.

His eyebrows rise. 'You're pretty sure? I'm sorry,' he says with elaborate sarcasm, 'but what does that mean?'

Not at all certain I'm doing the right thing, ignoring all sorts of warning signals, I hear myself say, 'We've looked. Everywhere. We can't find any money.'

'You can't find any money. I'm sorry, but that's hardly our problem. Why shouldn't it be in some bank somewhere?'

He has me there, of course. He also has me deep in admissions that would appal Jack. 'We did find a hidden account. But it was empty.'

He puts on a knowing expression, as if to say: well, you would say that, wouldn't you?

'We tracked the money some of the way,' I tell him, 'but I'm afraid it seems to have been lost. All of it.'

Now he is taking me more seriously. '*Lost?*'

'It seems so.'

'You're telling me you *know* it's all gone?'

Deeper still. I tell him we're as sure as we can be.

He searches my face, as if to gauge the truth of this. 'Great!' he hisses bitterly. 'Bloody great!' His mouth twists into a childish grimace, which, perversely, serves to make him appear more human and less frightening.

'I'm very sorry . . .'

He glares at me, not trusting himself to speak. Finally he manages: 'So what are we meant to do exactly? Forget it ever happened?' He twists his head to stare furiously out of the window before coming back with, 'There's no way we can do that! We can't just write it off like some bad debt! I have to tell you that the trustees intend to instruct lawyers,' he presses on. 'Not to mention the police.' He is angling for some greater reaction from me. 'And they're absolutely right!' he cries in a final outburst. 'It's theft! And of the most craven and disgusting sort!'

In the pause that follows, he pulls back a little, he says almost contritely, 'I'm sorry. I didn't mean to . . .' He makes a gesture as if to claw some of his remarks back.

But we both know he meant every word.

Leaving, Jack's warnings reverberate through my mind and I wonder if I haven't given too much away.

'He didn't get enough support, that was the trouble!' Anne declares emotionally. 'He just didn't get enough support!'

She looks to Charles and, briefly, Diana, but I am aware that her comment is aimed at me. It's a theme she has hinted at several times in the last hour but not openly voiced until now. We are sitting in Anne and Charles's drawing room indulging in desultory speculation about why Harry should have taken his own life.

Charles mumbles tensely, 'I don't think that's quite right, dear. I really don't. I think there were all kinds of pressures . . .'

Anne's voice rises again. 'But if he'd been able to *talk* to someone. *That's* what's so dreadful . . .' Unable to bring herself to look at me, she directs her resentment at Charles. 'Someone should have realised. *Someone.*'

I suppose I should defend myself – I think Anne is hoping I will – but I don't want to be drawn into an argument that will distress us both.

Diana drawls some inaudible comment. Forced to repeat herself, she rasps crossly, 'Never a talker, Harry. Never. Not to anyone.' She blows a dismissive breath through drooping lips and reaches, fumbling, for a cigarette. She has shown little emotion apart from irritation, as though she would like to get hold of Harry and give him a piece of her mind.

The room is hot and close. The curtains are partially closed, though whether against the sun or as some mark of respect for Harry I'm not sure. In the reduced light the densely patterned fabrics seem heavy and overblown, the gilt-framed landscapes dark and stormy, and, on the ancient Persian rugs, the sleeping dogs are like lumpen black shadows.

Charles says, 'I think we just have to accept that he was good at hiding his worries. After all, he hid them well enough from us.'

'What are you talking about?' Anne retorts tearfully. '*I* knew something was wrong! *I* knew! It was just that I didn't want to interfere. I thought I'd be getting in the way. I thought I wouldn't be *welcome*. But I knew all right!' Her tremulous voice rises into an accusing silence.

'Whatever any of us did or didn't do personally,' Charles says, 'is rather by the way now. I really don't think there's any point in going over it time and again. He was obviously determined to do what he did—'

'How can you say that?' Anne returns sharply. 'Harry wasn't the sort of person to give up. When did he ever give up?' She glares at us emotionally, daring us to answer. 'He must have felt so *lonely* to even *think* of doing such an awful thing,' she cries in a tone of high reproach. 'That's the worst of all. Not having anyone to turn to!'

'Anne, *please*.' Charles purses up his face in rare exasperation, and Anne closes her mouth abruptly, looking wounded.

I get up and Anne's liquid eyes follow me as I position an ashtray under Diana's toppling ash. Before I can retreat, Diana's long claw-like fingers close on my arm. 'You were hard on him, you know. You shouldn't have been so hard on him.'

I stare at her, too astonished and hurt to speak.

'Couldn't live up to it all,' she declares.

I don't try to ask her what she means by this, I just pick up my bag and with a tense goodbye leave the room. Charles catches me at the door.

'Ellen dear – don't take any notice. Please. They're just upset.'

I breathe hard and nod. I let him walk me to my car.

'It's the sense of having been so useless,' he goes on. 'That's what's makes us all so *cross* with ourselves.'

'Yes.'

'They didn't mean it.'

'No.'

He squeezes my hand.

'I'm sorry about the candidacy,' I say, remembering that condolences are in order.

'Oh, there we are,' he says phlegmatically. 'I didn't really fit the bill, did I? I mean, I'm a bit of an anachronism. Small-time landed gentry dabbling in politics – outmoded. Jack's much more the image – thrusting and successful and all that. I think they've made a wise choice.'

'Yes,' I say, 'I think they probably have.'

When I get home the children are watching their favourite soap and Molly is scraping burnt debris out of a pan.

'Bloody press,' she declares, abandoning the pan. 'Kept phoning. So I put a message on the answering machine saying we were unavailable and not taking messages. Is that all right?'

I tell her that's fine.

'Oh, and your father called earlier. He didn't seem to know what was going on. I wasn't sure what to do, so I sort of told him. Sorry, I just thought maybe . . .'

I tell her that she did the right thing, that I'm glad it was someone else who told him. My father will be finding the idea of suicide embarrassing, even threatening, and I'm sure he would have had great difficulty in finding something to say to me.

Molly pours coffee and cranes at the jotter pad by the phone. 'Oh, and Margaret got a fax at the office from Richard Moreland – in Saudi Arabia, is it? – saying he couldn't get through, and could you fax him back.'

'Could you ask Margaret . . . No—' I pick up my coffee, I start for the study. 'Thanks. I'll call her myself.'

Margaret is not at home but I leave a message on her machine asking her to fax Moreland in the morning and tell him what has happened. Though I miss my daily talks with Moreland, I'm not sorry to be communicating with him at one remove. I can't entirely forget that it was he who led the police to Harry's body, that I have him to thank for this sword of doom that hangs over my head, and just at the moment I feel rather confused about that.

While I'm speaking into Margaret's tape, I remember something I was going to ask her yesterday. I thought of it on my way back from Jack's, while I was still smarting from the sense of inadequacy he always seems to produce in me. Reaching into a drawer, I take out the Majorcan hotel bill with Meacher's name on it and check the date – it was some five years ago – and ask Margaret if she could look it up for me in the office diary and tell me what was happening around that time.

When I return to the kitchen Molly is getting ready to leave.

'Sure you'll be all right?'

'Sure,' I say.

'You know, I keep thinking . . .' She hesitates, she puts on a expression of studied puzzlement. 'This suicide thing – don't take this wrong – but I just never thought he had it in him.'

In the end it is easier to shut ourselves away for a few days. I inform Josh's headmistress that he won't be attending school until further notice; I ask Molly and Jill if they would be kind enough to shop for us; I have the answering machine refer calls to Margaret, who phones in twice a day with the messages; and Jill's husband frees the hinges of the ancient gates at the end of the drive with a hammer and chisel and swings them shut for the first time in living memory, although, strictly speaking, we are acting illegally by barring public access to the ancient bridle paths which criss-cross the estate.

I'm glad of our isolation. I enjoy walking with the children and doing things we used to do when they were younger and I seemed to have more time, like setting nature projects and reading aloud. I rally them to these pursuits in a relentless way, all heartiness and positive thinking like some scout-mistress. It's not that I'm insensitive to their moods, I'm just anxious to show them that life goes on, that, while we need to come to terms with these new events, it's also important to draw strength from each other.

I tell neither of them about the post-mortem, which Charles informs me is being carried out on Wednesday morning. Nor do I tell them that the operation to lift the yacht is under way until, after a failed attempt on Wednesday afternoon, it is finally accomplished late on Thursday. Not understanding the possible significance of this – and I do not explain it to them – they listen to this news with curiosity but no alarm.

Later we discuss the funeral, which I'm hoping to arrange for early next week; how it should be, the sort of hymns Harry would have liked. Twice I give Josh the option of staying away, but this causes him to glare at me accusingly, as if I am trying to deny him his rights from some deep and dishonourable motives of my own. I am careful not to suggest it again.

We talk about suicide too, or rather I talk about it and the children listen. I tell them how people with lots of problems can get so worried about them that their bodies get worn down and stop working properly and send all the wrong chemicals round the brain and then the brain stops working properly and these people become very ill, though neither they nor anyone else may realise it, and that this illness is as real as if they had broken a leg or needed an operation. I try to explain how, even though Daddy loved us all just as much as he ever did, the illness was so bad that it blotted out his memory and his feelings and, though he never wanted to leave us, he felt he had no choice. I consider telling them about the insurance money and how, if everything had gone to plan, it would have been his legacy to us, but on balance I decide against this.

With difficulty, because it's something that disturbs me too, I also tell them about attitudes to suicide, how people who don't understand about illnesses of the brain think that it's simply a lack of will, that only weak people kill themselves, when in fact you have to be very strong to do it. How some people like to suggest it's the dead person's fault, when it's no one's fault at all. How families can feel very guilty, as though they might have been able to prevent it, when it can be quite impossible to foretell. I say that none of us could have guessed what Daddy was going to do, that he gave no clue.

Such a painful discussion was never going to be easy, and

both children are upset by it, albeit in different ways – Katie looks cross, as though she would rather not hear about it at all, while Josh seems overwhelmed by the unfathomable mysteries of the adult world. But I know I'm right to force them through it, that before they face other people they must understand how unfairly the outside world may judge our tragedy.

Friday is the kind of day when the world seems to have rolled to a gentle halt. The heat hangs over the wheat fields, a single whisp of cloud floats in the haze of the sky, and the river is dull as an old mirror. In the late afternoon, as the haze thickens into a sulphurous band that blurs the horizon, I think about Moreland. I wonder whether he's back at his cottage yet, and if so, whether he's waiting for his wife there, or has brought her down with him from London. I wonder if she's as striking as her photograph; I wonder if, for all her attractiveness, she is good to him.

We decide to eat supper on the terrace. As the children carry out the last of the dishes and bicker amiably over who should go back for some forgotten cutlery, the doorbell sounds.

'I hope this isn't inconvenient, Mrs Richmond,' says Dawson, standing in the porch, 'but I was just passing. A few words?' He is looking hot and uncomfortable, his skin glistening, his hair damp at the temples. Sitting heavily at the kitchen table, he cranes his neck and runs a finger inside his collar.

I put a glass of iced water in front of him and invite him to take his jacket off.

He meets the suggestion with slight disapproval, as if I am encouraging him to break some rule, and briefly shakes his head. Clasping his hands together, he settles his elbows on the table.

'Perhaps you could tell me, Mrs Richmond,' he asks in a monotone, 'would you have described your husband as a meticulous man? Something of a planner?'

For some reason, this wasn't the sort of question I was expecting. 'Well . . . in business things, yes. He had to be. Otherwise . . .' I shrug. 'Not especially. It depended . . .'

'He had made a will?'

'Oh yes.'

'And he had insurance policies?'

'Yes.'

Dawson sips at his water and brings his slow eyes back to mine. 'And there was no note, Mrs Richmond?' he says quietly. 'You would have told me if there was a note, wouldn't you?'

'There was no note.'

'No,' he agrees as though the question was hardly worth asking in the first place. 'No . . .' He contemplates the table for a moment. 'A thorough man, though?'

'Well, I . . . On things that mattered.'

'And what sort of things mattered?'

'Well . . .' I face multiple images of Harry. 'Oh, the usual things, I suppose. Work, money, career – his political career, I mean.'

'And his family, I imagine.'

I tilt my head questioningly.

'He would have been concerned about you and the children.'

'Well, yes.'

'Did he talk about that? About your future?'

'From time to time—'

'In the period just before he died?'

'Not really. No. Not then.'

'But he must have had some worries about you. Respecting your financial situation.'

I see where this is leading. 'He didn't talk about it. Not particularly.'

Dawson rests his thumbs against the flattened bridge of his nose and squints briefly at me before saying, 'Your husband was very thorough when it came to his death, Mrs Richmond.'

A beat of alarm. 'Oh?'

'Perhaps you could suggest a reason?'

'When you say thorough?'

'He didn't talk about insurance policies at all?' Dawson says, ignoring my question. 'In the period just before his death?'

'No.'

'But the life policy was substantial?'

'Well – yes. So I'm told. I never knew much about it . . . It wasn't something we discussed.'

'Ah.'

The unknown pulses high in my chest. I ask again, 'You said he was thorough?'

Dawson's eyes lock on mine. 'He sawed through two plastic pipes, wide pipes that would let the water in rapidly. He then' – a pause – 'shut himself inside . . .'

I absorb this carefully. 'You mean . . . ?' I wait until he spells it out for me.

'So as to be sure he wouldn't be found.'

Ah. We are back to the unthinkable things that unrestrained bodies do, the way they rise, the way the currents pick them up and carry them off to more public places.

'And you think he did all this for a reason?'

'Most people leave notes, Mrs Richmond. They like the world to be in no doubt as to what they have done, and why. It gives them an easier mind.'

'But not if . . . ?' I want the thought finished for me.

'Well, the circumstances would be different if a man was thinking of his wife's financial welfare, wouldn't they, Mrs Richmond?' Catching my remaining uncertainty, he explains gently, 'For his wife to claim on the insurance, he would need to go out of his way to hide the true nature of his death. Go somewhere he wasn't likely to be found. Leave no note.'

I nod sharply, humbly. I lower my head.

Dawson drains his water and lumbers to his feet. 'Thank you for your time, Mrs Richmond. I very much appreciate it.'

On the way to the front door, I slow down. 'The post-mortem,' I ask, 'that's all . . . *over*, is it?'

'It will be shortly.'

'And . . . there's no doubt, I suppose . . .' I wait but he gives me no help. '. . . about what happened?'

He gives me a sorrowful look. 'Mrs Richmond, it wasn't an accident.'

I press a hand to my head as if to restore my brain. 'No. No, of course not . . .'

I watch him climb into his car beside one of the blank-faced young officers who came before. Without thinking, conditioned to a thousand leave-takings, I give them a hearty wave as they drive away.

Returning to the children, I find myself tipping Katie a soft wink.

It is only later, when I am alone, that I give a shape to the small glimmer I am feeling, and realise that I am allowing myself to believe that the worst is over.

FOURTEEN

'I'm afraid it won't be possible to fix a date *quite* yet, old thing,' says Charles, coming to a halt near the edge of the ditch and casting me one of his more oblique looks.

We are talking of the funeral.

'Why not?' I ask.

He clasps his arms, he blinks rapidly, his mouth turns down. I notice how very overheated he looks, and how very worn, his eyes drooping, his skin scored with an old man's lines, and I wonder what sort of a time he's having at home with Anne. 'Apparently these things always take time,' he says. 'No way round it. The police have to finish all their inquiries before they can, you know ... actually sign things off.'

I suppose he means, before they can release the body. I look out over the ripening wheat which stands motionless in long furry waves. For some reason I had made up my mind that we would be able to get the funeral behind us. I wish someone had told me sooner.

'I thought the police *were* finished,' I say.

'Oh, I'm sure they *are!*' Charles insists, as if he can reassure me by force of will. 'I think it's just a matter of paperwork. Red tape.'

Red tape. I can only think of the post-mortem. What else could it be? I can only imagine it isn't over and done with after all, a thought that has me draining the last of the wine from the warm glass I'm clutching stickily in my hand. I have already had one more glass than is good for my thinking, and probably my judgement as well.

'And the inquest?' I ask.

'Likely to be adjourned again.' He screws up his face apologetically. 'The coroner's office can't give a date for the hearing proper. All depends on the police again. How long it takes them to wrap things up. Got the impression the police aren't too speedy in these matters. Could be weeks. Even months.'

Momentarily confused, I have a grim thought. 'The funeral, that won't take—?'

'Oh no! Oh no! That'll be much sooner. Much sooner. Different lot of paperwork.'

'Paperwork . . . But what paperwork, Charles?'

He seems surprised at my persistence. 'They just talked about *formalities*. I rather assumed . . . They didn't give any details.'

But it has to be the post-mortem. What else could it be? I have a sense of powerlessness.

I look back to the terrace, to where Molly and Margaret sit under an umbrella with their coffee, to where Katie lies face down on the sunbed, plugged into her Walkman, and Josh stands by the barbecue poking at it with some sort of stick. As I watch he throws something onto the embers which makes them flame up and causes him to step back smartly and look around to see if anyone has noticed.

'I was going to put the house on the market,' I murmur.

'But . . . you can, can't you? I thought things were clear now.'

Now that there's a death certificate, he means. Now that, legally speaking, I'm a widow.

'I was going to wait until after the funeral,' I explain. 'I didn't want people all over the house.'

'Of course you don't. But surely, a bit of a delay won't hurt—'

'Things have changed,' I explain. 'I was relying on the life insurance, you see. That was virtually the only money I had. But suicide doesn't pay.' The irony was completely unintentional, and I give a bleak chuckle.

Charles's blink rate shoots up. Beads of sweat dance on his

eyebrows. 'No. Well, in that case . . .' I can't tell whether it's my attitude that embarrasses him, or the talk of money.

We start to walk again, following the edge of the lawn towards the rose garden and the heavy mantle of blooms, which hang vivid in the sluggish air. Now and again Charles pushes out his lower lip and funnels a draft of air upwards over his glowing nose. He is wearing his customary weekend outfit which, irrespective of the season, consists of baggy trousers and a long-sleeved, heavy cotton, check shirt designed for altogether sharper weather.

'I've been wanting to say Anne's really sorry for what she said the other day,' he says, growing awkward. 'She was upset, you know.'

I tell him what he wants to hear. I tell him I didn't take it too seriously. 'But she may have had a point, you know. Maybe I wasn't supportive enough.'

His head comes up sharply. 'No, not at all! No, I thought you were superb with Harry. A great support!'

'I was hard on him towards the end.' Why I tell him this I'm not sure. Perhaps I need to know what Charles thinks of me in the light of Harry's suicide. Perhaps I want to prepare him in some small way for the truth.

'They were difficult times, Ellen. You mustn't blame yourself. I really don't think Harry could have asked for more.' He moves his hand as if to touch mine, then swings it back diffidently. 'You were always so *loyal*.'

Loyal. Still this immaculate picture of me. Even if I suddenly announced that I drove Harry to it, I doubt he'd believe me.

We pause in front of a bed of crimson floribunda roses, their heads hanging low in the heat. At last I broach the question I have been wanting to ask Charles for some time, and for which I have engineered this stroll.

'I wanted to know—' My stomach floats upwards. 'How did they identify Harry's body?'

His damp face contorts with dismay. He makes a nervous sound. 'Ellen . . . Dear girl, what can it matter now?'

'I'd like to know, that's all.'

'But . . .' He gestures helplessly.

301

I try to explain that not knowing is far worse than anything else. Far, far worse.

His shoulders hunch forward, he fights some inner battle, Reaching a decision, he says with a sigh, 'Well . . .'

I wait.

'Dental records,' he offers at last, his voice gathering strength. 'Partly. And partly direct identification.'

I digest this slowly. 'Direct? But who by?' But even as I ask this, his expression gives me my answer. I touch his arm. 'Why didn't you say? You should have said.' I add, 'How awful for you.'

He brushes my pity aside with a shy gesture, a man who likes to think that in circumstances such as this feelings are something of an irrelevance.

I have a vision of the mortuary, of Charles staring down. I feel sympathy for him, but also, it has to be said, relief for myself, because he was there and now he will be able to tell me what I want to know.

'Was it . . . bad?' I ask very quietly.

He gives a brisk shake of the head.

'You could tell . . . that it was him?'

Enlightenment passes over his shaggy features; he thinks he understands why I am putting us through all this. 'Oh yes. There was no doubt it was him, Ellen. No doubt.'

'I mean, he wasn't . . . ?' I wait for help. Getting none, I murmur, '. . . damaged?'

Another wave of comprehension. 'Oh no! No . . .' he says gently, 'the *damage* was in the chest, Ellen.'

He still hasn't grasped what I'm after. I know perfectly well where Harry was shot. It's the rest that worries me.

'I meant, after all that time in the sea, wasn't he . . . ?' But I can't say it.

Charles is there at last. 'Oh no. He was remarkably . . .' It takes him a moment to find the word. '. . . *untouched*.'

'But I thought . . .'

He looks as though he might try to spare me the details but, catching my expression, he pushes his shoulders back, he says in oddly formal tones, 'Apparently the water's the critical factor – the water temperature, that is. And it was pretty cold. Also . . .' He describes a circle in the air. 'Being enclosed . . .' He waves the hand again, but feebly.

'Enclosed?'

'Being inside the cabin.'

'That made a difference?'

He fastens his mouth down and nods.

Finally I have it; the closed hatches, the sealed cabin, the lack of creatures that might swim in and – I use this careful word of ours – *damage* him.

No wonder the post-mortem isn't finished yet.

'Thanks for telling me.'

Charles's eyelids flitter. His tired face folds itself into a smile. 'Dear thing,' he says gruffly.

We head back across the lawn, which, after a brief revival during the rains, is growing large yellow patches again. The tableau on the terrace has shifted, I notice. The children are sitting together on the sunbed, Margaret has vanished and Molly is standing with her arms folded, glass cradled in one hand, waiting for us.

'I thought I'd take this lot for a swim,' she calls as we approach, tilting her head in the children's direction. Only when I am much closer does she tell me in a low voice which Charles cannot hear, 'The police have just arrived. Margaret's got them in the study.'

I glance quickly towards the children.

Following my gaze, Molly says matter-of-factly, 'I haven't mentioned it to them.'

I ask half to myself, 'But what do they want?'

Molly peers at me. 'You all right?'

I pull myself together. 'It's the way they come unannounced.'

I go to the children and try to sell them the swimming idea. I remind them that we have been offered the use of a pool by friends while they're away on holiday. But one glance at Katie's face and I can see that, though Molly may not have told her about the police, she has picked up the fact that something is going on.

'I've got to go and talk to the police for a while,' I explain immediately.

Katie gives me a hard stare, as if to ask whether I'm keeping anything from her. Even after all this time, she still has these moments of doubt. I touch her shoulder soothingly. 'It's just a routine thing. It won't take long. But why don't you go and swim?'

I can see the effort it takes her to summon her optimism. 'Okay,' she announces suddenly, getting to her feet.

Josh clambers up after her. I would speak to him, I would reassure him too, but he has gone before I have the chance.

Entering the study, I am met by the gaze of one of Dawson's blank-faced young officers. Dawson himself is standing at a bookcase, squinting at titles. He is wearing a suit in an eye-catching shade of mid-blue with a slight sheen to it.

He turns unhurriedly. 'Mrs Richmond,' he says with a small gesture of greeting, 'sorry to bother you again.' We meet in the middle of the room. 'But I was wondering if you could spare me some of your time? A few formalities. I would hope to have you back within a couple of hours or so.'

'Back?'

'We'll need to go to the station.'

'Oh,' I say, giving myself a second or two. I glance at Margaret, who is looking cross on my behalf, then back to Dawson. 'It can't wait?'

He makes a regretful face. 'No.' It seems to me that there is a doggedness in his gaze which wasn't there before.

'And we can't do it here?' I ask.

'Not really. I'm going to need a statement, you see. And that can't really be done elsewhere.'

'A statement,' I echo.

'A standard requirement.' He makes a reassuring movement, a spreading motion of his hand. 'We have to put things on record.'

But why now? I wonder.

I say, 'Then . . . of course.'

'Oh, and . . .' Dawson says in the casual tone of an afterthought, 'you might like to speak to your solicitor. See if you would like to have him with you. Many relatives do in these circumstances.'

In the pause that follows, the young officer shifts his weight slightly, and I find myself looking into a face that seems to have borrowed its studiously stony expression from a dozen bad films.

'But if you'd prefer not . . .' Dawson lifts his mouth into a meagre smile.

'I think perhaps . . .'

Dawson tilts his head.

'. . . that I will call him. If you don't mind.'

'Of course not, Mrs Richmond. That's your privilege.'

The room is box-like, with a narrow window set high in the wall. It is painted cream with a black floor and stained wood skirting, and has the sickly smell of industrial cleaner and room deodoriser. The furniture consists of a rectangular table, with one end pressed up against the wall, and, around it, the four chairs on which we sit, and, by the door, a fifth chair on its own. A battered tin ashtray, emblazoned with the name of a popular lager, empty of butts but caked with stubborn ash, lies on the table before me, alongside the heavy circular stand which supports the thin shaft of the microphone. The recorder itself sits on the edge of the table, against the wall. The formica surface of the table, shiny and otherwise unmarked, is scored by a single groove as if something very sharp has been dragged across it.

A uniformed policewoman has brought me tea in a plastic cup. Leonard, at my side, has accepted some water which he doesn't touch. The young officer opposite him stares out at me over the rim of his drink, while Dawson, facing me on the other side of the microphone, stirs sugar into his coffee.

'Not the most comfortable of surroundings,' Dawson says with a grunt of apology. 'But the recorder saves us having to stop every few minutes to get things down on paper. Saves a lot of time.'

I nod my understanding, though I am finding this more unsettling than I imagined.

The overhead light drains Dawson's skin of colour and accentuates the fractured ridge of his nose and the pouches beneath his eyes, so that when he offers me a quick smile the warmth, if it is there, is lost.

'Just have to get the recorder going,' he says. He presses a button or two, and, in a lumbering monotone, gives the date, the time, the place, his and the other officer's name, and my name and the fact that I am giving my statement in the presence of my solicitor, Mr Leonard Braithwaite.

'Have to go through all that, I fear,' Dawson says, instilling his voice with sudden intimacy, 'otherwise we can't transcribe from tape to paper. Can't use it for the record.' He clears his throat, he sips his coffee. 'Now ... I'll have to ask you to go over one or two matters that we've already covered, so you may have to bear with me.' The washed-out smile again. He settles his forearms on the table, he clasps his hands loosely together. 'Perhaps we could start with Mr Richmond's general state of mind in the weeks before 26 March. How would you describe it?'

I tell him what I told him before, about the pressures on Harry, the disappointments he'd suffered, the debts that he kept to himself and which I only found out about later. Going through it again, I hear myself honing the story, embellishing it in small but significant ways, painting Harry a little closer to despair. I don't like myself for doing this, but that doesn't seem to stop me.

Dawson leads me onwards with an interest that is methodical, often kindly, but never less than attentive.

'And the day of his disappearance, he gave no sign of being particularly depressed?'

'No more than usual, no.'

'There was no indication that he had any desire to take his own life?'

'No.'

'And he had never talked about taking his own life at any point in the past?'

'Never. It never entered my mind. I suppose it should have. I suppose if I'd thought—'

'Perhaps we could just go through the events of that last day, Friday, 26 March.' His low voice, steady and smooth, coaxes me forward. 'How did the day start?'

I have to think for a moment. 'We got up at about eight. Maybe just beforehand. We had breakfast. I went to the supermarket to get some food—'

'What time was that?'

'Nine. About then. I must have got back – I don't know – about quarter past ten? Harry was loading the car with gear for the boat. I sorted the food out, put it in boxes, took it out to the car. Then we drove down to the quay.'

'And when was that?'

This preoccupation with time. I try to think. 'At about . . . it must have been eleven-thirty.'

'There was a lot of this gear to load then, was there?' He asks in a tone of mild puzzlement.

'Not that much. Clothes, charts, food. It was only a weekend trip. Two, three days at the most.'

'But it took until eleven-thirty to load?'

'Well, yes. Harry kept getting sidetracked.'

'Oh. In what way?'

'Phone calls, that sort of thing.'

'Ah.' He nods, he drains his coffee. 'Business calls?'

'I think so. I just heard him on the phone.'

He cants his head slightly to one side. 'You never saw a shotgun in the car that day?'

I take this slowly. 'No.'

'Not something you'd miss really, not something that size,' Dawson remarks more to himself than anyone else. 'Would you think?' he asks, coming back to me.

I lift my shoulders. 'Harry'd already loaded a whole pile of waterproofs and boots and things like that. It could have been hidden underneath something, I suppose.'

Dawson gets a distant look as if seeing the possibility of this for the first time. Fixing his gaze on me again, he says gently, 'The firearms licence was for two shotguns, to be kept in a locker at the house. When did you first realise that one was missing?'

I work backwards. 'Three weeks ago? Whenever it was that the police officers came for the inspection.'

'No one had looked in the locker since your husband left on his final trip, since 26 March?'

'No. Harry was the only one who ever opened it.'

Seeming to lose his concentration for a moment, Dawson twists his cup slowly in his fingers.

I turn to catch Leonard's eye, wondering if he is happy with the way this seems to be developing into a question-and-answer session, but if he is concerned he gives no sign, and merely raises his eyebrows as if to say, not long now.

Dawson is asking, 'Did Mr Richmond ever leave a gun on the boat at all?'

'I'm not sure. It wasn't something I ever asked about.'

'And Mr Richmond didn't mention it?'

'No.'

It must be air-conditioned in here. I am beginning to feel chilled.

'So you loaded the car – could you take the story on from there?' Dawson's tone has softened again, as if he has just reminded himself of my situation and the need for a sympathetic approach.

'We drove down to the quay. I waited in the car while Harry went to fetch *Minerva* from her mooring and bring her in to the quay—'

'Forgive me—' Dawson asks with exaggerated politeness. 'But that took how long?'

'I suppose half an hour. No, a bit more. Forty minutes perhaps. Then we loaded everything on to the boat.'

'And you didn't notice a gun at this stage?'

'No.'

'And you would have, do you think, if it had been there?'

'Well ... I honestly can't say. Harry carried some of the heavier loads. It could have been in there. I wasn't really looking. The weather was appalling. It was bucketing down.

308

We were trying to get the job finished as quickly as possible.'

'Of course. Please . . .' He bobs his head. 'Go on.'

'When everything was in the boat I sat in the car while Harry stowed things away inside. Then I helped him get away. Untied the ropes.' I anticipate the next query with: 'It must have been about a quarter past one.'

'And he was heading where at this point?'

We have covered this twice before in the past, but I suppose that counts for nothing now that we are setting down the definitive version, and I am doubly aware of the need to get it right. I explain how *Minerva* could not stay at the quay on a falling tide, how Harry had to take her out to the mooring until the time was right to go downstream, how he was aiming to get to the mouth of the river at about six that evening and make a night passage round to the South Coast.

'And that was the last time you saw your husband, was it, Mrs Richmond, when he took the yacht away from the quay?'

The question throws me. I'm not sure what lies behind it. For an instant I read suspicion in his expression, I seem to detect an undertone to his words; then, forcing myself to recognise the improbability of this, seeing instead Dawson's lumbering adherence to step by step procedure, I confirm that it was indeed the last time I saw him.

'And did you see him stop at the mooring?'

I shake my head. 'It was raining so hard. I couldn't see that far.' I reach for my cup and slide it closer.

'So you never saw the yacht stopped at the mooring?'

This sounds like the same question. 'No.'

Dawson lifts a blunt finger and scratches at the chipped surface of his cheek. 'So what did you do then, Mrs Richmond, after he'd gone?'

'I went home.'

He waits for me to elaborate, then prompts: 'And what did you do there?'

We have never covered this before. 'I gave my son his lunch, I helped him with his project, I did some chores. Not very much really.'

He gives a series of slow professional nods, like a doctor listening to a long-winded patient. 'And later?'

'I dropped my son at Jill Hooper's and went to have supper with Molly.'

We establish Molly's identity as Miss Molly Sinclair, and her address.

'You spent the evening there?'

I nod. This being insufficient for the demands of the tape, he raises his eyebrows patiently and waits until I have given voice to a yes.

'And you left Miss Sinclair at what time?'

I sip at the tea which is tepid and bitter. I make a show of searching my memory. 'It must have been about ten,' I say finally. 'I thought it was later, I think I may have told you it was later, but it just seemed that way because we started the evening so early. I'm sure it can't have been later than ten.'

Dawson leans slowly back in his seat, and flexes his shoulders like someone easing a troublesome back. He gives a sudden smile, as if to apologise for the distraction. 'You went straight home?' he asks, finding his coaxing voice again.

'Yes.'

'Arriving when?'

'Well, it must have been ten-thirty or so, I suppose. If I left at ten.'

'Once at home, you stayed in the house?'

This, too, is new territory. 'Well – yes.'

'You didn't go out again for any reason?'

My heart gives a solitary tap against my ribs. 'No.'

'You didn't go down to the river?'

'No, I . . .' Then, as understanding comes: 'I never thought Harry might still be there. It never occurred to me.'

'And now – do you think Mr Richmond *was* there?'

Does he expect a guess? An opinion? 'I don't know. He hadn't said anything about staying. He seemed set on going that night.'

A pause. I cradle my cup with both hands, though the tea offers little warmth. I see Leonard glance at his watch and wonder if he will try to limit the length of the interview. I hope

310

so. I'm not sure I can go on much longer without making mistakes.

Dawson dips into the silence. 'After you'd returned home that night, did you hear anything at all? Anything unusual?'

'Unusual?

'Any sound. Anything you particularly noticed?'

But I sense he has a particular sound in mind.

'Outside, you mean?'

He nods.

'Not that I remember.' I look at Leonard and back to Dawson. I make a gesture which suggests it would be helpful to know what sort of sound I am meant to be remembering.

Ignoring this, Dawson continues on some predetermined course. 'The day of the twenty-sixth, did Mr Richmond injure himself in any way?'

'Injure?'

'Incur any knocks, bruises, that sort of thing? That you know of?'

So this is what they have found at the post-mortem. This is the worst they have found. A bubble of relief ripples up inside me.

I shake my head. 'But he was always bumping himself on the boat. Coming back with bruises.'

'But there was nothing you noticed that day of the twenty-sixth? Nothing he remarked on?'

'No.' I look to Leonard, wishing he would follow up with the obvious question. Finally I ask it myself. 'Why? Was there something . . . ?'

Dawson looks doubtful about answering this, though whether from a desire to spare my feelings or ingrained caution it's hard to tell. 'A bruise was found,' he states with magisterial solemnity. 'On the side of the head.'

For an instant, imagination and memory mix, become indistinguishable. I see Harry in the boat's saloon. I see him falling sideways, his head meeting the corner of the folded table. The next moment the picture shifts and my imagination casts it quite differently, and I wonder how I could have conjured up so sharp an image.

Perhaps Dawson reads something of the strain in my face because he glances up at the wall clock, then at his watch, and says, 'We can leave it there, if you like, Mrs Richmond. Finish off another day.'

I nod mutely.

Dawson scrapes his chair back and makes as if to rise. Then, straightening his fingers in a gesture of recollection, he leans forward again. 'Did, er, Mr Richmond have any particular enemies that you know of?'

I almost laugh. I thought they only asked questions like this in films. 'Not that I'm aware of.' Even my answer sounds like something from a script.

'Nobody who wished him harm in any way?'

I blink incredulously. Can he be suggesting that Harry's death might have been suspicious? That a cutout villain – some business rival – felt so aggrieved that he somehow plotted against Harry? The idea is so fantastical that I don't know what to say.

Dawson takes his answer from my face. 'No?'

'No.' I emphasise this with a firm shake of the head.

Dawson leans into the microphone and signs off.

Leonard helps me stiffly to my feet. As Dawson comes round the table, I find the courage to ask, 'That sound you thought I might have heard – you didn't say what it was meant to be?'

Coming slowly to a halt, Dawson lifts his heavy head and frowns at me, as if weighing me up afresh. Finally he says impassively, 'A person has stated that he heard a sound on the river late that night. He thought it was a gunshot.'

There is a deep pause. It is left to Leonard to break it.

'But that can't have anything to do with this matter, surely? If it was on the river.'

'Quite so,' says Dawson evenly. 'But as I'm sure you'll appreciate, we still have to make the appropriate inquiries.' He inclines his head towards me. 'Sorry to have kept you so long, Mrs Richmond.'

'Not at all.' Producing what I hope is a suitable response, I give a brave little smile.

*

I had forgotten about the anonymous letter with its newspaper clipping. Or perhaps I hadn't forgotten, but had pushed it to the back of my mind. After supper, gripping a second glass of wine that Molly has pressed into my hand, I leave her and the children watching TV and take myself to the study. I locate the letter half hidden by an opera brochure at the back of the drawer.

I read it in the context of Dawson's questions. An enemy? The writer of this cowardly little note certainly qualifies. But venom is a long way from wishing someone harm, and further still from doing something about it. This pitiable person would probably run a mile from any thoughts of violence. But if Dawson is set on the idea of enemies, if the gunshot and the bruise are lodged in his mind, then this, at least, would give him something to focus on.

There are dangers. It could complicate everything irredeemably. It could harden Dawson's thinking, move him permanently away from the idea of suicide, make him determined to search out new evidence. Perhaps I'm crazy, perhaps without this, Dawson would simply drop the whole idea of enemies.

Yet even as I think this, I feel he will not. It is the gunshot. People don't fire shotguns around here late at night. The occasional poacher maybe, once in a blue moon. But it's sufficiently rare for Dawson to be thinking, not surprisingly, that the gunshot could have been the same one that killed Harry. That something happened to Harry while the boat was still in the river.

. . . *Betrayed by Scum. Britain stinks for Real heroes . . . the Right man dEad now.*

I fold the letter and place it on top of the desk. The more I wonder whether it would be wise to show it to Dawson, the more undecided I become. I sit staring out into the garden, and wonder why things are moving so rapidly in the wrong direction. Though is it the wrong direction? Maybe not. This is the worst of it: I can't make up my mind.

I am roused by voices coming down the passage. Molly's burble, the low murmur of a male voice.

I realise: it is Moreland. I jump up, I check the drawers are closed. My own instincts fluster me; sometimes I forget what I am trying to hide and what I can safely reveal.

Molly, chattering brightly, leads him in. He is looking handsome in jeans and pale-blue shirt. He seems both unexpected and familiar, a new friend that I have known for ever. I feel a fast-beating pleasure, but also a sense of distance which I know it would be wise to maintain.

He grips my arm briefly, his only concession to sympathy, though for some reason this affects me more than any extravagant gesture.

'They've lifted the yacht?' It's a question but also an expression of concern.

I explain roughly what has happened and what the police have told me so far, how until today they saw it as a carefully planned suicide, set up to be undetectable, so that I could claim the insurance money.

'Until today?' Moreland prompts.

'Now they seem to want to know if Harry had any enemies.'

I am aware of Molly's eyes on us, picking up signals, trying to work out what if anything is in this relationship which I have told her so little about.

'The trouble with the police,' she declares, claiming Moreland's attention, 'is that they're not very bright. Once you've grasped that, you've grasped everything.'

While we discuss the IQ of the police she continues to examine Moreland with open interest until, with a show of tact, she takes herself off to catch a favourite programme.

'How are the children?' Moreland asks as soon as she has gone. I had forgotten this way he has of making me feel that I am being cared for, of making me feel, moreover, that I want to be.

I tell him that it's hard to be sure how they are coping. Katie seems to have accepted the fact of Harry's suicide, but Josh has gone quiet and won't speak much. Not, at any rate, to me.

'And *you?*' He makes a concerned creased-up face.

'Oh, I'm all right. Well...' I make a wide gesture, I give a wry laugh. Why pretend? 'I wish the police didn't have these odd ideas. They seem to be looking for something *unusual* about Harry's death.' Unusual. I don't know why I say this. Everything about Harry's death was unusual.

I start to recount Dawson's questions, partly because it seems natural to tell Moreland, partly because I'm curious to hear his reaction. I settle in Harry's seat while Moreland wheels the typing chair over and, sitting at the side of the desk, slides an elbow across the leather and props his head against his hand. I had forgotten how beautiful his hands are, how he looks at me with an expression that seems to understand everything I am feeling.

'Perhaps Harry did have enemies,' I say. 'But ordinary enemies. Business enemies. With all the deals he did it would be funny if he hadn't fallen out with a few people along the way. He could be' – a stab of disloyalty – 'abrasive. But for someone to actually want to *do* something about it? A contract killing or something? I assume that must be what's in Dawson's mind. It's mad!'

'He didn't say why he was asking? What had given him the idea?'

'Not really. Except . . .' I make light of it. 'Oh, there was a gunshot. Someone is meant to have heard it late that Friday night. But it could have been poachers,' I declare, testing the argument, gauging the sound of it. 'There are plenty of poachers around. Or it could have been a farmer taking pot-shots at rabbits in his headlights. Anything.'

But a spark of interest glitters in Moreland's eye. 'This person, did he hear where the shot came from?'

'He thought, the river.'

'What time was this?'

'Dawson didn't say.'

'What about the kind of sound? Was it loud, a bang, or more of a crack?'

But I don't know this either.

Moreland absorbs my limited information with an oddly speculative look, as if he were matching it to some previous knowledge. 'Did Dawson say anything else?'

'No.' As an afterthought I add, 'Well . . . there was this . . .

315

bruise apparently. He asked me if Harry'd bumped his head that day. I told him Harry was always bashing himself on the boat, that he wasn't very good at holding on when the boat lurched, that sort of thing. At the end of a weekend, he was always covered in bruises.'

Moreland listens with concentration before losing himself in some distant thought.

'What worries me about this talk of shots and enemies is that it'll get back to the children,' I sigh. 'You know how these things travel. I wish Dawson would leave it alone.' I wait for Moreland to agree with me.

'I realise it's difficult for you, Ellen. But I think he has no choice. I think he has to follow everything up.'

So here I have my independent appraisal: Dawson isn't likely to let go.

I look down at the cheap envelope lying in front of me. Realising that I may yet regret this, with some sense of going against my better judgement, I slide it slowly across the desk towards Moreland.

I don't say anything. I wait for him to take out the letter and the tattered press cutting and read them.

'When did this come?' His voice has darkened.

I tell him it was shortly after the memorial service.

'You haven't shown it to Dawson?'

'I didn't think it was important. You think . . .' I lift this into a question.

He gives me a reflective look before returning to the letter and reading it again. 'I think perhaps he should see it.'

'But this is just some pathetic little man, surely? Someone with a chip on his shoulder?'

He makes a who-can-tell face.

'Who's Joe Congreve?' I ask, though I have already guessed the answer.

He tucks the cutting inside the letter. 'He was the soldier from Harry's unit who got killed.'

So you know his name, I think. You know more than you let on. 'Tell me,' I say.

Moreland considers, he eyes me as if he is weighing up what

I can take. 'Some of Harry's unit felt very aggrieved about Congreve's death,' he begins gravely. 'They felt that he was exposed to enemy fire unnecessarily. That the order to send him out on his own was' – he chooses the word with care – '*flawed*.'

'And they blamed Harry?'

'Feelings run high at times like that.'

'But ten years later?' I protest.

'I'm sure you're right,' he agrees suddenly, 'there's probably nothing in it. But I think the police should see it all the same. I could take it along, if you like. Fill in the background for them.'

I sigh, an agreement of sorts.

Moreland slips a hand over mine, and his grip is warm and firm. I glance down at his hand. When I look up again it's to find him frowning and smiling at the same time, a mixed message if there ever was one.

FIFTEEN

Katie has never talked to me about the 'bad-bad' time, the day four weeks before Harry's death when he finally got to her. She has never told me, and I realise now she never will. She told Bob Block, of course, but under the terms of the confessional. Before then she used to encourage Bob to tell me selected elements of her story, to act as impartial broker of the more difficult emotions. But not for this. She knew, I think, that it would hurt me too much.

But then I had already worked out when it must have happened. There was a weekend when Katie came out from school and I was away most of Saturday evening at one of Molly's fund-raising events. A friend of Katie's called Lucinda was meant to be staying the evening. I don't know why Lucinda left early, or when precisely Harry drove her home, but she wasn't there when I got back. Perhaps Harry engineered her departure, perhaps he planned it in advance. Perhaps, seeing the opportunity, he was simply incapable of resisting it. Who knows? Even now I'm not sure that his actions can be judged by any normal standards. I think that by this time he had sunk so deep into his own nightmare that his actions were inexplicable, even to himself.

But whatever led to it, at some point after he had driven Lucinda home and Josh had gone to bed, he must have got Katie on her own.

When I came back at midnight and put my head round the study door – a move I undertook with caution at the best of times – he cast me a dismissive half-glare and declared impatiently that Lucinda was long gone and both Josh and Katie were in bed asleep. I was too tired to question this, too preoccupied to wonder why Katie wasn't up, watching her favourite late-night programme. All I wanted, I remember, was to sink into bed.

The next day we all drifted, barely connecting. I hardly saw Harry at all. Josh disappeared into the garden. Katie failed to appear for lunch. When I knocked on her door she announced she had stomach ache and wouldn't be getting up. Her voice was thick, her face puffy. I thought she must be coming down with something, I offered to call the doctor, but she wouldn't have it. All she'd agree to was to take some paracetamol washed down by a fizzy vitamin C drink. When I drove her back to school that evening, there was a blankness in her face.

Yes: that was when it happened.

I worked it out for the first time during that endless night on the boat, waiting for the dawn. It wasn't a great feat of deduction, not then, not after the events of the evening. I remembered how, soon after that Sunday when Katie had stayed in bed, she had failed a maths test and dropped out of the house play, how she had become monosyllabic on the phone. How, when Mrs Anderson noticed her sudden weight loss and sounded the alarm, I pronounced on the subject of anaemia and vitamin deficiencies – anything to avoid more painful truths – and took Katie to our doctor who, finding nothing physically wrong, suggested a touch of anorexia or school phobia or a mixture of both, and prescribed anti-depressants. I didn't argue. Even if school phobia was wide of the mark, I was forced to face the larger truth of what he was saying, that Katie was disturbed in some inexpressible way. As I saw it then, there was only one thing that could be disturbing her, and that was our troubles at home – Harry's depression, my clumsy attempts to keep things running smoothly, and overlaying it all, our silent warfare, which, in my simplicity, I thought I had managed to conceal from both Katie and Josh. I should have known that children pick up on these things, that someone as intuitive as Katie was bound to absorb this tension and take it into her vulnerable heart.

Katie swallowed the antidepressants for a day or so, but when she next came home from school the tablets weren't in evidence and I think she must have thrown them away.

I believed love and communication offered the best medicine anyway. Having told Katie too little, I overcompensated and proceeded to tell her what I later realised, with some agony, was far too much. I spelt out Harry's troubles as far as I knew or guessed them, I emphasised the terrible pressures he was under, I explained how the situation was taking its toll on me as well and, if I wasn't my usual self, it was because I tended to worry too much. I implied that our problems were at a critical stage. I spoke to her as an adult, I didn't try to hide anything – except the affair with Caroline Palmer – and in so doing I can't rid myself of the suspicion – some days it's a certainty – that I helped bring about our disaster. I think I laid such a burden of responsibility on Katie, I painted the picture so dark that she felt she couldn't add to my problems by even hinting at what had happened, that if she said anything it would only make life that much worse for all of us.

She was right in a way. It would have made life worse. But – and how could she ever have known? – not a fraction as bad as it would become as a result of her keeping quiet. Poor Katie: trapped.

I remember sitting with Katie in her bedroom as I catalogued Harry's woes, and the way she kept her eyes firmly on her lap, the way she wouldn't look at me. When I asked her if she understood what I was saying, her only response was a faint nod. At the time I felt she was being less than sympathetic. When she wouldn't answer my hug, I thought she was being unnecessarily difficult. Though, loving her as I did, not wanting to aggravate the anorexia, I didn't say this. I took care to let her know that she had our unconditional support. I told her that we'd always be there for her, that all she ever had to do was call, that in difficult times that was what families were for. Ironic, really.

And then – more ironic still – I looked around her bedroom

which had been newly decorated in her favourite colours, lemon yellow and pale blue, with Osborne & Little chintz cushions and frilly curtains, and, sitting there on the bed, I thought how pretty it all looked and how, here at least, she must feel safe and secure.

In America, during those first weeks, this scene kept coming back to me, part of my regular programme of self-torture, in which I became Katie, I became fifteen and hurt and bleeding, I was there in the bathroom wiping the blood from my legs, I was hand-washing the sheet and hiding it in among the other laundry. I was degraded, diminished for ever. And then I put myself through the final betrayal, sitting in the lemon-yellow and blue bedroom, listening to my mother tell me about my stepfather's problems, how they were so great that he deserved all my understanding and support. And with this, both I and the person that was Katie died a little more inside.

The need to punish myself was very deep. For a while it became an obsession. I flooded Bob Block with self-reproach, I bombarded him with tears and mortification. But in time even guilt wears itself down into something more manageable. And, as our return to England grew nearer, so my instincts for self-preservation reasserted themselves. If I was to have any hope of protecting the children, I knew I had to get some sort of grip on the future.

Katie brought it home to me once when we were in Yosemite Park, in a designated viewing area where we were permitted to get out of the car and admire the scenery.

Reading her mood, I asked: Okay?

Fine, she said without much enthusiasm.

Tell me if you want to.

Her head was down, her arms were clasped tightly around her waist. She took a long time to answer.

Sometimes I feel bad about . . . how I feel. Sometimes I don't feel the way I should . . .

She was talking about Harry's death.

I can understand that, I said.

But it's *awful*. It's awful to think like that.

It's natural, though. I often feel the same.

321

You do?

Yes. Sometimes I'm glad he's dead.

She wasn't quite ready to believe this. She shook her head.

No, I said. *Really*. He was so ill, darling, he was so *unhappy* that I actually think he's better off. Happier.

Harry's illness featured heavily in our discussions then. Bob Block had encouraged us to fasten on to it, both as an explanation for his behaviour, and as a means of coming to terms with our feelings about his death.

But Katie was not to be moved from her mood of self-condemnation. She said, I still feel . . . it was all my fault.

Your *fault*, baby? How could it possibly be your fault? It was never your fault.

But, Mum, I—

You did *nothing*, Katie. *Nothing*.

But I did! she cried in frustration. I *did!*

This was old ground, though not yet sufficiently well travelled for Katie's needs.

Listen, I said sternly, there are some things that it's right to blame yourself for, and others that it's just plain wrong to even think about blaming yourself for. You *know* which is which.

Bob Block had taken her through this many times. But that didn't stop her from giving me a look that was pure child, and asking miserably, You really think so?

I really think so.

She took what reassurance she could from this, which wasn't perhaps a lot just then, and looked away to where Josh was hanging over the rail that corralled tourists away from the edge of the gorge.

But I keep thinking, Mum. If something happened to you . . . she said, voicing the dread that never leaves her.

To me? I laughed.

Yes.

Nothing's going to happen to me.

I couldn't bear it.

Oh yes, you could, I said firmly.

But in my heart I knew she was right. She would fall apart.

This reminder came just in time. It concentrated my mind

during those last days before we came home. It forced me to go through everything that had happened, to work out where we were vulnerable, and how I could best protect us; it made me realise how vital it was to get my story right.

Now Katie seems overcome by the same lethargy that gripped her before Harry died. I noticed it creeping over her at the weekend. She has lost the wish to do anything. She certainly shows no desire to get back to school. Her headmistress, having fired off a stiff note of disapproval, following it quickly with lavish expressions of sympathy at what she described as the nature of Harry's death – this arriving only two days after the discovery of Harry's body, a gauge of the efficiency of the local grape-vine – finally, two days ago, made an offer to have Katie back.

But Katie doesn't want to go. She can't say why. She doesn't seem unhappy exactly, but she has distanced herself from me. For the last two nights she has stopped coming into my bed for our nightly chat, she has stopped searching me out, and though she accepts my expressions of love, she does so passively, without focus.

I can't seem to lift her out of this mood; perhaps I'm the wrong person to try. But with the weekend over, Molly is back at work, and Margaret, who only comes in on Mondays now, isn't close enough to her. Josh has gone back to school, grumbling loudly but, I think, secretly relieved to be away from the house.

So we are alone together, Katie and I, but subtly apart. I would like to share my worries with her – how often have I sworn to her that I would? – but, having laid that kind of burden on her once before, I'm not about to do it again. Besides, how can I tell her that my reassurances might be meaningless? That I'm not so sure I'm going to be around for her after all? That, despite everything I have tried to do for us, luck might to be turning against me after all, and that I live in hourly expectation of being found out.

Maurice pulls at the handle and the door follows a slow

backward arc into the underside of the roof. Sunlight floods the lower shelves along the rear wall of the garage, with their cargo of dusty boxes and old awnings and spare oars, and slants down over the rolls of carpet and unwanted furniture along one side.

Dawson steps in and looks at me questioningly.

I indicate the right-hand corner, which is in deep shadow, and follow him across the floor. We stand in front of the green tubular bag with its overflowing bulges of grey rubber.

'This is it?'

'This is it,' I confirm.

'It's what you'd call an inflatable?' Dawson asks with the air of someone who is keen to learn.

'Yes. Well – we used to call it the Zodiac. That's the make. A Zodiac.'

'And this is what Mr Richmond used?'

'Sometimes.'

'Not all the time then?'

'No. He used the dory a lot.'

'To get out to the yacht?'

'As a tender, yes.'

Dawson draws his heavy brows down and rubs his chin in a gesture of incomprehension that is almost theatrical. 'Forgive me, Mrs Richmond, but you'll have to explain these terms to me. I am a nautical moron, you see.'

'Sorry. For getting out to the mooring and back again.'

'That's a tender, is it? Something for getting backwards and forwards?'

'Well, I think so. But don't rely on me. I'm not so brilliant on these things myself.'

'Aha.' We share our moment of nautical inadequacy. 'What about, er – voyages?' Dawson continues, using the word self-consciously. 'Did Mr Richmond take the inflatable along with him then?'

'He didn't go on many long trips,' I explain. 'Two at the most. And they weren't even that long. Round to the next river. Down to Burnham.'

'But he took the inflatable on those occasions?'

'I don't know, I'm afraid. But I suppose so.'

'You didn't go with him?' he asks benevolently.

'Oh no. I used to get nervous and very seasick.' My half-chuckle emerges as a choking sound, as though I were feeling sick again now.

'And when the inflatable wasn't on the yacht, where was it kept?' Dawson picks at each word, feeling his way through what is still unfamiliar territory.

I think for a moment. 'Down at the quay. Sometimes. Or here. It varied.'

'So on occasion, when it wasn't in either place, it would be safe to assume it was on the yacht?'

I shrug.

'You don't think so?' His mouth shapes itself into a smile of professional inquiry.

'I just don't know. It was Harry's department. He never told me what he was doing with the boats.' Reaching some threshold, I say in exasperation. 'Forgive me, but I can't see what this has to do with anything. I find it – upsetting.'

'I'm sorry to put you to the bother, Mrs Richmond.' His expression is opaque and intractable; he doesn't intend to answer my question, nor does he intend to stop asking his own.

He directs his interest to the shelves, casting a look along the back wall, before turning to face the light, peering out into the drive with creased eyes, to where Maurice is standing beside Dawson's acolytes, the flat-faced police officer from before who, I have finally grasped, is called Fisher, and a chubby constable who looks about sixteen. Beside a van are two more officers, wearing paper overalls.

'The morning of Saturday, 27 March, you went down to the quay and you found the inflatable there?' he says. 'Is that right?'

'Yes.'

He looks back at me. 'You expected to find it there?'

'Well – yes. Harry had asked me to pack it up and put it away.'

'I'm sorry—' Dawson inclines his head towards me as if he has got hard of hearing. 'He asked you to—?'

'He asked me to take care of it.'

'Though that was usually his department?'

'Yes.'

'What did you think about that?'

I frown my lack of understanding.

'About him asking you?'

I wonder what he expects me to say to this – that I thought it was unusual? Or is he after a more personal reaction, like annoyance? 'I knew he was short of time. It was no problem. And Maurice helped.'

'Ah yes.' Dawson regards Maurice solemnly. 'You carried it up from the quay, did you? You and Mr – er, Crick?'

'We drove it up in the Volvo, yes.'

He takes this in with a slow nod, and turns to take another look at the swollen folds of grey rubber discharging from the mouth of the taut green bag. 'Looked normal, did it, when you found it?'

'I'm sorry?'

'The inflatable. Nothing to notice about it?'

'No. A bit muddy, that's all.'

'Muddy? Was that usual, for it to be muddy?'

'It's a very muddy river,' I explain. 'So – yes. Most things get muddy.'

He puts his face close to the dinghy with its largely mud-free skin.

'I gave it a bit of a clean,' I say, anticipating his question.

He looks at me with something like disappointment. 'Water? Soap? That sort of thing?'

'Water and a sponge. Then Maurice gave it a proper clean up here, before he packed it away.'

Dawson contemplates the dinghy one last time before offering me a formal smile and starting back towards the light. 'Oh,' he says matter-of-factly, 'you wouldn't mind, would you, if we took it away for a short while?'

I raise my shoulders powerlessly.

In the garage entrance Dawson stops suddenly and splays

326

out a hand, as if remembering something. 'Oh, and would it have had a motor, the inflatable?'

'There's a small outboard somewhere, I think. But it was hardly used.'

'Ah. It wasn't with the inflatable then, when you collected it from the river?'

'No.'

'So people would have—?'

'Rowed.'

'There'd be oars then?'

'Yes.'

He looks back into the interior expectantly. 'And where would they be?'

I had forgotten the oars. I call across to Maurice and ask him where they are. Immediately he lopes past us and is only restrained from pulling the oars out from where they stand in a dark corner behind the shelf ends by Dawson's hasty intervention.

Dawson gives instructions to the officers in overalls and goes to talk to Maurice while the men wrap first the Zodiac then the oars in copious plastic and carry them to the van. They wear rubber semi-transparent gloves, like medics.

'Oh, one last question,' Dawson says, tramping back across the gravel towards me. 'The – er, *dory*. Where was it exactly when you saw your husband off that day? On that Friday, 26 March?'

'Inspector...' I sigh, I don't try to hide the fact that I am finding this a trial. 'I don't know. I really don't know.'

'But you would have noticed if he had attached it to the back of the yacht?'

'Probably. Possibly. It was raining. I wasn't really looking.'

'It would help if you could remember, Mrs Richmond.'

Before I can stop myself I sing out testily, 'It would help if I knew why.'

Dawson glances down at his feet. When he looks up again, he regards me with altogether cooler eyes. 'The point is, Mrs Richmond, we have to consider all aspects. We have to consider the full range of possibilities.'

'I do see that,' I say with a sigh. 'But when you say possibilities . . . it worries me.'

He says solemnly, 'We have to eliminate the possibility of another person or persons being involved, Mrs Richmond.'

Out comes my incredulous laugh, a small explosion of sound that pierces the silence. 'But that's ridiculous.'

Dawson makes a regretful gesture, as if he would like to be able to agree with me. 'That letter was not very pleasant, Mrs Richmond.'

'But it was nothing very serious, Inspector.'

'You say that, Mrs Richmond, but we don't know that for sure, do we?'

I don't feel strong enough to argue this again – we have already been through it once in the house. And I don't want him ticking me off a second time for not having told him about it before.

I clasp a hand to my head, I rake my fingers back through my hair.

'Please don't upset yourself, Mrs Richmond. It's purely a matter of following up on available information,' he explains, reverting to police-speak. 'There's a person we need to trace and eliminate from our inquiries.'

This is new. I am confused. 'A person? Who?'

I have to press him before he says grudgingly, 'The person we believe most likely to have written the letter. I can't tell you more at present, Mrs Richmond, though I will, of course, keep you informed.'

'But why do you need the inflatable?' I indicate the Zodiac wrapped in its plastic sheath inside the open van.

'It's just a question of checking everything out, Mrs Richmond. Tell me again, Mrs Richmond, where you found it exactly, that Saturday after Mr Richmond's departure?'

'By the quay.'

'In the place you would expect to find it?'

I realise I am getting myself into a corner that I might regret. I say vaguely, 'There wasn't really a normal place for it.'

'But you found it easily enough? By the quay?'

Mistake, Ellen. Mistake. But I am committed now. 'Yes.'

'And the dory? You didn't notice it attached to the yacht when your husband left?'

'Well, I . . . Maybe.'

'You're saying that you did, Mrs Richmond?'

'No, what I'm saying is that I'm not sure. Does it really make any difference?'

'A great deal, Mrs Richmond. If he didn't have the, er, *dory*, with him at that time, then that would certainly be significant.' Even in my jumpy befuddled mood I can see that the dory could not have found its way to *Minerva* by itself, that if Harry left it at the quay, then someone else must have taken it out to the mooring.

Dawson pulls a finger and thumb down the edge of his lapel, he takes on a studious look. 'It is anyway an *odd* choice of vessel to take to sea, the dory, so I believe. Being of a large and more solid construction. Something you would not choose to take behind a yacht under normal circumstances. I gather this, er, style of vessel is extremely difficult to, er, *tow* along behind . . .'

Moreland. I hear your voice here. I can see you painstakingly leading Dawson through it.

'. . . and that it would slow progress a great deal. And that in violent weather it would be something of a liability. That it could even sink. Or . . .' He searches for the expression. '. . . turn turtle.'

'But if you're intending to kill yourself the circumstances are hardly normal,' I point out.

Dawson considers this. 'No,' he agrees finally. 'Which is why' – he lifts his chin, he squints down the bumps and curves of his nose at me – 'it would help if you could place the, er, *dory* on that Friday in March.'

A slam. One of the overalled officers is fastening the rear doors of the van. Beside him Fisher laughs, his face disjointed by a scornful smile.

'I'm sorry,' I say to Dawson.

'It was of course quite a large vessel as, er – *tenders* – go. You don't think you would have noticed if it was attached to the back of the yacht?'

'I suppose so, but... No, I can't be sure.' I turn my eyes heavenward, showing suitable despair at my own inadequacies. 'Sorry.'

The salesman's smile, in which all disappointments are carefully concealed, returns to Dawson's face. He nods slowly. 'If anything comes back to you, perhaps you would . . . ?'

'Of course.'

He walks me to the front door, inclines his head in thanks and starts towards his car. I hear him stop, the scrunch of his feet on the gravel. 'Oh, one thing I meant to ask,' he calls, strolling back a short way. 'There was a ship-to-shore radio on the yacht, I believe. But would Mr Richmond have had any other means of communicating? A mobile phone, for instance?'

My breath is tight. 'He owned one, certainly.'

'And he had it with him that day?'

I lift my hands. I give a weary laugh. 'Inspector, you keep asking me these things. And I simply don't know.'

A three-line letter from Gillespie, who wants to know if I have had a chance to study the financial plan, and, if so, if I'm ready to give him a decision.

I place the document with its impressively printed title on Harry's desk in front of me, I study the introductory remarks, I turn to the ranks of figures with a growing sense of hopelessness, I am lost by page three.

I push the document away, a child who doesn't want to face the unpleasant. I lower my forehead to the desk and rest it on the cushion of my fingers. Thoughts of Dawson and the dinghies crowd my brain. It occurs to me that he will probably have removed the dory from the boatyard and taken it away as well, though I'm not sure what he thinks he will find there, when the dory has been overhauled and repaired and burnished, when the gouges have been filled and the alien black paint rubbed away.

And the inflatable, what is he hoping for there? I am back at the quay, sluicing and sponging at the stubborn mud. I am standing on the garage apron, watching Maurice apply the hot

330

water and detergent, standing over him as he starts his systematic circular scrubbing.

Tired, I slip momentarily into a nightmare where I am slithering about in blood and mud, unable to extricate myself from the dinghy, and in the far-off house Katie is sobbing.

'Under the circumstances, which the trustees have agreed are somewhat exceptional, they are prepared to accept an offer along the lines we discussed.'

It is Tim Schwartz's turn to sound as though he is using notes.

'Hello?' he says when I don't reply. 'Hello?'

'Yes, I'm here.'

'But they have asked if it would be possible to make a higher initial payment.' He sounds crisp, the reluctant messenger.

The call has caught me in the kitchen. I work my way round the end of the counter and slide a stool under myself. 'I'm not sure I can manage that.'

'Well, perhaps you could suggest a timetable of payments? A formula for discussion.'

'Well . . .'

'Some idea. Very rough.'

'I'll have to come back to you. Could I?'

A pause. 'Is there a problem?'

Hearing a sound, I twist round. It is Katie, who drifts past and heads for the fridge.

'I am rather tied up at the moment.'

'Ah. Yes.' A thin sort of sympathy. 'When you have a moment, then.'

'Yes, I'll try . . .'

'Mrs Richmond, forgive me but I seem to hear a note of doubt. You haven't changed your mind?'

Katie stands at the open fridge, head on one side, hand on hip and takes something from a lower shelf.

'No, not at all,' I say. 'No, it's just a question of finding the time.'

'I don't mean to press you, but when do you think that might be?'

'Umm . . . Next week?'

Katie pulls bottles out of the door and, emerging with her arms full of fruit, Coke and mineral water, swings the door shut with a deft movement of her foot. As she turns and starts back across the room, I notice she has a small tart covered with whipped cream jammed into her mouth.

'Shall I call you on Monday then?' says Schwartz. 'Oh, and . . .'

A muffled exclamation. Katie has ground to halt and is standing stock still, gaping at the section of tart that is sliding down the slope of her bosom in a trail of whipped cream, gliding past the tightly clutched bottles, until, dodging the fingers she struggles to put in its path, it drops stickily to the floor.

'The trustees asked me to convey their formal regrets,' Schwartz is saying, 'about your husband.'

I watch Katie, wondering which way this is going to go. Her shoulders droop a little, she glares at the long smear down her T-shirt and then, with perfect timing, unable to resist the comic opportunity, her face comes alive and she turns to me with eyes popping, brows raised high, lower lip thrust out, a caricature of injured innocence.

'I'm sorry?' I manage.

'The trustees. They send their regrets.'

Katie holds her pose, playing it for all she is worth. She has a cream moustache on her upper lip. The laughter rises irresistibly in my throat and I have a job to say, 'Oh, thank you. I mean – thank them.'

I sense Schwartz's confusion. Deciding, apparently, that I am near to tears, he says grudgingly that there is really no pressure on the timing, he could make it Wednesday if that would be easier.

Ringing off, I give Katie her laughter and applause. Not a performer to have her head turned by such easily won acclaim, she takes this with cool grace, but I fancy her eyes glint with satisfaction.

Still laughing, I hug her, bottles, cream and all.

She guffaws into my neck.

Mercurial Katie. Still my girl.

I pull back. Seeing the emotion in my face, she drops her eyes, she begins to turn away.

'Don't, Katie. Don't, sweetheart.'

She pauses, she makes a face, she wages some internal debate. 'When the police come . . . I get frightened.'

I'm silent for a moment. 'Yes,' I murmur with feeling. 'Yes, so do I.'

And she comes back to me then, and we lean against each other, two battle-weary warriors resting between skirmishes.

Jack calls, 'Come up! Come up!'

The idea of visiting Jack's bedroom is not something that fills me with enthusiasm, but since he warned me that this was the only time he had to spare, I don't seem to have much choice. Climbing the stairs, I think of all the females who must have trodden this path over the years. Did they go in hope? I wonder. In love or lust? Did they imagine they would be the ones finally to catch him?

The bedroom is sparse: a large bed, and on the wall above it a large and intricate Eastern print which looks vaguely erotic, though I don't examine it closely enough to find out, a side table, a trouser press and a wall of built-in cupboards.

'Here.'

I find him through the far door, in a bathroom tiled in a startling blend of red and navy. He blows me a kiss through a beard of shaving foam. He is wearing a striped robe which gapes at the chest.

'Congratulations again,' I say.

He beams and waves me towards a seat on the lavatory, whose lid he closes with a flourish. 'Hasn't quite sunk in yet,' he says, grinning quietly. 'And I've still got to win the damned seat for us, haven't I?' He turns back to the mirror and, raising his chin, pulls the razor up his neck, removing a neat strip of white.

'So . . . ?' Half turning, he peers down at me.

'So . . .' I take a long breath; I tell myself that this will only be hard if I make it so. 'I still need that money.'

He rinses the razor under the tap, and, squinting into the mirror, removes another band of foam. 'Just tell me,' he says with an edge to his voice, 'are we going to have a rerun of our last conversation?'

'No,' I say tightly. 'No . . . I don't think so.'

'Good,' he drawls. 'Good. So what's it for this time?'

'It's for me.'

He slides me a look in the mirror. 'What does Gillespie say? Has he said you need it?'

I am so nervous my stomach is pushed high against my ribs. 'I haven't discussed it with him.'

'So we *are* going to have a rerun,' he says with undisguised irritation.

'I'm asking you as a friend, Jack.'

'And I'm turning you down as a friend, Ellen!'

I feel a pull in my chest, a lurch that is close to anger, and it carries me forward. 'Jack . . . I feel that we have a collective responsibility about this charity. A duty to try and put the matter right.'

'Duty!' The razor jolts to a halt, his eyes bulge at me from the glass. 'You have to be joking!'

I know that if I'm to get through this, I'm going to have to avoid his eyes. Fixing my gaze on the dark glazed tiles to Jack's right, I say cautiously, 'You see, it seems to me that Harry's troubles started with Ainswick, that if Ainswick had been doing all right he would never have been tempted to – take short cuts.'

Jack gives a harsh contemptuous sigh. 'It was his own fault! I told you, the Shoreditch idea was a disaster.'

'Yes, I realise . . . But there were so many other things that seemed to go wrong. Not getting permission for the bypass land—'

'I explained about that.' And his voice carries a warning.

I plough on, I tell myself I'm not going to be frightened of Jack any more. 'Yes, I know what you told me. I know. But you left a few things out, didn't you? When you got the bypass land, it was Meacher who promoted the development for you, wasn't it? You know him well. But when I showed you that hotel bill, you pretended you didn't recognise his name. And then it occurred to me ... That Majorcan holiday. You said Harry had arranged it, you suggested it was Harry who dealt with Meacher. But the date on the hotel bill ... it was five years ago, almost exactly, and I checked with Harry's diary. He was here then. He wasn't away. He didn't go to Majorca with Meacher.'

'No, well, he didn't have to, did he?' Jack says tautly. 'He just paid for it.'

Forgetting to avoid his eyes, I look into the mirror and say, 'But *you* went, Jack. You went to Majorca with Meacher.'

He turns and reaches slowly for a towel. 'Now what gives you that idea?' And there is a ring to his voice, part threat, part caution. He rubs the towel slowly over his chin, and above it his gaze is very hard.

'Well ... Margaret looked it up in the office diary.'

He drops the towel over the edge of the sink, he folds his arms, he says in a voice of exaggerated wonder, 'Now, why would Margaret want to do that?'

'I ... asked her to.'

'You asked her to!' He drops his arms, he advances until he is standing over me. Faced by his gaping wrap, I get slowly to my feet. 'And why did you ask her, Ellen?' he demands caustically. 'What was the purpose of this little bit of detective work?'

'I wondered why Harry had kept the bill, I suppose.'

'You wondered. And have you decided on the reason?'

I look away, I take my time. 'I think maybe he knew it was significant.'

'Ah. You think *maybe* he knew it was significant,' he repeats with relish, like a vindictive teacher leading a pupil towards ritual humiliation. 'And what do *you* think, Ellen? Do you think it's significant?'

I make an ambivalent face.

'Why would it be *significant*, Ellen?'

'Perhaps he thought' – I throw up a tentative hand – 'that Meacher was more of a friend of yours than he was of his.'

335

Jack regards me unblinkingly, his mouth spreads into an imitation smile. 'Tell me, did you keep that bill?'

I don't reply, I look away, which is an answer in itself.

'I thought so.' He takes a pace back as if to get a better look at me, then thrusts his face close again. 'There's a word for people like you, you know.'

I brace myself.

'Well, this *is* a threat, isn't it? It sounds very much like one.'

'Jack, it's not a threat.'

'Oh, isn't it? Then why didn't you destroy the bill?'

I think about this. 'I felt I couldn't.'

'That's right,' he says, proving his case, 'you felt you couldn't.'

I sigh, 'It's not like that.'

But Jack is nodding tightly, as though he has got my measure at last. 'So what's the arrangement, Ellen?' he says, with an elaborate air of enquiry. 'I pay off Harry's debts and you take good care of the bill, is that it?'

'You make it sound . . .'

'How do I make it sound?' He spreads his hands in mock innocence. 'How, Ellen? Like you are doing a deal on me, like you are twisting my arm?'

'I just feel that we share responsibility.'

'Responsibility? Now there's that big word again!'

Suddenly I am tired of his bullying. 'Okay,' I say in exasperation. 'If you like – I *am* twisting your arm. All right. Yes. *Yes*.'

He nods with the satisfaction of the inquisitor who has finally got the admission he wanted.

I take a moment, I calm myself. 'But I would never do anything with the damned bill, Jack. I'm not interested in creating more problems. I was only trying to point out that maybe Ainswick had more than its fair share of bad luck, that if things had gone better then Harry probably wouldn't have done what he did. I was just trying to point out that he didn't get the breaks he might have done. That maybe you could have done a little more to help.'

Jack doesn't try to argue with that. His aggression subsides a little. 'So . . .' he says crisply. 'I'm meant to do this out of the goodness of my heart, am I?'

I don't answer that one.

He gives a mirthless laugh. 'A bloody philanthropist! Well, let me tell you, I've got more than enough good causes already.' He returns to the basin and picks up the towel and presses it hard against his face.

He is still smarting because I have put him at a disadvantage.

'Jack, it's more than that,' I argue sombrely. 'It's for me and the children too. I can't bear the thought of it coming out. I really don't think I could stand it.'

'But I told you—'

'Not even the slightest whisper. I couldn't bear it.'

'Aahh,' he says, as if this made sense at last and he never believed my altruistic motives in the first place. 'So the image is not to be tarnished. The pristine Ellen is not to be shamed.' He gives a sardonic little laugh. He crosses the space between us and, pausing to enjoy my unease, grasps my neck and kisses me full on the lips.

He pulls back. 'So I'm to be kind to you, am I?' There is acceptance in his face, but also the harsh glint of calculation.

It's very dark outside Moreland's cottage. The drive is empty, no lights show. I park a short way up the lane and wait. I angle the car seat back and close my eyes. The air is alive with hidden sounds. When the wind breathes in through the window I seem to hear above the faint rattle of the laurel leaves the ripple and swash of the tide against the river-bank at the bottom of the hill, to catch the distant rasp and pull of the surf at the river-mouth, and to feel once again the fear that came with the mist and wrapped itself around me, cold as death.

His car wakes me. Trying not to look too furtive, I walk to the gate and, keeping well back, peer into the drive.

A light springs on, the front door swings open, throwing a wide beam into the darkness.

He is alone. I feel relief, but something else too, a sort of satisfaction.

He twists round at my call, he gives an exclamation of

surprise. He comes to meet me and leans forward to kiss my cheek. Maybe I turn my head a little, maybe he does, but our lips almost touch and I catch, mingled with the male scent of him, a breath of wine.

'What's happened?' he demands. 'Has something happened?'

I make a stab at humour. 'Just about everything.'

Unsure of my mood, he leads me into the hall and inspects me under the light.

'No – nothing really,' I admit. 'Just ... Dawson came and took the Zodiac away and asked endless questions about the dinghies.' Then, unreasonably: 'You might have warned me.'

'I didn't realise. I thought...' But he leaves it unsaid. He is looking striking in a dark suit and cream shirt with the top button unfastened and the knot of his tie slackened, as though he had wrenched at them on the way back from wherever he has been, in sheer frustration at having to dress up.

'He seems to have got the idea there was something odd in Harry taking the dory,' I say with only the faintest note of irony.

'I did tell him I thought it was a bit unusual,' Moreland confesses.

'I thought you might have,' I say in mild rebuke. 'He also seems to have acquired a prime suspect for the anonymous letter. Someone' – I find myself mimicking Dawson's tone – 'he wishes to eliminate from his inquiries.'

Moreland has the grace to look a little uncomfortable. 'Yes,' he says, 'I told him about that too.'

'You had someone in mind then?'

'As soon as you showed me the letter I knew who might have written it.'

'I see,' I say stiffly. 'Someone you already knew about?'

'Ellen, I'd have told you before. But I thought it'd be unnecessarily...' He has trouble finding a word that won't offend me.

'Upsetting?' I offer.

He makes a face of apology, he concedes my right to feel injured.

338

'Perhaps I could have made up my own mind about that,' I say in a small voice. 'Perhaps I can now.'

'Yes.' He drags at his tie until it gives way altogether, he slips off his jacket and throws them onto a chair, as if to announce that this is going to take time in the telling. 'I'll make some coffee.' Inviting me to follow, he goes into the kitchen and fills the kettle.

'I told you,' he begins, 'that we stumbled on Harry's platoon that night?' Forgoing a spoon, he shakes instant coffee direct from the jar into the mugs. 'And his men didn't seem too happy and they felt bitter about Congreve's death?' He leans back against the counter, he folds his arms and beneath the fluorescent light his face takes on deep lines and harsh shadows. 'They were in a bit of a mess,' he says in a reminiscent tone. 'The first thing they did was to shoot at us. That can happen any time, of course. But this wasn't exactly the heat of battle. We were up near Teal Inlet, with no Argies for at least fifteen miles. We had the advantage of knowing that, of course – we'd been recceing the southern shore of Teal Inlet, three of us. But even allowing for the fact that the Paras' intelligence wasn't up to ours, they were pretty jumpy.' He shakes his head at some distant memory. 'Anyway ... We were on to them before they were on to us – they were making enough noise, God only knows – clattering, yakking. We gave them a shout, and the first thing the buggers did was to fire at us. Luckily, having suspicious minds and cautious natures, we'd kept our heads down. They realised their mistake soon enough, or someone did, and they called out for the password. When we'd finished cursing them, we called back and established contact. But even then, we didn't move until they'd made a firm promise not to blow our heads off.' The kettle boils and clicks off. He looks distractedly at the steam as it curls around his shoulder.

'We were glad to see them. We'd been on our own for three days, we were tired. We'd missed two RVs – rendezvous – we were facing a hard slog to get to our emergency RV. We were glad to meet up with our own side. Swap intelligence, get some kip.' He pours the water. 'But it was hard to sleep. For

339

me anyway. I kept hearing things that made my hair stand on end. I mean, open insubordination from three or four men, and the rest not saying a word, not telling the discontents to shut up as they would in any normal troop. And everything angled in our direction, so we'd have no doubt about how unhappy they were. As if they didn't care what sort of trouble they got into so long as they could tell someone how browned off they felt. And there was Harry, failing to control the situation. He made the odd attempt, but it was crystal clear that he'd totally lost it. I couldn't identify the troublemakers in the dark of course. But Harry must have known who they were all right. But he didn't try and bring them to book, didn't knock the situation on the head. I suppose us being there made things worse for him, but by the time I realised how bad it was, my mates were kipping, I didn't want to kick 'em awake and tell 'em we had to get going again. So in the end I made myself switch off and go to sleep as well.'

He pulls a carton of milk from the fridge and sniffs at it before raising it in offering. I keep to black.

Moreland scrabbles in a drawer for a spoon and scoops sugar into his mug. He takes a long time stirring it and when he looks up his expression is grave. 'I told you, too, that they felt let down. That, rightly or wrongly, they felt their mate's death might have been avoided.' He watches me to see if I need reminding of the implication of this.

'They thought it was Harry's fault?'

'It was just a few of them – but yes, they did.'

'And was it?'

He gives a single shake of his head. 'Who knows? My men got the story – or a story of sorts – which I heard later. But who can tell? When someone buys it in what seem like unfair circumstances, it's all too easy to shove the blame around.'

He takes my coffee from my hand and, tipping his head towards the door, leads the way through into the sitting room. We settle on either side of the cold hearth. I notice a couple of cigarette-ends in the grate, and on a side table a glossy fashion magazine, and on the mantel a vase of shop-bought flowers that are past their best.

'What we didn't realise was there'd been the most almighty scuffle before we arrived. A man called Atkins had gone all out for Harry. There was another incident of sorts while we were there, just before dawn as we were getting ready to leave. It didn't get so far as a scuffle, but it was pretty close. I heard retching, I thought someone was puking. But it was Atkins choking. His mates were sitting on him to stop him from having another go. He kept thrashing about. In the end I asked Harry what was going on. He said the man had gone mental. But my men told me another story later, that this man Atkins was Congreve's mate, and had tried to throttle Harry.' He pauses. 'I never told anyone about this,' he murmurs. 'I felt it was Harry's business. Nothing to do with me.'

I try relating this distant tale to my present situation, I try fitting Atkins into the scenario that Dawson is painting, but the whole thing seems to belong to another Harry, to a world that I have never quite grasped.

'So . . .' Moreland puts his coffee aside and leans forward, his elbows on his knees, his hands loosely clasped. 'Atkins seemed the obvious place to start.'

I never imagined a name would be put to the poison-pen letter. I never thought there would be a person to pursue.

'I don't see it,' I say firmly. 'Harry killed himself. Anything else is just ridiculous.'

'I know it may seem that way but . . .'

'Everyone keeps going on about the dory. Harry always loved the dory because it had a big engine and went like stink. Rowing irritated him. It was just like him to take the dory along when he shouldn't. Anyway' – I seize on the point – 'if he was going out there to kill himself, he wouldn't have cared which boat he took. It wouldn't have made any difference.'

'Why take a dinghy at all, then?' Moreland argues softly. Before I have time to feel outmanœuvred, he continues in his most gentle tone, 'And – I'm not sure if you know, perhaps Dawson hasn't told you' – he pauses questioningly – 'but there was something else that was odd. The inflatable – it was seen early that Saturday morning, stranded on the mudflats above the quay.'

341

And I told Dawson I found it at the quay. I say this aloud: 'I told Dawson I found it at the quay.'

'You must have a good neighbour, then. Someone who fished it off the mud and brought it back for you. But Wally Smith saw it there in the morning, first thing.'

Wally is the gamekeeper on the next-door estate. Stupid of me not to realise that someone would see it. Stupid. And such an unnecessary lie to tell Dawson. I am starting to make mistakes. I wonder if Dawson realises I have lied, or whether I can still extricate myself. I wonder how many other mistakes I have made.

'Dawson saw Wally?' I ask in bemusement. The idea of Dawson talking to my neighbours fills me with fresh insecurities.

'I think so. But Wally had told several people anyway.'

People? Or was it you, I wonder, who just happened to have heard about it and then passed it on to Dawson?

'So . . .' Moreland takes a slow breath. 'What with one thing and another – the letter . . . the bruise . . . the gunshot' – he gives each a quiet emphasis – 'you can see how it looks to Dawson.'

'Tell me,' I ask quietly, 'how it looks to him.'

He gives me an odd frown as if he can't quite make out the spirit in which I am asking this. 'Well . . .' He splays out both hands, palms down, he begins tentatively, 'Well . . . I suppose it could be that this person – Atkins or whoever – took whichever dinghy was still at the quay and used it to get out to the mooring. The attack took place, and then he decided to take the yacht out to sea—'

'Why would he bother to do that?'

Moreland concedes the point immediately. 'I'm not sure. Maybe there was a struggle and there was a lot of blood or whatever' – he doesn't flinch from this – 'some sort of evidence that couldn't be got rid of anyway. So he decides to make the whole yacht disappear. He casts off the inflatable, which drifts onto the mud bank, he keeps the dory, takes the yacht out to sea, starts it sinking, heads back to shore in the dory, lands on the beach, pushes the dory off again, it's found drifting the next day. And then . . .' He trails off. He makes a doubtful gesture, as if to admit that it doesn't really hang together.

I give a loud exclamation which takes Moreland by surprise. 'You mean that this soldier knew the river and all the sandbanks, knew how to start *Minerva's* engine, knew how to start the dory's outboard?' I laugh again. 'I hardly think so.'

Moreland smiles with me for an instant before saying, 'Well, the engines wouldn't have been a problem for Atkins. He comes from a family of offshore fishermen. But the river . . . yes, that does seem a bit much.'

I stare at him. 'You've been checking up on him?'

'I made a call today, yes.'

'And Dawson – he's been checking too?'

'I would think so.'

I have a vision of this man Atkins under arrest for a crime he didn't commit. 'But you don't think there's anything in it?' Then, almost pleadingly: 'Do you?'

'I think . . .' He shoots me a considered look. '. . . that it's pretty unlikely.'

I feel relief. 'And you've told Dawson?'

'I pointed out a couple of things, yes. I told him a Para would never choose a shotgun. Not his thing at all. More like a knife. And then why wasn't he seen? Someone must have seen him, if only when he made his way back from the shore.'

'From the shore?' I echo.

'If he landed the dory on the beach, he'd have had to get away, get back to his transport. I don't think Dawson had thought of that.'

'No,' I murmur, miles away.

'And as you say, why bother to go to all the trouble of sinking the yacht?'

I look away, disentangling my thoughts with difficulty. 'So does Dawson understand that? Does he see . . . ?'

'The problem is, it wasn't the first time that Atkins had put pen to paper. Margaret told me – has told Dawson – there'd been malicious letters before.'

'*Before?*' I am still the actor, but I have stepped sideways into a strange play where I have been given a part without lines and

343

the other players seem to be making up the story as they go along. 'Why didn't Margaret . . . ?' I lift a knowing hand. 'No, don't tell me – she didn't want to upset me.'

Moreland keeps a diplomatic silence.

'These letters,' I ask, 'how many have there been then?'

'At least three, she says.'

And she told you about it, I can't help thinking. In view of the writer's military connections, I suppose she would, though this doesn't entirely quash my sense of aggrievement. 'And they were from this person?'

'They weren't signed exactly. But they were from the same person.'

The coffee has sent me into a sweat, I feel the heat spreading down my back, dampening my shirt. The room seems oppressive. I hear myself exclaim, 'God! God!' I sink back in the chair and cover my eyes and rub them viciously.

I hear Moreland get up. He squats in front of my chair. 'Ellen, don't . . .'

'But this is all so ridiculous,' I cry. 'I thought we knew where we were. I thought we knew Harry had killed himself.'

'I know. I'm sorry. I feel partly responsible—'

'Well, yes, you are!'

He flinches slightly. He takes a long breath. 'But I never intended to do anything – to uncover anything – that would hurt you in any way. I promise that was the very last thing I intended.'

'No, well, I'm sure.' I hear the peevishness in my voice, and gesture it away. 'Tell me something . . .'

He shifts his position, resting an elbow on the chair arm and propping his chin on his knuckle. He has this expression, this way of looking at me, that is so full of reassurance and goodwill and something like affection that there are times when I feel I could tell him literally anything, that, whatever I chose to confide in him, however much I was asking him to overlook, he would make the necessary leap of faith.

And then there are the other times when I glimpse the unbending integrity that runs through him like a rod, and it's like a warning, and I pull back, heart beating, from the brink.

344

'Tell me . . .' I search his face. 'Why have you bothered with all this? Why have you gone to so much trouble?'

He looks wary. Or reticent.

'I mean, it's not that I'm not grateful. Well, perhaps grateful isn't quite the right word,' I say drily. 'Appreciative. But Harry wasn't a particular friend of yours. In fact . . .' I almost say: I can't believe you liked each other at all. '. . . you weren't close. And the debt – well, that wasn't really such a big thing, was it? So . . .' I shrug. 'Why?'

He considers this for a long moment. He looks down, and when he looks up again there is something new in his eyes, something I have never seen before, a brighter, more uncertain light. 'It was partly the debt,' he says slowly. 'In the beginning anyway. Partly, the professional challenge. Proving that I could locate the yacht. Thinking, in my arrogant way, that it was bound to help your financial situation.' He glances down again, and I sense a nervousness in him, and suddenly I know what's coming, and I feel a nervousness too.

'But then . . . it was concern for you and the children.' His eyes stay on me, and I read in them all manner of things that I am half frightened, half hungry to read; and I have this sense of rushing forward into something that I don't want to prevent.

I can only think of repeating, 'Concern?'

The language of this new dialogue doesn't come easily to him either. Finally he says, 'I wanted you to be all right.'

Sensing that the moment might slip away, not wanting it to, unable to think of what to say, I reach up to touch his hand where it rests against his face, and it seems to take forever for my hand to reach his, I watch it moving with infinite slowness and all the time I am aware of him watching me and my heart beats so high in my chest that I think he must hear it. Reaching his hand, I touch it lightly with my fingertips.

His twists his hand around mine and grips it against his cheek.

'I meant well, Ellen.'

'I know.'

'I just wanted you to be free of it all.'

'I know.'

He kisses my hand. And his eyes, with their strange light, are still on me, and the space between us is so full of feeling that it's like a heat.

My head roars with a sense of freedom and certainty. In the past, love has always been a considered thing for me, a blend of emotion and judgement and desire. But this is much simpler. This is disconnected from the future, and I have no doubts.

Suddenly I want him desperately. I want him to fill the lonely spaces around me, to smooth my pain.

I move first, but he is only an instant behind me. We come together, and I put all the signals he needs, if any more be needed, in the way I open my mouth to his. I shift closer and slip an arm round him and grasp him hard, like someone who has no intention of letting him go, which, just now, I don't.

We don't so much kiss as consume. Our mouths stretch wide, our tongues search and reach past each other. I slide down off the chair until we are kneeling against each other.

After a moment I feel him pull away; I try to follow him with my mouth.

'Ellen, Ellen . . .' He cups my chin in his hand. 'We should talk about this.'

I narrow my eyes at him. 'I don't think so.'

'My situation is . . . complicated.'

I shake my head. I go for his lips again.

'Tricia and I have talked of separating. In some ways, we have already, but—'

'It doesn't matter.' I smile to show him that I really mean this. I put my fingers against his lips.

'But I don't want you to—'

'I won't.'

He laughs close to my mouth. 'But you don't know—'

'Oh yes, I do.'

He would try to say more but I don't let him. I cover his mouth with mine, I lick the edge of his cheek, I drop my hands and grip the perfect roundness of his behind. Then, in a gesture that might have surprised me a short time ago, I make

346

the move that will take us past any last opportunity for retreat. I get slowly to my feet, he rises with me. I pull his arms around my back, I lean my body against his, I signal that I am ready to be taken by the hand and led upstairs.

So brazen have I become. So open.

We undress with the lights on. His body is beautiful, lean and smooth. In the moment before he reaches for me, he takes my face almost roughly in his hands and says, 'I never meant you any harm, Ellen.'

Later, as we lie hot and damp in the darkness, still half entwined, he tries to talk of the future again, but I deflect him, I speak of other things.

It's only later still, when he has walked me out to my car and we are standing in the pre-dawn chill, postponing the moment of separation with soft kisses, that he succeeds in silencing me.

'I'll try and talk to Dawson,' he says, 'but I think it may be too late. I think he's rather hooked on the idea of finding a villain for the plot.'

SIXTEEN

'They want to see us at one-thirty,' Leonard complains at the other end of the line. 'Very short notice. I said it was rather *inconvenient*. An objectionable young police officer – *Fisher*. Most impolite. So unnecessary. Shall I put them off? I feel like putting them off,' he adds, showing rare pique.

I suspect that they aren't to be put off so easily and I tell him not to bother to try, that I'd rather get it over with anyway. I ask him if he wouldn't mind picking me up, although it will put an extra forty minutes on his journey. I know – though I don't explain this to Leonard – that driving will be beyond me.

I make a joke of it to Katie, I tell her that they're hauling me in for a grilling. I say to come and bail me out if I'm not back by midnight. She isn't fooled, of course; she can see that this front of mine is paper-thin. Oddly – but perhaps not so oddly – she rises to the occasion. She relishes the opportunity to take charge of me; it is almost as if she has been looking forward to it. She helps me choose something to wear; a loose-fitting jacket, cool slacks. She brushes my hair and thrusts lipstick and eye pencil into my hand and stands over me while I put them on. She marches me downstairs and forces me to consume orange juice and toast.

Katie my protector, bossy and capable. Through the haze of tension that presses in on me, it occurs to me that I have been denying her any role but that of victim, that in trying to shield her I have been reinforcing her sense of powerlessness, and this is something she would like to be free of.

On the doorstep she gives me a brisk kiss, she wags a finger in front of my nose. 'Don't let them bully you,' she says.

I hear little of what Leonard says on the drive to Ipswich. Something about proving the will, the price the house is likely to fetch, documents he is preparing for me to sign.

Inside the police station the desk is busy. While Leonard tries to attract the attention of one of the three officers who are helping people find their way through forms or listening dead-eyed to involved tales of woe, I take a seat between a sprawled unshaven man with stained trousers and a plump black woman with a sad smile whose look seems to say we are all going to be here a long time. When Leonard finally manages to get his message across and someone has spoken into a phone, we are asked to wait. If there is air-conditioning in this part of the building it isn't working too well and the heat contains odours of fried food from long ago and too many unwashed bodies in too small a space. Leonard paces back and forth, stopping regularly at the desk to ask how long we will be kept waiting. Coming back to me, he stoops and mutters, 'Outrageous for you to be treated like this. In your circumstances.'

My circumstances. That's just it; I have the feeling they have changed.

It is shortly before two when Fisher finally appears and leads us down the soundless corridors to the same chill interview room as before. Dawson rises heavily to his feet and comes round the table to shake my hand. His face looks pouchy and tired. His smile is brisk and impersonal.

While tea is being fetched no one speaks much and when Dawson trumpets into a handkerchief the sound fills the room.

This time, as soon as the uniformed policewoman has brought the tray of plastic cups, she occupies the chair by the door, and I notice that, in addition to Fisher at the table, there is another young officer who takes a seat against the wall.

349

When everyone is settled, Dawson faces me and we go through the usual business with the tape recorder. Dawson's voice is muffled and nasal from a congested nose. A pause while he arranges his hands neatly on the table, then he lifts his chin and, offering me an unreadable expression, says, 'Mrs Richmond, I have to inform you that as from this morning we are treating the death of your husband as a suspicious event.' He gives this a moment to settle before adding, in case I haven't got it: 'In effect, we have begun a murder inquiry.'

I see Leonard's hands jerk, his head come forward. His mouth moves soundlessly before he manages to gasp, 'There must be some mistake—'

This is not perhaps a remark to endear itself to Dawson and I wonder if Leonard, fine drafter of wills and conveyor of house titles though he is, isn't going to find this situation beyond him.

Without offering a reply, Dawson brings his grey eyes back to me. 'I realise this has come as something of a shock, Mrs Richmond. I'm very sorry indeed.' Then, as if remembering the correct procedure for such circumstances: 'Would you care to take a moment or two before we continue?'

I realise some reaction is expected of me, though the dryness in my throat, the troop of butterflies cavorting in my stomach are real enough. I whisper incredulously, 'I don't see ... I can't ...' I drop my head, I squeeze my eyes shut. Coming up again for air, I ask unsteadily, 'But *who? Why?*'

'These are matters we are seeking to establish.'

'But – you have some idea?'

'Our inquiries are only at a preliminary stage. We can't say as yet.'

'But ... you're sure it was ...?' I ask emotionally. 'That someone ...?'

'We have reason to believe so, yes,' he says solemnly.

I say *'God!'* several times.

'Would you like a moment?' Dawson offers again, creasing his eyes against some nasal tickle.

Realising I'm unlikely to get much comfort or advice from

Leonard, at least for the time being, I shake my head. Dawson's face contorts suddenly and he twists away to sneeze into a hastily opened handkerchief. Unexpectedly, without any warning at all, a tear rolls out of my eye and plops onto my hand. I look down in surprise and brush the dampness from my eyes with the back of my hand.

Dawson, having missed this, crumples his handkerchief into a ball and says, 'As I'm sure you'll appreciate, Mrs Richmond, under the, er, circumstances we will be needing to make very rigorous inquiries. And that will necessitate going through everything with you again in greater detail. Obviously we would appreciate it if you could give us the fullest possible information.'

I nod mutely.

'If we could start with a couple of points?' This is more of a statement than a question. The avuncular civility has faded, and I catch the cool draught of his professionalism. 'The day you helped your husband prepare for his yachting trip, that is, Friday, 26 March of this year, did you at any time during the course of that day see a shotgun that might or might not have belonged to your husband?'

The question swells to fill my mind. Why is he asking me this all over again? I teeter on the brink of all the things I am about to say that can never be unsaid.

Dawson tilts his head. 'Would you like me to repeat the question?'

'No. No – I didn't see a gun.'

'Not in the car, not in the yacht?'

'I didn't go in the yacht,' I point out softly.

He acknowledges this with a small movement of his fingers. 'Around the yacht, then?'

'No.'

He dabs at his nose and makes a loose phlegmy sound in the back of his throat. 'You didn't see a gun anywhere then?'

The repetition takes an effort. 'No.'

He unfolds and refolds his handkerchief, a rumpled off-white cotton square that looks as though it has done long duty, and searches out a section to receive the next blow.

'Your husband owned two, er, *tenders*, I believe – a dory and an inflatable, the latter also referred to by yourselves as the Zodiac. Could you tell me which vessel, if any, was at the, er, quay that day?'

I shake my head. 'I don't remember, I'm afraid.'

Dawson looks down at the table and it may be my imagination, but I think I see annoyance tug at the corners of his mouth.

'Did you see either of these, er, *tenders*, anywhere else that day?'

'Not that I remember.'

Another pause, a cooling in the air between us. Fisher shifts in his seat but I am careful not to meet his eyes.

'Moving on,' Dawson says ponderously. 'Regarding the inflatable dinghy, also referred to as the Zodiac – could you tell me where you found it on Saturday, 27 March, the day after you helped your husband prepare for his yachting trip?'

This has come much sooner than I thought. I feel light-headed and it is an instant before I realise I am holding my breath. 'I'm glad you asked that,' I say in a forced tone. 'Because, um . . . very foolishly' – I feel my mouth twitch into the semblance of a smile which I swiftly extinguish – 'I didn't quite get that right before. In fact . . . I didn't tell you the truth.'

There is a silence like cold or darkness. Fisher glances at Dawson with a knowing flicker. Dawson, whether from anticipation or long practice, shows no reaction. His heavy lids blink once. 'Now why did you do that, Mrs Richmond?' he asks in a lugubrious tone.

'I thought . . .' I shake my head at my own stupidity. '. . . it would only muddle everything. That . . . you'd start to take this Atkins idea seriously.'

In the corner of my eye, I'm aware of Leonard frowning at me in dismay.

'Ah,' says Dawson drily. 'You didn't think we should do that then?'

'I thought the whole Atkins idea was quite mad, frankly. Nothing to do with Harry and what happened. I thought if I told you about the dinghy—'

'The inflatable?'

'—the inflatable, then you'd think there was something in it, and everything would get stirred up again. Just when it was all beginning to quieten down. Just when I was getting the children settled again. I thought it would only confuse things . . .' I trail off, gesturing my penitence. 'I didn't realise.' I add humbly, 'I'm sorry.'

Dawson takes a long troubled breath, the schoolmaster faced by the errant pupil. 'Mrs Richmond, you must have realised the *seriousness* of failing to mention this.'

I give a remorseful nod. 'Well, *now* . . .'

'At the time?'

'No, I . . . really didn't.'

Dawson snorts, clearing some obstruction from the back of his nose. 'So where did you find the inflatable?'

'It was sitting on the mud.'

'Where on the mud?'

'Upriver from the quay a way.'

'How far exactly?'

'I'm not very good at distances. Umm – fifty yards? A bit more?'

'You could see it from the quay?'

'Yes.'

'And what did you do?'

'When I saw it? Well, I thought it had just drifted there, hadn't been tied up properly. And I went and fetched it.'

Dawson unfurls the dismal hanky again. When the blast of his hooting has died away, I can hear above the faint hum of the recorder the sound of someone shouting in the corridor outside.

'May I ask how you fetched the inflatable back exactly?' He affects the look of someone in need of enlightenment.

'Well, I waded out through the mud and I paddled it back to the quay.'

353

'Paddled? Forgive me, I want to be clear. Is that the same as rowing?'

I answer dutifully, 'No. What I did was to sit in the front of the dinghy and use one oar as a paddle, first on one side then the other. I've never been very good at rowing.'

'It was hard, paddling?'

'No. The current was with me.'

'The current was with you?'

'The tide.'

'Ah. It changes, does it?'

I wonder if he is having me on. 'The current moves downriver when the tide's going out, and upriver when the tide's coming in. I had to learn that,' I say with a short laugh, sounding too eager.

'When you were doing this paddling, and later, at the quay, did you notice anything unusual about the inflatable?'

'I'm sorry?' We both know that I heard, we both know that I am putting the moment off.

His eyes are watering. He blinks rapidly to clear them. 'Was there anything in or on the inflatable that caused you to take notice of it?'

'You mean—?' But he doesn't help me. 'Well, there was mud,' I say. 'I'd brought a lot of mud in . . .' I lift my shoulders. 'Nothing else. What else should there have been . . . ?' I look to Fisher, to the officer by the wall, as if they might give me the answer. 'What sort of thing?' I am sounding anxious again.

No one answers me.

'You gave the inflatable a clean up?' Dawson continues.

'I got the worst of the mud off, yes.'

'And the oars? They were there in the inflatable when you found it on the mud, were they?'

I think carefully. 'Yes.'

'And you used them to paddle back?'

'Well, just the one, yes.'

'And were they muddy as well, the oars?'

'I didn't notice. I don't think so.'

'And there was nothing else about them? That you noticed, I mean?'

It comes to me then. The oars. It is the oars. I didn't clean the oars well enough and they have found Harry's blood on them.

'Did you wash the oars as well, Mrs Richmond?'

My nervous inappropriate smile springs up before I can suppress it. 'They may have got a splash of water. But no. I mean, I didn't sponge them or anything like that.'

It is definitely the oars. And realising this, I try to grasp where this might lead, I'm swayed by new uncertainties.

Reaching some juncture in his own thoughts, taking his time, Dawson inserts a handkerchief-clad finger up each nostril and submits his nose to a thorough clear-out. He gives a heavy sigh. 'Pity you didn't tell us about this before, Mrs Richmond,' and when he looks up his expression has hardened, and my confidence falters and I am not at all sure he has believed a word I have said.

There's a cry a child makes that kicks at your deepest instincts, that has you sprinting, sick with nameless terror, towards the source, ready to defend, fight, tear, rip, kill. Once when Katie was five she got lost in a crowd and when her scream rang out it turned my heart to ice. Another time, when she was about seven, her cry took me pounding across a friend's garden and into battle with a terrier that had her by the sleeve of her dress. I dragged the dog's jaws apart with a strength I never knew I had, and which came, I think, from sheer necessity.

When Katie got through to me at Molly's that Friday evening, the sound she made down the phone wasn't a cry exactly, more of a wail, but, with her frantic sobs and the realisation that for some reason she wasn't at school but at home, I was soon racing out to the car and fumbling with the ignition and pushing my foot flat against the floor in mindless reaction. During the journey to Pennygate I talked myself out of the more excessive scenes of doom and disaster, I told myself that Katie often got things out of proportion, but as soon as I got into the house and called out and heard Katie's answering cry from upstairs, the terror came thudding back.

She was sitting in my half-filled bath, fully clothed, the water dark and murky.

I kept asking what the matter was, I kept asking until my voice became like a chant in my ears. For a while she was completely incoherent, shivering hard, rolling her head, sobbing in juddering spasms through a mouth that was pulled back in a long grimace. When she finally managed something intelligible, it was just a few garbled words. But if I had been slow in the past, if I had managed to close my mind to everything I didn't want to see, I quickened up then, I got there in a single wrench of understanding, and it was like stepping off a ledge into nothingness.

For a while the anguish was so great that I clung to Katie, and together we rocked back and forth, sending waves across the murky water.

Then she shivered more violently, and I helped her out of her clothes and drained the cold dirty water and poured hot clear water and helped her bathe herself. I wrapped her in a large towel and put her in my bed and held her tight against me and stroked her hair and told her over and over again that I loved her. And all the time I was shrivelling inside.

I gave her sleeping pills, two strong ones, and as soon as she began to quieten down, I asked the questions that I half dreaded to ask. I kept my voice low, low and calm; I began with what I hoped were the less disturbing things. What made you come home from school? How did you get here? For a while it seemed she wouldn't answer, and when she finally did the words came spasmodically, in blurred moans and gulps. At last I made out: 'Said you were there . . . promised . . . *promised*. Said . . . you were . . . fetching things. Promised . . .'

The rest came in equally uneven snatches, but finally I understood that Harry had phoned her at school, had promised her that I was there with him, that the two of us wanted her to come over for supper, that she was to get a taxi.

I absorbed this in agonising lurches. He had said I was there. He had lied to her. But it was more than that; he had done it, I realised, to deceive her into thinking she was safe. In understanding this, I also understood, with the shock of the obvious, that Katie had known she was at risk, that she had been living in fear.

And then there was only one question to ask. It was all I could do to keep my voice under control as I whispered, has this happened before?

When she didn't reply I asked her again. But she turned her head deeper into the pillow and blocked me out, and her action was an answer in itself.

I felt emotionally sick, I wanted to vomit all the love I had ever felt for Harry clear of my body. I wanted to void all my feelings and be rid of them for ever. And fuelling my despair and revulsion was my own sense of failure. I could only think that I had let this happen, that I should have seen.

And then I thought of the way Harry had lured Katie away from school, I thought of the planning he had put into it and something shifted inside me and I felt this peculiar coldness, a gathering of altogether fiercer emotions.

I had reached the age where I thought I knew everything there was to know about myself, I thought my boundaries had been marked out for me, that I had experienced every kind of happiness of which I was capable, every kind of anger. But when I thought of Harry and what he had done, my emotions sped out into entirely new territory, and I felt this rage. It was nothing like the occasional flashes of childhood heat I'd felt when provoked by my mother, it was nothing like the weary anger I'd felt at the more testing times in my marriage. This was a worm of resentment and fury that uncurled inside me, feeding on itself until it filled me up, I was bursting with it, and it drove every other thought from my head.

Leaving Katie to sleep, I pulled on a coat and slipped out of

357

the side door and through the gate onto the track. As I strode rapidly down to the quay, stumbling now and again, jarring my legs in the darkness, fresh realisations came to me, I saw new layers of deceit and betrayal. Muttering aloud, my voice like a second presence, I pushed on, unstoppable.

At the quay there was only the dory, its heavy engine shipped, and no key for the ignition. But then I saw the way the tide was running and remembered the paddles that were always kept under the back seat, and, buoyed by determination, I cast off and struck out into the stream and let the current carry me away. It was dark, there was still a heavy mist, but I never doubted I would find *Minerva*. My rage would carry me there.

Dawson is called away and, returning briefly, suggests a half-hour break. Leonard and I go for a walk in the heat of the street and look unsuccessfully for somewhere quiet to sit down.

'This is so terrible,' Leonard keeps murmuring in hushed tones as we trudge towards some tea shop that is meant to be a couple of streets away. 'So *terrible*. But in some ways perhaps it's a *consolation* to know it wasn't suicide.' He looks anxiously for my response. Getting none, he says in his practical voice, 'Do you want me to tell the family?'

The thought of anyone else knowing is painful. 'Not yet.'

'The newspapers – I'm afraid they'll find out.'

The tea shop has gone, another victim of the recession, and we turn back.

I agree: 'The family then,' and the enormity of what is happening comes home to me.

When we reassemble in the interview room it is with a sense of familiarity, everyone in the same seats, the tea and tape recorder ceremonies unfolding with the smoothness of ritual.

Dawson's cold seems to have worsened. His eyes have acquired a glassy look, the skin around his nostrils has become red and inflamed, from time to time his voice croaks or seizes altogether. The weary cotton handkerchief has gone, replaced by a box of tissues which he dips into with faint reluctance.

Leonard, determined perhaps to make up for his earlier confusions and inadequacies, makes a statement about the unacceptability of keeping me too long, considering it is already late in the afternoon. It is, in fact, five.

'No one will be kept longer than necessary,' Dawson says thickly, tidying some papers on the table in front of him and turning his attention to me. 'Mrs Richmond, could we just go over a few things concerning that evening of Friday, 26 March?' His manner has hardened, and I have the feeling that it isn't just his cold which is aggravating him. 'You went to Miss Sinclair's for a meal at about six p.m.?'

I agree.

'What time did you leave Miss Sinclair's?'

'I think I said – it must have been about ten.'

'Are you sure about that?'

'Well . . . it could have been earlier. I don't remember.'

He gives me an odd look, as though he knows this to be untrue. 'You went straight home?'

'Yes.'

He coughs uncomfortably, as if his chest is causing him pain. 'And then?'

'I did a few chores and I went to bed.'

'What time would you have got to bed exactly?'

'About twelve, I suppose. Something like that.'

'Did you receive any phone calls that evening after you got back?' And suddenly he is staring at me intently. And I too am very still, because while I have been dreading this, I have also been preparing for it. I know my lines, there is no problem about that, but I am short on rehearsal and I'm not sure my delivery will be up to scratch.

I make a show of searching an imperfect memory. 'I don't remember any, no.'

'Nothing at about eleven-fifty?'

'I don't think so. But I could well have been in the bath, and then I might not have heard the phone. In fact, I often don't hear it. I usually have the radio on, you see. When I'm in the bath.'

'So if there'd been a call at eleven-fifty, it would have gone unanswered?'

'The machine would have picked it up eventually.'

'I see.' This emerges as a croak. 'And then you would have played the message back at some point?'

'Yes. In the morning, probably.'

He clears his throat with a loud hawking sound. 'And was there a message the next morning?'

I shake my head. I blow out my lips. 'It's hard to remember after all this time.'

His eyelids droop. 'Would you have remembered if it had been a call from your husband, Mrs Richmond?'

I stare at him. I whisper, 'Of course.'

'There was no message the next morning from your husband?'

I am still staring at him. Coming to with difficulty, I shake my head.

'You're quite sure about this?'

'Yes. But I don't understand . . . you're saying my husband called that night?'

Dawson pulls in his lips and says in a significant tone, 'A call was made from your husband's mobile phone to your home at eleven-fifty that night.'

I am openly bemused.

'And you're saying there was no message?' Dawson asks.

'No.'

'Would anyone else have played the message tape back?'

I shake my head uncertainly. 'They shouldn't have.'

'So what could have happened to his message, do you suppose?'

I hunch in my chair. I raise a baffled hand. 'Perhaps he didn't leave one.'

'The call was logged at six minutes, Mrs Richmond.'

A clammy sensation creeps over me. It is all I can do not to freeze entirely. I had no idea it had been so long. I look away, I feel a trickle of sweat inside my shirt, and the longer I founder, the more I sense I am giving myself away and the greater the swell of panic. For an instant I have an urge to admit to everything, to get it over and done with, but somehow I manage to drag my eyes back to Dawson's and slowly shake my head.

'You have no explanation?'

'No.'

'There was no one else in the house who may have taken the call?'

Another rush of anxiety: he knows about Katie. He must know! Everyone knows! Then, slowing down, playing his voice back in my mind, I hear his note of pedantic enquiry, and I tell him calmly that there was no one else in the house.

He doesn't argue; he doesn't repeat the question.

In my relief I have a momentary vision of Katie lying half-comatose in my bed, of the phone ringing, of her reaching groggily to answer it. I see myself back on *Minerva*, clutching the mobile to my ear, repeating myself time and again, getting nothing but wild incoherent mumblings until at long last she seemed to understand what I was saying. Back in a while, back in a while. Just sleep, darling, just sleep. It's going to be all right, I promise it's going to be all right. Not such an important message perhaps, but vital to me. I couldn't have left her without a word; I had to know the drugs were working and she was going to sleep.

We go over the foibles of the answering machine, the frequency with which it has lost messages in the past. I tell Dawson it has jammed occasionally, that it is impossible to tell when it has lost messages.

We return to the bath I took that night, how long I stayed in it, how loud I was playing the radio.

Then it's back to the answering machine. And again. The same questions in slightly different form. How it could have lost a message. Whether I think it lost Harry's message that night.

And every time he repeats a question, I feel it's a small step closer to the end, because I sense he doesn't believe me. It is his determination against mine, and I'm not sure that mine is the stronger.

Dawson picks up one of the papers in front of him. 'Your

husband also called your daughter's school at' – he brings the sheet a little closer – 'six-thirty.' Lowering the paper, he regards me with raised brows. 'Were you aware of that?'

'No. But then he can't have spoken to her.'

'Why not?'

'Well, she would have told me,' I say unsteadily. 'In fact, the last time she spoke to him was on the Tuesday. She said so.'

'So who would your husband have spoken to then, on the Friday?'

I shrug lightly. 'Oh, one of the seniors, I expect. You phone the house and leave a message with one of the senior girls on duty, asking your daughter to call back.'

He screws up his face and presses his fingertips to the side of his head in a practised show of puzzlement. 'So she would have got a message?'

I am falling, falling. And in danger of taking Katie with me.

'No . . .' I grab at something, anything. 'Often they can't find her. She's somewhere else in the school. The message gets lost. So you call back and . . .'

He leans forward and cocks his head to hear me better.

'. . . you just try again.'

'Just try again,' he echoes ruminatively. 'That's how it works, is it?'

I nod breathlessly.

I must look odd or ill because Leonard glances at me anxiously and Dawson asks me if I want more tea and raises an empty cup to the policewoman. Suddenly everyone is in motion, stretching, standing up, collecting cups, and I have gained recovery time. Dawson retires into a corner with a bunch of tissues to hoot and trumpet in private. Leonard gives me a bleak look and pats my arm.

When the fresh cups stand in front of us and the door is closed once more, Dawson sinks solidly back in his seat. Beating a fist against his chest, he says, 'Apologies. Hope I'm not blowing germs your way.'

'You should take something for it.'

He looks at me blankly.

'My grandfather always used to say, take a candle and a

362

bottle of brandy to bed. Light the candle and when you see two flames, blow them both out and sleep through till morning.'

He regards me with slight puzzlement until, getting the humour, such as it is, he gives an awkward mirthless smile.

'Now . . .' He pulls his face down into an expression of gravity, as though I needed reminding of why we are here. 'Perhaps we could move on to the period leading up to Friday, 26 March? The few weeks prior?'

Debts. Anonymous letters. After the phone call ordeal, I greet these subjects with something approaching relief.

'May I ask' – and his tone is contrite, as if he wished he didn't have to mention it at all – 'how things were between you and your husband?'

I grip my cup more tightly. 'Well—' I say eventually, 'we were under a lot of strain. All his business worries, the debts, not being able to talk about them . . . Our relationship certainly suffered, yes.'

'There were no other problems between you?'

Ah, I have the drift now. I see where this is leading. I make a non-committal shrug. 'Well, every marriage has its ups and downs.'

Dawson draws in his lips, he takes his time. 'Were you aware that your husband was having a relationship with a woman named Caroline Palmer?'

Now who has been talking? I wonder. Margaret? Or Jack?

I say it straight out. 'Yes.'

'How long had you known about it?'

'Since October.'

'And how did you feel about it?'

'I was upset. When I found out. But then I realised it wasn't serious, I realised it was something that would pass. I learnt to live with it.'

'You, er, tackled your husband about it?'

'No.'

He contemplates the table. 'Not once?'

'No.'

'Why not?'

'I didn't think it would do any good.'

363

Dawson frowns before rubbing a tissue mercilessly across the end of his nose. 'But you were unhappy enough to, er, keep tabs on your husband, to keep an eye on him?'

Jack: it is Jack who has told them.

I can't decide whether I should try to deny this. I hear myself say, 'For a while, yes.'

'You were jealous, in fact?'

Where is this leading? But even as I wonder, a part of me already suspects. 'Upset,' I correct him. 'I was upset.'

Dawson's look suggests that I am trying to split hairs. He says heavily, 'Didn't you take to trying to find out where Mr Richmond was? To phoning your husband's flat in London? To calling friends to ask them where he was?'

Yes: definitely Jack. He was the only person I ever called to ask where Harry was. He was the only one who knew how I felt about Caroline Palmer. I wonder if this is Jack's way of getting back at me over the charity money.

'There was a time,' I admit, 'when I needed to know where he was. A time when I was particularly upset.'

'When you were jealous?'

I give in. 'If you like.'

Dawson pulls his shoulders back, a gesture of satisfaction. 'And, er, the reason your husband was trying to get the yacht round to the South Coast, that was connected, wasn't it?'

'He was going cruising.'

'Wasn't he in fact taking it there to act as a weekend meeting place for himself and Miss Palmer?'

'He may have been.'

'And this was a fact that you were well aware of?'

'Well – I guessed.'

'You knew?'

'As good as,' I concede.

'And you wanted to prevent it if you possibly could?'

There is a pause, a collective holding of breath, as the implications of this question fill the room.

I am being accused.

Leonard finally feels moved to say, 'Inspector, is this really necessary?'

364

Dawson leans closer across the desk and says in a low voice, 'I'd be grateful, Mrs Richmond, if you would answer – did you try to prevent your husband from leaving?'

I blink tearfully. 'No.'

'Why didn't you tell me the truth about the inflatable dinghy straight away, Mrs Richmond?'

'I told you . . .'

'But the real reason?'

I shake my head, I make a gesture as if to say, why are you asking me this?

Dawson sighs. 'Mrs Richmond, that phone call from your husband' – and his voice is heavy with regret – 'you did in fact answer it, didn't you?'

Leonard moves as if to intervene again and is cut short by a rapid twist of Dawson's hand. I feel the ground slipping away from under my feet and there's nothing to hold on to.

'No,' I breathe.

He turns an ear to hear me better. 'I'm sorry?'

I repeat my denial in a stronger voice.

Dawson leans back in his chair, coughing roughly. Recovering, he gives me a mournful stare. 'Perhaps you'd care to think things over, Mrs Richmond?'

'There's nothing to think over,' I say, with a bravado I do not feel.

'Shall we say ten o'clock tomorrow?'

'Josh?' I try putting a hand on his shoulder, but he shakes me off with such force and resentment that I pull back to the edge of the bed and look helplessly towards Katie.

I make one more attempt. 'I really do think they've made a mistake, honey,' I say, with a sincerity that rings falsely even in my own ears. 'I just don't believe that anyone would want to hurt Daddy. I just don't believe it. I think the police had it right before, that there was no one else involved, there was just . . . *him* . . .' I trail off, aware that I have lost the will to fight even on this front, which is almost the most important one of all. We have been here for half an hour, the three of us, going over the same ground – or rather Katie and I have been picking the

365

police's ideas apart while Josh has lain rigid, resistant to all offers of love or comfort.

Katie says, 'I think they watch too many films, the police. I think they fancy themselves zooming around finding clues and arresting people and looking cool and all that stuff.' She paces to the head of the bed and looks down at Josh, inert on the duvet with its bright red and green racing car pattern. 'Hey?' She nudges him gently. 'Hey?' She ducks her head down to get a look at his face. Getting no response, she pulls a face as if to say she'd do better on her own, and, feeling defeated, needing no second prompting, I retreat.

The thing is, I don't blame Josh for giving up on us. He would have had to be blind and deaf not to realise that Katie and I had a separate agenda in America, he would have had to be totally insensitive not to feel excluded. Perhaps, with this final shock, he's run out of faith. What can I say to him? Believe me, Josh? Why should he believe me when I don't believe myself any more?

Moreland is late. Like a child I go to the window in the hall and look out, as if this will be enough to bring his car into sight. Waiting there, I lean my head against the glass and feel the blend of clarity and confusion that exhaustion brings.

Clatterings take me to the kitchen, where I find Molly, bent over a saucepan, stirring briskly.

'I'm not sure anyone's going to be hungry,' I tell her.

Her head comes up, she stops. 'No,' she agrees immediately and switches the gas off and chucks the spoon down as if the idea were so obvious she should have thought of it herself. 'No,' she sighs. Wiping her hands on her apron, she reaches for the cigarette smouldering in the adjacent ashtray and inhales long and hard. 'Drink?'

I wouldn't mind something but decide against it. I need to clear my mind, not muddle it. I have this notion, based on nothing but the shallowest of hope, that if I think hard enough some ideas might yet come to me, that against all probability I might yet persuade Dawson that I have nothing to tell him.

'What is it, honey?' Molly cocks her head at me, blowing a plume of smoke expertly past her nose.

I have been staring. 'I want to ask you something,' I say after a moment's thought. 'A sort of favour.'

Molly stubs out her cigarette. She makes one of her more extravagant gestures, all wide arm movement and chinking jewellery. 'Anything.'

I draw her to the table and we pull out chairs and sit hunched knee to knee. 'The thing is, the police will probably come and talk to you again. If they do . . . would you . . . well, I'd be grateful if you didn't tell them about the call from Katie. That night?'

She knows the call I mean. She's already shaking her head. 'Haven't mentioned it before. No reason to mention it now.'

'Also . . .'

She urges me on. 'What?'

'You must say no if you have any doubts. If you feel unhappy about it . . .'

She brushes this thought aside.

'It's just . . . they might understand things better if you told them that I was worried about Harry.'

'Well, you were!'

'Yes. But I mean particularly worried that evening.'

'Of course.' She shrugs as if to say, is that all? 'Anything particular you were worried about? Was he ill? In a bad mood?' She's enjoying the challenge, but I think she's also relieved that I haven't asked for more.

'A bad mood, I think. Depressed. And that's why I left early.'

'Did you leave early?'

'It might have been before ten.'

'Oh. But you went to see if he was all right?'

'Yes.'

She presses her cheek to mine. 'No problem.'

'It's just that I don't want—'

Pulling away sharply, she holds up a hand. 'No, don't tell me,' she says. 'No need.' And she looks pleased with herself for this display of discretion, as if we were involved in some harmless game and she is proud of having grasped the rules.

The phone rings and, taking on her self-appointed role as guardian of the peace, she gets up to answer it.

'Charles – *hello*,' she says into the phone, rolling her eyes in my direction. Receiving my not-at-home signal, she proceeds to tell him I have taken a sleeping pill and gone to bed.

Ears towards the drive, I'm finally rewarded by the sound of a car. Slipping out through the kitchen door, seeing the scruffy black Golf, my worries are momentarily pushed aside and I feel all the half-forgotten emotions of a new lover, the blend of excitement and apprehension, the foolish hopefulness. Watching Moreland climb out of the car, I measure him against my image of him, and he hasn't changed. If anything he seems more familiar, like someone I have known a long long time, and I feel a surge of affection that at any other time I might easily take for love.

When he looks up, he doesn't have to tell me that something is terribly wrong, it's written all over his face.

'Have you got a while?' he says. He doesn't kiss me, he doesn't even touch me, he just stands there, looking grave and stern, and my throat is suddenly dry.

I nod wordlessly and go back to tell Molly I'll be away for a time. I return to find him holding the passenger door open for me.

When we're bumping down the drive I ask, 'What is it? What's happened?'

He frowns ahead, he answers with difficulty, 'I'd rather tell you when we get there.' He glances briefly towards me. 'If that's all right.' And his politeness is almost worse than anything else.

At the main road we don't turn left towards Woodbridge and Moreland's cottage, we go the other way, towards the sea. If I think of speaking again, I am silenced by the grimness of Moreland's profile, the tightness of his lips. We pass through one village and another, we turn onto a smaller road, and then into a lane that is barely wide enough for two vehicles, and suddenly I know exactly where we're going.

The sun is almost set, the land is darkening, and only the tops of the taller trees are brushed with gold. The fields fall behind us, then the last of the trees, and we descend onto a verdant table of reclaimed marshland, and then there is nothing ahead of us but the mass of the shingle bank that rises in a giant rampart against the sea.

The single-track concrete road dissects the flatland, wriggling briefly over two dykes, before slanting up the back of the shingle bank, with its bedding of sand and tussock grass. Halfway up the slope the road forks, carrying on towards a group of coastguard cottages which stand in incongruous isolation on the top of the bank, or turning left, up and over the top of the shingle. Taking the left turn, negotiating a barrier that says NO VEHICLES BEYOND THIS POINT, we rise over the brow of the bank, and the sea spreads out before us, filling the horizon, vast and broad and dark as pewter.

The top of the bank is wide. Before the sand and meagre vegetation give way to the mass of grey pebble, there are large brackish pools and, running parallel to the sea, a ribbon of pitted and crumbling concrete, a remnant of some World War II defence system. Moreland negotiates the concrete for a distance then, choosing his spot, points the car towards the sea and parks. When he turns the engine off, the silence is filled by the rumble and rasp of the waves dragging at the stones below. Hearing this, I am scrabbling to find my footing on the stones again, the salt is sharp in my eyes, the waves are pulling at my legs.

Moreland places his hands high on the steering wheel and leans his forehead against them as if he were deeply tired. Straightening up slowly, staring out to sea, he starts to speak in a voice that seems for all its control to be close to despair. 'A couple of days ago, when I was taking the Atkins idea seriously, when it seemed to fit everything, the dinghies and so on, before I'd thought it through properly, before *you* helped me to see that it was a non-starter...' He pauses and almost glances at me before fixing his eyes on the sea once more. '...I tried to work out how Atkins could have done it. The sheer logistics.' He makes a derisive sound and murmurs bitterly, 'Ever the detective!' Pushing himself onwards with an effort, he continues, 'I reckoned that Atkins would have had to come ashore somewhere along this stretch of beach before pushing the dory out to sea and making his way back to his transport. But where was he most likely to have landed? And how did he get back to his transport, assuming he had some? I couldn't see him taking the dory all the way back up the river. Too visible, too obvious. So where did he land? Much further north than here and he'd have had to swim the Ore or walk miles and miles to Aldeburgh or beg a lift on a military ferry, and still be a long way from his transport, assuming he left it somewhere near Pennygate. No, the way I saw it, if he had any sense at all he'd have come in somewhere near here and taken the path back over the marshes.'

He stops for no apparent reason and, turning away slightly, narrows his eyes as though examining something on the horizon. Concentrating again with reluctance, he resumes in a slightly brisker tone, 'So I asked around. The local lads, the fishermen, a bloke I'd met who has one of the coastguard cottages here as a weekend place. Anyone who might have seen anything. I even went back to the rambler, the one who saw *Minerva* motoring out of the river. But ... nothing.' He looks down at his hands, he squeezes his lips, and still he finds it easier not to meet my eye. 'Then the chap in the coastguard cottages called me today. He said there was someone in one of the other cottages, an old guy who lives there all the time, and I should speak to him. So ... I went there this evening.'

Beyond him in the middle distance, the cottages stand in ghostly silhouette, small Gothic follies against the fading sky.

Moreland turns at last, he looks at me, and his expression is at once appalled and sad, and I have a rush of feeling for him, for both of us, because I know what he's about to say.

'He saw a boat drifting early one morning, he wasn't sure of the date exactly, but it was about the right time. In March anyway. A weekend. A white boat, open, like a dory, though he couldn't be sure about that either. He didn't think there was anyone in it. He watched it for a bit. It drifted steadily north and then he lost it in the mist. While he was watching he noticed someone coming up over the shingle about where we are now, someone wearing a white waterproof jacket with some colour on it – green, he thought. He particularly noticed because the person staggered and fell and lay down for a while. He thought of going out to see if the person was all right but when he looked out again the person was getting up. He went down to the kitchen shortly after and saw the person passing the the back of the cottages and taking the path down onto the marshes.' Moreland's frown deepens, his voice trembles slightly as he says, 'He said it was a woman. He was quite sure it was a woman.'

The silence stretches out between us.

'Tell me he was wrong, Ellen.'

But I can't tell him that. It would be useless to try.

SEVENTEEN

'It was me.' I say it quickly as though this might lessen the impact.

Moreland twitches slightly as though an unseen insect has flown against his skin, he stares at me with faint horror and open bewilderment.

I look away. There are moments you fear and try to plan for, moments you think about so much that you can't focus on them any more, and then when they finally arrive they aren't as you imagined. I feel a sense of loss, but mainly I feel a bleak relief.

I make a gesture of appeal or apology. I say again, 'It was me.'

'You were on *Minerva*?' Moreland asks thickly.

But I can't answer this without answering everything. Needing more time, I wind the window down and let the breeze bowl in, cool and damp from the sea, filling the car with the low clamour of the pebbles clinking and rattling on the beach below.

'*How?*' Moreland demands. 'Why?'

I sigh, I begin emotionally, 'It was Harry. You may not have realised, but he was in a terrible . . .' But this is wrong. If I am going to get through this story with some self-respect, if indeed I'm to have any hope of being believed after the untruths I've told, then I must do it without the more unedifying dramatic trimmings.

'Can I go back a bit?' I ask rather formally.

He indicates: anything.

But the beginning still eludes me. I could start with Harry

losing his parliamentary seat, with Ainswick's troubles, I could even start with the affair with Caroline Palmer, but I'm not sure that these tales would add much to the story, which is straightforward enough. If only I can get it right. But I must get it right, for Katie's sake as much as my own. Lies are not so hard to tell, but they're extremely hard to fix in the memory accurately, so that they emerge unaltered every time.

'Harry ... was ... unhappy.' I begin haltingly. 'Things had been going wrong for a long time. He had been under terrible strain. He was very depressed. He felt things were never going to work out for him. He felt he was sinking deeper and deeper...' I am losing momentum. Gathering myself again, I continue, 'I couldn't seem to offer him any support. I couldn't reach him. He cut himself off from me. From everyone. I think...' I pause as though to consider this afresh. 'I think he was clinically depressed. I mean, from being something mental it had become physical as well. You know – the wrong chemicals in the brain. An illness. Needless to say, he wouldn't go and get help. That wasn't his way. He couldn't admit to anything that he couldn't deal with himself.'

I hate these half-truths, I hate my veneer of plausibility. Beneath it I feel transparent, I feel that Moreland must see straight through me, so that when I glance up I'm rather surprised to find him watching me with sympathy.

'That Friday,' I hurry on, 'I had the feeling that something was terribly wrong. I mean, worse than usual. He was in such a strange mood when we were loading the boat. Not there at all. Doing things mechanically. Half dead. I can't put my finger on it quite. A feeling of doom and despair. Hopelessness. And going singlehanded in that weather! I was sick with worry. I went down to the quay in the afternoon to see if he needed anything but of course I couldn't make contact. I mean, the boat was there on the mooring and I shouted and waved, but he never heard me. The mooring's quite a way out, it's hard to hear on the best of days. I tried calling the mobile phone but he must have switched it off or something. When I got to Molly's that evening I couldn't stop worrying. I kept thinking – well, that was it, I wasn't sure what it was, exactly. A feeling. A sort of foreboding, I suppose.'

Such a performance. The details, the embellishments. It seems I have an instinct for these things.

'So I came home early. I went down to the quay. It was very dark. I couldn't see *Minerva*, I couldn't see a light. I thought he must have gone. In a way I hoped he had – sailing always cheered him up, made him forget his troubles. And it was such a big challenge, taking the boat so far on his own; I thought it would give his confidence a lift, get him going again. But the weather still looked so horrible – wind and rain – that I rather hoped he hadn't gone after all. I thought it would be too much for him, sailing at night in that wind.'

Pausing, I stare out through the windscreen and Moreland follows my gaze. The sky is fading fast, the sea is dark as slate.

'I kept an eye on the weather for the rest of the evening,' I resume and he watches me again. 'Kept the windows open, listened for the wind. It dropped right away. I was relieved. I thought of Harry somewhere in the middle of the estuary with all those ships around, I thought he'd be much safer with the wind gone. I went to bed, feeling a bit easier about things. Then ... oh, about eleven-ten' – I have caught Dawson's obsession with precision – 'well, some time just after eleven, I heard the ...' I lift my head as if to hear the sound again. '... the *shot*. It was a long way off, muffled, but I knew what it was. A shotgun. I mean, I've heard enough of them. There's quite a bit of shooting around Pennygate in the winter.' I make an indeterminate gesture. 'I also knew ... somehow ... that it was Harry. I just ...' I lift a hand. '... *felt* it.'

The breeze stiffens, I turn my face to meet it. Moreland shifts forward slightly as if to keep sight of my face.

'I drove down to the quay and there was a light. It could only be *Minerva*. It was in the right place, the right distance away. I knew then ... somehow ...' I shake my head, I look down at my hands. 'So I went out. To look.' I sense Moreland's unvoiced question. 'It was the dory. I took the dory,' I tell him.

374

'It was the only thing there. But I didn't know how to lower the engine into the water. I got the torch from the car, but I still couldn't work it out. And even if I had managed to get the engine down, I wasn't sure how to start it, whether you just turned the key or what. So I paddled. I saw the way the current was going and I realised I could go with it. I almost missed *Minerva*, though...' I wince at the memory. 'Almost got swept past. Had to paddle like mad. Just managed to grab the Zodiac and pull myself up to *Minerva*.'

I brace myself. The vision is very strong and, though I have been back to the yacht many times in my mind, now that I try to put the picture into words the scene has become doubly vivid, like an etching that has sprung into full and awesome colour.

'He was ... dead.'

Moreland nods in the manner of someone hearing what he has expected to hear.

'There was no doubt,' I whisper. 'I mean – that he was dead. I checked, I felt for ... you know, pulse and things. And...' The memories crowd closer still, my voice constricts in my chest, it's all I can do to say, 'His eyes ... were wrong. You know – open.'

Moreland nods again.

'The gun was beside him,' I murmur. We contemplate this in our separate ways before I continue in a new voice, 'I sat there for a long time. I don't know – an hour or so. Oh, I covered him up,' I add swiftly, as if this were an important point. 'I covered him with a chart; it was all I could find. It was wide...' But this is too painful and I abandon it with a shake of the head. I see the blood still. The astonishing redness of it as I bent over him. The way it glistened in the light. The awful gape of his mouth which seemed to yawn up in front of me even when I had turned away.

'Then I just sat there.'

Just sat there and wept, though I don't say so. Wept and railed and sobbed until my throat was hoarse, until, catching the sound of my own voice, I recognised the futility of it all and shuddered to a halt.

'I felt so frustrated and angry,' I relate calmly. 'I kept going over it all in my mind. I couldn't understand why he'd been so . . . Why he couldn't have *told* me . . .'

Moreland's hand arrives on my arm and grips it dutifully.

'That's what's so hard. That he never talked about it.' Saying this, I allow old emotions to rush in, I remember what enraged me so profoundly as I tied the dory to the rail and pulled myself onto *Minerva*'s deck, as I prepared to go into the cabin and confront Harry; it wasn't his failure to tell me about his troubles – I never really expected anything else – but the realisation that he had deceived both Katie and me with such dedication and skill, that he had never faltered in his determination to deceive.

Moreland's hand is strong and warm on my arm.

'I realised why he'd done it,' I announce with a sigh. 'The only thing that could have made him do such a thing . . .'

Moreland withdraws his hand and waits attentively, his face shadowy against the last streaks of light.

'The Rumanian orphans money – I think he was about to be found out. I think they were on to him, and he couldn't bear the shame.' I watch a ship far out at sea, its lights like pinpricks in the growing cushion of darkness. 'There were the debts as well, of course. And the pressures on his business. And . . .' I hesitate, 'other things. But it was the thought of scandal, I'm sure of it.'

After a time Moreland murmurs, 'What happened then?'

'Then?'

'On *Minerva*,' he prompts gently. 'What happened then?'

'Oh . . .' I pull myself back into the story. 'Oh, I thought and thought. *God*, I couldn't stop thinking. About what had gone wrong, about the terrible waste of it all, about the absolute sheer *uselessness* of what he'd done. And then . . . Then I started thinking about the children . . .' I glance at the childless Moreland, in sudden doubt of his understanding. 'About what this would do to them. How they would be saddled with having a suicide for a father. How people would always whisper about it behind their backs. How it would become a label, stuck there for ever. How they'd never be free of it. And

I was angry.' I turn blindly to Moreland. 'I was angry with Harry for having been so selfish. I know it seems – *bad*. I know it was *wrong*, but – I just couldn't help it. I just felt – angry.'

'That's natural,' Moreland says flatly. 'I'm sure that's natural.'

'Then I realised, of course – the suicide was nothing. *Nothing.*'

This is the difficult part. If I am going to lose Moreland anywhere, it's going to be here.

'I realised that the shame of having had a father who'd killed himself was nothing compared to the shame of having had a father who was a fraud – someone who stole from orphans! Whose only decent action in the whole of his life was to kill himself – well, that's the way people would see it, wouldn't they?' I grimace involuntarily at the thought. 'I just couldn't bear it. The thought of the shame being visited on the two people who least deserved it. Who were least able to deal with it. I felt – and I know this wasn't fair, I know Harry was very ill at the end – but I felt he should have thought of that. He should have thought of the children. And since he hadn't, I realised I would have to instead.'

I sense in Moreland a sharp curiosity as to what's coming next, and, though it may be a product of my shaky confidence, the first stirrings of incredulity too.

'I kept thinking about the children,' I hurry on. 'How I'd do absolutely anything to spare them the shame of it. How they had their whole lives ahead of them. With Harry dead, it seemed to me that they were all that mattered, that my first – my only – responsibility was to them.'

Searching the shadows that mask Moreland's eyes, I seem to glimpse scepticism. But then his cheeks crease into a brief smile of encouragement, and I realise that he is still with me.

The breeze is fierce and cold on my neck, I wind up the window almost to the top and the swish and claw of the dancing stones fades into the sound of our silence.

'Then I realised there might be a way of protecting them after all,' I say. 'I'm not sure how it came to me. Thinking about the charity, I suppose. Imagining how the trustees might be persuaded to forget the whole thing. I thought that if I could pay them back then they might agree not to say anything, that the fraud would never get out. Harry didn't have any money of course. I knew that. But I thought perhaps I could borrow some. Or sell things. Or . . . and then I realised.' I give a bitter laugh. 'Harry had a life insurance policy. I wasn't sure how much exactly, but a couple of hundred thousand at least – enough to repay the charity – well, that's what I thought at the time. And then I realised – the final irony! – it would never pay out! Not for suicide. They never do, do they?' I attempt a sardonic laugh that rings unpleasantly in my ears. '*God!* I couldn't believe it. I sat there – *sick*. I felt this unbelievable hopelessness. This sense of complete defeat. Even the insurance – no good! I just felt it was the end for all of us, not just Harry. And I think perhaps I was still in shock. I don't know. But I must have been because otherwise I could never have done what I did. I couldn't even have begun to think of it.' I press my head back against the seat. 'Well . . .' I say meekly. 'You can guess the rest.'

Moreland's voice is low, close to wonder or disbelief. 'You took *Minerva* out to sea?'

'Yes.'

'You . . .' He hardly knows how to put it. '. . . sank her?'

I nod faintly.

While Moreland absorbs this with a long dazed intake of breath I replay what I have just told him in my mind, and the more I go over it, the less convincing it sounds. I see nothing but holes, I see the sheer unlikeliness of the great thinking session I'm meant to have had in the cabin in the presence of my husband's body, and I have this urge to go back and embroider over the thinner patches, to make a more convincing job of it. But some cautionary instinct holds me back, something tells me that this will only smack of uncertainty and desperation.

'Tell me,' Moreland says with some awe, '*how*? How did you manage it?'

'The boat?'

'The whole thing.'

I rub a hand over my face. 'You may well ask. By guess and by God as much as anything else. And by frightening myself to death.' My voice shakes at the memory.

'But you'd never been out of the river.'

'No.' I give a rocky laugh.

'Tell me then. Tell me how.'

Here is the other Moreland, ex-Royal Marine, master seaman and survival expert: the compulsive matcher of facts to evidence.

This part of the story isn't hard to tell; it can be lifted complete from my memory, a series of desperate moments linked by intervals of more absolute terror. Though, wary as ever, I check the journey for pitfalls before starting out. 'Well...' I say at last, 'I had all night, you see. To prepare. *Minerva* was ready to go. Harry had done it all. The electrics were on – something he always talked about, getting the electrics on, but something I wouldn't have had a clue how to do on my own. And the key was in the ignition. I tried it and the engine started first time. I went back to the house first, though. I took the Zodiac and rowed back to the quay and went up and got some things. Warm clothes, waterproofs ... And a saw. I took the saw from the garage.'

'You knew how you were going to do it? With a saw?'

'Oh no. I mean, I wouldn't have known. But ages ago Harry got me to help him with some repairs. Well, *help* ... I just stood there giving moral support really. This was back when he first had the boat and was still keen on doing these things himself. He was taking a pipe off one of those things that brings water into the boat – a sort of nozzle thing—?'

'An inlet.'

'An inlet. Anyway when he eventually got the hose off, the water gushed in. Just gushed in. He hadn't turned the wheel thing off properly—'

'The stopcock.'

'The *stopcock*. It was jammed. And while he was trying to get it to work the water kept gushing in. He managed to shut it off eventually, but it gushed in for quite a time. I mean, so fast. I'd seen how long it had taken him to get the hose off. He had to put heat on it and things, it was a terrible job – and Harry was quite strong – so I knew I'd never be able to do it that way, that I'd have to find another way. I thought a saw would be easiest. The pipe was made of that soft bendy plastic. I didn't think it'd take very long to cut through it.' Hearing this, I'm struck by the calculation in my voice. I say, 'But I didn't plan it, not like that. I mean, the whole thing just sort of *happened*. It was...' But it's hard to explain my thought processes, and in the end I don't try.

'When I got back to *Minerva* the dory was the most difficult thing. I had to make sure I could get it to work when I needed it. It took me for ever to get the outboard down into the water. I tried everything. I thought it was just a matter of pressing some lever. I didn't realise you had to lift the outboard and operate the lever at the same time. And it was so heavy, the engine. I got there finally, but it took a long time. And then *starting* it. I'd never had much to do with the dory. I'd ridden in it but never driven it. I wasn't sure what you had to do. There was meant to be a key hidden under the back seat – I'd seen Harry put one there anyway – but when I looked it wasn't there, and I thought I'd have to go all the way back to the house to find a spare. I almost gave up then. But ... I couldn't.' I rub my fingers savagely over my forehead. 'I was in a state. Frantic. Not thinking straight. All I knew was that I had to do *something*. I wanted to make things *right*, you see.' I glance at Moreland as though for reassurance. 'Impossible, of course. Nothing could be right, but I still felt I had to try. I felt it was the only way any good could come out of what was otherwise an absolute disaster.'

In the pause that follows Moreland glances away, his profile unreadable. Beyond him, a car's lights sweep over the coastguard cottages and, coming to rest behind them, die abruptly.

'In the end I found a key for the dory on *Minerva*. In the chart-table drawer, right there with all the other keys. I tried it, but nothing. I mean the key turned, but nothing happened. The thing seemed dead. I'd seen the way Harry pushed the

380

handle forward when he started it, the handle by the steering wheel – what is it?'

'The throttle. Well, throttle and gear combined, probably.'

'The throttle. I tried it every which way, and finally got the engine to turn. But it still wouldn't start. Eventually I found that knob – you have to push it in, don't you?'

Moreland nods. 'To put it out of gear, yes. It wouldn't start in gear.'

I tap a finger against my temple in a gesture of dull-wittedness. 'Well, I got there, finally. It took long enough. But I finally got it started.'

I am deafened again by the howling outboard, which seemed to fill the river, an invitation to everyone to come and investigate, or so it seemed. I'm back in a state of indecision about whether to let it run for a while – it sounded so sick and spluttery – or to turn it off again and have the cover of silence. I held out for a minute or so. The silence, when it returned, roared in my ears, almost as loud as the engine.

'I waited then. Under the hood in *Minerva*'s cockpit. Until there was enough light. I may have slept for a while – but I don't think so. When the time came I started the engine. I was shaking with fright. It was so bad that I was sick in the end. Had to go to the rail and heave. I felt a bit better then. I went and undid the mooring, and raced back to the cockpit and pushed the lever forward. I was so relieved when she started to move. I hadn't been sure she would, you see. I thought . . . I don't know.' My doubts seem unexplainable at this distance. 'She seemed to go more or less where I wanted. I'd worried about that too, about whether I could steer her. It probably sounds silly to you, but I'd never done it before, not really. Only when Harry told me to hold the tiller for a minute while he did something important. I'd got as far as the fact that you moved the tiller the opposite way, but that was about it. Anyway, I got the hang of it – well enough anyway. Then I was busy looking out for the buoys. I couldn't remember where they all were, I was frightened of missing one, but I knew about the colours, red to the right. I kept saying it: red to the right. There were posts, too. I wasn't sure about them, I just guessed, but the moorings weren't a problem. I knew you went between them at Waldringfield. I knew where the mud was just there.'

'I remember,' Moreland comments softly.

I had forgotten our trip downriver to Waldringfield. Something in his tone makes me realise that the incident with the sailing dinghy, the way I warned the boy away from the mud, has stayed sharp in Moreland's mind, that he had stored it carefully away, along with my unsuspected talent with knots.

'I wasn't so good with the Zodiac,' I murmur as if we were discussing knots now. 'I can't have tied it on very well. It drifted away in the night some time. From the mooring. It wasn't there in the morning, anyway. I found it later, when I got back.'

'On the mud where Wally Smith saw it?'

I respond vaguely; I have already moved on. I'm back on *Minerva*, coming to the narrow river mouth, I'm seeing nothing ahead of me but the empty sea. I'm feeling the first swaying movements under my feet. The shoals are ahead and the fear is tight around my stomach and I'm feeling sick again.

'Coming out of the river I had no idea where to go,' I resume. 'I just headed out. It was misty, I couldn't see very far. I knew there were shallows somewhere, everyone was always on about them. The *shoals*. But I couldn't see any markers. I thought there was meant to be a buoy somewhere, but I couldn't see it. So I just hoped and prayed. The waves got bigger – well, they seemed big to me. They made the boat roll and lurch. I fell over once. And then ... And then the water ahead was ... different. Flatter. Covered in ripples and small pointed waves.' I flutter my hand in the darkness. 'I knew immediately. I just – knew. I turned the boat away and tried going another way. And then I realised I'd turned too far, that the line ahead was the shore, that I was heading back again.' I frown. 'So I turned again. I probably went in a complete circle. And then I thought of looking at the compass. But I wasn't even sure how *that* worked. I had to think for ages about which direction I wanted. I couldn't work it out. I mean, I knew I should go east, roughly, but what was that on the compass?'

Moreland, thinking perhaps that I don't require an answer, takes a moment to spring to life. 'Ninety degrees.'

'Ninety ... Ah.' I remember the dancing dial, the way it moved in the opposite direction to the one you thought it would, the way it kept moving in one direction even after the boat had started turning in the other. 'Ninety. Yes, I thought it must be something like that. But it was too late by then' – the memory snatches at my voice – 'because I was in the shoals again.' I suffer the horrors of perfect recall, I see the peaking frothing water. 'They seemed to be everywhere, the waves. All around. In the end I pressed on because there was nothing else to do. I sort of *froze*. I can't explain. I was so frightened I just stopped thinking. Cut everything out. Went into a complete daze. Then—' I take a second to breathe. 'There was this awful crash. The boat stopped dead. I fell forward. It felt as though we'd hit a wall.' Reliving it, I pull back slightly against the seat. 'I thought we'd had it. I thought that was it, that the boat was going to sink under me there and then. I thought...' I sigh, I shake this off. 'Then she sort of skidded round and leant over a bit and I felt her bumping. I realised there was still a hope. I put the engine on faster – Harry used to do that when he got stuck in the river at low tide. It made an awful noise. I thought it was going to stop altogether. Or blow up.' I laugh grimly. '*Minerva* was shuddering and shaking. It was hard to tell what was happening, the water was swirling round so much. Then, I don't know, I had the feeling we were moving again, slowly, slowly. She leant over again. And then...' I exhale suddenly. 'We were free.'

I don't tell him about my diatribe, my screams to all the powers that be and ever were, to every god that might have been to hear my prayers and deliver me from my nightmare. I don't mention that I collapsed onto a seat afterwards, and sat there limply, muttering over and over to myself like some madwoman, moaning with relief and fright.

'I kept going,' I say, recovering with an effort. 'It was very misty. All around. I never saw another thing. I took a point on the compass – I can't remember what it was now. I couldn't stick to it anyway, I was all over the place. But I tried to come back to it now and again – roughly, anyway. And I just kept going. I don't know how long for.' This period is still a blur, a time when I lost the measure of many things. 'The boat lurched all over the place. The waves seemed enormous, though I don't suppose they were. One of the sails got itself unravelled and started flapping about. But I left it. I could hear things crashing around in the cabin, but I couldn't face going down ... I couldn't bear to...' I drop my face into my hands, I see Harry's body again, the chart that didn't quite hide the hideous wound. Raising my head, I catch the breeze through the top of the window. 'I just kept going.'

A faint luminosity comes off the sea, a suggestion of a watery presence amid the greater darkness, but inside the car all I can see of Moreland is the shape of his head, the line of his nose.

I plunge on before I have the chance to think about what comes next. 'Finally I realised how far I must be getting from the shore. I stopped. I ... got everything ready. I pulled the dory in and tied it alongside. I got the outboard going, to be sure it would work...' I break off, eyes burning, confused again by the lucidity of my actions then, which seemed to have a momentum of their own, quite independent of my chaotic thoughts. 'I thought of giving up again. Doing ... such a thing. I realised there'd be no going back, that it was quite – irrevocable. I realised that in some ways ... it was a terrible *terrible* thing...' I draw in long breaths, I drop my head onto my chest. 'Because Harry would never be buried properly and ... his body would be ...'

I must be whispering, because Moreland leans closer. 'I'm sorry?'

I lift my head, I say more distinctly, 'I thought of ... him there. Of the things that would happen to him ... And I couldn't bear it. That's why I closed the hatches when I left. Closed them tight. To shut him in. I couldn't bear...' This thought drifts into the ensuing silence. I try to push the image of Harry's body from my mind, just as I tried to escape it on *Minerva*.

I force myself on. 'The pipes, they didn't take long. I cut

384

through two in the end. The water poured in. It wasn't long before it started coming over the floorboards.' But again I have difficulty in going on. Tears are dripping slowly onto my hand. 'Then I said prayers for him – every prayer I could remember. And I said goodbye. From everyone.' I wipe a drip from the end of my nose with the back of my hand. 'And then ... I went. I left *Minerva* pointing east – well, what I hoped was east – and put the engine lever forward so she'd keep moving.'

'And you put the auto-pilot on?'

It seems there's nothing that Moreland doesn't know or guess.

'I pressed a button and hoped, yes. I didn't know if it was going to work.'

'The boat wouldn't have kept straight otherwise.'

'Ah?' I say, only half listening.

Moreland lifts a hip and, pulling something from his pocket, presses a handkerchief into my hand. I blow my nose hard. I mop up generally.

'You found your way back?' Moreland's tone is reverential, though whether for me or Harry I can't tell.

'Back? Yes.' I make a sound of disbelief. 'By sheer luck. I was in such a state, I didn't think, I just set off. The mist was bad and when I looked back *Minerva* was fading fast, and then of course I realised I had no way of finding the shore, that I was going to get totally lost.' I groan at my idiocy. 'I turned back straight away. But even then I couldn't see her – *Minerva*. She'd disappeared – in those few seconds while I was turning. I panicked. I thought I'd be going in circles for ever. I thought ... well...' I laugh shakily at the memory of everything that went through my head. 'But then I glimpsed her through the mist. Just. *Just*. It was a job getting back on board. I tripped over the rail. I fell on my shoulder and bashed my head. And then I nearly lost the dory! Nearly let go of the rope!' I hear Harry correcting me: the *painter*, Ellen, it's called a bloody *painter*. 'It was awful going back on board. *Awful. Minerva* was getting lower in the water. And...' I close my eyes involuntarily, I see the water lapping around Harry's body and this is almost the most terrible memory of all. 'I searched,' I say

385

through a throat that is seized tight. 'I searched and found a compass. And then I left again.'

The waves popple and hiss and whisper below. Listening, I remember my first sight of the beach, the long line of the shingle as it emerged shadowlike from the soft wall of mist. I wasn't sure what I was seeing, I didn't care, I headed straight for the deepening line. The shingle was steep, it was hard to land. The pull of the water was very strong, the way it surged up the stones, and dragged and sucked back. I had to go in up to my armpits to turn the dory round and push it out to sea. A wave took my legs from under me, I fell, the water went over my head, and I imagined what it was like to drown.

'Well,' Moreland murmurs, sounding dazed. 'Well...' Then: 'You're going to have to tell them, Ellen.'

These things are so easy for Moreland; you simply establish the honourable path, and follow it.

'They'll think I did it for the money,' I tell him.

'What?'

'Well, I did partly. Remember.'

'But if you explain about the charity—'

'No. Never. I can never do that.'

'But *something*, surely?'

'No.' I say with sudden vehemence. 'They'd dig it all out. The fraud, the debts – it would become public property. There'd be a terrible scandal. Then everything I did would have been for nothing. For *nothing*.' I add more calmly, 'And then they'd be bound to charge me with something, wouldn't they? They'd have to, I'm sure they would. Failure to report a death, perjury – something like that. It'd get dragged through the newspapers with the rest of the scandal, and the children would have two parents to be ashamed of.'

He tilts his head in understanding or mystification. 'All right,' he says, sounding troubled. 'Tell them you did it for the children then. To spare them the fact that it was suicide.'

I ask seriously, 'Do you think they'll believe that? Do you think so?' I'd like to think it was possible, but voicing it, the chances seem increasingly remote. 'I think they'll find it hard to believe I went to all that trouble just for the happiness of my children. I think money will figure much larger in their thinking. The fact that I was trying to claim the insurance. That's fraud, isn't it? I think they'll find it hard to believe it wasn't the main reason I wanted to hide Harry's body.'

'You underestimate yourself, Ellen. I think you're the one person who can talk of protecting her children and be thoroughly believed.'

'You think so?' I almost laugh aloud. 'I'm afraid I don't quite have your faith. You're forgetting, I've told them an awful lot of lies. Why shouldn't I still be lying? In fact . . .' I give a strange excited laugh. '. . . since they're convinced it was murder, why shouldn't it have been me?'

'Come on, Ellen. Don't be silly.'

'It's not so silly,' I say, feeling frightened. 'Think about it.'

'Come on.'

My voice wobbles. 'I'm perfectly serious.'

'But why would you have wanted to kill Harry?'

'Ah. Well, we were going through a bad patch, you see. He was having an affair.'

'Oh.' Moreland digests this slowly. 'Oh,' he says again. 'But that's hardly a reason to kill someone.'

'Isn't it? I thought that was precisely why lots of people killed each other.'

Not judging this worthy of a reply, Moreland blows dismissively through his lips.

With a leaden feeling, I tell him, 'The money's not all, I'm afraid.'

I feel him scrutinising me through the darkness. 'What do you mean?'

This is the difficult part; this will involve a leap of trust which I'm not entirely sure I'm ready to make. I put the decision off a little longer by telling him about the Zodiac's oars, how the police have found Harry's blood on them, how they interpret this as a sure sign of foul play.

'Well, that's explainable,' Moreland states. 'You used the Zodiac, you obviously must have had some blood on your hands.'

Blood on my hands. What a ring it has.

387

'Yes,' I agree. 'But then . . . there was a phone call. From the mobile phone on the boat. To the house. Late that night. The call was answered, they know that. They thought it was Harry calling me. I persuaded them that the answering machine picked the call up and lost the message. Or rather, I failed to persuade them. I don't think they believed me for a moment. If I tell them what really happened, that it was me on the boat, that I made the call, they'll want to know who I was calling.'

'And? Who was it?'

'That's the trouble. I can't tell them.'

Moreland makes an uncertain movement. 'I don't understand.'

My senses reach out through the darkness towards him. To trust or not to trust? I hover on the brink. Suppressing the last quiver of doubt, I make the leap. 'It was Katie. She'd come home from school unexpectedly.'

'*Katie*. But why can't you tell them that?'

'Because she's on the point of a nervous breakdown already. And if they question her, she'll almost certainly have the real thing.'

Moreland's confusion is almost tangible. 'Katie? But why?'

'She was completely devastated by Harry's death. You may not have realised. She almost flipped. I had to take her to a psychiatrist. She's still very shaky.'

I leave him with this for a moment. Then I murmur, 'I can't risk Katie. I can't risk Josh either. Whatever I've done wrong, the truth would crucify them.'

'But Ellen. *Ellen*.'

'I know, I *know*. Don't tell me – it's a mess! I know . . . But trying to explain it will only make things worse! And what's to stop them making something really bad of it? The blood on the oars. Why shouldn't they think I did something much, much worse?' I leave the worse thing – that is, murder – to float unspoken before us.

Moreland leans forward and, gripping the wheel high on the rim, stares out through the windscreen, shoulders hunched, like a demon driver in full flight. Then, some internal debate resolved, his shoulders fall and he sinks back.

'Then you mustn't tell them,' he says tightly. 'You mustn't tell them anything.'

Reprieved. I allow myself a moment of thanksgiving, an inner smile of relief.

'You must hold on . . .' He's thinking aloud. 'If you just hold on they'll lose interest. They're bound to, sooner or later.' He turns to me. 'Stick to what you've already told them. Don't budge an inch. Don't show the slightest doubt. I mean – don't overdo the confidence, but don't let them rattle you either.'

'They frighten me,' I tell him truthfully.

Moreland's hand finds mine. 'Just stick to your guns.'

'I get so scared.'

'I'll be here for you.'

I am suddenly breathless. 'You will?'

He takes my head in his hands, he kisses my forehead solemnly. 'Oh yes, dear Ellen. Yes.'

EIGHTEEN

Christmas approaches, and life unwinds gently before me. Sometimes when I'm out shopping, I pause and give up silent thanks. Or when I'm cooking, or at the Project, or at my drawing-board. I close my eyes, I feel this surge of gratitude, I savour my sheer good fortune. I tell myself that I'll never take anything for granted again, not the obvious things, not the simpler things, and certainly not the fact that I'm free to lead the uneventful life I have wanted for so long. I stop and ask myself what I have done to deserve so much, and I'm not sure. But if gratitude in any way contributes to luck, then I feed it regularly, with reverence.

Even greater rushes of feeling come at me when I'm lying close to Moreland in the night. This is partly the euphoria of love, of course, which has been an undreamed of bonus of these last few months, partly my belief that nothing bad can happen to me while Moreland and I are together. And indeed, nothing has. Richard manages to give me a disproportionate belief in myself, to fill me with much of his very considerable confidence. During the long summer, when Dawson was still pressing hard, Richard talked me steadily through my worries, rehearsed me carefully before each interview, persuaded me that I was capable of holding out against Dawson. Having committed himself to the idea of protecting me, he has applied himself to the job with single-minded devotion. Counsellor, supporter, lover, friend; always there for me, just as he promised.

When I stop to consider my luck, I also ask myself what I've done to deserve Richard, and I don't know the answer to that either.

I've heard nothing from Dawson since October. Officially, the investigation is still open, still a murder inquiry. But since Atkins was found to have an unshakable alibi and no other suspects have come to light, since in effect nothing is happening or is likely to happen, the team has been wound down from what I believe was once thirty officers, to twelve, then five, and though no one will confirm it, I'm told that no officers are actively working on the case at present. That isn't to say Dawson has given up. I know he hasn't. He told me as much at our last meeting. It had been the usual question and answer session, we had gone through our lines like performers in a long-running play, our voices flat, almost bored, we had trailed off into an inconclusive silence, when Dawson brought his palm down on the table, a gesture of finality, and announced that he would walk me out to my car.

'There's a tradition,' he said as he held the car door open for me, 'that a case stays open until it's closed.' He eyed me speculatively. 'You can rest assured, Mrs Richmond, that as far as I'm concerned this case will remain open for as long as is necessary.'

'I appreciate that very much,' I said without a trace of irony. 'Though you know how I feel about the murder idea.'

He inclined his head in acknowledgement. 'Just as *you* must appreciate, Mrs Richmond, that I really can't be satisfied with suicide.'

'Perhaps we'll just have to accept that we'll never know for sure.'

'That doesn't bother you, Mrs Richmond?'

'No,' I announced after some thought. 'Not any more. All I want now is a quiet life.'

'Ah. But we don't always get what we want, do we?'

But I have got exactly what I want, that's the amazing thing. The niggling fear never quite leaves me, of course, but then I never expected it would. It is anyway a pale shadow of what it was in the summer. While the murder inquiry was in full swing I couldn't rid myself of the dread that some new evidence would come to light, something ugly and irrefutable; that Dawson would discover Katie was at home that night, that the old man in the coastguard cottages would realise the significance of what he'd seen and go to the police, or that it would occur to Dawson to question him and the other people who have a view of the shingle bank. None of this ever happened, but the accumulated tensions of this and my other worries erupted in a long bout of flu which left me weak and depressed. It was several weeks before I got over it, and some of that time I was in such a shaky state – mind as well as body – that if it hadn't been for Richard I'm not sure I wouldn't have stayed in bed and turned my face to the wall.

Now, my energy has come back, I can sleep for as long as six hours at a stretch, and without nightmares, and more often than not I reach the morning with a sense of hope and optimism. The only time I can't sleep is when Richard is away. In October when he was in Saudi for a week, I went out and bought a dog from the nearest dogs home. Jiff is a mutt of unknown parentage and all the things I said I wouldn't have, large and long-haired and an indefatigable transporter of mud onto furniture, but he's affectionate to the point of idiocy and when I'm alone lies warm and woolly on my bed.

I finally moved out of Pennygate in September, a week after the sale was agreed and two months before completion. I went to a cottage ten miles inland, in a small village where people leave you pretty much to yourself. The place is only rented, it could do with some paint, the windows are draughty – Richard has had to attack them with putty and tape – but it has a cosy feel to it, a certain well-worn charm, and the fires draw well. When Richard and I lie in our bedroom under the eaves we hear scufflings in the thatch. Richard mutters darkly about vermin, but I find it rather companionable to share a roof with the local mice. The cottage stands alone on the fringes of the village, half-way up a narrow dead-end lane, so that few people have reason to come past the gate.

This suits me fine, since I still have something of a phobia about the press and treat anyone looking over the fence with suspicion.

The press had a field day with the murder story, so Molly told me later. Every national newspaper and the evening bulletins on both main channels. There were reporters camped at the end of the drive, and photographers who used the ancient rights-of-way to walk to within a few hundred feet of Pennygate and zoom in on the cars parked in the drive. First the house phone, then the business line, had to be left off the hook, and someone at the police station must have tipped them off about my next visit to Dawson because when I drove up with Leonard there were four or five photographers waiting.

Such interest couldn't last, thank God, but if I'd hoped for a rapid return to peace and quiet I was soon put right by a persistent piece of unpleasantness, a journalist from one of the tabloids – I later discovered he wasn't fully accredited – who pounced on me one day in the village and kept reappearing at regular intervals like a bad smell that won't go away. He had a leering grin, a greasy collar and a battered trilby. We called him The Bookie. Once he tried to talk to me when I was shopping with Richard and got more than he bargained for – Richard's language was startlingly succinct – but the episode left me nervous for a time. The last thing I needed was a story of the widow-quick-to-take-lover type. But maybe Moreland frightened him more thoroughly than I realised, because nothing appeared. Not then.

Once I had moved into the cottage, I slipped into a quiet almost hypnotic routine, which I have been following with enthusiasm ever since. I do two afternoons a week at the Project as a volunteer. I have no particular skills to offer young offenders, except perhaps to listen. I think I must listen quite well, or maybe the boys recognise some fellow feeling in me because, now they've got to know me, most of them seem happy to talk. I don't say a lot, I ask the occasional question, but I take them seriously and, when provoked, give as good as I get, which they seem to appreciate, albeit guardedly. They

393

are, as they say themselves, full of shit. Boasters, liars, smirking gloating vandals, kids who would steal – have stolen – from their own grandmothers, even supposing they know who they are. They have only a distant curiosity about the notion of right and wrong, like package-tourists who view foreign customs as quaint and nonsensical. But, as in all the best hard-luck stories, the boys have their redeeming features. Most have never had anything that resembles a proper home, some have been abused, all have been neglected. Without exception they can barely read and write. It seems to me that they went wrong because there wasn't any other way to go, and I of all people can sympathise with that.

Molly is so busy with builders and plumbers that I hardly get to see her at the moment, except to share her frustrations and woes at the delays in opening the new half-way house. But at least it is going ahead; the planning permission came through in July. Molly is convinced that her coffee-and-charm sessions with her tame councillor won the day, and she may well be right. I certainly wouldn't suggest otherwise.

I spend four mornings a week at the drawing-board. I've had quite a few commissions now; well, three – a logo for a women's boutique in Ipswich, the design for an estate agent's news sheet, and – a major job – a corporate image for an expanding transport business. It was hard getting back to work, harder still to feel confident. I had to give myself imaginary briefs and work through dozens of ideas before I felt I could accept a paid commission. I still haven't got to the stage where I feel I can go out and market myself – the jobs so far have come through friends – but I'm getting there. I'm beginning to recapture a sureness of touch, a certain satisfaction.

On Wednesday mornings I write the children between two and three sheets of A4 each. I try to get the letters into the post by one-thirty so they'll arrive on Thursday and break up the week for them. Most parents don't bother to write, they just get their children to phone, but I like to put things on paper.

Not only does it make me cover a much wider range of thoughts and ideas than I ever would chatting aimlessly on the phone, but it makes for an altogether more powerful statement. Devotion, commitment, a readiness to take pains; all the things I want the children to know and feel when they open those thickly packed envelopes.

Katie has done better at school this autumn, her marks have climbed from rock bottom to borderline acceptable. She may even scrape some results next summer, though I'm not banking on that. More importantly, she has been much calmer and outward looking, as though she has decided to put the past behind her and get on with life, a development that fills me with tentative relief.

I'm not so happy about Josh. In fact, I feel very confused about him. He has gone to a boarding school in Norfolk, some forty miles away. Friends tell me I have been wise and far-sighted to let him go, sometimes I even manage to persuade myself that it was a sensible decision, but most of the time I'm cross with myself for giving in. I feel it can only force us apart, and that frightens me.

He seems to have settled in well enough – the staff haven't mentioned any problems anyway – but when he comes home a dark tension settles over him, an unvoiced indignation. Much of this resentment gets pushed my way, he gets quite difficult on occasion, but, as I try to remind myself, parents always get the brunt of these things. I try to give him the benefit of the doubt, I think of it as a stage he is going through, some lingering reaction to all the dramas of the summer; a cry for attention perhaps. But I can't pretend I don't miss the easy, loving boy I used to know.

The rest of the time? I walk, I shop, I cook, I wait for Richard to come home. Recently his work has taken him to London and often he doesn't get back until late. I wait like a bride, table laid, supper in the oven, heart lifting at the sound of every distant car, breath tight at the thought of the moment when supper will be over and we climb the stairs to our cosy bed under the eaves.

I don't think about the future too much; I feel it's unlucky somehow. It is enough that Richard loves me, that he has finally separated from his wife, that he has promised he will never leave me.

I have something approaching peace of mind. I am far luckier than I deserve.

A couple of weeks ago Charles came to see me. He sat stiffly by the fire and sipped at his whisky with the uneasy manner of a UN official undertaking difficult negotiations.

'It would be nice if we could all get together again,' he said wistfully.

I reminded him that it wasn't me who was holding things back, it was Anne, and he nodded sadly at that. He could hardly disagree.

Anne doesn't actually come out and say so – not to me anyway – but I know she thinks I haven't told the truth about Harry's death. She doesn't go so far as to point the finger of blame at me – even she, with her overblown imagination, doesn't believe I'm a murderer – but she thinks I'm covering up in some way. *Obstructing the course of justice*, she has been heard to say. What motives I'm meant to have for this I don't know. A secret lover, perhaps, whom I was entertaining at Pennygate that night when the call from Harry came through. Or a lover whom I'd sent to kill Harry and who was phoning from the boat to tell me he'd completed the job. The fact that this lover has never appeared, that I've taken up with Richard, doesn't seem to figure in Anne's thinking, but then she doesn't approve of my relationship with Richard anyway. She thinks I've been indecently quick off the mark. And then, if I've been an unfaithful wife, what's one lover more or less anyway? Who knows? Anne's mind is unfathomable.

'Perhaps you and the children could come over for Boxing Day?' Charles suggested. 'Tea, or something?'

I told him I didn't think it'd be a very good idea.

'The children then. Anne would love to see them. And so would their grandmother. They've bought them all sorts of presents.'

But I didn't like the idea of the children going to Anne and

Charles's on their own. I didn't want them picking up disturbing messages about me.

'I'm sorry,' I said. 'Perhaps when Anne's feeling better about things.'

Charles accepted this with a small sigh. 'I'll do what I can.'

At the door he asked me how I was managing generally.

'Just fine,' I said.

'Money all right? All sorted out?'

'All sorted out,' I said.

This wasn't strictly true, but it's not something I discuss with anyone but Richard and my new accountant, a discreet and hard-working young man from Woodbridge. Now that the largest assets are sold, it's clear that I'm going to be left with very little. Pennygate got a poor price, barely enough to cover the various mortgages, the furniture and pictures achieved disappointing prices at auction, and the yacht insurers have refused to pay out because the yacht was 'scuttled'. Leonard has fought this, just as he has pressed the life insurance company, citing the police's decision to treat the death as murder, but the company insist that while there's any doubt about the manner of Harry's death it's against policy to pay out. Leonard remains determined, but I have written all the insurance money off. Things are going to be tight, but I'll manage.

The Rumanian orphans got their first cheque in July. For a time I worried about raising anything like enough money for the next instalment, but, having thought it through, I have decided to go back to Jack and ask him if he can find something in his charity budget for next year. I don't feel too bad about this. His various companies have gone from strength to strength, he has acquired another prime site on the outskirts of Ipswich and I read in the local paper that he has sold an office block in the middle of town, presumably at a profit.

He has also managed to pick up a couple of bargains. In October, two months after Ainswick went into liquidation, I asked my new accountant to find out what had happened to Ainswick's assets. He discovered that within a month of liquidation the receiver had sold the Shoreditch building to a company called Redfern, who sold it on almost immediately to a Hong Kong investment company. Redfern, it turned out, is a wholly owned subsidiary of Conquerall Properties – a telling name – which is registered at Companies House as a private company ninety per cent owned by Jack Crawley.

Ainswick's parcel of land near the bypass was also acquired by Jack at a knock-down price. Although, as chance would have it, it now seems that the land might not be quite so useless after all. According to an obscure notice in the local gazette – brought to my attention by Molly's councillor – Jack's company has successfully applied for a change of use for this plot, along with the granting of the all-important access across the intervening council-owned land.

Jack with the golden touch.

I know I should feel bitter; sometimes I do. Whichever way you look at it, the children and I have been cheated.

But what am I going to do about it? Looking at it bluntly, my options are extremely limited. I could take legal action, I suppose, but I suspect that, being Jack, he will have covered himself very carefully and it will be extremely hard to prove anything. These cases can take thousands in legal fees and drag on for years, without any guarantee of success. And I mustn't forget that when it comes to fraud I live in the largest glass-house of all, and that it might be extremely unwise to start throwing stones.

No, taking everything into account, I prefer to think that things will get balanced out in other ways, that when the children and I need anything, Jack will help us out. Indeed, he's already agreed to pay Josh's school fees, and, if I have trouble in finding Katie's fees next term, which is very probable, then I have no doubt he will help us again. Ever since I found out about the bypass land, I haven't felt too bad about going back for more. Jack has no children, he is very rich; I like to think that contributing to our welfare makes him happy.

One thing about the murder inquiry – the only advantage, one might say – is that Jack has been keen to keep his distance.

As a suicide's widow I merited a certain pity, but murder has a taint to it, a suggestion of dark deeds and scandal, and I think Jack worries about his image. Our dealings have become brisk and businesslike, which is only appropriate when you consider the nature of our arrangement, about which neither of us has any illusions.

I decided some time ago: this was going to be the most complete Christmas ever.

Richard says I have missed my vocation and should have been a military logistician, the way I have planned it. Lists, highly targeted shopping expeditions, secret present-wrapping sessions. With the children due home in two days, I have done the decorations to death. Every mantel and picture is draped with holly and red ribbons, there are garish lights round the porch – Richard suggested I should go the whole hog and have them flashing on and off – while the tree fills an entire corner of the small living room, its branches laden with lights and glass balls and silver icicles and glitter that I brought from Pennygate. Beneath, I have laid out the presents so they look bulky and tantalising. Mistletoe hangs in the hall, and waiting on the children's beds are enormous green felt stockings embroidered with festive robins and pieces of fake holly.

On the food front, I intend to reach new heights. For Christmas lunch, I plan turkey with mushroom and olive stuffing, accompanied by roast potatoes, carrots and sprouts and bread sauce and gravy: the full trimmings. And afterwards, mince pies and brandy butter and plum pudding complete with lucky twenty-pence pieces. Though no baker, I have managed to make a traditional cake with frosted icing, decorated with (shop-bought) chocolate yule log, scarlet-sugared Father Christmas, and a 'Merry Christmas' in red plastic and *diamanté* that looks as though it too should flash on and off.

In the ten-day lead-up to the big day itself, I have planned all sorts of outings for the children: cinema trips, shopping expeditions, visits to friends, video showings at home.

Apart from persuading Moreland to dress up as that great chimney escape artist Father Christmas – a role he has firmly declined – I think I have covered absolutely everything.

Waking early, I watch the first glimmers of light creep in under the thatch and apply my mind to composing clues for a treasure hunt that I'm planning for an evening in four days' time, when some friends are bringing their children over to supper.

As soon as Moreland shows signs of life I try him with, 'I'm old and venerable, I hurry for no one, but young people regularly look up to me.'

Moreland mumbles, 'Grandfather clock.'

'Oh! Too easy then.'

'Too easy because I got it?'

'Well, I like to think I can fool you sometimes.'

'No chance.'

And he rolls over and pulls me close against him and kisses me just how I like to be kissed.

'The problem with you,' I say, hooking a leg over his waist, 'is that you're too bright.'

His mouth travels onto my neck. 'Just as long as you think so.'

We are well down the road to making love when the phone rings.

'Leave it,' Moreland breathes.

But even as he says this he gives up the idea and rolls onto his back to let me reach over and pick it up.

'Sorry, darlings,' says Molly's voice, 'but there's something in the paper. I think you might want to see it.'

'What sort of thing?'

'A story.'

'Bad?' I ask.

'Well – not too good. Listen . . . I'll bring it over.'

We're up and dressed by the time she arrives. The story is splashed across two pages of a popular tabloid. I don't need to read the byline to realised that The Bookie has finally sold his story. It doesn't take long to get the gist of it. Under the

400

headline *SO WHO **DID** KILL YACHTING MP?*, the story, based on 'exclusive information', states that the police have finally ruled out an SAS-style revenge killing and now believe that the murderer was someone well-known to Harry Richmond. Evidence from 'exclusive sources' points to a well-planned attempt to conceal the crime.

There is a lot of background detail, a rerun of the story so far, then the revelation of the 'exclusive' evidence. The blood on the oars. The inflatable left high and dry. The shotgun blast. The late-night call to the house.

If Harry Richmond was killed by a shot heard at 11.30 p.m., as police believe, then who made the late-night call from the boat to the house? The Bookie demands. *And who took the yacht out to sea and sank it?*

I feature quite heavily. I was up at the house through the latter part of the evening but 'claim' that I didn't hear the phone call. I rescued the inflatable from the mud the next morning but 'claim' that I didn't think it was worth reporting.

Then, as if that wasn't damning enough: *Ellen Richmond has been interviewed eight times by Ipswich police.*

We all know what that means in tabloid-speak. It means that the police are convinced I'm guilty but can't find enough proof.

'I don't think anyone takes any notice of this sort of thing,' says Molly, protesting too much.

But they do, they do. And Richard knows it too, because he is grim-faced as he puts an arm round my shoulder. The paper, for all its gossip and slick journalism has an enormous circulation and is read by politicians, the media, most of my friends and probably half the village.

And I thought the risk had passed. I sink into a chair. I accept a black coffee. I half listen to Richard as he tells me that these stories blow over in time, that thinking people take them with a pinch of salt.

I say abruptly, 'The children.'

I catch Katie on her way out to her first class. Luckily she has seen and heard nothing. The newspaper is one that the girls in her house take regularly, but with the end of term disruptions no one has read it yet.

When I give her a rough outline of the story she groans and sighs and says angry things about newspapers and journalists. Then, more plaintively, 'How *could* they? Why don't they leave us alone?'

I ask her if she wants me to come and collect her a day early.

'No, I don't think so,' she says uncertainly. 'No. That would mean we minded, or something.'

'You're sure? The girls are bound to see it. They might say things.'

'No, I'll be fine,' she says in an altogether tougher voice. 'No problem. We always knew, didn't we? I mean, there was always a chance of this sort of stuff. But are you okay?'

No problem, I declare, adopting the jargon. I tell her that it's like water off a duck's back, that friends are the only people I care about and they're not going to take this sort of thing seriously, that it'll blow over in time.

'You're not on your own?' she asks.

I tell her I have Molly as well as Moreland. Positively surrounded, I joke weakly.

I don't feel such urgency about reaching Josh. I'm pretty sure he doesn't get to see newspapers at his age – not gossipy rags like this anyway – though I leave a message for his housemaster anyway.

Both Moreland and Molly offer to stay with me, but I send them off to work and sit at my drawing-board, tinkering fruitlessly with ideas for a bathroom fittings brochure.

The phone rings solidly. I monitor the answering machine – a couple of reporters, friends I'm not ready to talk to – and pick up the handset only when I hear the voice of Josh's housemaster.

'I guessed it'd be about that,' he says when I explain. 'I'm afraid one of the day-boys must have said something already. We have no control over what day-boys read.'

'Josh—?'

'He's rather upset.'

My heart lurches. 'What did the boy tell him?'

'I don't know. It didn't seem the time to try and find out.'

'Is he very upset?'

'Well, he is in a bit of a state, yes.'

I ask if he could arrange to get Josh packed, as I'll be picking him up and bringing him straight home.

When I arrive Josh is sitting in the dormitory next to his trunk, which one of the matrons is packing for him. He is like a small statue, pale and immobile. His eyes are puffy from crying. He gives me a strange glance as I go to hug him, as though he can't believe I'm here.

Driving back, I hold his hand as often as I can, I tell him everything I told Katie. I say it's a lot of nonsense, the stuff they put in the papers, that as far as these editors are concerned it's anything for a good story, that we have to be strong, the three of us, and rise above hurtful things.

I ask what the day-boy said, but the question so obviously disturbs him that I don't press it. Back at the cottage, he picks at his lunch without interest. His movements are minimal, as if he will attract less attention that way. I go through everything I told him in the car for a second time, but it's like pushing against glass, I don't feel I'm getting through. I try a couple of other approaches, but I realise with a sense of failure that I don't really know what to say to him. In the end I light a fire and leave him curled up on the sofa with Jiff, watching an old film.

I manage to track Moreland down at the boatbuilders in Ipswich. He says he'll come straight away and I move restlessly around the house until he arrives. Typically he has stopped on the way to buy me flowers and a card on which he has written a supportive message.

I give him a punishing hug. I say humbly, 'You're the best present I ever had.'

'Just remember – the press don't matter. Nobody can possibly matter except the people we care about.'

'Keep telling me.'

'I'll keep telling you.'

'Thanks. For being here, I mean.'

'Oh, it's no great hardship really,' he smiles.

He kisses me, and I cling to the sense of safety that only Richard can bring me.

Just as typically, Richard has brought something for Josh as well, an adventure magazine and some favourite chocolate-coated nuts. With conspicuous tact I leave the two of them alone in the living-room and lose myself in the kitchen.

They emerge after fifteen minutes and Moreland announces, 'We thought we'd change and go into town for a burger. If that's all right?'

'Saves me cooking!' I say with nervy joviality.

Watching them leave, it seems to me that Josh has brightened up already.

I spend the time sewing and watching TV and monitoring the answering machine. After eight, I start to listen for the sound of Moreland's car.

Jiff leaps up at one point and barks frantically, but it's only the rain pattering against the window. Later I go out to replenish the wood-basket. The night is very dark and there's a doleful wind. Somewhere at the edge of the garden branches creak and rub complainingly. And beyond everything, way off in the dim distance, I seem to hear the sea on the shingle once again.

I pause, I listen, and I shake a mental fist at the trickery of the wind. The shingle is all of fifteen miles away. I laugh. I think: You won't get me that easily again! Nothing will! I'm free of all that. Newspaper stories won't harm me, nor Dawson's little campaigns. I feel too strong to be frightened any more, and the realisation is like a small revelation.

I return to the warmth and light, a crab scuttling happily into its shell.

At nine I decide Richard must have taken Josh to the cinema. Or they have met up with friends. No, the cinema; otherwise they would have phoned. By ten, my apprehensive nature has pushed its way to the surface and I'm beginning to remember how treacherous and narrow the roads are, how it only takes one crazy driver to cause an accident.

Thirty minutes later I hear the slamming of a car door, and, all fears forgotten, I hurry to let them in.

Moreland carries a sleepy, blinking Josh over the threshold and, forestalling questions with a shake of his head, takes him straight upstairs. Wordlessly he helps undress him, and I don't interfere.

'Good night, my darling.' I lean over the bed to kiss Josh.

'Night, Mummy,' and he puts his arms around my neck and turns his cheek to meet my lips and there is a relaxation in him, a warmth to his embrace which thrills me.

'What did you say to him?' I whisper to Moreland in the passage.

'Oh, nothing in particular. Listen . . .' He glances away. 'I have to go and write something. Could we talk about it later?'

I look at him. I have this feeling. 'Later?'

'It'll only take half an hour. But I've just got to get it done.' He smiles briefly, but his eyes don't smile with him.

'Is there something wrong?'

'I want to tell you what Josh said. But it'll take a while to explain properly. And I've really got to write this thing first.'

'Something's wrong,' I repeat.

He makes a gesture of impossibilities, and my heart sinks at this small evasion.

'What is it?' I press.

'I promise – just half an hour.'

I look into his face and I see all kinds of messages that frighten me to death.

'But I want to know now.'

'Half an hour,' and I can see he is not going to be moved.

Giving in, I say with a small smile, 'No longer?'

'No longer.'

He turns away and I let him go. I have a bath, I lie on the bed with a book in front me and cover the same passage time and again. I can't rid myself of a sense of foreboding.

When Richard has been gone twenty-five minutes I hear a sound, a door closing. When he still doesn't come, I start to get off the bed. As I swing my legs down I hear a car. I sit there and I hear it drive away from the house. I leap off the bed and race downstairs and throw open the front door.

His car has gone.

I stand there until I begin to shiver. Retreating, I look in the living-room, I look in the dining-room where Richard does his paperwork. I turn back into the hall.

Then I see it. On the table by the door, an envelope, with my name written in Richard's clear script.

There is no 'Dear Ellen'.

I have to tell you what Josh told me this evening. You were right to be concerned about him. He's in a bad way, mainly because he's terrified that you're going to be arrested and taken away, and he feels very confused about that. He has good reason to think this might happen, because he saw you on the night his father died. I will try to put it down exactly as he told me. He said that his supper at Jill's made him ill and he got up to be sick. He saw lights at Pennygate. Thinking you must be home and wanting to see you, he pulled some clothes on and sneaked out of Jill's and came across to find you. Inside the house, he heard crying. He was frightened and hid in the kitchen. When you came into the kitchen and took a key from the dresser he hid behind the door. He didn't say anything because he thought you'd be cross with him. He saw you go into the boot room and come out with a shotgun in your hand and leave the house. He called to you then, but you didn't hear. He followed you as far as the edge of the garden and saw you go on down to the river. He waited for a while then went back into the house. He waited at his bedroom window for a while, to see if he could spot you coming back. Then he heard the sound of a shot.

This is what he told me.

I'm afraid I told him something I shouldn't – I told him I was sure there was an explanation. It was wrong of me to abuse his trust in this way, to raise his hopes artificially, but I couldn't bear to let him see how utterly shocked I was, or for him to think bad things about his mother because of me. Poor little blighter will find out all about betrayal soon enough.

Unless your concern for your children is entirely pretence, I suggest you think of a story to tell Josh. It'll have to be something pretty convincing. Otherwise he's going to spend the rest of his life wondering what happened that night, believing you killed his father, and that will screw him up for ever.

I don't think I'm in the market for more lies myself.

I'm sorry I couldn't tell you this to your face. I didn't think there'd ever be a situation I would run from, but I was wrong.

I'll get my stuff collected, if you'd be good enough to pack it.

There is no signature.

NINETEEN

The best that can be said for moving house is that it weighs your mind down with so many trivialities that you don't have time to think of other things. I got the timing wrong though. I should have left the move until late September, when the children will be gone and another dreary winter will be looming ahead and I'll be only too glad of something to keep me busy. As it is, we moved two weeks ago, towards the end of August, just when I had intended to spend what they call quality time with the children, and to help Katie get herself organised for America. I don't know who drove each other madder during the move, the children or me. They couldn't believe how disorganised I was, and I suppose I did rather leave things to the last minute, but their ideas of packing were pretty bizarre too, with whole drawers left unemptied and miscellaneous debris left under beds. In the end they took charge, which was no bad thing. I needed a bit of leadership.

Now we're beginning to settle in, I tell myself it's good to be in our own place, bought and paid for, thanks to a little help from my friends and a building society. I give myself all the arguments about laying the foundations of a solid future, about the importance of providing the children with a firm base. I ignore my own restlessness, which scratches at me like rough cloth. But constant travelling wouldn't be the answer. It's not a change of scene I'm after, but a quieter mind, and that's not so easy to find.

It was Molly who goaded me into moving. I think she got fed up with seeing me in that dank cottage during the long winter.

She pushed me into looking at houses in March, I made a fruitless bid for a half-timbered cottage south of Woodbridge at the beginning of May, and found this in June. It's tiny, the kitchen's a cheap add-on, far too many things needed doing to it – the builders were in for five weeks – but the living-room is south-facing, the garden sunny, and Jack thought it was a good buy, and you can't get a much higher recommendation than that.

We're still camping. Boxes remain unopened, and I can't muster a great deal of enthusiasm for finding fabrics or getting coat hooks screwed on walls, so the interior is spartan and likely to remain so for some time. But the kitchen and bathroom function, I have a place to put my drawing-board; we can live.

The summer holidays are almost over. In three days Josh goes back to his boarding school where he has developed an unsuspected talent for art, aided and abetted by an inspirational teacher called Mrs Daly, who keeps telling him he could be really good, which is very pleasing.

The day before that, Katie leaves on an exchange visit to a college near San Francisco. It's only for a term, she'll be back by Christmas, but you'd think she was setting off on an uncertain voyage to an unknown continent. Cards and messages arrive daily, her friends send her such weight savers as jars of marmalade and framed photos of themselves, she has stocked up with packets of her favourite muesli. When she isn't spending hours on the phone, squawking with excitement, she is railing at the inadequacies of her new clothes, about which she was ecstatic just three weeks ago.

I hold a farewell lunch for her. The day is warm enough to have it outside, which is just as well since we're too many to fit comfortably inside the cottage. We sit at two trestle tables put end to end and covered in white cloths, like a French wedding party. In the best tradition of such feasts, the family have assembled for the occasion. Charles sits on my right, Diana on my left, and Anne on the far side of Jack. I didn't really expect Jack to come – he's always telling me how busy he is – but I think he has a sneaking liking for family gatherings and, now that he's had time to get used to the idea, a pride in his role as uncle-figure and benevolent provider. Not that anyone is meant to know about that, though some seem to have guessed, a fact for which Jack himself is probably responsible. Molly tells me that he has been dropping hints in various quarters, and I can just imagine him murmuring with a suitable show of modesty, *well, I do what I can, you know*.

Having guessed about my financial arrangements, some people have drawn quite the wrong conclusions. Only the other day, when I mentioned a lingering debt, Anne said, 'Can't Jack look after that?' I gave her a questioning glance and she raised her eyebrow slightly and gave me a knowing look as if to say, you can't think I'm a total fool. And I have heard there are whispers in other quarters.

Jack doesn't help this kind of rumour by dropping in on me at odd times, rather in the manner of a wise investor inspecting an asset. He is still wary of being seen with me in public – I remain something of a talking point, I gather, and the talk isn't entirely free of speculation – although this prudence only serves to lend his furtive visits, in which he is careful to park his highly conspicuous car down a side lane, a somewhat suggestive air.

But I don't care what people think. I'm content that Jack and I have reached an understanding that has become almost amicable. And so long as the faintest whiff of scandal attaches to me, I know that his interest in me will never step beyond the proprietorial, which suits me very well.

This doesn't prevent him catching my eye and throwing me his most charming low-lidded smile.

Anne and I have also reached an understanding, though it's an altogether more uncomfortable and less well-defined arrangement. We go to pains not to offend, we address each other courteously, we try to smile, and as I look at her now, she raises her glass and calls, 'What a wonderful day!' But I have no illusions about what this show of family unity costs her. She still thinks I am guilty of something. I catch it in her face sometimes, and I get the impression that she shrinks when I come near.

'What's she talking about?' croaks Diana, who's getting increasingly frail and confused. 'It's cold. *Cold.*' And for an instant it could be Harry, there is such a similarity in the intonation of the voice, in the profile of the nose they shared. I lift her cardigan from the chair back and drape it round her shoulders, and wonder briefly what Harry would have been like in old age.

Molly, in a flowing cotton number, sits on the far side of Charles, next to one of Katie's three school friends, pretty fresh-faced girls wearing the mandatory sloppy T-shirts and torn jeans and long hair which they constantly scoop back from their foreheads with a nonchalant rake of the fingers. Their languid movements and flashing eyes are directed towards a young man called Biff, whom Katie invited as a 'sort of friend'. Biff has startling blue eyes and a quick smile and seems to be saying fascinating things. Josh is delighted by Biff too, not because of anything he's saying, but because his name rhymes with Jiff, and every time someone mentions Biff's name the dog, who's confused enough about moving house, jumps up and barks, which sends Josh into paroxysms of laughter.

At the far end of the table sits Katie, the loveliest of them all, with her gleaming hair and smiling eyes, all ethereal composure broken by eruptions of exhilaration. Watching her, I think of the wonderful time she's going to have in America, of the life that stretches before her, and I tell myself that everything I did was worthwhile, every last awful deed, and that I don't regret a thing.

I tell myself this, though it isn't strictly true. I do have regrets, and the greatest is Moreland. It's at moments like this, when I'm surrounded by family and friends, or at night when I'm alone in the emptiness of my bed, that I feel his loss the most. I tell myself that there was always going to be a price to pay, that I should count myself lucky that it's not a great deal worse, that I could have been caught and sent to prison for an unimaginable number of years, that indeed I'm fortunate that

411

Moreland's sense of honour will not permit him to go to the police. I tell myself that I will get over him in time, but the pain lingers, an old wound that I pick at in my dreams and reopen constantly.

After Moreland left I learnt that time is a lumpy commodity, that it passes with plodding slowness or in bursts of distraction that are all too brief. I learnt that there are ways to reduce your awareness of being alone, that having the TV on all the time provides a permanent backdrop like auditory wallpaper, that you can believe a dog is almost human if you talk to it often enough and with sufficient feeling, that if you make yourself cosy and comfortable, and warm your bed with an electric blanket and plant a TV at the end of it, you can fool yourself into believing life's treating you well.

'Ellen?'

They're all laughing at me.

'Miles away!' Charles says affectionately.

'Sorry,' I say, sitting up and smiling back.

Jack is on his feet, wine glass in hand. He raises an eyebrow at me as if to check that I'm finally paying attention before announcing in his best parliamentary voice, 'A toast. To Katie. May she have every success at her new school.' Needing no lessons in timing, he leaves it a second before adding, 'And not get into too much trouble.' Amid laughter, he raises his glass.

'Katie!' everyone cries, and she glows with pleasure.

Her glance slips my way. I lift my glass and silently mouth her name. We exchange a look in which nothing is left out.

Packing has never been one of Katie's stronger points, and we spend most of the next morning trying to fit an impossible quantity of gear into her case.

'Can Biff come with us to the airport?' she asks casually.

'Well, I suppose so. Does he really want to come all that way?'

She flashes her eyes at me as if I'm crazy to ask. 'Course.'

'You like him?'

'Oh, *Mum.*' She puts her hands on her hips with an expression that says: you of all people!

I retreat hastily, I throw up my hands. 'I didn't mean ... I meant – he's nice? He's going to be a real friend?'

She gives me the benefit of the doubt. 'Yeah. I mean, he's *okay*. And he wants to come, so ... Damn! My Walkman's packed up.' She pushes the buttons repeatedly. 'Batteries flat!'

'We can buy some at the airport.'

She doesn't answer but marches next door into Josh's room, and I make a mental note to replace whichever batteries she is pinching from her brother. I hear her pulling open drawers and rooting around, then a long silence. After a time I put my head round the door. She is standing by a half-unpacked box reading what looks like a letter. She turns and holds it out to me. 'Here.'

I'm about to admonish her for trespassing, but something in her expression gives me a beat of alarm, and I reach out and take it.

I stare at Moreland's handwriting. The letter is addressed to Josh, and dated June, towards the end of the summer term. I don't mean to read more than a line or two, but it's impossible to break off, and I go through to the end. It's a newsy letter peppered with anecdotes and enquiries in the tone of someone who's written many times before, and had replies too.

'Did you know?' demands Katie.

I shake my head.

'How dare he! The ratfink! What a cheek!'

I read the beginning again. *Dear Josh, Cricket was never my game either! All that standing around for hours waiting for the ball to come your way and then when it does, and you have to make a catch, you have two dozen kittens because you're so terrified of missing it.*

'You should tell him to get lost.'

I fold the letter and slowly shake my head.

'After the way he left! You should tell him to mind his own business!' She studies me for a moment, she reads my expression and sighs. '*Mum* – he was a rat!'

'No.'

'He just walked out!' And there is still hurt in her voice,

because, despite giving him a hard time, she liked Moreland too.

'He didn't walk out. I told you, I asked him to go.'

She doesn't want to contradict me, but she doesn't believe me either.

'There were good reasons. Really.'

'Sure,' she says dismissively.

And suddenly I don't want Katie to think that Moreland is just another man who lets people down.

'He had a conflict of interest,' I explain, pushing the letter back into the chaos of the box.

'Oh yes?' she says archly.

And, facing her again, seeing how grown up she has become, I tell her what I have never told her before. 'He thought I helped Harry to kill himself. Or worse, that maybe I pointed the gun.'

She digests this. 'Why?'

'He found out I'd been lying to him. He found out' – and I say it in a tone of total acceptance – 'that I took the shotgun down to the river that night. Before the shot was heard.'

Understanding comes to Katie's face. 'Josh told him?'

'But you mustn't blame Josh.'

'Oh, Mum,' she sighs, 'why didn't you tell me?'

Because I didn't want to upset her. But I don't say this, I just shrug.

She studies me again, and all kinds of conflicting emotions pass over her face. Then, moaning slightly, she comes and puts her arms around me. 'Oh, Mum.' After a time she pulls back and takes another reading of my face. 'You mind,' she accuses me.

'No. It wouldn't have worked anyway. Really. If it hadn't been that, it would have been something else. *Really*. We just weren't suited.'

She shakes her head with high drama. She is at an age where she puts love on a pretty high plane, and you either love someone with burning passion or not at all.

I am beginning to wonder if I have made a mistake in telling her the truth.

'You could still tell him. Why don't you ... ' She wrestles with a decision, she contorts her mouth, finally she says, 'You could explain a bit about ... you know, *me*. I mean, I wouldn't mind. If it was just him.'

But she would mind, I know that she would. 'That's a very sweet offer, darling, but I honestly don't think it would make any difference now.'

'Why not?'

'Oh, all sorts of reasons. Too late. Too much water under the bridge.'

And because he wouldn't be so ready to believe me, because he would see the holes in whatever story I tried to give him and shoot it down in flames, though I don't say this.

'I wouldn't mind. If it made a difference.' She is mildly offended at having her gesture turned down.

'Sweetheart ... No. Really.' And I'm careful to remove all trace of regret from my voice.

This doesn't stop her from acquiring the troubled look she always gets when the past comes back to haunt her and she doesn't quite know how to cope with it, and I say quickly, 'Come on, let's go and finish the packing before it drives me completely crazy.'

There's something about going away that brings out the chaotic in Katie. Having stayed up late – I don't know what time she finally turned out her light – she is almost unrousable in the morning. When she finally gets up she drifts around unproductively for at least an hour before managing to get dressed. Then, just to drive me to distraction, she announces fifteen minutes after we're meant to have left for the airport that she's lost her air ticket. By the time we finally get the show on the road – Josh, Biff, Katie, plus air ticket – we're half an hour late and I'm driving with white knuckles.

But we make up time and the tension drops away and I start to chuckle at the children's convoluted jokes. At the customs gate I am the model parent. I don't say too many embarrassingly motherly things, I am practical and briskly loving. It's Biff I feel sorry for. Katie, having sent him across the terminal to post a letter, then rewards him with the most perfunctory of farewells, a brief, 'See you!' and the sort of distant gaze that stars bestow on fans when they're finding adulation a bit of a bore. Josh and I get the hugs and grins.

Waving her off, I feel happy for her, but at the same time I'm not in the mood to talk, and I'm relieved when the two boys discuss dogs and sport most of the way home.

With only a day to get Josh organised and packed for the new school year, I'm thrown straight back into name tapes and missing sports gear and shoes that suddenly don't fit any more. As we sit beside the trunk ticking items off against the list, Josh tells me what shoes will double, which sports shirts are unnecessary, and I'm struck by how much his confidence has grown since the winter.

I still tremble at the thought of what Josh witnessed, it still wrenches my heart to think of the burden he was carrying for all those weeks. Until his father's body was found I like to think he'd largely blocked the memory out, that he didn't in any way interpret what he'd seen or match it to events. But later, when the gun was found beside his father, I hate to think what went through his mind. I have never pressed him on the subject so I can only guess, though this, of course, is almost worse.

It was hard holding out against Dawson, but the most challenging story of all was the one I had to construct for Josh. Not only did I have to explain my actions, but I had to do it without destroying Josh's belief in me and in the memory of his father. This was a tall order. Abuse was never on the agenda – no ten-year-old could cope with that – and I could hardly pretend I'd taken the gun down to the boat and let Harry commit suicide in front of me, so in the end I hatched an entirely different scenario that relied on Harry's death being purely accidental. When Josh gets older he may see the gaping holes in this version of events and if he ever questions me I'm going to have to think of something better, but in the meantime he seems more than satisfied. I think he was desperate to grasp any explanation, however unlikely, so long as it relieved him of the guilt of seeing what he saw, and the anxiety of my possible arrest.

Now, like any other boy who's coming up to eleven, he's preoccupied with school and friends and seeing the latest videos, and if the past still bothers him at all, he doesn't seem to dwell on it.

On the drive to school, I hover on the point of asking him about Richard. I am curious to know how long the correspondence has been going on and whether Richard ever says anything about me. But in the end I never quite say anything. I would hate to put him on the defensive, to make him feel that I've been prying, or to put him in a situation where he feels he has to lie to me.

I come home to a house that is empty save for a prancing Jiff, and immediately plunge into gloom. Molly, who knows my moods all too well, has arranged to come over later, armed with wine. But this does little to forestall my sense of loss and isolation. It still baffles me as to how I have managed to find myself in a strange new village without either of my two wonderful children. No doubt I'll pull myself together in a couple of days, I'll get back into the routine, I'll put some theatre dates into my diary and persuade myself I have a social life, but the truth is I'm useless at being alone and always have been.

Allowing my self-pity a short unimpeded burst, I sit disconsolately in the bare living-room eyeing the new paint where it's run and the floorboards where they're still hopelessly uneven, before dragging myself upstairs to do something useful like stripping the children's beds.

I have not been into Katie's room since she left. An envelope sits prominently on the pillow. I feel a leap of affection and gratitude at her thoughtfulness. It is just like her to leave a farewell message when I need it most.

Then I read what she has scrawled on the front of the envelope.

Mum. Don't be cross with me. But this is like a present from me to you. I thought about it very carefully, and it's definitely what I want to do. I love you, Mum. You've been the best.

Fumbling, I tear open the envelope and pull out four sheets: photocopies of a letter in her own handwriting. My heart lurches as I skim through it. I double back a couple of times, but there's no mistake. I feel dizzy. It's all here, she has left nothing out. I am breathless with astonishment.

Then all emotions are swept aside by an eruption of fear as I realise the enormity of the risk she has exposed us to.

'Oh, Katie,' I cry.

Trying to contain my anxiety, I reach for my address book, I start for the telephone, I stare at my watch, I go back to the letter, I return to the telephone and dial Moreland's number.

Before it can ring, I drop the receiver back into the cradle.

The phone will not do: I will have no peace until I find the letter and watch it burn.

The street where Moreland lives lies in a maze of similar streets to the south of Clapham Common, in an area of road-bumps and chicanes and other deterrents to through traffic. The terraced houses are grey-bricked and bow-fronted and packed close together behind tiny front gardens with no trees. Nearly all have been gentrified, with white-painted windows and bright glossy doors and flower tubs, prudently chained to walls.

There are so many cars that I have to park in the next street and walk back. Moreland's house has a blue front door and a smart brass knocker which needs a polish. There's no one at home. Through the uncurtained bay window I see a sofa covered in a modern pattern, a simple standard lamp, a large pastel print on a white wall. I can't see through the letter box which has a flap over the back of it.

I go and sit in the car for a while, then, as lights start to blink on, I cruise back and find a parking place just two doors away on the opposite side.

At nine, people are still coming home from work, smart professional girls, young men in pinstripes, nobody over forty. TVs go on, curtains are drawn, people stand with drinks in their hands. And still I'm filled with irrepressible fears. My thoughts skid between the efficiency of the postal service and the arrangements Moreland is likely to have made for his mail if he has gone away. Perhaps his wife is back. Perhaps she

418

deals with the mail, perhaps she will eventually open the door to me.

By ten I am badly in need of a loo and relinquish my parking space to drive to the nearest half-respectable pub to use the facilities, squalid as they are.

When I return there are lights burning in Moreland's house.

I park in the first available slot and walk back and knock firmly.

I hear an internal door and firm footsteps approaching. I feel myself being scrutinised through the spyhole, then there's the sound of a heavy lock turning and the front door swings open and a startled Moreland stands under the light.

Before he has a chance to say anything, I blurt out, 'I need to know if you've got a letter from Katie.'

I notice how tanned he is, how clear his eyes are, as though he has just come back from holiday.

His stares at me, his mouth moves a couple of times as though he would answer if he could remember the question. Then, taking in what I have said at last, he glances over his shoulder, he throws out a hand. 'I've only just got back. I don't know.'

He gives an uncertain smile which is poised some way between warmth and doubt. Then, reading the urgency in my face, he says, 'Hang on a minute,' and steps back into the hall and picks up a pile of letters from a side table. He comes back, shuffling quickly through them.

He holds up an envelope and I see Katie's writing and feel a great surge of relief. I nod rapidly.

'Why don't you come in?'

'No,' I say hastily. 'No, I . . . I just wanted to know that it hadn't gone astray. And that you'll promise to destroy it.'

'Should I?'

'She wants you to.'

'Oh. Am I allowed to read it first?' He says this lightly, not expecting a refusal.

'I'd rather you didn't.'

He frowns at this. 'What about Katie – does she not want me to read it either?'

419

I hesitate before shaking my head.

He says not unkindly, 'Is that a no, she doesn't want me to read it, or a no, she's not against me reading it?'

When I don't reply, he says with a touch of his old sternness, 'You'd better come in.'

'No.' And I'm already retreating down the path. 'I'll come back in a minute,' I call, 'when you've decided.' And I walk quickly away before he has the chance to say any more.

I sit in the car, recovering slowly. My nerves are so taut, my emotions so extreme, that it is some moments before I stop trembling. Through this haze of feeling, I imagine Moreland switching on the standard lamp and settling back on the patterned sofa and unfolding the letter. I see him starting to read.

I reach into my bag and draw out the copy that Katie made late that night on my desktop copier, and, as Moreland reads, I read with him by the sulphurous light of the street-lamp.

Dear Richard, I was upset when you left us that time. Mum tried not to show it but she was very upset too. It's hard when your Mum has a boyfriend. You have funny feelings about it. You don't like to think of sharing your Mum with anyone, which is sort of selfish, I know, but you can't help it. And after everything we'd been through I didn't want anyone around <u>ever</u>. But I have to say you were okay, always dead straight with us and great with Josh and if I gave you a hard time sometimes, I'm sorry. I never really meant to. I just felt very protective about Mum. She's been so great to me. Not just my Mum, but my best friend too. The reason I'm writing to you is – there's a line crossed out – *because I think what happened at Christmas was unfair on her. It's not right for you to think bad things about her because it just isn't true. It probably won't make any difference now, but I want you to know what happened and I'm trusting you not to tell anyone, for Mum's sake and for mine. In fact, can you promise right now to burn this the second you've read it?*

Such trust, my Katie. Even after everything.

What you have to know is that my stepfather had been abusing me. Mum didn't know and I couldn't tell her. I felt so ashamed and confused. I thought it was my fault somehow, that if I pretended it wasn't happening it would go away. I've had therapy since then and I

420

can talk about it now, but then I felt so miserable I wanted to crawl away and die. I know now that Dad wasn't well, that he was sick, and that helps, to understand that. I also know that what he did was very wrong, but I didn't understand that either, not then. I know that may seem crazy, but victims often feel that way, they feel it's all their fault. When it started I just prayed for everything to be all right again. I thought perhaps if I just kept out of the way, then Dad would forget about it.

That night, he phoned me at school from the boat and said to come and join him and Mum for dinner. He said Mum was just getting some food from the house and that I was to get a taxi over and if Mum wasn't at the house, then to come down to the quay and he'd pick me up in the dinghy. He promised me faithfully that Mum was there. I didn't think he was telling me lies because she'd said she'd be down there most of the day, helping him get the boat ready and everything. And he kept promising, he kept saying she was there.

Yes, he was a brilliant liar, Katie, he could fool anyone.

Harry spoke to my housemistress and got permission and I took a taxi over. There was no one in the house when I got there and I never thought of checking the calendar to see where Mum was. I just went straight down to the quay and Harry was waiting for me. Half-way to the boat I suddenly thought, what if Mum isn't there? But it was too late then. And Harry seemed okay. Like he didn't say anything to make me realise.

Then I got on the boat and saw Mum wasn't there. I asked Harry to take me straight back. I begged and begged him. He said to calm down, not to be hysterical, that he wasn't going to hurt me, but then he did bad things to me. I mean, he raped me. I'd never fought him before, not when it happened the other times, but I fought him that time. He kept saying he loved me and cared about me, but he wouldn't stop. I got something, a lamp, and hit him on the head but he still wouldn't stop and when he did stop he said terrible things which weren't true, awful things about me, and I went crazy. I must have gone a bit mad because I don't remember much, but I got a knife. I didn't mean to hurt him so much, I just wanted to hurt him a bit, and to make him stop and not do it again. But the knife went right in. I hardly pushed at all but it went right in and Harry fell down and went white. It's hard to write this because you're probably thinking what a terrible *person I am. I can only say that I didn't mean to kill him and that it's the worst thing that ever happened to me in my whole life and that if I could bring him back right now, I would.*

You didn't have to do all this, Katie, you could have left some of it out. And thinking this, I am filled with strange pride.

I couldn't believe it but he died just like that. I couldn't believe it, but he did. He wasn't breathing. I tried things, but it was no good. And then I totally panicked. I could only think of getting Mum. I got the rubber dinghy and rowed to the quay and ran up to the house and saw that she was at Molly's and called her. She came straight over and gave me sleeping pills and put me to bed. Then she rushed down to the boat. When she came back she didn't say anything to me about what she was going to do, but everything she did after that was to try and protect me. Everything. She took the shotgun and went back to the boat to make it look like suicide. She said it wasn't a hard thing to do, to use the gun, because he was already dead. She says that, but I think it must have been very hard really.

My eyes fog up, my throat seizes. 'Yes, it was hard,' I say aloud. 'Very hard.'

Poor Mum, she thought that would be enough. She didn't realise.

'No, I didn't, I didn't,' I sigh, gripped by helplessness again.

I don't know what went wrong, she wouldn't really talk about it, but for some reason it was no good. She realised they'd guess straight away what she'd done. Then she had the idea to take the yacht out to sea.

You make it sound so easy, Katie. But it took hours and hours to work out.

And she took the boat out to sea and sank it. It was an awfully hard thing for her to do when she hates the water and doesn't like boats. She didn't tell me everything that happened, but I think she nearly got lost and thought she was going to die too. It was so brave of her and I think she was crazy to do it, but I'm glad she did. I couldn't have got through this without her, I just couldn't.

I should say that Mum couldn't have told you all this even if she'd wanted to because she promised me a long time ago that she would never tell a living soul for as long as she lived. She told me so I'd feel safe, and it helped a lot, though I was always frightened that the police would find out. But she said that at the very worst they'd accuse her of trying to conceal a suicide. She said she might go to prison for a few months at the most, but it would be a small price to pay and whatever happened I was never to own up because she'd never ever forgive me if I did. I was terrified of her going to prison and it's just great that it hasn't happened because I couldn't have taken it.

I can never forgive myself for what I did. I know it was wrong. But then what Harry did was very wrong too.

'Yes – wrong,' I echo, as if she could hear me now and needed support.

While I'm in America I'm going to have more therapy. I know this won't make things right either, but at least maybe I can work my way through everything a bit better then.

It's been hard for Josh too. He saw Mum take the gun, though we never realised until Christmas. It must have been awful for him thinking Mum had done something bad. As soon as we realised what he'd been thinking we told him a bit of what happened, as close as we could anyway without making him feel too bad about Dad. I told him that it was all my fault. I didn't say about the abuse. Mum felt it'd be too much for him. I made it sound like an accident instead. I told him that Dad had been drinking, which was true, and was maybe on pills as well, and had been in a foul mood. And that I'd been no better, that I'd said a lot of stupid things that had made him even madder, that he grabbed me to tell me off, but the boat rocked and he stumbled and we both fell and I had a knife in my hand because I'd been chopping things for supper. I made it sound like a complete accident, so you must never tell him the truth. Poor Josh. It's been hard for him, not just thinking those things about Mum but feeling left out. He thinks we should have told him the truth at the beginning and perhaps we should.

I've told you everything because I don't want you to think badly of Mum. She's too good for that. But writing this letter is scary. It's a big thing for me to tell someone. You always seemed like someone I could trust, so I hope you won't let me down, and will burn this straight away.

I got your address from Mum's desk. And then I called you two nights ago and didn't say it was me (if you were wondering who the call was from). I wanted to check you were there.

It will probably drive Mum crazy, me having written, but I wanted to.

Katie.

PS. Could you write to me in America (P.T.O. for address) and let me know you got this all right and everything?

I fold the sheets carefully and put them back in the envelope. I sit in the long silence, I start slightly as a sports car engine roars into life close by. I watch a long-haired blond woman walk past with a long-haired blond dog. I give it another five minutes before I make my way back.

This time Moreland opens the door almost immediately. Without a word, he takes me gently by the arm and leads me inside and closes the door. He grasps my hands and, lifting them to his mouth, kisses them in a gesture that would be flamboyant if it weren't so full of feeling, then, with another courteous old-fashioned movement, he signals me to follow him down the passage and into the kitchen.

The letter lies open on the table. Still without saying anything, he takes a metal wastepaper basket which he must have brought from another room and, placing it in the middle of the floor, he suspends the first page above it and puts a lighted match to it.

'I should have guessed,' he says solemnly.

'But why?'

'The call you made to Katie from the boat. Her nervous breakdown.' He gestures hopelessly with the burnt match. 'The way you were so desperate to protect her.' He sets the next sheet alight.

'But no one was meant to guess.'

He won't be mollified. He says in a tone of disbelief, 'I should have realised.'

I hand him my copy. 'You'd better burn this too.'

He holds the papers in his hand. He starts to speak only to halt abruptly and throw me an unhappy glance, before winding himself up to try again. 'All this time – ever since Christmas – I was tortured by the thought of how wrong I'd been about you. I couldn't believe I'd been so badly taken in. So thoroughly deceived.' And his face tightens at the thought. 'But you know, the worst thing – the *worst* thing – was thinking how carefully you must have worked everything out, how you must have planned it all!'

'Planned it . . . ' I smile faintly. 'No, Harry was the planner.'

'Taking the yacht out to sea,' he continues urgently, as if he must explain himself with all possible speed. 'It was *that* more than anything, Ellen. The more I thought about it, how tough you must have been to do it, the more I persuaded myself you were capable of anything.'

'But I had to take it, you see. I had to take the yacht.' I gather myself for one last excursion into the past. 'The suicide; when I decided to try it, I realised I had to make it look right, that if I was going to do it at all I mustn't make a mistake. I knew it would only take one thing, just one thing, and I'd be found out. I'd read somewhere about traces of powder or whatever it is people get on their hands when they kill themselves. I knew you had to get that right. So . . . I put his hand on the barrel of the gun.' I stare at the wastepaper basket, at the last wisps of smoke. 'I wrapped his other hand round the trigger. I wiped my fingerprints away. I thought I'd managed it.' I pause, seeing again the terrible sight in the cabin. 'Then I realised' – I press my fingertips against my temple, I give a bitter laugh – 'I realised it was all for nothing. I'd missed the most obvious thing of all. You see, there was no bleeding. I shot him and there was no bleeding. I realised they'd know straight away. They'd know he was already dead when he was shot.' I look away to a draining-board that is cluttered with upturned saucepans and draped with a dish-cloth that is none too clean. 'And that wasn't all,' I say, and the visions crowd in on me. 'When I pulled the trigger, I wasn't holding the gun tightly enough or something, because it jerked a bit to one side and' – I grimace – 'it didn't cover the knife wound. Well, I *thought* it didn't. They never found it, in fact, the knife wound, so I must have . . . *managed* it after all. But I thought they'd find it. I thought everything would be an even worse disaster than before. And then . . . ' I gesture inevitability. 'I was faced with having to do something. With having to hide the whole terrible mess.'

Moreland is very still, I feel him watching me. And then his hand is squeezing mine hard and he is saying my name in a ragged voice before he turns slowly back to his task and, taking the copy letter, sets light to each page in turn.

We watch the last page fall flaming into the bin.

He says, 'You knew I wouldn't hesitate, didn't you? To burn this?'

'I knew. But I had to be sure. I couldn't help it. You may have noticed, I have a tendency to worry about these things.'

His eyes flash with affection. 'I had noticed.' He throws the burnt match into the bin. 'I'll write to Katie,' he says, 'I've kept the address.'

'I know you'll say the right things.'

'What worries me' – and he fixes me with that uneven look again – 'is what I can say to you.'

I think about this for all of a second. 'I think that you could tell me that you'll come and see us sometimes. I know Josh would love it. And Katie, too.'

'And you?'

'Me probably most of all.'